Liz Byrski is the author of se~~veral~~ fiction and non-
fiction books, the latest of whic~~h is~~ *~~S~~ome Thoughts on
Women and Ageing*.

She has worked as a freelance journalist, a broadcaster with
ABC Radio and an advisor to a minister in the West Australian
Government.

Liz has a PhD in writing from Curtin University where she
teaches professional and creative writing.

www.lizbyrski.com

Also by Liz Byrski

Fiction
Food, Sex & Money
Belly Dancing for Beginners
Trip of a Lifetime
Bad Behaviour
Last Chance Café
In the Company of Strangers

Non-fiction
Remember Me
Getting On: Some Thoughts on Women and Ageing

LIZ BYRSKI

Gang of Four

PAN
Pan Macmillan Australia

First published 2004 in Macmillan by Pan Macmillan Australia Pty Ltd
This Pan edition published 2014 by Pan Macmillan Australia Pty Ltd
1 Market Street, Sydney, New South Wales, Australia, 2000

Cataloguing-in-Publication entry is available
from the National Library of Australia
http://catalogue.nla.gov.au

Typeset in Palatino by Midland Typesetters
Printed by McPherson's Printing Group

The characters in this book are fictitious and any resemblance to real persons,
living or dead, is purely coincidental.

Papers used by Pan Macmillan Australia Pty Ltd are natural, recyclable products
made from wood grown in sustainable forests. The manufacturing processes
conform to the environmental regulations of the country of origin.

ACKNOWLEDGMENTS

I would like to thank my family and friends who have, for so long, encouraged me in my writing. Special thanks to my son Neil for many patient readings of early drafts and to Carolyn Polizzotto for those clarifying discussions about the journey from non-fiction to fiction. Thanks, too, to my agent Sheila Drummond for her faith in my work; to Cate Paterson at Pan Macmillan for giving my manuscript a home; and to editors Sarina Rowell and Jo Jarrah for their thoughtful and professional treatment of *Gang of Four*.

5W–Women Welcome Women World Wide is an international friendship organisation for women. I would like to thank the women of 5W for allowing me to feature the organisation in this book, and encourage readers to visit the website at: www.womenwelcomewomen.org.uk

ONE

There was a moment when she first woke, a moment free of any sense of the day ahead; a moment before she opened her eyes and when all she could feel was the warmth of the early sunshine falling on her face through the open curtains, and the soft heaviness of her body relaxed after sleep. A moment of innocence before reality interfered.

Isabel got up, pulling on the cotton wrap that lay crumpled on the rose velvet chair. The chair had belonged to her grandmother and later to her mother – it was part of her history. She stared at it, seeing herself at five in the pink organza fairy dress her grandmother had made for Christmas, climbing onto the chair and claiming it as her fairy throne. Perhaps having the chair in her own bedroom nearly fifty years later wasn't a particularly good idea. She might swap it for the one in the spare room, maybe get it reupholstered.

Doug stirred, rolling onto his side. 'Up already?'

'Things to do.'

'Mmm. Want me to help?' he asked, closing his eyes again and pulling the bedclothes around him.

'No, it's fine – I'm better on my own.'

He nodded, eyes still shut, reaching out his hand to her. 'Merry Christmas, darl.'

Isabel took the outstretched hand and bent to kiss his stubbly cheek. 'Merry Christmas.' He was almost asleep again.

Alone in the kitchen she switched on the kettle and opened

the fridge. The turkey, trussed, stuffed and covered with a damp cloth, sat pale and bulky on a middle shelf. She glared at it, took out the milk and closed the fridge. It was only half past six, plenty of time yet. She took her coffee out onto the deck, gazing across the jumbled rooftops to the grey-green smudges of Rottnest and Garden islands. A couple of yachts, their sails gleaming red and white, raced towards the open sea. Down in the town the bells were ringing for early mass.

A perfect morning, a perfect Australian Christmas Day 1996. But the weight of the day wrapped itself around her, and she was ashamed of her own ingratitude. She had a husband, children and grandchildren who loved her, a beautiful home, enough money. What sort of person was she to feel so overwhelmed with gloom and resentment on Christmas morning? It would be the same as last year, and the year before and the year before that, as many years as she and Doug had been married – this would be the thirty-fourth. Had she really cooked that many Christmas dinners, served thirty-four turkeys in the sweltering sunshine, ignited thirty-four rich dark puddings and carried them to the table swathed in brandy flames? Children had been born and grown to adulthood, and now they came with their partners and their own children. And through it all she had been there cooking the Christmas dinner, performing the same rituals, while her mother and stepfather grew older and sicker and finally died, and while Doug's parents grew younger and more energetic, like an advertisement for superannuation funds. And here she was, doing it again. In the lounge the tree sparkled with tiny white lights, towering above the mound of presents. The weeks of work, shopping, wrapping, cooking and planning would be as nothing by the end of the day. And she would still be here, with this leaden exhaustion, this resentment, this longing to be free of the responsibility, free of the burden of their expectations.

She remembered the delicious promise of that waking moment and wanted it back. She wanted to stretch it, examine it, turn it over, see what she could make of that crystal clear sense of lightness and freedom. It followed her as she dried herself after a shower and wandered back into the cool bedroom. How tempting it would be to stretch out on the bed, close her eyes and let Christmas pass her by. The taste of stillness and solitude haunted her all morning, even as she spread the cloth on the table and counted the cutlery. There would be one less this year. No Eunice, no extra space needed for her wheelchair, no one reminiscing about crisp European winters, roasted chestnuts and snow-clad city streets bright with decorated trees and horse-drawn sleighs. Isabel sighed, put away the extra set of cutlery and spread the place settings a little wider. Her mother had died in November; there would be more room at the table this year.

Deb and Mac came first. She heard them from the bedroom, their voices preceding them up the steps as they argued above the children's excited squeals. The house was filled with noise and movement. Danny and Ruth thundered along the passage to the bedroom, pausing breathless in the doorway.

'C'mon, Gran, it's Christmas,' said Danny from behind a Spider-Man mask, a red and black cape swinging from his shoulders. 'Look what Father Christmas brought me.'

'I got a fairy dress,' said Ruth, trailing behind in ruffles of pink net.

Isabel got up and hugged Danny. 'I barely recognised you, you look so scary,' she said, and she picked Ruth up and set off with them to the lounge. 'Do you know, Ruth, I had a pink fairy dress like that the Christmas I was five.'

'I'm four,' said Ruth thoughtfully, her tinsel tiara lurching at an angle.

'Well, you must have been a very good girl for Santa to give you a fairy dress when you're only four.'

The others all seemed to arrive together, Luke with his girlfriend Cassie, Kate and Jason explaining that they would have been earlier but they had to phone Jason's mum in Noosa, and Doug's parents struggling under a load of parcels.

Christmas Day drew Isabel into its net, trapping past and present, blurring their boundaries until her limbs felt leaden and her face ached with the effort of smiling. They sat around the table surrounded by the debris of Christmas dinner, the dirty plates, the drying pudding, the torn crackers and paper hats.

Luke raised his glass to her. 'Fantastic dinner, Mum!'

The others followed, her family, eleven faces she knew so well and loved so much, flushed with food and wine, their smiles weary with pleasure and contentment, paper hats at rakish angles, the little ones sliding wearily off their chairs.

'To Mum – thanks for making it all happen, this year, last year, next year,' Luke said and they echoed his toast.

Isabel smiled into the stillness as they drank. 'Thank you, I'm glad you enjoyed it . . . but . . . well, maybe not next year.'

Confusion and disbelief hung in the silence.

'I mean, maybe it would be nice to do something different,' she said, nervous suddenly at speaking such heresy. She looked down to the far end of the table where Doug was cutting a piece of cheese.

'Different?' said Luke, his glass still raised.

'Well, we might want to go away somewhere, your father and I, perhaps . . .' Her voice faded as Doug looked up from the cheese in amazement. 'Well, me,' she went on. 'Maybe I might . . .'

'Your mother's got post-Christmas stress disorder a little early this year,' Doug said, putting the cheese on his plate and picking up his glass. 'We'll be here! Here's to next year and the year after that and . . .'

'Next year,' they said, raising their glasses again, relief visible in every smile.

And Isabel raised her glass and drank, but in that moment she knew that next year she would not be there. Speaking it had made it inevitable. Those few words had changed everything and there was no going back.

'I keep meaning to ask you what all that stuff was on Christmas Day,' Doug said, swinging the car into his parents' driveway. It was New Year's Eve and they were on their way to another ritual meal.

'What stuff?'

'About not being here next year, going away.'

'I need a change,' she said. 'We could go away perhaps, do something different.'

He switched off the engine and opened the car door. 'We've always done it,' he said stubbornly. 'It's a family tradition, like tonight with Mum and Dad.'

'Yes,' she said, stepping out of the car. 'But that doesn't mean we have to keep on doing it. It doesn't mean we can never take time out.'

He clicked the remote control irritably and the car doors locked with a snap. 'It's important,' he said. 'To all of them, the kids, the parents, everyone.'

'You mean it's important to you.'

'Yes, if you like – me too.'

'And what about me?'

'You never complained before.'

'No.'

'Well, there you are then. You need a rest, Iz.' He put his arm around her shoulders. 'Why don't we go down south for a few days? You could phone that nice place with the spa.'

Isabel turned to see his profile in the fading light and wondered, not for the first time in thirty-four years, how it was possible to feel so totally misunderstood by someone you had lived with and loved for decades.

The councillor for the North Ward paused. He had been on his feet repeating himself for ten minutes. Isabel stared at him hard, willing him to wind up, but he shifted his weight from one foot to the other, picked up another sheaf of correspondence and took a deep breath to begin again. She peered at him over the top of her half-glasses.

'Yes, thank you, Councillor Williams. As you've said, it's a complicated issue with serious budgetary implications. I suggest we refer it to the finance committee for consideration and ask for a report at the March meeting. Those in favour? Against? Thank you, that's carried then.'

Shocked by the speed with which his plans for a day centre had been dispatched to the finance committee, Councillor Williams grunted irritably and resumed his seat. The relief was palpable; councillors began to pile their papers together.

'Well, that brings us to the end of the agenda, Councillors. The next meeting is on Monday the twenty-fourth of March. I declare the meeting closed at ten minutes past ten.'

The chamber buzzed with noise and movement as people got to their feet and began to leave the chamber. The council's CEO, Sam Lewis, slipped his files into his briefcase. 'You're unusually brutal this evening, Madam Mayor,' he grinned. 'Mr Williams didn't know what hit him.'

'I feared we might be here till midnight,' Isabel said. 'Old Mr Martino was already asleep and I think I heard him snore. Another five minutes and at least half the chamber would have been snoring with him.'

'You don't have to convince me,' Sam replied. 'I'd lost track of what he was saying a couple of minutes after he started. Can I buy you a drink?'

She shook her head. 'Thanks, Sam, but not tonight. I'll be in on Wednesday morning if we need to discuss that issue about the heritage register.'

'Fine,' he said. 'But, Isabel, before you go, have you – well, have you thought again about running for a third term?'

'I have and I'm not. I've had enough, Sam. I need a break and it's time the council had a change, anyway.'

He shrugged, stopping at the door of his office. 'I still hope you'll change your mind.'

'No way,' she smiled. 'I've got other plans.'

It was after ten but she wasn't ready to go home. She needed time by herself. She considered a coffee on the cappuccino strip but dismissed it – she would be a sitting target for anyone with a council gripe. Almost without thinking she drove across the intersection, and headed towards the refuge. It was a rambling old fibro house with a metal roof and wide verandahs, half hidden behind a tall, thick brush hedge which was starting to encroach on the pavement. There would be complaints from the neighbours, so she'd have to remind Loretta to get it trimmed. They got enough complaints about the residents and their unwelcome visitors without having to cope with complaints about the hedge.

Isabel pulled into one of the four parking bays at the front, switched off the lights and wound down the window. The sound of the Bee Gees floated across the garden, and through a lighted window she could see a couple of women dancing to the music. The double wooden doors were open, protected, like the windows, by steel security doors, a safeguard against the angry, sometimes violent men who were prone to roll up in the middle of the night demanding access. Over the entrance was a small curved sign announcing 'Isabel Carter Refuge for Women'. Isabel gazed at it with affection. She had fought, first as a private citizen and later as a councillor, to get the city to fund a refuge and then to buy the house, and she was prouder of it than of anything she had done since.

She got out of the car and wandered over to the seat beneath the big peppermint tree, remembering the tears of pride in her mother's eyes as the then mayor cut the ribbon and declared the refuge open. 'Be proud, darling,' Eunice had said, gripping her daughter's hand. 'Your passion drove you to do a wonderful thing.' She had hung on grim-faced as Doug and Mac struggled to manoeuvre her wheelchair over the gravel, but her pride in her daughter's achievement was obvious.

A face peered out of the window into the darkness, then moved away. Seconds later the woman stepped out onto the porch and shone a torch beam towards the tree.

'It's okay, Loretta, it's only me loitering out here,' Isabel called.

'Thank goodness,' Loretta said, lowering the torch beam to the ground and walking towards her. 'Whatever are you sitting about out here for? We thought you were an aggrieved husband planning a break-in!'

Isabel leaned back. 'Sorry. I needed time to think. I've just finished a council meeting.'

'D'you want a cup of tea or something?'

'No thanks, I'm fine.'

Loretta switched off the torch and they sat together in companionable silence.

'I might go away for a bit,' Isabel said.

'A bit? What's that mean? How big a bit?'

'Several months . . .' She hesitated. 'A year, maybe.'

'That's a big bit. Doug got some flash posting somewhere?'

'No, no I'm going on my own. Time out . . . time to myself.'

'Well, I guess if anyone needs time out it's you.'

'I haven't told Doug yet.'

'I see . . .' There was a long pause.

'I'll tell you more later, when it's clearer. Don't mention it, will you? I haven't told anyone else yet.'

'Sure. If there's one thing you learn from working in a refuge, it's when to keep your mouth shut.' She put her hand on Isabel's arm. 'You're okay, though?'

'I'm okay, just need a break, time for me. You'll still be here?'

'You know me – they'll carry me out of here feet first but not for another couple of decades. If you're asking me if I'll be here to look after things, you know I will.'

Isabel swallowed hard on the lump in her throat.

'Thanks, Lori. I don't think I could go if you weren't here.'

'Lord bless us, of course you could, I'm not indispensable. Let me know the plan of action when you're ready.'

Isabel opened the car door and slid into the driving seat. 'I will, thanks again. Oh and, Loretta –'

'Yes, I know, the hedge needs cutting. The guy's coming the day after tomorrow. We'll be all neat and tidy by the weekend.'

For a while Isabel had struggled with the feeling that her overwhelming need to get away had to be directed to some serious and important purpose, but eventually she came to the conclusion that this was just what it should not be. For more years than she could remember, she had been occupied with serious and important purposes; with work, raising children, helping with the grandchildren, looking after her mother and stepfather, and fitting everything around Doug's job, fighting for the refuge, the council. What she wanted was an end to purpose, time to drift, time free of other people's needs and expectations.

She got out the old wooden box filled with her mother's post-cards – Lisbon, Granada, Seville, Monaco, Nuremberg, Vienna, Berlin – and spread them on the table alongside the map of

Europe in her old school atlas. As a child she had marked the locations on the map as the postcards arrived, charting Eunice's travels with the dance company from one exotic location to another. More memories sprang out as Isabel studied the map: Bruges, where women sat making lace in the streets; a story about eating raw herring by the canals in Amsterdam; and dancing on the broken bridge at Avignon.

They were dream places far away from the stifling heat of her grandparents' home in the hills with the chook pen in the back yard, the Coolgardie safe, and the tiny sleepout that was her bedroom. When the mail came, Isabel and her grandmother sat together in the swing seat on the verandah to read it. She could feel it as if it were yesterday; the comfort of Grandma's warm body, the smell of face powder and rosewater, and the sound of seat posts creaking as they swayed. Each card was a promise that her mother might be back soon. Isabel studied them, hoarded them, first in a biscuit tin and later in the wooden box her grandfather had made especially for the purpose. By the time Eunice gave up dancing and came back to Australia with a new husband, Isabel was eleven years old and her collection of postcards filled the box.

Not only was her new father a stranger but her mother had become a stranger too. No longer the glamorous, exotic dancer of the postcards, she was a tired, disappointed woman in her thirties with injuries to her legs and feet that would confine her to a wheelchair by the time she was forty-five. Isabel's father had been killed in action a few months before she was born in 1943. When the war was over, Eunice somehow managed to get herself to London for an audition and was soon touring Europe. She had left Isabel with her parents, promising to be back in a year or so. But she was still dancing in 1953 when she met Eric at a cocktail party in Monaco. He was an under-secretary at the British consulate with a promising career in the foreign office. They were married that year, and just a few weeks later their car was hit by a drunk driver as they rounded a steep bend on a narrow road between Nice and Grasse. Eric escaped unscathed but Eunice's feet and legs were crushed. For months she languished in hospital before she was well enough for Eric to be able to get her on a ship back to Australia. Slowly she learned to walk again, but she always needed a stick and as she grew older, arthritis locked her joints to rigidity. By the time Isabel was eleven, she was living in Perth with a mother she barely knew and a stepfather who adored her as if she had been his own daughter.

Isabel scanned the international listings of women who offered accommodation to other women travelling alone. It was a network she had joined years before but never used, although she had played host to women visiting Australia – a Turkish woman had stayed once, and one from Bratislava. Finally she worked out the cost of the trip and added twenty-five per cent for emergencies. Eunice's legacy would more than cover it. She wondered briefly if there was something distasteful about using the money so soon after her mother's death. People might think she had been waiting for Eunice to die so that she could get away. But she had spent too much of her life wondering what people might think. It had stopped her doing so many things, and driven her to do others. She looked at the important dates in her diary: the expiry of her mayoral term, Doug's birthday, Kate's birthday . . . but if she looked at all the dates there would be no right time to leave. She might just as well close her eyes and stick a pin in the calendar. Monday 12 May, the pin said. She wrote it in her diary and dialled the number of the travel agent.

Isabel knew that everyone thought she was a good organiser. She had a dogged quality, an intellectual and emotional stamina that enabled her to stick with things, to retain the grand vision as well as to struggle with the tedious detail. She wanted to go through all Eunice's papers before she left – it would be good to take some of the diaries with her – but first she would have to think about organising things at home for the time she was away, although organisation was the easy part. The rest would be much harder. How do you tell your husband and children that, much as you love them, you are leaving them for a while? That for the next twelve months they must carry the burden of servicing the complex web of relationships that sustains the family? How do you tell your closest friends that you are no longer content just to discuss this midlife angst, this restlessness, this longing for solitude, but plan to turn it into action?

Isabel woke at night with her heart thumping in her chest, sweating over plans that were thrilling by day and terrifying by night. She stared at herself in the bathroom mirror and wondered how she had arrived at this point. This plump woman with fine blonde hair twisted into a knot at the back of her head, the unmistakably pale Celtic looks – who was she? Eunice's daughter, Doug's wife, mother to Luke, Debra and Kate, mother-in-law to Mac and Jason, daughter-in-law to Jack and Freda, grandmother of Danny and Ruth, closest friend of Robin, Sally and Grace . . . But who was she really? Who would she be away from all those relationships, those roles, those responsibilities? Who was Isabel Carter?

'You can't be serious,' said Grace. 'You can't honestly mean you're going away for a year, leaving Doug, the kids, everything?'

Isabel knew it would be tough and that Grace would be the toughest, but she had decided to tell her friends first. She needed a test run, a chance to talk about it before she told Doug and the family. They were waiting for an explanation. Robin, with that thin, intense look, leaning forward, her hands curled around her coffee cup, as though listening to a submission by opposing counsel. Sally, leaning back to run her hands through her wild hair, her glasses perched on top of her head, and Grace, immaculate as ever, crossing her legs, folding her arms and turning slightly in her chair, her body language oozing disapproval.

Isabel paused as the waiter piled their dirty cups onto a tray and took the order for more coffee. She felt a great wave of embarrassment and vulnerability. These were her closest friends. They had supported each other through personal and professional crises, parents dying, and children leaving home, job changes, house moves, political activism, diets and really bad haircuts. Suddenly they seemed like strangers. She had hoped that they would see it as she did, that she wouldn't have to explain. She swallowed hard and began to shred a paper napkin with nervous fingers.

'Look, we're constantly talking about how we feel, about anger, frustration or needing solitude. We're always joking about menopause and midlife crises and . . . well, we joke but it's serious too, and sometimes I feel it might swallow me up, like I might wake up one morning and find that all those feelings are smothering me and I can't actually draw breath.'

She paused, hoping that one of them might pick up on her lead but they said nothing. 'I've been living the same life for decades, married to Doug, being a mother then a grandmother. I feel so desperate that one day I'll be dead and it will be all I've ever done. Sometimes I feel as though all the important things in my life have already happened.'

'But your life is changing all the time,' Grace said. 'You've said it yourself. Okay, you've lived here for thirty-odd years, and been married to Doug, but in that time you've had jobs, had children who've grown up and left home. Look at what you're doing now. You're the mayor, for heaven's sake! All sorts of things have happened to you.'

'But that's exactly what I mean,' Isabel said. 'It's happened to me, life has happened to me. I haven't directed it, I haven't made things happen. I've just responded to things, fate, nature, opportunity . . . whatever you want to call it. Doug, his job, the kids, their kids. I did what I had to, and it's precious to me, all of it, but now I want to do something different. Something just for me, something I've chosen.'

'The refuge didn't just happen, being the mayor didn't just happen,' Grace persisted. 'You chose those things, you had to campaign for them, and look what a fantastic job you're doing.'

'My second term is up at the end of April and I've already said I won't run again. Six years as mayor and five as a councillor is enough – for me and for the council. You're right in one way, Grace, but those things were an outer journey, this is different. I'm not sure if I can explain it but I think now I'm ready for the inner journey.'

The silence was long enough to make her uncomfortable.

'I'm not quite sure what you mean,' Sally ventured. 'Are you saying you're going away and not coming back?'

'No, no, not at all. I just mean that I want a break, an adventure, something totally different and totally on my own, away from here. I want a year of my life all to myself. I am so tired of running around doing what other people expect me to do, and what I feel I *ought* to be doing.'

She was close to tears, almost at the point of apologising for considering it, but she could not let it go. 'And I want to see the places where Mum was, get some sense of her life there. Grace, you've often talked about going off somewhere quiet, to the country, having time to do your patchwork, starting the organic herbs business. You even did a business plan. That's your dream.'

Grace turned to her impatiently. 'Honestly, Isabel, I think you've gone off your rocker. Of course I talk about it but I couldn't afford it. I need to work for at least another eight years. I don't have a husband anymore, and Ron and I weren't good savers. He didn't leave me a fortune, you know.'

'I think it's wonderful, Isabel,' Sally said. 'It's so exciting and romantic going to all those places where Eunice danced. I bet you've been planning it secretly for ages.'

Isabel smiled at her in relief. 'Well, I've always wanted to do it but somehow it didn't seem possible. But then Mum died and there was her money and I realised this was something I could do. Christmas finally decided me. That was when I actually started to plan it seriously. You know, I feel that I've been making it possible for other people to make their journeys – Doug, the kids – now it's my turn.'

Robin skimmed the froth off her coffee with a teaspoon. 'I think it's wonderful too,' she said. 'I was reading another one of those books on menopause, and there's a chapter in there about tribal communities where the women go away for a year when they reach menopause. They spend time grieving for the loss of childbearing and then preparing for the new phase of their lives. It's a ritual.'

'I thought she wanted to get away from the rituals,' Grace sniffed. 'And don't tell me Isabel is grieving because she can't have more kids. We're all thankful we don't have to worry about that anymore.'

Sally reached out to put a conciliatory hand on Grace's arm. 'Hang on, Grace, what are you getting so upset about? Anyone would think that Isabel was asking *you* to go away for a year. I'd love to do something like that. Move right out of my own life for a while.'

Grace pulled her arm away in irritation. 'I see, Sally, so you're going to chuck everything in and disappear up a mountain for a year or so? Give up teaching art, get into rock painting and become a hermit? Go on some mystical retreat?'

'I don't really see it like that,' Sally said slowly. 'But I've often thought of taking time out – a sort of sabbatical, away from everything and everybody.' She turned to Isabel. 'It's more than a sabbatical or retreat, really, isn't it? An emotional and spiritual journey.'

Grace pushed her coffee cup aside. 'I think you're completely mad,' she said. 'Do you honestly think you're going to enjoy traipsing around Europe on your own for a year? What would you do? You've got a husband, a lovely home, you're respected here. You can't really mean you'd risk all that simply to go off on some inner journey. What about your kids, and the grandchildren? What about Doug, what does he think about it?'

There was a silence and Isabel stared at her coffee.

'Oh my god, you haven't told him yet, have you?'

She swallowed hard and shook her head. 'I wanted to talk to you three first. Sort of nut out the issues, to help me when I talk to him.'

'So how do you think he'll take it?' Robin asked gently.

'He'll be devastated, of course,' Grace cut in. 'He'll think she's leaving him.'

'Are you?' Robin asked.

Isabel shook her head. 'No, not leaving him in the sense that Grace means. I'm just stepping out of my life for a while. But I'm coming back. Of course I'm coming back.'

'What if he isn't there when you do come back?' Grace asked, leaning forward. 'What if he's gone off on his own journey? How would you feel about that?'

Isabel looked at her, pondering the question. 'Pretty devastated,

I suppose, but I would think that he had a right to do it. And I'd hope that he'd come back too.'

Grace laughed. 'You're mad! Robin, come on, you're the rational one – make her see sense.'

Robin paused, looking from Isabel to Grace. 'Actually, she sounds perfectly sensible to me,' she said quietly. 'It's a risk, but one she's prepared to take. It's exciting, really, an adventure. Like that movie *Shirley Valentine*, the bit where she talks to the wall and asks whether this is all there is, when she feels sort of betrayed by life.'

'Oh, Robin, really, *Shirley Valentine* was a great movie but that character was a downtrodden housewife. You're single, a brilliant lawyer with a beautiful home and plenty of money. You have what a lot of women would kill for – and so does Isabel – and you can hardly compare poor old Doug to that domineering, oafish husband in *Shirley Valentine*.' Grace shifted her chair further under the shade of the café awning. 'Isabel's hardly oppressed and downtrodden, she's always been free to do what she wanted.'

Robin had flushed with embarrassment at Grace's first onslaught but now she bounced back. 'Since when did you become the reverend mother, Grace?' she snapped. 'I can recall many conversations where you talked of feeling burnt out and wanting to be left alone. I think I can recall times when you talked about how nice it would be to get away and not have all the responsibilities of being a successful nineties woman.'

'But that's just talk,' Grace responded. 'It does us good to have a whinge from time to time, gets it off your chest. I've never said I wanted to go off on some inner journey to transform myself.'

'Nor have I,' said Robin. 'But right now the idea is very tempting. I'm feeling really exhausted and . . . well . . . scattered. I'm just longing for solitude and space for myself.'

Grace picked up her bag, searching for her sunglasses. 'I can't believe we're having this conversation.'

Sally leaned across, putting her hand on Isabel's arm. 'I think that if you can do it, if you can handle the family side of it, it would be the most wonderful thing. But in any case, Isabel, you don't need our approval.' She paused, grinning sideways at Grace. 'You don't even need Grace's approval.'

'Well, that's for sure!' Grace said. 'I'm off. I've promised to babysit for Tim and Angela. I'll see you all soon.' She looked across at Isabel. 'In the meantime I look forward to hearing that you're nominating for a third term. I'm ready for another session of doorknocking. Why don't you book a couple of weeks' getaway down south, that'll give you time to yourself. Bye now.' They watched her weave her way between the tables to the door, shoulders square, slim hips swinging with determination.

'Phew!' said Robin, refilling their water glasses. 'Whatever got into her this morning?'

Isabel leaned back in her chair, exhausted by the tension. 'I knew this was going to be difficult, but I didn't really expect such hostility. I seem to have upset her dreadfully. I'll give her a call later.'

Sally shook her head. 'Let it go, Isabel. She'll sort it out, it's not personal.'

'I know, but I didn't want to upset her, or any of you – sorry.'

Robin reached out to squeeze her hand. 'There's nothing to apologise for. I honestly think it's wonderful. You're very strong, Isabel. You must have thought about how difficult it will be with Doug, and probably the kids too.'

'Of course,' she said. 'I've thought about it endlessly but I keep coming back to the feeling that I am actually entitled to some time to myself after all these years.'

'I suspect they'll tell you that you can have time to yourself at home, that they'll give you space,' Sally said.

'Or, like Grace, they'll suggest you go away on your own for a couple of weeks,' Robin added.

'It's not enough,' Isabel said, hearing the note of desperation in her own voice. 'I need more.'

As they walked slowly from the coffee shop a gentle breeze swept in from the sea and whispered through the pines bordering the park that wound down to the beach. They paused in silence, looking down on the creamy white sand and the glittering blue expanse of the ocean, ruffled now to a slight swell of waves edged with crisp white foam.

'Sometimes I look at this and think I'm in paradise,' Isabel said. 'And then I look again and think it's a prison that I've chosen. Somewhere so fortunate and beautiful that to yearn for something else, for change, would be disloyal and ungrateful.'

'There's nothing ungrateful or disloyal about wanting time away, time to yourself,' Sally said. 'In fact, it can even be about renewing your relationship with the place and the people you're retreating from. But I don't think Doug and the family will see it that way. They'll feel threatened, so they'll almost certainly see it as selfishness.'

'Is that how you see it?' Isabel asked.

'Not at all.'

'Me neither,' said Robin. 'Look, I'm single, but I'm longing to be free from all the claims on my time and energy, so with all your commitments you must feel all that multiplied by thousands. I envy you having the courage to do it.' She put on her sunglasses and searched for her car keys. 'When will you talk to Doug? This week?'

Isabel nodded. 'Yes, it's not fair to leave it any longer. I've booked for the middle of May. I'm dreading telling him.'

Sally took her arm as they strolled across the car park. 'We could meet next Saturday. Talk over how it went.'

TWO

Friendships hang together like a house of cards. One person takes a deep breath, the cards shift and flutter, none is untouched. Isabel took the deep breath and the cards shifted. They had known each other for years; Isabel first met Sally when she bought one of her paintings at an exhibition. Grace and Sally met at yoga and Robin and Isabel met when they sat beside each other at an International Women's Day breakfast. They were extended family, easier to get along with and often more reliable than their own families. They were sounding boards, shoulders to cry on; they had given each other support, encouragement, understanding without judgment. They called themselves the Gang of Four. A dramatic action on the part of one was bound to affect the others.

Grace could not quite explain the anger and sense of panic she had felt since Isabel dropped her bombshell. The following week she sat behind the large Tasmanian oak desk in her very comfortable office wondering why she was feeling so bad. Ever since the Sunday morning conversation she had been overwhelmed with pointless, unfocused anxiety.

At fifty-five Grace was almost the same age as Isabel, older than the other two, and widowed ten years earlier. She had started her working life as a nurse and risen from the wards to become head of nursing education at the university. She had status, respect, high blood pressure, a passion for patchwork quilts (of which she owned some fine examples), a very active social life and a troublesome shopping habit. She was a small-framed woman with an olive complexion and thick, dark hair that she wore in a short, chunky bob. She liked the way that grey was starting to break up and soften the colour. Grace had a natural elegance and she dressed to enhance it. Today she was wearing an olive-green linen suit that had cost her an arm and a leg. She fingered the linen nervously. That particular arm and leg had been earmarked as an extra contribution to her negligible superannuation, but the long skirt cut on the cross and the neat shape of the jacket had seduced her.

Grace leaned back in her revolving chair. She couldn't have felt more shaken if Isabel had slapped her in the face. She pulled out the bottom drawer of her desk, kicked off her shoes and put her feet in the drawer. It was a habit she had developed years earlier as night sister in a tiny hospital in rural New South Wales. Her feet got so cold in the early hours that she kept a stone hot water bottle in the bottom drawer of the desk and rested her feet on it to warm them. No need for a hot bottle in the middle of summer in this office, where the temperature was so finely controlled that it gave no indication of the season. But Grace still derived a degree of comfort from putting her feet in the drawer.

She gazed at the campus lake and the sloping lawns where, on weekdays, students spread themselves on the grass pretending to study, and on Saturdays wedding groups posed for photographers before heading off to their receptions. She thought of Isabel talking about how often she cried with inexplicable anger and resentment, about tears shed with a sense of hopelessness. Grace was used to helping people get their feelings under control. As a ward sister, and later a director of nursing, she had been firm but compassionate, respected and popular with the nurses, able to combine the distance of authority with a reassuring presence. But Grace had never learned to manage her own feelings, or perhaps she had learned to manage them by cutting them off at the roots. In fact, she was so completely out of touch with her own feelings that she didn't know what was hidden away inside. And she never cried. Never. Not even when she was alone.

Occasionally her friends challenged her about the time bomb ticking away inside her. 'That's nursing training,' Grace would say with a grin. 'Can't feel too much when the patients are dying or their limbs are dropping off all around you.' But it wasn't just the nursing training. 'People rely on us,' her mother used to say. 'The vicar's family has responsibilities, even you, Grace. We all have a role to play, dear, we learn to put others first.' Her father was an Anglican minister, her mother a quiet, restrained woman who made being the vicar's wife into a full-time job. It was a somewhat chilly and constrained household, functioning on politeness and a policy of not rocking the boat.

'One day,' Sally had said to her, 'all those repressed feelings are going to come up and hit you square in the face.'

'Probably,' said Grace. She knew intellectually that Sally was likely to be right, but she didn't understand it at a gut level, so she let it flow in through one ear and straight out the other. 'But then I'll have my friends around to help, won't I?'

Even when Ron died Grace barely shed a tear. They had been married for twenty years, and while it wasn't the love story of the century, it wasn't that bad either. Ron's death was slow and painful: the chemotherapy had not only failed to halt his cancer but had poisoned his system with nausea and cramps. Grace took two years off to nurse him at home and when the end came she was sad and relieved, but she wasn't sure which emotion was dominant, because she could only register them as names of feelings rather than identifying and experiencing them. But she did know that no longer having to be a nurse at home seemed like a new lease of life, and in her occasional quiet moments she apologised to Ron and hoped that wherever he had gone (up, she thought, rather than down) he could hear and forgive her for being glad about getting her life back.

Right after the cremation she snapped out of being an efficient home nurse to being an equally efficient grief counsellor for her son, her mother-in-law and her sister-in-law. And almost immediately she returned to work. Ron's long illness and her home nursing had wiped out their savings. She swiftly became director of nursing and was soon offered the job at the university. So here she was, on this clear, warm March day, head of nursing training, member of numerous boards and committees, mother of Tim, a computer scientist, mother-in-law of Angela and grandmother of Emily, nearly four, and legal representative for her father, who had Alzheimer's disease, and her mother-in-law, who had Parkinson's, both in nursing homes. Here she was with her feet in a drawer unable to stop this scary, fluttery feeling in her stomach that had haunted her since the weekend. Well, at least it was on the inside, no one could see it, and so she could pretend it wasn't happening. Hopefully it would soon go away and she would get back that familiar tense-but-safe feeling with which she was so comfortable. Come to think of it, perhaps it wasn't Isabel's irresponsible scheme. Maybe it was simply that she was attempting to give up coffee – it was almost thirty-six hours since she'd had any caffeine.

Grace took her feet out of the drawer, and went to her secretary's office and surveyed the coffee pot, which was, as usual, comfortingly half full and hot.

'I don't know how it is, Denise, that you always manage to have fresh coffee in the pot, it's always hot and never tastes as though it's been standing for ages. It's an extraordinary talent.' And she filled both their mugs and put Denise's down on the desk beside her keyboard.

'Not really,' said Denise, who was twenty-eight, deeply attached to Grace and saw her as a fine role model. 'It's easy – you and I drink it so quickly it never has to stand there and get stale. Although I must say you seemed to be ignoring it the last couple of days, so I had to drink your share.'

'I got a bit carried away with the idea of giving it up,' Grace admitted, sipping the very strong Arabic blend. 'Or at least cutting down. Do you think we drink too much coffee?'

'Grace, you're the nurse, I'm just a minion. What do you think?'

'I think we probably drink too much coffee,' Grace replied, feeling the comforting lift of real caffeine flooding through her system. 'But it doesn't seem to be doing us any harm. After all, we both exercise and neither of us drinks or smokes, so I think we can probably tolerate it okay.'

'Best rationalisation I've heard,' said Denise. 'Are you okay? Your hand looks a bit shaky.'

'Rubbish,' Grace snapped, turning back to her office. 'Steady as a rock. Could you get me the midwifery standards files, please.' And she went back into the office and put her feet straight in the drawer.

Sally, meanwhile, was taking a party of Year 11 students to the art gallery. She was covering for a colleague who taught Year 11 photography and who had come down with shingles two days earlier. Sally, who found it hard to say no, had agreed to take both the photography group and her own art students to the exhibition with the help of a student teacher. The idea was that the photography class would go around the photojournalism exhibition with the student teacher while Sally took her own class around the gallery's permanent exhibitions. But Sally had done those exhibitions many times before and she wasn't in a mood for Charles Blackman or Sidney Nolan or Arthur Boyd, or even any Aboriginal artists. So she told the student teacher to take charge of her group while she went to the photojournalism exhibition. It was the sort of outing that many teachers dread, because of the potential for the kids to get lost (inadvertently or deliberately), upset gallery patrons and staff, and generally be obnoxious or simply boisterous and high-spirited. But Sally was popular with the teenagers and she rarely had discipline problems.

She was a striking woman who looked younger than her forty-nine years, and she wore her unruly grey-blonde hair to her shoulderblades, controlling it with two large tortoiseshell combs. She had started life as a mousy child with mousy curls that had gone blonde in her teens and turned rather suddenly to grey in her early forties. Even Grace, who believed that as a general rule women over forty-five should wear their hair short, made an exception in Sally's case.

She had a talent for distinctive clothes, most of which she made herself. 'You're into textures, aren't you?' sales assistants would say, more as a statement than a question, when they baled her up in fabric shops, fingering offcuts of velvet, short lengths of paisley patterned wool, or the ends of rolls of embroidered silk.

Sally was indeed into textures but she was also into colours. Rich colours, purples and aquamarines, burnt orange and cerise, olive, lime and cobalt, and she mixed them courageously. She was easy to spot from a distance, swinging along in skirts made from panels of different fabric, long, loose jackets, chunky silver jewellery, or unique colourful pieces that she picked up at craft exhibitions. She looked interesting, somewhat eccentric, and more confident than she felt. In fact, she was in many ways rather conservative and surprisingly conformist, painfully shy but good at concealing it, and certainly interesting. She was the only one of the Gang of Four who had managed to stay single all her life.

At eighteen she had left Australia with a group of friends for the great Aussie descent on London, and lived in a shared house in Islington where she never knew if she would come home from art school to find her bed occupied by a new arrival. In England she had fallen in love. Simon was fifteen years older, a product of Harrow and Cambridge; he was a lawyer with a tiny mews cottage in Gray's Inn. He also had a seriously bad memory because he forgot to mention to Sally that he had a wife, two children, three labradors, a horse and an elegant house with six acres of land near Bristol. When Sally found she was pregnant, she was naive enough to think that she and Simon would work things out together. His angry instruction to 'get rid of it', the five hundred pounds in an envelope he stuffed into her hands and the parting shot that she'd better not try to contact him 'or else' were shattering. Unable to face Australia she stayed on in London for a couple of years, moving to a pleasant flat shared with another girl in Earl's Court and trying to repair her ravaged life.

She was almost twenty-two when she finally made her way back home to rural Victoria. A couple of months later, the town and the house where she had grown up seemed stifling after London, and she moved to Melbourne, completed her degree, and soon had a quiet and exemplary career as an art teacher. Towards the end of the seventies she had lived with an Irish mining engineer and had moved with him to the west. From time to time she thought she loved him and perhaps she did, but not enough. They parted with some acrimony when he wanted her to move again, this time from Perth to one of the most remote communities in the Pilbara.

A few years later she fell headlong into a chaotic relationship with a fellow teacher. Harry was an alcoholic, delightful when sober, fascinating and entertaining after a couple of drinks, abusive, melancholic and incredibly tedious when drunk. As he was drunk most of the time it was an extraordinarily painful and complicated period, and on reflection Sally wondered why it had taken so long to extricate herself. Even now, five years later, Harry had not really let go. For her part Sally was relieved to be alone, except for those very occasional days when she wondered just how it would be to wake up beside someone she truly loved.

Sally had not slept well since the day Isabel broke her news. It had made her restless and envious. The night before the gallery trip she had sat up late finishing a Doris Lessing novel, *The Summer Before the Dark*, which increased her restlessness. It was after one before she put out the light, she was up at six and she was a woman who needed her eight hours a night. She worried about Isabel having to break the news to Doug and her children, and she worried for Doug, of whom she was fond, and for Debra, Kate and Luke, whom she had known so long they seemed like nieces and nephew. But most of all she wanted Isabel not to change her mind.

The student group dissolved into the crowd and Sally browsed the catalogue and paused for a while in front of pictures of the women of the Save Our Sons campaign. She studied the passion in their faces, the tension in the bodies, the press of the crowd marching behind the leaders. Photography was art but very different from the art with which she spent her days. That morning she was moved by the intensity of the photographic images; spontaneity and transience transformed into something fixed and lasting. There was so much the camera could do that brushes, oils or pastels could not. It wasn't that one medium was more or less than the other, simply that she cherished the difference and had long yearned to know both.

'Were you at those demos, Miss Erskine?' said a voice over her shoulder.

She turned and smiled. 'Yes, Adam, I was in the anti-Vietnam marches, but I was too young to have a son there.'

'I know that,' Adam said, adding conspiratorially, 'I just wanted to get away from the others and see some of the photos.'

Sally nodded and they moved on side by side, past images of election campaigns, of Mrs Petrov at Darwin airport, of Gough Whitlam maintaining his rage on the steps of the old Parliament House.

'I always wanted to do photography,' Sally said in a rare moment of self-revelation.

'Yeah!' Adam nodded. 'Great, isn't it? Takes you right into the moment. Why didn't you?'

She shrugged: 'You know how it is, life takes you on a certain course and you get caught up, suddenly the time has gone by and you never got around to it. Come to think of it, you don't know – you probably haven't had time to experience that yet.'

Adam shifted his backpack from his right to his left shoulder and shoved his hands into his pockets. 'No,' he said. 'But Mum and Dad used to talk like that. Dad used to say he wished he'd learned to play the guitar. He used to say that when he retired he was going to buy a guitar and learn.' Sally turned to him in concern. 'Yeah! Well, he never got to retire, did he? I thought about that, at the funeral, you know. I s'pose I should've been thinking more uplifting stuff but all I kept thinking about was Dad waiting all those years to have time to learn the guitar.'

He shrugged and looked down at the floor, and Sally realised he was trying to get a grip on his voice, fighting back the tears that threatened to embarrass him, just as he had the day she had sat with him on the wall outside the art room. That was on his first day back at school after his father had died after falling from a cooling tower in the power station where he was supervising a routine repair job. 'Adam . . .' she began.

He looked up quickly. 'It's all right, Miss Erskine, I'm all right, not going to blub in the art gallery.' He grinned and blew his nose. 'Y'know, I'm going to do the things I want when I want, because you don't know what might happen, do you?'

Sally looked at him thoughtfully. 'No, Adam, you don't, and

even if you have a long life you could end up still not having done the things that were important to you.'

Adam drifted away and Sally wandered on, paying more attention now to her thoughts than to the photographs. She came to an abrupt halt in front of a picture of a two-tier traffic bridge broken apart, the upper level collapsed onto the lower, trapping cars and their occupants. She bent to read the caption and caught her breath.

October 1989, Loma Prieta, San Francisco. A 250-ton section of the Oakland Bay Bridge collapses in the earthquake.
Photograph: *The Oakland Tribune*.

There were other shots of the earthquake: a couple climbing cautiously down the crumbling masonry, a three-storey apartment block collapsing as its footings broke loose, burning buildings, people searching for their possessions in piles of rubble, exhausted relief workers gratefully accepting coffee from a proffered flask. And in the background the familiar span of the Golden Gate Bridge and the broad expanse of San Francisco Bay.

Sally sank down onto one of the low benches and stared at the photographs, her heart beating faster, a prickly sensation heating her skin, not just a hot flash, this was something different. San Francisco, the photographs unleashed a confusing welter of memory and emotion. Such eerie synchronicity: San Francisco, the conversation with Adam. Sally shivered in the warm gallery and then looked around her. She had lost track of her students and must round them up again. She took a long last look at the photographs and walked out to the central staircase where an hour and a half of restraint was starting to tell on the students, who were becoming noisier by the minute.

'Come on now, guys!' Sally said. 'Keep the noise down. It's time we got out of here and you can go and get something to eat.' And she led the way down the gallery stairs and out into the plaza, where they spread out on the stone benches by the fountain and ate their sandwiches.

'Good, eh?' Adam grinned at her, signalling back at the gallery.

'Very good,' she smiled. 'And you're right, Adam. You must do what you want when you want it.' And she sat on a stone seat and began to unwrap her salad sandwich.

Robin couldn't wait to get out of court. For one thing she was dying to go to the toilet, but mainly it was because she was feeling claustrophobic. The prosecution's closing argument had been exceptionally long and tedious, and Justice Simpson had delivered a ponderous and deeply flawed summing-up. The jury was almost obliged to return a guilty verdict, and there would have to be an appeal on grounds of misdirection.

As soon as the court rose she bolted for the toilets and then, picking up her papers, turned back to the robing room and got out of her wig and gown.

'If only the good Lord would save us from the likes of Justice Simpson,' said Malcolm Wells, who was prosecuting the case Robin had been defending. 'You must be hopping mad, Robin.'

'I really thought he'd lost it this time,' she agreed.

'You'll have to appeal, of course. You've got grounds,' Malcolm said, pre-empting the jury in words as Robin had already done in her thoughts.

She nodded. 'Meanwhile, my client gets to cool his heels in jail.'

Malcolm shook his head. 'Well, I've got to say you put up a very strong case. Without Simpson's interference you could have been certain of an acquittal. That police evidence was always problematic.'

'He should have retired years ago.' Robin sighed irritably, pulling on her jacket. 'He's been a real worry recently.'

Malcolm Wells removed his wig and smoothed his hands over his thinning hair. 'I know that a couple of other counsel have considered filing complaints with the chief justice. We should get together and make a complaint,' he said. 'See you in the bar? The jury'll be out for at least a couple of hours.'

Robin shook her head. 'No thanks. I'm going to have a walk, need the fresh air. I've got a bit of a headache.'

She did have a headache, but she was going out because she wanted to be alone. She was desperate to shake off the claustrophobia that had descended on her since Isabel had broken her news. And she also wanted to make a call without being overheard. Slinging her bag over her shoulder Robin walked out of the court building and across into the park, where dozens of pigeons and a few seagulls were harassing the tourists and city workers eating their lunch in the shade of the peppermint trees.

Robin was a dark horse. That's what her friends said. It's what her mother used to say. 'Our Robin, she's a dark horse, that one, and no mistake,' Mrs Percy would say, standing at the old earthenware sink in the stuffy kitchen of the little house in south London. 'Secrets, secrets, nothing but secrets with that girl.'

It was a survival tactic. The second of seven children, sharing a bedroom with three sisters, the only way Robin got any privacy was by keeping her cards close to her chest. She had learned that the greatest power resided in those who had the least to say, and she knew when to keep her mouth shut. In that corner of Battersea, privacy was a rare commodity and Robin knew its value. In Australia in the nineties she still put a high price on it, now more than ever because she had something to hide.

She found a shady spot on the grass and, leaning back against the tree trunk, dialled the number that connected her to the private phone on Justice McEwan's desk. 'Me!' she announced when the judge picked up the phone. 'Jury's just retired.'

'How was it?' McEwan asked.

'Bloody dreadful, honestly, Jim. Lionel Simpson is really losing it.'

'Misdirection?'

'To a gross degree. Even Malcolm Wells commented on it.'

'You'll have to talk to some other people and get a complaint to the chief justice.' He paused. 'Shall we meet at your place?'

'Mmm. Six o'clock, okay? I've got some fresh trout I could grill.'

'Sounds wonderful,' McEwan said. 'Take it easy, darling, you sound terribly harassed.'

'I'm furious. Ashby is innocent. And a homophobic judge has misdirected the jury. This poor man is going to spend five or six months in jail while this is sorted out.'

'We'll talk about it tonight over the trout . . . or something.'

Robin grinned. 'Yes, or something . . . it's over a week since I saw you.'

'I know,' he replied. 'Probably won't recognise you. Good thing your distinguishing features are engraved on my memory! I'll be there at six.'

Robin closed her eyes and rested her head against the tree, savouring the moment of peaceful isolation amidst a crowd of noisy strangers. She pushed her fingers into the grass and its moist warmth filled her with a longing to be out of town, to be somewhere still and silent, where she could rest and run. Run along a forest track or a cliff path, run so hard that she got the red mist in front of her eyes, and her lungs started to burn and her calf muscles screamed for mercy. Running along the beach at five o'clock every morning was never quite enough to force the knots of anxiety from her chest and gut, and clear her head. Isabel's announcement had resonated with the book Robin was reading. The author had done what Isabel was doing, taken time out of her life, found a remote cottage on the Welsh coast and retreated to it. There she ran daily along the cliff tops, and dedicated her time to writing a novel about the life of Beethoven. To Robin it sounded like ecstasy.

The problem for dark horses is that they have to carry so much in their heads, plans for protection, plans for evasion, contingency plans, camouflage and evidence; evidence they have collected in case they need it in arguments with themselves. On her forty-fifth birthday Robin had decided to change by the time she was fifty. She put quite a bit of mental energy into working out what she wanted to be like at fifty: calm, steady, more open, and enjoying a less stressful life. She would cut down on work, fit in some long weekends away, spend more time with her women friends. She visualised being like Sally, colourful, warm and wise, with that easy flowing energy she seemed to radiate; or perhaps like Isabel, thoughtful, outspoken and full of moral courage. Her five-year plan had been to simplify her life, but six years later she was just as busy, just as stressed and had complicated her life by falling in love with Jim McEwan, who was married.

About once a month Jim and Robin had intense and painful conversations about their future. They lived in one of the most isolated state capitals in the world with a population of around a million. It was a parochial environment, conservative and inward looking. The circle they moved in was small and the ensuing scandal would damage both of them. Were they ready to risk their careers, their status, their reputations, in order to be together? What would they do? Ideally, they'd move out of town. Jim would let his wife take the house, Robin would sell her house by the beach and they would live together in peace and harmony in the karri forests of the southwest, or by the wild and craggy white sands of the Great Southern.

The conversations had been the backdrop of Robin's life for four years. Should they make a move now or wait a while? And what about Monica, Jim's wife? How would she cope? She and Robin had once worked together, could they really inflict this on her and the children? And then there was Robin's career to consider. She was likely to be invited to take silk this year, but there were times now when her private life seemed more precious than her career goals. Time and again they discussed it, moving each time towards taking action before one of them would draw back in caution. They were just about due for one of these conversations.

Robin was an outstandingly good lawyer, a hard worker, conscientious and intelligent, but it wasn't easy for her; she wasn't naturally brilliant and she had struggled to get where she was. At sixteen she had been a typist in a solicitor's office in Battersea. Pregnant at seventeen, she had married in haste to protect her own and her family's reputation. But the baby was stillborn. Robin and gentle, well-meaning but boring Tony had been left facing each other across the breakfast table in a one-bedroom flat in Putney, with nothing in common but memories of uncomfortable lust in the back seat of a Morris Minor, and a dead baby.

The divorce took ages but it was amicable and Robin, still

typing, had gone to night school to get her A levels. When she was twenty-five, and the day after she got her results, her father, after a lifetime of disappointment on the football pools, finally managed to put the crosses in the right places. Thanks to the combined efforts of Watford, Liverpool, Queen's Park Rangers and Wolverhampton Wanderers doing what he alone had predicted, Frank found himself in possession of a cheque for seven hundred and fifty thousand pounds, which in those days was a not-so-small fortune. Robin was able to stop trying to calculate how many years it would take her to do a law degree part time and do it full time at London University. From there it was a short step to articles and then the Bar. And in 1984, when a former colleague set up a practice in Australia and invited her to join his chambers, she couldn't get on a plane fast enough.

She had done well, made money and had an architect-designed house of rammed earth and jarrah, with huge windows and a view of one of the best beaches on the west coast. She had more work than she could handle, a wardrobe full of black and charcoal suits for court, regular attacks of acute indigestion, occasional severe migraine headaches, several original works of art by significant local artists, a large ginger cat called Maurice, and the love of Justice McEwan.

The mobile rang. The jury was back. Robin looked at her watch. Only thirty-five minutes – what did that mean? She got up, brushed the grass from her skirt and headed back to the court building, a slim woman in a charcoal grey suit and a white blouse, tired eyes hidden behind black-framed Ray-Bans, sleek dark hair cut to fall to the collar now ruffled by the afternoon breeze. She imagined running along a cliff path on the south coast, and not having to stop. Running for her emotional life, her spiritual life, her physical life, running until her body ached and all she could feel was the pull of her muscles, the beat of her heart and the rasp of her own breathing. She would talk to Jim again, this evening. Last time he was the one saying it was time to do it. Now she would agree with him. She had had enough. Forget taking silk, forget ambitions for the judiciary, forget Monica. She was too worn out to cope with it all anymore. At fifty-one surely

31

it was time to reach out for bliss, time for change, renewal – transformation, even.

But did taking off with one's lover constitute an inner journey or renewal, and what would the other three say about Jim? None of them was a prude but Robin suspected that while they would relish the falling in love, they might have something to say about an affair with another woman's husband. She would be a failed feminist . . . again. What price ideology when it comes to passion? Robin shook her head to free it of the imagined reproaches. Was that really how it would be or was it just her guilty conscience working overtime?

THREE

'A year?' Doug said, swinging around so fast he knocked over his glass of wine. 'I thought you were talking about three or four weeks. You can't mean a year.'

Isabel went inside for a bucket of water to sluice the wine from the floorboards of the deck. It was early in the evening, and they were sitting watching the sunset. She had steeled herself to tell him, having backed off from it the two previous evenings when he came home with a pile of files to read before a meeting with the minister. Now the meeting was over, and he had come home relieved, able to think of other things. She knew it must be tonight.

She watched as he wrapped the broken glass in an old newspaper and put it in the bin, his face flushed from bending, his fine grey hair falling forward across his forehead. She looked at him with the love and knowing of thirty-four years; she was about to hurt him dreadfully. They went back out to the deck. The sun had sunk a little lower, the sky turned a duller shade of rose.

'Now, tell me again,' he said.

And so she told him again. A year alone, wandering around Europe, the places she'd always wanted to visit, the need to get away from everything, from everyone, an inner journey, solitude, reflection, renewal.

'You're leaving me,' he said. 'That's what this is about.'

Isabel put her hand on his arm.

'No, Doug, I'm not leaving you. This is not about you, it's about me. I've been looking after everyone, everything, for years. I just want to have some time looking after only myself.'

'But you've always been able to do what you wanted,' he said, his face tight with distress, his eyes fixed on the horizon.

'Within the limits imposed on me by our situation, the family, your job, the need to look after Mum and Eric. I have fitted my expectations and my aspirations around all that. Now I want to expand the horizons.'

'You would leave us all for a year? A whole year? You can't mean it.'

She poured herself another glass of wine. 'You left us for a year.'

'That's unfair, that was work. The department loaned me to the Vietnamese government.'

'Yes, and you were mad keen to go. Couldn't get there fast enough and so involved with it that you didn't even bother to use the two trips home they wrote into the contract for you. If I hadn't flown up there and forced you to take a couple of weeks off, I wouldn't have seen you at all that year. And the kids didn't see you at all.'

'You never said you resented it at the time, now you're throwing it back at me.'

'I didn't resent it at the time and I don't resent it now. I'm simply pointing out that it was okay for you to go away for a year then, so it ought to be okay for me to go away for a year now.' She was struggling to stay calm.

'It's different.'

'How?'

'You're choosing to go away for no reason –'

'I'm going for a very good reason, which is that I want to, that it's a challenge, it's something I need to do. Just the same as when you went to Vietnam, the same as when you went to PNG for six months. The opportunities were there. It would have made sense for you to send someone else but you wanted to do those things and you did them. This is just the same.'

'What about the children?'

'They're adults, all three of them.'

'They need their mother here, you're not being fair.'

'Doug, that's ridiculous and you know it. They're adults. If they can survive their father going away for a year when they were in their teens, they can certainly survive their mother going away for a year when they're grown up and married. It's not as though I'm going forever. I'm not leaving you or them.'

They sat in silence as the sun slipped down behind the horizon and the rose glow faded to lavender and then grey. She took his hand but he would not return her grasp. The conversation began again. It went on and on; explanations, justifications, exaggerations, recriminations. Isabel was bone tired and nauseated. She could put her arms around him and tell him that it would be all right, she wouldn't go away, she would stay here, that nothing would change, but she knew it wouldn't work. It would be a bandaid for him and a fatal wound for her.

She had always done the emotional search and rescue in this relationship, she had carried that side of it for thirty-four years, managing the way they related to everyone, rescuing Doug from the various family dramas, shielding him, smoothing things over, making him feel better. She had always been the one to offer the olive branch after an argument, to broach the silence, to make the first concession, to suggest a compromise. She loved him dearly but she was exhausted with being responsible for his feelings. He looked at her now, waiting for the rescue that always came. But this time there was none; she could not rescue him from herself. The exhaustion ate into her limbs, her neck and head ached, and she wanted it to be over, for him to understand. Even to have him angry would be a release.

'All right,' he said, getting up and walking to the edge of the deck. 'All right, supposing I agree to this –'

'I beg your pardon?'

'I said, supposing I agree to this –'

But she cut him off again, her exhaustion replaced now by anger. 'It's not a question of you agreeing to it, Doug. I'm going whether you agree to it or not. I'd like your agreement, I'd like your blessing, but I don't need it.'

'But we're married, you're my wife –'

'Yes, and this is the twentieth century. I'm not some chattel in your custody.' She stacked the glasses onto the tray and walked away from the dark of the deck into the harsh light of the kitchen.

The estrangement was agonising. They lay in the darkness as far apart as possible to avoid inadvertent touching, each occasionally holding their breath to hear from the other's breathing that they were still awake. The tension was stifling. The luminous green figures on the radio alarm clock showed the minutes turning to hours. Isabel thought she might never sleep again. She considered moving into one of the other rooms but knew it could only make things worse. It was ten past three when she felt his hand move across the chasm of the mattress and settle on hers. She turned hers palm up to hold his fingers.

'I'm sorry,' he said in a whisper. 'I love you. I'm frightened of losing you.'

She turned and rolled towards him and they held each other. 'You're not losing me,' she whispered against his shoulder. 'I love you too. Love doesn't rely on proximity.'

'You may be different when you come back.'

'Yes. You were different when you came back from Vietnam.'

'Was I?'

'Mmm. Very different, but you still loved me, and the kids.'

He paused, his hand stroking her shoulder. 'I suppose I was . . . or . . . I mean . . . I knew I was different but I didn't know you knew it.'

'I'm a witch. Remember you told me that on our honeymoon, when I knew you were panicking about money?'

She felt his smile through the darkness. 'Yes, I remember. I've become very dependent on you. So used to you always being there. The kids too. I don't know how they'll take it.'

'That'll depend to a great extent on how they see you taking it. You can make it easier or harder, for them and for me.' She paused. 'Will you help me?'

Doug gave a wry half-laugh that turned to a splutter. 'Christ, Isabel, you want a lot. You want to bugger off for a year and leave me and you want me to help you make it okay with the kids too.'

'And your parents.'

'Shit! God knows what Mum'll say.'

'Will you?'

'I'll make a deal with you,' he said, taking her hand in his again. 'I'll help you on one condition. I want to visit you once. Just once, please, halfway through. I'll come to wherever you are.'

She hesitated, but he was not asking for much. 'Of course.'

He held her tighter. 'Do you remember that poster Kate used to have on her bedroom wall? It had a picture of a white horse on it and it said, if you love something let it go and it'll come back.'

She nodded. 'I remember.'

'Does it always work out like that, d'you think?'

'I don't know. All I can tell you is that I love you and I need you, and that I have every intention of coming back.'

Two weeks later Sally and Isabel drove into the car park from opposite ends at the same time and ended up with their cars nose to nose, which meant that one of them wasn't following the arrows.

'Have you seen Grace?' Isabel asked as they walked towards the glass-enclosed terrace of the café.

'I had lunch with her last week,' Sally said.

'And?'

'I assume you mean how is she feeling about your plans?'

Isabel nodded. 'Yes, and is she still mad at me?'

Sally paused, thinking for a moment as they settled at a table for four. 'She's mad about something. She's in that manic state, you know how she can be, irritable and very stressed. She knows she was unfair. She's restless, uneasy. I think she's genuinely concerned for you – and for Doug, and how it will all work out.'

They sat with their chairs turned to get a good view of the beach, which, despite the brilliant sunshine, had been emptied of its regular sun worshippers by the strong hot wind that was whipping up sand in stinging flurries.

'I hate this wind,' Robin groaned as she flopped into a chair, just minutes after Grace. 'It makes me so tense and irritable.'

'I don't need the wind to make me like that.' Grace smiled ruefully, looking straight at Isabel. 'I can manage it all on my own!'

There was a subtle difference in the energy around the table, an unfamiliar tension. They tried talking about mutual friends, Robin told them about taking Maurice for his cat flu injection, Grace mentioned a concert at the university she thought the others might enjoy.

'I've told Doug,' Isabel said abruptly. 'I've got my leave pass.'

'How was it?' Robin asked, casting a sidelong glance at Grace, who was showing an intense interest in her fingernails.

'At the beginning, really awful. He was hurt and angry and he didn't understand. I came so close to backing down . . .'

'And?'

'Well, then he just seemed to let go. I was so strung up, we'd talked and argued for hours and ended up barely speaking. Then quite suddenly it was as though all the stuff that had gone before dissipated, almost like we were on opposite sides of the street and he suddenly crossed to my side.'

Grace sniffed and looked out of the window.

'Is he okay now?' Sally asked.

'He seems to be. He said he wanted to come and see me once, halfway through the year.'

'And you agreed?'

'Oh yes. Something had changed by then. It was as though he stopped thinking about how it would affect him, and started thinking about me.'

'What about the kids?' Grace asked.

Isabel gave a slight laugh. 'Doug came with me to tell Deb and she had a fit! Cried and shouted at me, said I was abandoning them, that I didn't care about her and Mac and the kids. I almost lost it with her but Doug stopped me, told Deb not to be so selfish and we left. I haven't heard from her since. Doug's spoken to her but he didn't volunteer what she'd said so I thought I wouldn't ask. Kate was fine but then she's always been one to take herself off to different places. She thought it was a great adventure. She and Jason are off to Sydney next month because he's got work there.'

'And Luke?' Sally asked.

'Funny, really; he gave me a metaphorical pat on the head and suggested that I'd be back home in a month once I'd got it out of my system. It was like he was the parent and I was some wilful teenager leaving home.'

'So when do you go?' Grace asked.

'The twelfth of May at seven in the morning. I'm heading to Lisbon first.'

There was a silence around the table as they registered what it would be like not to have her around, not to be able to pop in to the house where they were always welcome, throw themselves down among the magazines on the couch, and talk about anything from government spending to painting their toenails.

'You're an inspiration, Isabel,' Sally said. 'I'm so pleased for you.'

'Are you really sure?' Grace began. 'I mean, Isabel, a year's a long time, you might find your life, your relationships, are radically changed when you get back. You're fifty-four. You may have to start over again in all sorts of ways.'

'I know, Grace, and I know I'll be different too. But it's something I have to do or I'll always regret it.

'I think it's terrific,' Robin said.

'I have to do it,' Isabel said, a lump rising in her throat. 'If I don't make a stand and do this for myself I'll always resent it.'

Grace had been looking out of the window. 'Isabel, I'm sorry,' she said, turning to face her. 'Really sorry for the way I behaved last time. I think you're crazy, I think you're taking a terrible risk and I'm afraid that in a couple of years time you're going to regret it horribly. But . . . well, it's obviously really important to you. So anything you need, anything I can do to help . . .' She paused. 'You only have to ask.' She looked around at the other three. 'I know I couldn't do it. I have a job, responsibilities, the kids need me around, babysitting and so on. I have two oldies to look after, I'm involved in all sorts of things. I wouldn't want to give it up, not any of it – I love my life.'

Sally smiled at her across the table. 'Tim and Angela have their own lives, Grace, and the oldies are in excellent hands at the hostel and the nursing home. And, anyway, no one's asking you to give it up. But I've been thinking about it all week. I felt really envious of you, Isabel. I feel I'm ready to grow into something else but I can't because I'm too involved in other people's lives.'

'Ours, you mean?' Robin asked.

'No! Not you guys, because it's not a one-way street with you three. It's give and take; something is always coming in as well as what goes out. But I've got myself too many hangers-on, people who seem to drain all my emotional energy and don't give anything back.'

'Harry?' Isabel asked.

'Harry, and my sister and her kids. It's been a nightmare since her divorce. And there are various students and ex-students with whom I haven't maintained the boundaries very well. I'm not good at saying no, or protecting my own space.'

'Harry would be devastated if you went away,' Robin said.

'Well, maybe he'll have to get used to the idea,' Sally said with more confidence than she felt. 'It's been over for years but he still hasn't let go. He's always on the doorstep wanting something, or wanting to do something for me or with me. He stops drinking, then he starts again and each time he tries to involve me. I guess part of the problem is that I'm still really fond of him and for some ridiculous reason I feel a bit responsible for him.'

'Co-dependence,' Isabel said, 'it's hard to break out of, especially while he's close by. In that respect alone it might be good to get away, break the pattern. You can't go on always being there for him.'

Sally nodded: 'Exactly. It's really getting to me but it's as though I'm colluding in it and then, of course, I resent it. It's the same with the others, I sometimes feel I'm conspiring with them to suffocate myself.'

'Don't say you're going to opt out of your life as well,' Grace said.

'I've been thinking about it. I could take my long-service leave and some unpaid leave.'

'Where would you go?' Robin asked.

'San Francisco. I always wanted to go there. There's a . . . well, a friend there I haven't seen for years. And you know I always wanted to study photography. There's nothing to stop me, really. You inspired me, Isabel.'

Isabel grinned and squeezed Sally's hand. 'So where would you study?'

'There's a course I'd like to do at the University of California at Berkeley, and there's quite a good chance I could get in. The money's a bit of a worry. Long-service leave would pay me for six months, but the other six months I wouldn't have an income. I could rent my house out but it probably wouldn't cover the rent in California.'

'What about the money your father left you?' Robin asked.

Sally nodded. 'Exactly – that's what I thought. I mean, really, I suppose I should invest it, but this would be such a wonderful thing to do and that money could cover the fees and keep me for the other six months. I think I could manage. I might be able to sell a couple of paintings . . . what do you think?'

'It's brilliant,' Robin said quickly. 'Really brilliant. Do it, Sally, do it! You know I told you I've been reading yet another of the endless menopause books and this one's rather good. The woman who wrote it calls it "the retreat of the crones". She's that English woman, Leslie Kenton, you must've heard of her. She went off to some remote place in Wales for a year and she ran every day and she wrote a novel about Beethoven.'

Grace shifted uneasily in her chair. 'So you'll be the next one will you, Robin?'

Robin leaned back shaking her head. 'I wish I could but it's just not possible right now. My life is so complicated.' Robin knew it sounded pathetic. The truth was that although her work made the situation complex, the real difficulty in changing her life lay in the monumental secret she was hiding. Secrecy suddenly seemed like an unbearable burden but she didn't know how to divest herself of it.

'I'd love to do it. I'm tired out and sick of work. I'd love to go south, Denmark or Pemberton, somewhere like that and just rest and run. Leslie Kenton ran along the cliffs. When I read that, I felt she was running to cleanse herself.' She paused, embarrassed, and then began again. 'It was as though the running forced stuff out of her, not just physically but emotionally too. Going away for a long time, cutting myself off, is the only way I could do it. But . . . well, I can't do it right now.' She sat back pulling her coffee cup towards her, tearing open a sachet of sugar.

'Why not?' asked Isabel with disarming directness, and Robin felt totally exposed.

'Obviously her career, for one thing,' Grace cut in. 'Mightn't you be offered silk, Rob? You deserve it, it must be a possibility and it's what you've always wanted.'

'It was, but I'm not sure if it still is,' she said. 'Certainly if there was only that to consider then I would opt for going away, but it's more complicated. There's this case I've got, you know the one, Gerry Ashby's case. We lost it last week. Justice Simpson misdirected the jury outrageously and I have to prepare an appeal and lodge it quickly. Gerry's in prison and I want him out, I want to see him get some justice. It'll be several months, even a year, before I'll be free of that.'

'Couldn't someone else take it on?' Sally asked.

'No.' Robin shook her head. 'It's my case, my responsibility. Gerry's whole life is on hold because of this –'

'And his life is more important than yours?' Isabel asked.

'I feel responsible,' Robin said, knowing how inadequate it sounded. 'I know you think it's an excuse, and perhaps it is.' She shrugged. 'Maybe I just don't have the courage, or maybe the time isn't right.' She wanted to put her head in her hands and weep. She did want justice for Gerry, he was a friend as well as a client, but Sally was quite right, someone else could handle the appeal. She really wanted to disappear, be free of it all, but disappearing would seem like putting pressure on Jim, a way of trying to force his hand; even telling him how much she wanted to run away would seem like emotional blackmail. As she looked around at the others she saw that Isabel knew she was lying. Robin flushed deeply and looked away, hoping she would not confront her.

'I think that the time being right is very important,' Isabel said. 'You want to do it but the time isn't right for you. It would be madness to do something like this unless it felt absolutely right

42

in every respect. In a few months you might feel quite differently. I think you've got to be totally single-minded about it, as though nothing can stand in your way.'

Robin looked at her with relief. 'I think so,' she said slowly. 'I just need to give it more time.'

'Sanity prevails,' said Grace. 'One middle-aged backpacker, one tentative photographer and two rational stay-at-homes. I'm heartily glad I don't feel the need to shake off my skin and go racing round the world.'

Isabel knew that Robin was lying or, rather, withholding something. She also knew that Robin had realised she knew, and so she wasn't surprised when, a couple of days later, Robin called her and said she needed to talk.

'Lunch?' Isabel suggested.

'Early evening would be better,' Robin said. 'What about a walk on the beach?'

The sun hovered just above the horizon tinting the sky rose and tangerine as they wandered barefoot at the water's edge. Along the beach, families were picnicking in the sand, cooling off after the day's heat. Isabel relished the soft evening air on her neck and arms, the damp sand under her bare feet. She was longing to be gone but the longing was shot through with moments of intense anxiety, and the feeling that by choosing – needing – to go away she was being ungrateful, as though she might be risking something that could never be restored.

'There are beautiful beaches close to Lisbon,' she said. 'Luke's girlfriend, Cassie, worked there teaching English. She's been helping me work out where I'm going.'

Robin took a deep breath. 'Look, the other day – there's something I want to tell you. I . . . I wasn't being totally honest.' She stopped, indicating some flat rocks nearby and they walked over to them and sat down.

'It's very difficult and I don't really know how to start.' Robin was staring nervously at her bare feet and twisting the laces of the Reeboks she was carrying.

'I think you're trying to tell me about Justice McEwan,' Isabel said quietly.

Robin's head shot up. 'You . . . you know?'

'Well, I've heard the gossip.' Isabel smiled. 'And I admit that I have assumed it to be true.'

'How long have you known?'

'Oh, I don't know, a year, maybe more . . . I'm not sure now.'

'But how did you know?' Robin asked, confusion adding to her anxiety.

'This is a small town, Rob, we move in a fairly limited circle. Jim McEwan has a high profile and you're not entirely unknown yourself. You know how stories get around. Doug heard it and he told me.'

'But we've been so careful,' Robin protested, her heart thumping fiercely in her chest.

'I'm sure you have,' Isabel said. 'But it's very hard to hide. One person says something to someone else and so it goes, and people always find things that confirm their suspicions.'

'You never said anything.'

'No.'

'Why not?'

'I suppose because you didn't. You didn't want me – well, us – to know, otherwise you would have told us.'

'What about the others?' Robin asked. 'Do they know too?'

'I suspect not,' Isabel said, picking up a handful of sand and enjoying the way it trickled through her fingers. 'I've never mentioned it.'

'A year or more,' Robin said quietly. 'What must you have been thinking all that time? I guess you must be shocked.'

Isabel turned to her. Robin's face was a pale oval in the fading light. 'I've been worried for you, Rob,' she said. 'I wondered how it was, how you were coping with it all. I hoped that it was worth it for you. But shocked? No – why would I be?'

Robin felt a surge of relief at being able to talk about something she had hidden for so long. She wanted to blurt out every detail, every fear and frustration, every jealousy, the intensity of her feelings for Jim, but she kept a grip on her voice. 'Because of what we've always talked about. About married men and the women who have affairs with them, about deceiving other women, about sisterhood and not doing things that undermine other women. About not being able to build happiness on someone else's misery.'

'Ah! I see what you mean. Sisterhood, and everything that it entails. You have sinned against feminism, is that it?'

Robin nodded and pulled a handkerchief from the pocket of her shorts. 'Exactly. It goes against everything we believe.'

Isabel took her hand. 'That's the way life is, Rob. It's easy to have all those ideals and beliefs when we're not being challenged at a deeply personal level. But we only really find out how we feel when something thrusts its spanner into our own lives. Then it's not so easy. You have integrity, Robin, you're a loving woman, and I am assuming this is not just a casual fling.'

'It's not a fling for either of us,' Robin said. 'But you can imagine the complications. We talk about it all the time, we search for painless solutions and there are none. So we talk about it again and still end up doing nothing, not ending it, not being honest about it, and hoping something will happen. In the end, of course, we'll just have to *make* something happen one way or the other.'

Robin put her face in her hands and Isabel slipped an arm around her shoulders. They sat in silence as the sun slowly melted into the sea.

'I feel too old to be doing this,' Robin said. 'There's something undignified about having an affair with a married man at my age. This should be a thing of the past, somehow it ought to be more straightforward.'

Isabel smiled. 'We're never too old to fall in love, and who knows where the chemistry will strike? Jim's about the same age as you, isn't he?'

'A bit older – fifty-three.'

'No one thinks it's undignified for a man of his age to have an affair,' Isabel said. 'Robin, I bet even you haven't thought it's undignified for Jim.'

Robin managed a smile. 'No, of course I haven't. It's just the "mistress" thing – the "other woman".'

'You're sounding very fifties. You're not in Battersea and this is the nineties. I think you can stop judging yourself so harshly.'

The sun was gone now, the sky turning rapidly from pearl to charcoal, and the temperature had dropped a couple of degrees. The cooler air was a relief, and they walked back to the water's edge and stood where the soft ripples lapped around their feet.

'I could eat something,' Isabel said. 'Shall we walk up to the salad place?'

Robin nodded and they headed towards the path away from the beach.

'What do you think about the others, Grace and Sally?' Robin asked as they reached the top of the path and stopped to put on their shoes. 'Do you think they'd be shocked? They'll disapprove?'

Isabel brushed sand off her feet, dragged on her sandals and straightened up, looking at her friend in the shaft of light from the restaurant across the street. 'I can't speak for them,' she said. 'But how would you feel if it was one of us?'

Robin paused for a moment. 'I think,' she said, 'that I would feel as you seem to feel, only I doubt I could have put it as well as you've put it to me tonight. I'd be concerned for them, I'd understand, I'd empathise, I suppose.'

'So then why do you feel that your friends, all three of whom love you dearly, would be any less generous to you than you would be to them?' Isabel asked.

'Shame, I guess,' Robin replied after a long pause. 'It's my guilt and shame that makes me feel that way. I suppose I disapprove of myself.'

'That's the hardest thing of all,' Isabel returned. 'I've been worried about you. I hope you're being honest with Jim about what you need and not just accommodating his situation. Promise me you'll take care of yourself?'

Robin nodded. 'I promise. I do feel more aware of it, more able to name it all since you started this ball rolling.' She reached out to hug Isabel. 'I'll miss you so much.'

'Me too,' said Isabel. 'Deciding to go away has really made me appreciate what I'm leaving behind. I hope I like the reality as much as I like the idea.'

'You haven't been to yoga for weeks,' Sally said to Grace over the phone. 'Don't you miss it?'

'I suppose so,' Grace said, 'but I just have so much on at the moment, there doesn't seem to be time.'

'That's the time you need it most. Come with me on Friday morning. The six o'clock session. We can have breakfast before we go to work.'

'Er . . . well . . . now, Friday . . .' Grace began.

'Please, Grace,' Sally said. 'Indulge me. I'll be gone soon – and in America I'll *have* to go to yoga on my own!'

'I can't believe you made all this happen so quickly,' Grace said. 'One weekend you're talking about it and by the next weekend it's organised. Long-service leave, unpaid leave, registered for the course . . .'

Sally thought there was something plaintive about the way Grace's voice trailed away. 'Well, I had to move quickly so I could get into the course. And the school had had a request from an art teacher in England who wanted to work here for a year, so I knew they'd be okay if I disappeared for a while. It suddenly all seemed to come together. Are you okay?'

'Of course!' Grace snapped back. 'Why wouldn't I be?'

'Oh, I don't know. You just sound a bit tense.'

'Well, you know me – tense is the story of my life!'

'Yes! So come to yoga?'

'Sure. I'll make the most of you while you're still here. It's bad enough Isabel going but you too . . . I'll miss you, Sally. I'm just realising how much.'

At seven o'clock on Friday morning they came out of the church hall and walked in the crisp early sunshine along the cappuccino strip. Grace sat at a table while Sally went inside to order and returned with a tray heavy with coffee and almond croissants.

'I can't believe you're going so soon. It still doesn't seem real. We've all been doing the same things for so long and now everything's changing,' Grace said, helping to unload the tray.

Sally sat down, drawing her coffee cup towards her. Autumn had given the mornings a slight chill and she was glad she had put on her emerald jacket. 'That's what I wanted to talk to you about,' she said. 'I was thinking about how much I'll miss you and I realised that I have some things I need to say to you.'

Grace pulled a long face, her coffee halfway to her lips. 'That sounds ominous. Am I in trouble?'

A young man with a large, hairy dog sat down at the next table and the dog promptly settled beside Grace and put a heavy paw in her lap. Grace picked up the paw and patted the dog on the head. 'You're gorgeous,' she said, 'but I have to go to a meeting in this skirt,' and she pushed the dog away, brushing the hairs and dust from the burgundy silk. 'I sometimes think of getting a dog,' she said as the young man pulled his dog to the other side of the table out of their way. 'But then I think it would just be something else to look after and, anyway, you can't have a dog in a flat.'

'Grace, I know you're not going to like this, but I have to ask you to bear with me,' Sally said.

Grace nodded to her to go on.

'I know you say you don't want anyone to worry about you, but I do, I love you and I have to talk to you about it before I go. You're incredibly capable, and very efficient and all that. But I see you taking on more and more, getting more and more stressed and tense. You're stretched to your limits and show no signs of stopping.'

Grace's fingers tapped impatiently on the table and Sally, unnerved, spoke faster hoping to hold her attention: 'You must let go of some of these things, the committees, the people – all the things you do. Oh God! I just sound as though I'm lecturing you and I know you're annoyed.'

Grace creamed the foam off her cappuccino with a spoon and transferred it to her mouth. She was silent for a long time. So long that Sally, who knew it was best to keep quiet, almost opened her mouth to speak again.

'I don't really know how to do that,' Grace said suddenly, and Sally thought she could hear a tremor in her voice. 'I've never learned how to live without the sense that I'm in control of everything that moves. I wasn't quite so bad when I was on the wards because even as a sister you can't be in control, even as a director of nursing. You can't program the patients to do as you want, you can't control the doctors, but most of all you can't ever control what will happen with people's illness. I sort of got used to that but in my present job it's easy to have the illusion of control.'

Sally looked at Grace in amazement. She had expected to be told to mind her own business, but here Grace was actually implying that things weren't quite perfect. 'Why do you feel you have to be in control?'

'Because it's safe and it's powerful, that feeling that other people rely on you to know what to do. It's like a drug – at least, it is to me. But now . . .'

'Now?'

'Well, I don't know, really. It's just all this sudden change. It's what you've been telling me for ages, that I can't really keep going on like this. It's as though my life has become a bit slippery and I'm losing my grip. But I don't know what to do.'

Sally was shocked to see what looked like fear in her eyes. She took Grace's hand across the table. 'Now that I've opened this up I don't know what to say,' she admitted quietly. 'Except that I appreciate you telling me. I know that's not easy for you.'

'No, it's not one of my strengths, but I do realise how much I've relied on having you and Isabel and Robin around me. Now it all feels a bit rocky, as though a whole lot of stuff deep inside me has started to rise to the surface. When I think of you and Isabel leaving I feel as though I'm being cast adrift.'

'Just because I'm going away it doesn't mean that our friendship is less important to me,' Sally said. 'I'm sure that's true for Isabel too.'

'Oh, I know that,' Grace said. 'But it's made me realise that I am nowhere near as much in control as I thought I was . . . it really doesn't make any sense. I always thought everyone needed me, and now I'm starting to think that perhaps it's the other way around.'

The tables were beginning to fill with regulars settling to drink their coffee and study the morning papers. A few early tourists drifted in to consult their guidebooks over breakfast. Sally, who only ever stopped here when she was with someone else, suddenly felt how bleak it would be to sit there alone. The familiarity was deceptive. She was filled with the uncomfortable sense that she was about to desert Grace at a really important time, a time when she needed support.

'Maybe I should think about therapy,' Grace ventured. 'What do you think?'

'I wanted to suggest that but I thought you'd have a fit,' Sally said.

'I guess I haven't been very open . . . in the past, I mean . . . you've often warned me . . .'

'It doesn't matter about the past,' Sally said, hugely relieved. 'The thing that matters now is the present. There's a terrific woman in West Perth. I'll phone you later in the day with her number.'

'I never thought this would happen to me,' Grace said. 'Needing therapy . . . okay for other people but not for me! But I do think I need someone to guide me through it.'

'You know I worried that one day you would just crack up, or get ill from stress. I kept thinking you'd have a stroke. Please do something about it soon.'

'I won't have a stroke,' Grace said with a smile. 'But ring me with the number. I'll call this week.'

FOUR

When Grace told Sally that she would call the therapist she honestly intended to do so, but somehow events overtook her. That same week she had to cope with a very important meeting of the midwifery standards committee, and there were staff problems to sort out. Angela, her daughter-in-law, got a virus, so Grace went to help out with Emily. Before she knew it the twelfth of May had arrived and she, Robin and Sally were at the airport with Isabel's family, waving goodbye and wiping away their tears. Then she flew to Sydney for a nursing conference and a couple of weeks later she was at the airport with Robin to say goodbye again, this time to Sally. Somehow the therapist got lost.

'I know you haven't phoned her yet,' Sally said in the airport toilets, half an hour before she got on the flight to San Francisco. 'But promise me you'll do it soon.'

'Of course I will,' Grace replied. 'This week – I promise.'

'Keep an eye on her, Rob,' Sally said, nodding towards Grace as the three of them walked towards the entrance to the departure lounge. 'She's a health hazard.'

'We'll keep an eye on each other, won't we, Robin?' Grace said, hugging Sally.

'Absolutely,' Robin said, her eyes filling with tears. 'But we'll miss you. It seems so strange without Isabel – what'll we do without the two of you?'

'Work less. Relax more. Don't take on anything else – either of

you!' Sally said, wiping away her own tears. 'Take care! And write
– promise you'll write!'

'We'll write!'

But of course Grace didn't phone the therapist, and several
weeks after Sally's departure, the Post-it note with the therapist's name and number was still stuck on the fridge and other
things were demanding her attention. Just a few days after Sally
left, June, Grace's mother-in-law, died and Grace moved into her
top-level organisational mode to deal with the funeral and the
administration of her estate.

'Gone then, has she?' Grace's father commented when she
told him. 'Shame, really. She was my only daughter, you know.'

Grace took a deep breath and wondered for the umpteenth
time just what went on in the mind of a person with Alzheimer's.
'*I'm* your only daughter, Dad,' she said patiently. 'I'm Grace, June
was my mother-in-law, Ron's mum. Do you remember Ron, my
husband?'

'Course I do, course I remember Ron. Blackfella. Came from
the Western Desert all the way to my church, brought his dog.'

Grace gripped the arms of her chair and prayed for patience.
'No, Dad, Ron was not a blackfella, and anyway, these days we
say "Aboriginal people" or "indigenous Australians".'

'Nothing wrong with blackfellas, you know. Don't care what
you call them, God loves 'em same as the rest of us.'

Every time Grace argued with her father she ended up feeling
guilty and ashamed of herself. The Alzheimer's had stripped him
of his independence, his sense of authority, and his mobility. Even
his faith was sometimes absent. Why couldn't she just let him be?
What did it matter if he thought Ron was black? What did it
matter if he confused her with June or with her own mother, or
thought he was eating breakfast on Friday when he was having
afternoon tea on Wednesday?

'What you need to understand, Grace,' the geriatrician told
her, 'is that for people with Alzheimer's, the world is wrong. They
have no insight into their own behaviour. Arguing will get you
nowhere. Just go along with what your father says, enter into the
fantasy. It'll keep him happy – far better than arguing.'

Grace wanted her father to enjoy whatever happiness was left to him, and each week as she drove to the nursing home she told herself over and over again that she would be different. However, argument came more easily to her than entering into fantasy, and her father's harmless delusions would have her on the edge of her chair within minutes. As she left he would be planning a sermon he would never give, jotting down confused phrases and half-remembered quotations on a piece of paper, and she would be in a high state of anxiety, cursing her own need for things to be absolutely right.

'You're such a control freak, Grace,' Isabel had said. 'This is a wonderful opportunity for you to learn to let go.' Isabel's step-father had died with Alzheimer's a few years earlier. 'You can't control what your father thinks, so stop torturing yourself.'

'But all my training says that people should be given the correct information, told the truth and allowed to take informed decisions,' Grace groaned. 'It's all about rights.'

'Maybe, but there comes a time when you have to accept that a person is no longer capable of making decisions or seeing reality. You can't force your father to believe something just because you know it's true.'

The Sunday that Tim and Angela broke the news, Grace had been to see her father in the morning, and arrived at their house, a mass of tension, looking forward to taking Emily for a walk by the river. It was a chilly July afternoon and she sat on the pure white sand of the foreshore while Emily waded into the shallow rippling water in her red wellies. Grace missed Sally desperately, and missed Isabel more than she had anticipated. She hadn't fully appreciated quite what the Gang of Four meant in her life until everything changed. Her friendship with Robin had only existed as part of the group. Now it seemed that they were stuck with each other and Robin was preoccupied, probably with the appeal but also, Grace suspected, with her secret love life. It irritated her that Robin thought they were all too blind to see what was going on. She was offended by Robin's secrecy. Did she think her friends would spread gossip about her, or was she afraid they would admonish her for her illicit affair?

Grace had been at school with Monica McEwan. Perth was like that, so small everyone seemed in some way connected to everyone else. She had never liked Monica since the day when, aged twelve, they and some other girls had been caught smoking behind the drama hall. Monica, who was the ringleader and who had supplied the cigarettes, told the principal that the cigarettes belonged to Grace, and so she had taken the bulk of the punishment. Even so, Grace was wary of being unfair to Monica over the Robin–Jim affair. She hated it when a wife was demonised as some sort of justification for betrayal. Had the subject been up for discussion she would have taken care not to say anything derogatory about Monica, but in her heart of hearts she thought Monica deserved everything that might be coming to her.

Grace stood up, brushing the sand off her immaculate jeans. 'Emy, darling, come on out of the water. Let's go home.'

Emily turned, lurching slightly in the water, and waved a bent stick. 'Ganma, come water!' she cried. 'Come water.'

Grace smiled, walking to the water's edge, and bent to pick her up. 'No water for me, Emy,' she said. 'I don't have lovely red boots like you. We're going home. Mummy's making brownies for you.'

Emily pressed her face close to Grace and planted a large wet kiss on her cheek. 'Emy love Ganma.'

'And I love you too, darling,' Grace said, hugging her and breathing in the delicious scent of young skin and baby shampoo. 'You're my sunshine.'

'Shunsine,' Emily repeated. 'Shunsine, Ganma.' And Grace set her back on her feet and they walked hand in hand towards the car.

She had thought there was some tension in the air when she arrived from the nursing home but they were halfway through lunch before Tim plucked up the courage to tell her.

'I know it's a long way, Mum,' he said cautiously, watching

the look of horror on Grace's face. 'But there's a direct flight from Perth to Tokyo, and it's only for two years.'

'But Japan! I'll never see you. And why would you want to live in Japan?'

'It's the job, Grace,' Angela said, sitting down beside her. 'It's a wonderful opportunity for Tim, for the three of us. We'll have a rent-free apartment, and there's a huge away-from-home allowance. It means we'll come back here at the end of the two years with heaps of money in the bank. And we'll be back in time for Emy to start school.'

'But Japan!' Grace said again. 'It's so . . .'

'It's a very sophisticated and civilised country, Mum,' Tim ventured. 'We'll have a two-bedroom apartment in Kyoto. You'll be able to come and visit us.'

Grace felt like Alice in Wonderland in the rabbit hole, small, lost and as though she was tumbling from a great height into endless unfamiliar space. 'Will you come back at all? I mean, before the two years are up?'

'We get a trip home for four weeks each year,' said Tim. 'And if you come over a couple of times, well, that won't be so bad, will it? You know we'll miss you but we're so excited about it.'

The wise and generous mother in Grace knew she should be thrilled for them. The devouring, possessive, insecure woman wanted to howl. She wanted to whine and sulk, to ask how they thought they would manage without her help, and how they could leave her alone. She paused, her body tense with shock and distress.

'Of course,' she said shakily. 'Of course it's a wonderful opportunity. I understand, I do, really, it's just that it's a bit of a shock. I'll miss you all so much, Emy will be so different . . . but of course you're right.'

Angela took her hand. 'We'll call often and email. I can scan pictures of Emy into the computer and send them – I'll do it every week.'

Grace smiled. 'I know, Angie, I know. When are you actually going?'

Tim shuffled his feet and looked more uncomfortable than ever. 'Actually, they want me up there urgently – next week, in fact. I'm leaving on Thursday. Ange and Emy are coming up two weeks after that.'

Grace's head spun. She looked at the battered fluffy rabbit on the floor and Emily's tiny bare toes, which were curling under her feet as she concentrated on getting some round plastic people into a red and blue toy bus. 'So soon,' she said, swallowing hard. 'Well, you must have heaps to do, so how can I help?' And she pushed down the urge to vomit.

Robin dreamed she was driving somewhere in Portugal trying to find a remote village like the one on Isabel's postcard. She had no map and no idea in which direction she was travelling. It was hard to see the road because she was crying but she knew that if she could only get to the village everything would be all right. Isabel would be there; she'd know what to do. She turned a corner, speeding downhill, and suddenly a woman stepped out into the road and waved at her to stop. It was Isabel. But when Robin put her foot on the brake, nothing happened, the car just raced on and then plunged to the edge of a steep cliff, where it stopped suddenly, hanging perilously with its front wheels over the edge. Scared of tipping it, Robin moved slightly in the driving seat and woke, her heart thumping with fear and a cold sweat prickling her skin.

It was five o'clock. She always had bad dreams if she fell asleep in the afternoon. She shivered slightly, pulled the doona further up the bed and curled closer to Jim's back. They must have slept for about an hour. He'd said he needed to leave by seven because he'd told Monica he was playing golf and then going for drinks at the club. Robin tried to shake off the residual anxiety of the dream. She didn't know much about the meaning of dreams but she thought she knew what this one meant. She had dreamed it several times in the last month, and each time she woke determined to tell Jim how she felt, and each time she changed her mind.

She buried her cold face in the warm curve of his neck, tasting his skin with her tongue. He stirred slightly at first and then, waking, turned towards her smiling, his eyes still shut. 'What time is it?'

'Five – just turned. Heaps of time.'

'Yes. Would you like some coffee?'

'I'd love some coffee, but I'd like a kiss first,' he said. He opened his eyes and, slipping his hand behind her neck, pulled her down towards him.

Robin could feel her resolve dissolving into his mouth. 'I want to talk to you,' she murmured, moving away.

'That sounds ominous.' Jim grinned, reaching out to stroke her back as she got out of the bed. 'I'll definitely need coffee to gird my loins.'

'Keep your loins there and ungirded,' Robin said. 'I'll bring the coffee in here. It's cold this afternoon.'

He was sitting up in bed reading the Sunday paper when she came back with the coffee and she paused momentarily, watching him from the doorway. He looked older than his fifty-three years, but he was fit. Spare frame, square shoulders, strong neck and a lean face topped with crinkly grey hair made him look more like a sports coach than a judge. He looked up, blue eyes smiling. 'Excellent room service!'

'Every service available at a price,' she joked, handing him a mug of coffee and climbing back into the bed beside him.

'So, talk away.' Jim tossed the newspaper onto the bedroom floor and sipped his coffee.

Robin took a deep breath to quell the butterflies in her stomach. Jim reached out and covered her cold hand with his warm one. 'Heavens, Rob, you're frozen. Here, put this on.' Leaning over the side of the bed and balancing his coffee with one hand, he grabbed his sweater from the floor.

She pulled the dark blue cashmere over her head and felt its softness settle comfortingly around her. She didn't know how to begin. 'These conversations we keep having . . .'

'Mmm?'

'The conversations about us, you telling Monica, us taking the risks . . .' She paused briefly. 'Well, we always end up doing nothing and now I feel . . . I can't . . . I can't cope with it anymore.'

Jim set his coffee mug down on the bedside table and took her hand in his. 'Go on.'

'That's it, really. I can't cope with it anymore. I feel absolutely wrecked. Wanting you so much, the secrecy, living for the times when you can get away, not being able to go out together, not being able to do anything normal. Most of the time I'm eaten up with jealousy and anger because I feel trapped, as though my life is completely controlled by your marriage. I'm powerless. Only you can change it. I'm sorry if you think I'm neurotic and unreasonable but I can't do this anymore.'

Jim held her hand tighter and looked out of the window where the sky had darkened to a dull grey, and the wind was whipping up waves that crashed to the beach in showers of white foam. 'You're not neurotic or unreasonable. Not at all.'

Robin started to shake with emotion. Jim got out of bed, closed the curtains, switched on the heater and a bedside light and climbed back into bed, putting his arms around her. 'What do you want to do?'

'I want you to leave Monica now ... for us to be together. I don't care about the gossip. I don't care about my job. I worry more about your job, but at the same time I feel quite desperate, as though I'm fighting for my life.'

The silence was painfully long. Her heart pounded in her chest as Jim rested his cheek on the top of her head.

'You're right,' he said. 'I'm so sorry to have put you in this position for so long. I'll talk to Monica tonight.'

Robin checked her watch. It was two minutes later than the last time she checked. Ten thirty-two. She felt weak and nauseous. The night stretched before her like an eternity. It was more than three hours since Jim had left, promising to talk to Monica as soon as he got home. Would it be a civilised discussion, or a dramatic scene? Surely Jim and Monica wouldn't just go to bed as usual after he'd told her he was leaving. He would call her, or more likely pack a bag and come back. They must still be talking. She knew it was too soon to hear from him but the waiting was driving her crazy. She wished she could talk to Isabel. The silence was torture. She wrote a note and put it on the kitchen bench, where Jim always dropped his car keys. Then she grabbed her waterproof jacket from the laundry, went out the front door, down the path, and started walking briskly along the footpath to the beach.

The salt-edged wind from the sea stung her face and whipped her hair out of her hood. Half closing her eyes she saw what she had seen every day for weeks, the image of a woman running along a cliff top towards a small cottage, a woman running for her life. She started to run hard and fast against the wind, until she could feel nothing but the burning in her chest and the pounding of her feet on the pavement. Then she turned and ran again, all the way back to her house where the lights glowed soft and welcoming through the rice-paper blinds and where Jim's car would probably be in the drive, or his reassuring voice on the answering machine. But the drive was empty, and no light blinked on the answering machine. Robin took a hot shower, washed her hair and crawled into bed. She buried her face in the pillow, breathing in his scent, wondering what was happening ten kilometres away in that strange and threatening other life that he had, until now, shared with Monica.

At six o'clock the next morning Robin dialled Grace's number. 'Can I come over?'

'What? Now?' said Grace, who had also had a sleepless night and was feeling like death.

'Now – I need to talk.'

'Well, so do I. Come on over. I'll make coffee. Do you want something to eat?'

'Nothing,' Robin said. 'Just coffee – I couldn't eat a thing.'

'Are you okay?' Grace asked.

'Not really. What about you?'

'Terrible,' Grace said. 'Sounds like mutual counselling.'

'Uh-huh! I'll be there in twenty minutes.' Robin put down the phone, threw some cold water on her face, pulled on her clothes and went out to the car. It was a bleak morning with a sharp chill in the air and fine rain falling from a solid grey sky.

Grace opened the door in her dressing gown. 'My god! You look like you were up all night.'

'I was. How about you?' Robin asked, wishing desperately that she hadn't come, wishing it were anyone but Grace.

'Same, really,' Grace said. She put mugs and the coffee pot on the table. 'Tim and Angela are going to Japan for two years.'

Robin raised her eyebrows. 'Work?'

'A really good job. Of course it's wonderful for them but I feel simply terrible. Silly, I suppose. Somehow it feels like a personal insult – and I do know how ridiculous and selfish that must sound. First Isabel and Sally go, then June dies, now this.' She forced a laugh. 'My life seems to be crumbling around my ears.'

Robin heard the false bravado in Grace's voice but was too distressed to respond with more than a murmur of sympathy. Grace paused, looking at her, feeling the embarrassing chasm of silence. 'Anyway, Rob, you're in a worse state than me. What's happened?'

Robin stared at the floor. She had been mad to come here. She had no idea how to relate to Grace alone, intimately, when they were both in pain. Had Grace known about Jim it would be easier but first she must explain all that and probably answer awkward questions. The fear that had prompted her cry for help now paralysed her, locking her into awkward silence. Grace began to pour the coffee.

'Take your coat off and sit down, Rob,' she said with uncharacteristic gentleness. 'Is it about Jim McEwan?'

'It certainly doesn't sound good,' Grace said, two mugs of coffee later.

'Am I stupid thinking he should have called, or come back?' Robin asked, desperate for explanations. 'I mean, I thought what would happen was that he'd go home, tell Monica, they might have an argument, or maybe a long talk, and then I'd hear from him. It's twelve hours. He can't have gone to sleep, surely, not after that. I tried calling him but his mobile's switched off.'

'He might have slept,' Grace said thoughtfully. 'Men are so weird. I know you were awake all night, most women would be. But a nurse I once worked with told me that the evening she told her husband she was going to leave him he was terribly upset, devastated. He cried, he begged her not to go and this went on for hours, until she couldn't bear it any longer. She went to have a shower and when she came out of the bathroom he'd gone to bed and was fast asleep and snoring. She paced up and down all night crying, and he slept right through.'

Robin looked at her in amazement and Grace leaned forward across the table and took her hand. 'The trouble with men, Rob, is that they're different. We expect them to be like us, especially the ones we love, but they're not. They're totally different. Once we accept that, once we stop expecting them to behave like women, life with them becomes a bit easier. It took me years to learn that and then Ron died.' She got up, pulling her white bathrobe in at the waist and tightening the knot of the belt. 'Even so, I would have thought Jim might have called by now – it's after seven.' They both stared at Robin's mobile lying on the table. 'Are you in court today?'

Robin shook her head. 'No, but I've got a case conference at nine.'

'Try him again now,' Grace suggested. 'If he answers I'll go upstairs.'

Robin picked up the phone, dialled and got the voice mail again. 'How did you know about Jim and me, anyway? Who told you?'

Grace rinsed the coffee mugs. 'I'm going to make some toast. I really think you should have something in your stomach. Someone said something, at work one day, I think. I can't really remember.'

'So it wasn't Isabel who told you?'

Grace looked surprised. 'Isabel? No. Does she know?'

Robin shrugged. 'Yes, has done for a while, apparently, but she only told me just before she left.'

Drying her hands, Grace shrugged her shoulders. 'She never mentioned it to me.'

'Why didn't you say anything?' Robin asked.

'Why didn't you tell us?' Grace countered sharply. 'Didn't you trust us?'

'It wasn't that exactly . . . it wasn't that I thought you'd tell anyone else, just . . .'

'Just what?' Grace's eyes darkened.

'I couldn't face what you might say. That you might think so badly of me. And anyway, you know Monica.'

'Everyone knows Monica,' Grace cut in before her finer feelings could stop her.

'Yes, but –'

'Oh, I know, I know what you mean. Sorry I was so sharp, but I've felt so annoyed that you never said anything. I guess you're just copping that flak now, when you can least handle it.' Robin looked away, studying her hands, and the silence descended again.

'Strange, isn't it?' Grace said quietly. 'You and I here like this.' Robin looked up in surprise.

'I mean, we've never been particularly close,' Grace continued. 'You were close to Isabel, me to Sally and those two to each other, but not you and me. Now they're gone we're . . . well, we're . . .' She couldn't finish the sentence.

'Stuck with each other?' Robin said, raising her eyebrows.

The moment of tension was palpable, but a slow smile spread across Grace's face and she nodded. 'That's pretty brutal.'

'But it's true. Isn't it?'

Grace put four slices of rye bread into the toaster. 'I miss them, both of them, individually and the four of us together,' she said.

'Me too,' said Robin, rubbing her eyes. They felt as though they were full of sand. 'There's a great big gap in my life. Do you think it will ever be the same again?'

'No,' said Grace. 'What we had is gone . . . well, changed. We'll still be friends, still be the Gang of Four, but it'll be different.' The toast popped up, making her jump, and she took it out, put it in a toast rack and handed it to Robin. 'Can you get the plates off the shelf, please. There's honey and Vegemite in the top cupboard.'

They sat facing each other across the breakfast bar. 'Why did you come here this morning?' Grace asked, spreading a minute amount of Vegemite onto her toast.

'Because, despite the distance between us, I trust you. You're tough, and you're honest . . .'

'And there was no one else?'

'That too,' Robin admitted.

'Same for me,' said Grace, turning to the window as she felt her face might be starting to crumple. 'Maybe this is where we get to know each other.'

Robin nodded. 'I guess so.' She paused. 'Thanks for being here, Grace.'

'Thanks for coming.'

And as Grace turned back from the window Robin thought she caught a glimpse of a tear in the corner of Grace's eye.

Grace was unusually late getting to the office. It was a nuisance because it barely left her time to prepare for a meeting at the health department, but although she had to rush she felt considerably better than she had at dawn. She had woken with the same Alice-falling-down-the-rabbit-hole feeling, but Robin's visit had given her a focus. Now, as she sorted the papers she needed for the meeting, she remembered how close she had been to losing her grip. She felt a strange sense of gratitude to Robin, whose acute distress had enabled her to turn down the flame of her own feelings and pull herself together.

'So when are they leaving?' Denise asked, leaning against the filing cabinet.

'Tim leaves on Thursday, and Angie and Emy a couple of weeks later.'

'You'll miss them.'

'Oh yes. But it's wonderful for them. And I get to go to Japan. They'll be living in Kyoto and it's supposed to be gorgeous. Angie showed me pictures on the Internet. I'm really excited about it.'

Denise raised her eyebrows. 'And Emily? You'll miss a big chunk of time with her. They change so fast at that age.'

Grace snapped her briefcase shut and put it down beside the desk. 'Well, I guess I'm lucky to have had so much time with her thus far – not all grandparents do. One must make the best of things. I'll be at the health department, in Stan Ledger's office, if you want me. I've got the mobile and I'll be a couple of hours.' Denise nodded and opened the door for her. 'If Robin Percy rings, can you tell her she can get me on the mobile. And can you ring Andrew Peters and ask him how much longer it's going to take to finalise this probate for June.'

'Yes, ma'am!'

'And Denise . . .'

'Yes, Grace?'

'If you have a minute could you ring around and find out the price of wheelchairs. I think my dad's going to need one very soon.'

Denise gave her a mock salute, and Grace smiled distractedly before closing the door behind her.

She turned into St George's Terrace, tapping the steering wheel in annoyance at the heavy traffic. She would just about make it. And when the meeting was over she would call Robin. Whatever had happened since the early morning Robin was going to need a lot of support. Briefly Grace wondered why she suddenly felt so much better. Thank goodness she was not into taking pills. She could have let herself fall into an emotional mess with all the things that had happened in the last few weeks, but here she was coping splendidly despite that wobbly bit earlier in the day. You couldn't let yourself fall apart when people needed you. No point being miserable about the kids, there was too much to do. Angie was always hopelessly disorganised, so she would just have to grab the reins. Grace slipped into a gap in the outside lane and cruised down to the traffic lights. She felt a surge of confidence and realised that the nice, hard, safe feeling in her stomach had come back. She wasn't sure what had summoned it, but she welcomed it with a sigh of relief and a quick reassuring glimpse at her reflection in the rear-view mirror.

*

'But I thought you'd realise,' Jim said, rubbing the bridge of his nose where his glasses had been resting. 'Darling, I'm so sorry. I had no idea you'd be so upset or worried.'

Robin twisted the strap of her bag into a tight coil and then let it unravel. 'I told you how I felt. I told you I was at the end of my tether and you said you would talk to Monica. You left my place last night to go straight home and talk to her.'

'Yes, but . . .'

'So why didn't you do it?'

'Well, as I've told you, I didn't feel I could. I got in, Monica was watching *SeaChange*, Chrissie and Mike were doing homework, the house seemed really calm and peaceful and I didn't feel I could just walk in and destroy everything.'

Robin's head was pounding. She felt physically sick and desperate for fresh air, and fumbled with the car window.

'Here,' said Jim, switching on the ignition. 'Now it'll open.' The air was typical of an underground car park, heavy with petrol and exhaust fumes. Robin's stomach heaved.

'The least you could have done was to let me know. I was frantic. Can't we go somewhere else to talk? Come back to my place.'

'I didn't appreciate you'd be so upset. I thought you'd realise what had happened.' He looked at his watch. 'It's turned six, Rob, I have a meeting at six-thirty. There isn't time. I'm sorry.'

'So when will you tell her?'

'I don't know exactly. But I promise to do it when it seems like a good time. When there's an appropriate opportunity.'

Robin threw up her hands. 'Jim, there is no good time to leave a marriage. It's always going to be awful, whenever you do it. And what do you mean by an appropriate opportunity? Do you think Monica's going to wake up on Wednesday and say, "Oh, by the way, Jim, if you want to leave me, today's a good day"?'

'You're being ridiculous and unfair.'

'And you think you're not? For almost four years you've been saying you would leave and we've been considering every possible scenario. Not anymore, this is the end of the road. You have to tell Monica now. You have to leave. I can't bear living in the shadows, having half a life, not anymore.' She rummaged for a tissue to wipe away the tears. Jim passed her a box of Kleenex, taking some for himself.

'I feel terrible having got you into this situation. It's so unfair on you.' He paused, reaching for the tissues again, and Robin could see how he was struggling to keep back his own tears.

'You didn't get me into this. I'm not a helpless child, I knew what I was doing. But we always planned that we would be together. You always said you would leave when the time was right. Well, the time is right now.'

Jim screwed the tissues into a tight ball and dropped them into the Greenpeace rubbish bag hanging from the cigarette lighter. 'Not for me. The time is not right for me. I'm sorry, Robin . . . I need more time.'

'Why, Jim? What's going to change next week, next month, next year? You've had four years. How much more time do you want?'

He shook his head, swallowing hard. 'I don't know. I can't answer that. I went home last night fully intending to tell Monica about us and ask her for a divorce. I've imagined doing it so many times, just walking into the house and saying it. But when it came to it, I couldn't do it. Robin, you know it's you I love. You know you're more important to me than anything, but last night I felt I would destroy them, shatter their world, not just Monica, the kids too. I can't do that to them.'

They sat side by side in silence staring ahead at the door in the wall that led to the back staircase up to the judges' chambers. 'You do understand, Robin, don't you?' he asked quietly, reaching for her hand. She snatched it away and pulled down the sun visor to look at her reflection in the mirror.

'Yes, I understand,' she said, rubbing her hands over her face. 'I understand perfectly well.' She reached into her bag, got out a comb and ran it through her hair. 'I understand that although you say you love me more than anything and anyone, you are not prepared to give up anything to be with me. You think you'll destroy Monica? It would take a full battalion of German tanks to destroy Monica and you know it.' She snapped

back the sun visor and turned to face him. 'But I am less resist-
ant, Jim. I love you and want you more than I ever wanted
anything in my life, but I can't handle this anymore.'

She opened the car door and gathered up her bag and jacket.

'I only have one life and I am not going to spend it as a lady
in waiting.' And she swung herself out of the car and slammed
the door behind her, turning back to look at him through the open
window. 'I can't imagine that I will ever stop loving you,' she
said, her voice close to breaking. 'But I have to look after myself.'

And without looking back she walked swiftly away from the
car and up the ramp to the street, where the rain pounded heavily
onto the pavement and a wave of water from the wheels of a
passing car drenched her legs.

FIVE

The railway line ran west from Lisbon, hugging the coast along the mouth of the River Tagus to the sea. On one side were neat back gardens filled with geraniums and bougainvillea, washing strung across balconies, and the service entrances of shops and small businesses. On the other side the Atlantic Ocean stretched to the horizon beyond the steep cliffs, sandy beaches and rocky outcrops. The route was dotted with small resorts running one into the other, old churches, and elegant houses of fading grandeur, peach and rose paintwork peeling in the sunlight, wisteria smothering the porches, and statues of the Virgin Mary watching silently from tiled alcoves.

Isabel sat on the ocean side of the train, staring out across the sunlit water, thinking of the beaches at home and trying to stave off the waves of panic that struck whenever she remembered that there were fifty-two weeks in a year and she still had another forty-nine to go. Her wonderful adventure was not evolving according to plan. And that, she thought, was the problem. The plan just wasn't good enough. Her time and energy had gone into organising the life she was leaving, making arrangements for everything to run smoothly in her absence, and in the chaos of those last weeks she had neglected her own journey. The careful sorting of Eunice's papers as the basis for an itinerary just didn't happen, and she had grabbed haphazardly at a few old letters and diaries, stuffing them into the bottom of her case. She thought she would have time later, to sort out her priorities, plan and read.

The stopover she'd allowed herself in Hong Kong would be a good time to start. But it didn't work out that way.

She hated the noisy, clamorous streets and the humidity that devoured her energy the moment she stepped outside the airport. She couldn't wait to move on, the physical and emotional upheaval of leaving home had left her too restless to focus on anything for more than a few minutes. Unable to concentrate, she tossed aside her books and maps and whiled away the time torn between anxiety about what might be happening at home and the enormity of what lay ahead. She wanted to be in Europe and to be a traveller, but she felt like the worst kind of whingeing tourist.

Lisbon's infectious spirit revived her. She was fascinated by the big, jumbled city with its gracious boulevards, winding cobbled streets and steep hills where trams and funiculars rattled day and night. She had chosen Portugal as a starting point because it had been one of Eunice's favourite places. From there she would go to Spain, then France and the Riviera, and Germany in time for Christmas: dark evenings, log fires, snow. There were pictures of Eunice in Munich, riding a sleigh drawn by ponies decked out with bells and ribbons. Isabel wanted a northern Christmas, the stuff of fairytales. The outline was drawn but the gaps remained to be filled.

She spent the first five nights at a hotel and then moved to the home of one of the women in 5W. Women Welcome Women World Wide was an international friendship network with several thousand members around the world. Women could contact each other to suggest a meeting and to ask for accommodation for a maximum of two nights. It was open to the hostess to offer a longer stay if she wished. Senhora Soarez's first-floor apartment was in a three-storey ochre and white building in a street near the Castelo San Jorge. From the window of the spare bedroom Isabel had a narrow view across the rooftops to the harbour.

Carmen Soarez was in her sixties and looked as though she had been upholstered into the dark, neatly tailored business suits she wore to her middle management job in a bank. She was hospitable, formal and restrained in her welcome, but after the first night she invited Isabel to stay on for a week. She accepted with relief but felt some pressure to make other arrangements, to avoid lurching from one short homestay to the next. Carmen was not very communicative and Isabel felt a sense of clumsy displacement. She was disoriented, saturated with new experiences, exhausted by change and confused by the landscape and the language. She was ashamed of her foolish assumption that a few words of Spanish and French would ease her way in a country in which neither was the native language.

She did some sightseeing, wandered through the markets, tracked down an art gallery featured on one of Eunice's cards, and stopped to drink coffee in a tiled plaza, staring at a fading black and white snapshot of her mother sitting in almost exactly the same spot. Armed with another rather dog-eared photograph she set out to find what appeared, from a note on the back, to be the home of one of Eunice's friends. Perhaps by some crazy chance the woman would still live there. But she had got hopelessly lost and returned to the apartment exhausted from trekking up and down the steep hills. What she needed was somewhere to be still and quiet, to make better plans and adjust to her new, albeit temporary, single state; to get used to the sense of time being her own, to the reality of her freedom. Perhaps she would be better away from the city. Perhaps the trip along the coast would reveal a place where she felt more at ease.

The train rattled on, stopping at every station, and Isabel got out at Estoril, the famed postwar haunt of exiled royalty and the idle rich. From there she walked the path along the sea wall, enjoying the midday sun and watching the waves breaking, white with foam, over the rocks, until she reached Cascais. Tourists browsed the market stalls in the square above the port, searching for bargains among the T-shirts, satin slippers, garish paper knives and crisp cutwork table linen. Isabel picked her way between the stalls, over the coiled fishing nets with their cork floats, and found a seat outside a café, where she ordered a salad.

Cascais was enchanting, and she felt better away from the city. At a nearby table a couple of younger women were tucking into fish soup. They wore white T-shirts and faded jeans with rope-soled espadrilles, like the ones on sale at the market stalls. They

70

were speaking English but their confident manner and the fast and familiar exchanges with the waiter in Portuguese signalled that they might be locals rather than tourists. They finished their soup before Isabel's order arrived and almost immediately one crumpled her serviette and stood up. She leaned over to hug the other before picking up her bag and setting off towards the centre of town. The other woman poured herself some water from the half-empty carafe and pulled a newspaper from a large leather shoulder bag. She had the ease and confidence of a woman comfortable in her surroundings; a woman who liked her own body. It was an ease that Isabel envied.

The waiter passed and Isabel asked for some butter, but he couldn't understand her.

'*Manteiga, Fernando!*' the English woman called out to the waiter. '*Senhora quiera manteiga.*'

'Ah!' He smiled. '*Manteiga!*' and he whisked off between the tables to fetch the butter.

'Thanks very much,' Isabel called. 'I'm afraid my Portuguese only extends to coffee and bread at this stage.'

The woman smiled. 'On holiday?'

'Yes and no.' Isabel hesitated. 'More like a sabbatical. I'm just finding my way around.'

The young woman folded her paper and stood up. 'Mind if I join you?'

Isabel moved her own bag off the chair and gestured towards it. 'Please do. Maybe I can pick your brains – you seem very much at home here.'

Close up she was older than she appeared from a distance, thirty-two perhaps, Debra's age. Slim and fit, with a pale English complexion that had taken on a light tan but still needed protection from the sun. Her corn-coloured hair was cut in a jagged Meg Ryan style that looked like rats' tails on some people and a million dollars on others. This woman was in the latter category. 'Sara Oakwood,' she said, stretching out a hand. 'I live here; at least, I have done for the past couple of years. Before that it was Birmingham, and I can tell you this is a whole lot nicer. You're from New Zealand?'

'Australia,' Isabel said. 'Been here two weeks and I could really use some advice.'

'Sure,' Sara said, ordering mineral water when the waiter returned with Isabel's butter. 'I live in Cascais now, but I've seen quite a bit of Portugal, mainly on foot and by public transport.' Isabel felt the stab of envy she always felt when she met young women living lives so different from her own. At Sara's age she had already been married for a decade, had three children, and had not been out of Australia. She sometimes wondered whether marrying young and having a conventional family life was some sort of reaction to Eunice's absence during those years in Europe.

'What a terrific thing to do,' Sara said as Isabel explained how she came to be in Portugal. 'How did your family take to the idea?' She listened intently to the story of Doug's initial resistance, Luke's pat on the head, Kate's encouragement and Debra's hurt and anger.

'She'll get over it,' Sara commented. 'She's just scared of you not being there – it's only natural. I think it's wonderful. My mum would never do it. She's really stuck in a rut, although she's divorced and got enough money. She could afford to just take off for a bit but she never would. So, what can I do to help?'

Isabel laid out her plans, or lack of them. There were places she wanted to see but didn't know what to expect and what sort of accommodation to look for. The women's network had contacts in Lisbon and Porto but she didn't want to have to keep moving every few days. She wanted somewhere to stay for a couple of weeks while she sorted herself out, made the transition from one life to another.

Sara leaned back and crossed her legs, grinning broadly. 'Would Cascais suit you?'

Isabel sighed. 'It's gorgeous here, it feels just right, but I have to be careful about the cost. I can't afford hotels all the time and these look quite pricey.'

Sara poured a glass of water. 'Would you be interested in sharing a two-bedroom villa? My housemate's away for a while. Her mother's sick and she's gone home to England. She's hoping I'll find someone to take the room and cover the rent while she's away. But of course she doesn't want to lose it to a long-term tenant. We live up there.' She pointed towards the cliff that loomed above the town. 'It's small but comfortable. I could show it to you . . . see what you think.'

The house was a white stucco villa with arched doorways and smooth terracotta tiled floors; a Portuguese doll's house with a balcony crowded with pots of rambling scarlet geraniums. Sara had given up her job as a reporter on a Birmingham evening paper and spent a couple of years backpacking around Europe before coming to Cascais to visit a friend. 'Just a week or so after I got here he got a contract to renovate some lighthouses along the Mediterranean coast, and he was off – so I rented the house. It was going to be for a few months but I loved it and I stayed.'

'Do you work here?' Isabel asked.

'Yes. Just! I just manage to make a living! I do some work for an English language paper in Lisbon, and some other freelance stuff. It's not much, but it's enough to keep me. Well, this is the room, and it's got its own little ensuite – what do you think?'

'I'm not sure how to say this, Isabel,' Sara began, 'but I think you need a bit of a makeover before you move off.' They were sitting on the balcony looking out across the moonlit surface of the sea and the pinpoint lights on the fishing boats. After two weeks at the house Isabel had shaken off the unease and confusion of her arrival and was learning to let go of her anxiety about home. Sara knew Portugal and Spain, and with the help of maps and guidebooks they had sorted out a route that would enable Isabel to see some of the most memorable places in both countries. Now she was able to relax, enjoy her surroundings and prepare for the promise ahead.

'A makeover? What sort of makeover?'

'You've got far too much stuff for a woman wanting to do the amount of travelling you're planning,' Sara said, resting her feet on the white wall of the balcony. 'And . . . look, please don't take offence but your clothes are all wrong!' Isabel looked at her in amazement. 'Sorry – I don't mean to be rude, but what you've got

73

is just not practical. You can't possibly cart all that stuff across Europe for the next year.'

'But I need all those things,' Isabel said, feeling her security blanket being ripped away. 'A year is a long time. I need winter and summer things, my books, walking shoes, all that stuff.'

'What you need,' said Sara, 'is the minimum. A few plain T-shirts, some comfortable pants, a light jacket, one of those rain-proof jackets that roll up really small, some walking shoes, some sandals – that's about it. That's the art of this sort of travelling. I mean, how do you think you're going to manage those two huge suitcases and the overnight bag on the bus and train, moving all the time?'

Isabel took a deep breath. 'I suppose you're right,' she began tentatively.

'No "suppose" about it – I *am* right. I've done it, I learned the hard way. The rule for this sort of travel is minimalism. You take as little as possible, discard things and replace them along the way. You take small sizes of toiletries or decant large ones into plastic bottles. And you need a new haircut.'

Isabel's hand shot up to her head. 'What's wrong with my hair?'

'Nothing's wrong, it's just impractical. You can't carry hairdryers and hot brushes and sprays and stuff. You want some-thing short and simple that you can easily wash and dry, without electricity. Sometimes the power goes off for twenty-four hours or more. You have to be able to manage without those things.'

Isabel sat in silence, shocked at the prospect of short hair and being separated from all those things that had seemed so essential when she had packed them.

'Look, you can't travel around looking like some civic digni-tary on an official town-twinning visit. You'll look weird and you'll be uncomfortable. How many pairs of shoes have you got in that bag?'

'Six.' Isabel grinned sheepishly. Sara spluttered into her drink. 'And a long black velvet skirt, a winter coat, two suits –'

'Stop, stop!' Sara put up her hand. 'Wherever did you think you were going? You haven't planned this properly at all. You'll have to leave most of that stuff here with me. I can send it on to you or back to Australia. Tomorrow we'll go shopping and then to the hairdresser. You'll just have to trust me. I promise you you'll look great and you'll be much more comfortable.'

She was ruthless in her assault on Isabel's luggage, salvaging only underwear, a couple of pairs of cotton pants and a fine black wool sweater. An hour later Isabel was the owner of four new T-shirts, a couple of light cotton shirts and another pair of cotton pants. Sara had banned linen, because it creased too much.

'Cream and black for the T-shirts,' she had insisted. 'And that sage green shirt and the same in black.' Isabel had never owned clothes like these, casual, plain, loose but shaped. 'I can't believe it,' Sara exclaimed. 'You come from the most easygoing place in the world but your clothes are so formal and conservative.'

'I've never been good at casual clothes,' Isabel said. 'I didn't think they suited me. And I always seem to be doing things that need me to look . . . well . . . dressed up.' But she surveyed herself in the fitting room mirror in a close-fitting cream T-shirt and khaki pants and was pleased at the effect.

'I'm surprised your daughters haven't got you better organised,' Sara said, stepping back to view her critically from a distance.

Isabel laughed. 'My daughters are rather like younger versions of me,' she said. 'I've obviously stunted their growth. But my friend Grace would be thrilled. She always said that shaped clothes would make me look thinner, and she'd love these colours.'

But it was the haircut that really transformed her. In the basement salon of an elegant hotel by the beach, a young man with the face of a thoughtful eagle greeted Sara with a hug. 'I've brought my friend Isabel to you, Tony,' she said. 'She needs a travelling haircut. Minimum fuss, maximum style, and youthful.'

And as Isabel was swathed in a black cape and escorted to the basins, Sara and Tony discussed the fate of her fine shoulder-length hair. Despite his Latin appearance Tony was a cockney, and he examined Isabel's hair, bunching it up, sweeping it to the side. 'It's rather fine, darlin', but there's plenty of it and it's not limp. I think we can do something rather specky with this.'

She watched anxiously as the long strands drifted to the floor, but by the time Tony was finished she could hardly believe she was looking at herself. The short crop framed her face, making her look younger and slimmer. Tony sold her the smallest folding hairdryer she had ever seen and a tiny pot of hair wax with instructions to use only a smidgen. 'You shouldn't really need it, but it'll make you feel better,' he smiled.

'I'd better buy you coffee and croissants to make up for brutalising you,' Sara laughed, taking her arm as they went out into the square. 'And tomorrow we'll go to Lisbon and hunt for that house you were looking for, although I think it's a long shot that you'd find your mother's friend still there. What was her name?'

'Antonia,' Isabel said. 'I've just got this photograph of the house and on the back it's got the address, and then "Antonia's house". And I'll buy the croissants. I feel like a new woman.'

They found the house with ease, a tall, rather forbidding-looking place alongside a bakery and halfway up a steep hill near the cathedral. 'It looks awfully shut up,' Isabel said, staring at the shuttered windows. 'In fact, it looks empty.' She hammered on the door and they waited in the street for some sign of life.

'Doesn't look too hopeful,' Sara said, looking again at the photo. 'But that's definitely the right house and, look, the bakery has the same name on it now as it does in the photo. We could try in there.'

Isabel shrugged. 'It's worth a try, I suppose. If you don't mind doing the talking.' She stood in the entrance as Sara took the photograph to the young woman behind the counter.

'She doesn't know anything,' Sara explained as the woman, photograph in hand, disappeared into the room at the back of the shop. 'But the bakery's been in the family for years; she's married to the present baker's son. Apparently the grandfather still lives here and might know something.'

The woman reappeared in the doorway nodding and beckoning, and they squeezed behind the counter and went out through the beaded curtain, past the bread ovens and into the yard at the rear of the house. An old man was sitting in the sun outside, a couple of chickens pecked at ants between the smooth old flagstones, and a cat dozed in the corner. The man smiled, pointing with his pipe to Isabel's photograph.

'He knows the family,' Sara translated. 'They are called Peralta. They're gone now – well, the parents have gone, dead obviously. There was a daughter who married and went to America, a son whose name he can't remember, and he doesn't know where he is, but apparently Antonia was the youngest. She still lives in Portugal.'

'In Lisbon?' Isabel asked. 'Does he know where?'

The old man shook his head. Isabel held her breath. Suddenly it was important to find this woman, to make that direct connection with Eunice's European life.

'She lives in one of the hilltop villages in the Alentejo region,' Sara said, waiting for the old man to go on. 'Either Monsaraz or Marvao. He thinks she has some sort of guesthouse. She comes to see him when she's in Lisbon. He thinks she's a writer or perhaps a translator.'

Isabel could hardly contain her excitement as the baker's wife invited them to sit down and brought out a tray of coffee. The conversation between Sara and the old man was fast and animated and they were soon joined by the baker himself, who remembered Antonia and her brother from his childhood. 'They were older than him,' Sara translated, indicating the baker. 'He thinks she'd be in her late sixties, perhaps older.'

Isabel was surprised by the urgency of her sudden desire to find the woman. 'But we don't know which town, and she probably married and has another name,' she said.

Sara shook her head. 'Apparently she has the same name. And don't worry, I know those tiny hilltop towns – if that's where she is, we'll find her. Trust me. I'm a journalist, I've tracked down people on far less information than this.'

From her seat at the back of the bus Isabel could see the village of Monsaraz perched on the hill, white houses with terracotta roofs clustered together at the top and thinning out away from the centre. Above them the russet and grey remains of a castle overlooked the misty green hills and plains that stretched to the Spanish border. Ten minutes and she would be there. The bus lumbered up the steep hillside, scattering a few grey and white goats onto the verge as it turned right beneath a stone archway and rattled to a halt in a cobbled square, where two elderly women, dressed entirely in black and with black scarves on their heads, leaned against a drinking fountain built into the wall of the church. Isabel followed the other passengers down the steps of the bus into the glare of the sunlight. The two women climbed aboard and the driver executed a tight turn and drove off back in the direction from which he had come.

The other passengers disappeared silently along narrow side streets and Isabel stood alone, looking around her in the mid-afternoon silence broken only by the fading rumble of the departing bus. She reached in her pocket and pulled out the directions Sara had written for her. The pale cobbles led between the white houses to the foot of a steep flight of steps. Isabel picked up her backpack, slung it over her shoulders, and began to make her way up the narrow street. She was thankful she had taken Sara's brutally frank advice. Without it she would have been staggering along here in uncomfortable shoes trying to handle two large suitcases.

Pausing for breath at the foot of the steps that led to a terrace of two-storey houses, she realised that the thumping of her heart was due to more than just the physical exertion. It was the excitement that had gripped her since she sat in the baker's yard. Sara had been as good as her word. It took her less than an hour to learn that Antonia Peralta had a pension in Monsaraz and to get the telephone number. 'Want me to call?' she had asked, grinning with satisfaction.

'Yes,' said Isabel. 'I mean, no . . . well, what I actually mean is, if it's a guesthouse maybe I could just turn up and stay there, talk to her when I get there.'

'I could call and see if she has a room – book it, if you like,' Sara suggested. 'It's a long way to go on the off-chance and the place is so tiny you could find yourself with nowhere to stay.'

'Yes, brilliant.' Isabel nodded in delight. 'Call and if it sounds okay, if it sounds like it could be her, just book me a room.' She waited, dizzy with excitement, while Sara made the call.

'It's her,' Sara said putting down the receiver. 'She answered with her full name. She takes a maximum of two guests in rooms in the house and there's a garden studio but that's already occupied. She only takes single people, no couples or families. You get dinner the first night. After that you shop and look after yourself. You can use the kitchen whenever you want and there's a lounge and terrace for the guests.'

'And you didn't say anything about –'

'I just booked the room,' Sara said and Isabel leapt to her feet in delight. 'You look like you won the lottery.'

'I feel like it. Isn't it weird? I didn't even think about it in Australia but now I so much want to meet her. Ever since we found the house I haven't been able to think of anything else.'

Sara handed her the paper with the address and telephone number. 'She speaks excellent English and you'll love Monsaraz. If you like peace and quiet, this is it. It's so quiet you can hear the neighbours breathe.'

It was the last building at the end of the terrace. A dozen blue and white tiles set into the wall formed a picture of the Virgin Mary, her hand raised in a blessing. Beneath the shutters, closed against the sun, narrow boxes overflowing with blue and white trailing daisies clung to the sills. The solid wooden door stood slightly ajar and Isabel tapped on it, softly at first and then more loudly. There was no sound from inside but the door swung further open at her firmer touch and she stepped inside the cool entrance hall, dark after the sunlight. In front of her a narrow stone staircase with a wrought-iron rail led up to the first floor.

'Hello!' Isabel called out. 'Hello, is anyone there? Hello!'

A figure materialised in the shadows at the top of the staircase.

'Senhora . . . I'm sorry, the door was open . . .'

'Senhora Carter! I'm so sorry,' the woman said, coming slowly down the stairs. 'I was working upstairs and forgot about the time. Please come in.' She halted at the half-landing to throw open the shutters and stepped through the shaft of light from the window. She was, as the baker had indicated, in her mid to late sixties and still stunningly beautiful. She wore a soft Indian cotton skirt with a white cheesecloth top, and her silver hair was wound into a loose knot at the nape of her neck. She held out her hand to Isabel. 'I am Antonia Peralta. You must be hot and tired after your journey. Come, I'll show you your room and then get you a cool drink, or perhaps you would prefer some tea?'

The white-painted room was tucked under the slope of the roof with narrow French doors opening onto a small balcony. Wooden floorboards were polished to a golden glow, the white iron bed made up with cream linen and a cotton cover patterned in cream, black and rusty red. There was a small wardrobe, a chest of drawers and a marble-topped washstand with a heavy blue and white porcelain jug and bowl. Beside the windows was a writing table with an upright chair and in the corner a deep armchair covered in the same fabric as the bedspread.

'It is not very large, I'm afraid, but I hope you'll find it comfortable.'

Isabel put down her bag and breathed a sigh of relief as she took in the cool stillness of the room and the calm of the landscape.

'Senhora Peralta, it's simply perfect. Just what I was hoping for, thank you so much.'

'*Antonia*, please – we are going to be housemates. You are Isabel, I think? You have your own bathroom just next door. It, too, is rather small but it has all the essentials. You must make yourself feel at home. I have only one other guest at the moment, a friend from Germany. He is a regular visitor and speaks good English. You'll find he's very quiet.'

She gestured to Isabel to follow her back down the stairs, walking with a dancer's grace. 'Later I will show you where things are kept. I think you know that I cook for guests only on the evening of their arrival, but you have the use of the kitchen whenever you wish. Tomorrow I will introduce you to our few shops and you can become self-sufficient.' She led the way into the kitchen where she took a tall jug of lemonade from the refrigerator, poured some into two glasses and handed one to Isabel, lifting her own in a toast. 'I hope you will enjoy your stay. I hope you like peace and quiet.'

The glasses chinked and Isabel smiled. 'I am desperate for it and I'm sure I'll love it here.'

They walked together back into the hall and through to a large room that combined a dining and sitting area. Glass doors led to a terrace, which looked out in the opposite direction from Isabel's room. 'Feel free to use this room. It is for guests, my own rooms are upstairs. The other guest accommodation is down there.'

Isabel looked over the terrace wall to what looked like a studio situated at the bottom of a flight of steps. In the open doorway a man dressed in shorts and T-shirt was sleeping in a cane chair, a light straw hat tipped over his eyes, an open book facing downward on his lap. At his feet a tortoiseshell and white cat stretched out on the warm tiles.

'Klaus, Herr Hoffmann,' Antonia explained softly. 'Tosca, my cat, is very attached to him. You will meet them both later. I have invited Klaus to have dinner with us this evening, Tosca will invite herself. I hope you don't mind cats.'

'I love cats,' Isabel said. 'And this house is beautiful. You've kept the original building but renovated it so carefully.'

'It was done by a friend,' Antonia said. 'I told him what I wanted and he made it work. I don't have many guests. Monsaraz is too quiet for most people but it suits those with a need to get away from busy lives. But you must be tired, we'll talk later. Dinner is at eight-thirty out here on the terrace.'

Isabel was tempted to blurt out her questions there and then but stuck to her decision to wait a while. Perhaps that evening over dinner she would produce Eunice's photograph of the house in Lisbon, but for the moment she would simply enjoy her sur-roundings. The adventure had begun. Now, at last, she could feel once again the passion that had driven her to make this journey. She sipped the lemonade and gazed out across the rooftops and plains to the next hilltop village.

'It's perfect,' she whispered. 'Like stepping back into the past. I can't tell you how wonderful it is to be here.'

SIX

Sally had been in Berkeley for four weeks before she finally opened the telephone directory and did what she had imagined doing since she stood in the art gallery looking at the earthquake photographs. That day, her skin prickling with goose bumps, she had pictured this moment – her finger moving swiftly down the 'M' pages of the San Francisco directory, slowing at the first Mendelson and then seeking out the 'O' initial, until she saw the address that she had held in her memory for twenty-five years. Would they be listed under 'O' or 'O & E'? Would they still be living there, at the address on the yellowing pages of the letter?

She almost stopped breathing – there it was under 'O & E', the same address in Hyde Street, Russian Hill. She wrote down the number and closed the directory. From the window of her apartment she could see across the rooftops of Oakland to the bay and the city of San Francisco, cream and gold in the hazy light of late afternoon. Strains of Ella Fitzgerald floated down from the CD player in the house upstairs and the volume swelled as Nancy opened the sliding doors to the balcony. Sally went back to the watercolour on her easel, picked up her paintbrush and put it down again, trying to calm the frantic activity in her mind. How should she do it? Should she phone or write? Was she really ready to cope with this?

The elegant outline of the Bay Bridge, linking Oakland and Berkeley to San Francisco, seemed sketched in charcoal above the still waters of the bay, thirteen kilometres of iron and steel. She had stood in the gallery in Perth, in front of the photograph of its crumpled girders and crumbling concrete, thinking about this place. Now she was here, in a small ground-floor apartment in a house clinging to a steep escarpment in Berkeley. A card in her purse identified her as a student of the University of California, her name on a list allocated her to a postgraduate unit in photo-journalism. She had attended the first five lectures and tutorials and appeared to be doing exactly what she came here to do, but Sally knew that she hadn't really started.

From the balcony above, excess water dripped through the timber slats. Nancy was watering the geraniums, and Chuck's voice began to compete with Ella and won – the music was turned down. She had seen a few hellholes in the search for a place to live, but the moment she walked into this comfortable space where shafts of afternoon sunlight filtered through the trees to trace delicate patterns on the polished wood floor, she knew it was the place for her. The rent was a strain, almost twice as much as she was getting in rent for her townhouse in Perth, and her long-service leave pay didn't translate to much in US dollars. If she was very careful, her father's legacy would just about see her through. She had been lucky with her landlords. Chuck and Nancy Parker were kindred spirits, intelligent, thoughtful and friendly, both in their sixties and still busy with their own teaching commitments at the university.

Sally stared at the phone wondering whether to call now. What would she say? After all these years how would she even broach the subject, and what chaos would she cause by announc-ing her presence just a few miles away across the bay? She glanced at her watch. After five. She would wait until tomorrow. What was one more day after all this time?

She picked up the worn envelope, addressed to her at the flat in Earl's Court that she had shared with Vanessa. Unfolding the pages, Sally stared at the neat sloping writing and the words that she knew by heart.

Dear Sally Erskine

*I have started this letter so many times and then changed my
mind, but for months I've known that I had to write to you. I
am not supposed to know who you are and you have a right to
be angry that I have discovered your name and address.*

*My name is Estelle Mendelson and three years ago my
husband Oliver and I adopted your baby. All I know is that
you were a single mother and that Lisa was born in London on
18 November 1969. I have thought of you and wondered what
it can have been like for you to part with Lisa.*

*I always felt that if you wanted to make contact with Lisa
there were ways for you to do it while we were living in
England. But last year we moved back to San Francisco, which
is our home town. We have taken Lisa away in a very final sort
of way. We both love her as if she was our own child, but we
intend to tell her at an early age that she is our chosen, not our
natural child. We will also tell her that her mother loved her
but could not care for her in the way she wanted.*

*So often I look at Lisa and wonder about you, how you are
and if you are happy. I am sending you our address in San
Francisco. If, one day, you want to make contact with Lisa we
will do our best to help, provided of course that it seems to be
in her best interests.*

*I hope this letter will feel like reassurance rather than an
invasion of your privacy. To have Lisa with us is the greatest
gift we could imagine.*

*Yours sincerely
Estelle Mendelson*

Sally folded the letter feeling the strips of sticky tape with
which she had repaired it, years after she first tore it up. She
could hardly remember the person she was then, and the
person she had been in 1969 when Lisa was born. When Simon
thrust the envelope of five-pound notes into her hand and
roared away in his cream Volvo, she knew she couldn't face an

abortion any more than she could face the pursed lips and disapproving sniffs of a small Australian country town. Her parents would be hurt and horrified, her older sister self-righteous and condemning. None of them must ever know. Despite his point-blank refusal to use condoms, Simon had blamed her entirely and, because he was so much older and a man, Sally believed he was right to. She struggled through the pregnancy, designing greeting cards at a small company in Islington, until the day she was shocked by a sudden intense contraction two weeks before her due date.

Lisa was born on a dark November morning when the streets of London were black and treacherous with freezing rain. Her body exhausted and her heart breaking, Sally lay in the hospital bed holding the tiny blue-eyed baby and fighting back the tears that threatened to overwhelm her. Kissing the top of her downy head, she handed Lisa to the social worker and turned her face to the window and the dark abyss of the hospital car park, listening to the dismal tap of the woman's shoes as she walked away down the hospital corridor.

Three weeks later Sally took Simon's money from its envelope and caught the bus to Oxford Street. In the fabric department of John Lewis she bought dress lengths of wool and velvet, silk and cotton, enough to make herself a whole new wardrobe. From there she headed to Selfridges, where she had her wild curly hair highlighted and restyled. The next day she saw a flat share advertisement in the *Evening Standard* and caught the bus to Earl's Court. She loved the flat and really liked Vanessa, who had inherited it from an aunt. She paid a month's rent in advance for a bedroom with casement windows, a steeply sloping roof and a white shag-pile carpet, which was just like one she had seen in a magazine at the hairdresser's. The next day she moved in and two weeks later she had a new job in a bigger greeting cards company. She had bought herself a new life and she closed the doors on the past, sealing away her pain, refusing to allow herself to feel her own grief. Two years later, with the money she had saved and a determination to get a degree and become a teacher, she made her way back to Australia.

Estelle Mendelson's letter arrived the following Christmas. Sally took the train to her parents' home for the holiday, a two-hour trip from Melbourne, where she was studying and working as a part-time waitress. The airmail envelope from London was sitting on the hall table, inside it a Christmas card from Vanessa and the envelope from America. 'It came a week ago,' her mother said. 'I didn't bother to forward it, knowing you'd be here shortly.'

Sally stood in the lounge reading the message in Vanessa's card and wondering who could have written to her at Earl's Court, and who she might know who had gone to San Francisco.

'Everything all right, love?' her mother asked, glancing up from the kettle to see Sally's face white and set, the pages of the letter fluttering in her shaking hands. 'Not bad news from Vanessa, I hope.'

Sally stuffed the letter in her bag and, mumbling about putting her things upstairs, fled to her old bedroom where she sat bolt upright on the bed staring at the familiar rose-patterned wallpaper. She felt as though she had been stripped naked. This letter had lain on her parents' hall table for a week. Anyone could have opened it and discovered her shameful secret. The social worker had promised her total confidentiality, it had been the one fragment of consolation, the thought that her family would never know. Sally tore the letter in two and then into four pieces, but stopped herself from throwing it in the wastebasket. She'd have to dispose of it tomorrow, put it in a bin on the street. If she dumped it here someone might discover it. Carefully she put the torn letter back into its envelope, folded it and zipped it into the side pocket of her handbag. But the next day there was no opportunity to go out and although it seemed like a bomb waiting to explode, the letter stayed put.

Christmas and New Year passed in scorching heat and it seemed easier just to pretend it wasn't there. She spent the days in the garden, chatting with her mother and sister, and watching her nephews playing under the sprinklers. And in the evenings her father and brother-in-law charred steaks and sausages on the barbecue, and neighbours turned up with six-packs and flagons

86

of wine. When she caught the train back to the city the letter was still in its hiding place and when, months later, she finally went to dispose of it safely she couldn't quite bring herself to do so, its dangerous potential dissipated by the passing of time. She kept the torn sections folded in the envelope until one day, more than a decade later, she realised that the letter had lost its power. She got it out and stuck the pieces back together.

In her twenties Sally had cast Estelle Mendelson as a nosy, interfering stranger with the power to destroy her life. But time had changed the way she viewed the world, and the letter that had once filled her with fear and rage, at this point seemed generous, even courageous. Now Sally gazed at her painting and the view beyond it. Was she a fraud? She had grasped at the motivating force of Isabel's decision but she had done it dishonestly. It was true that she had always wanted to learn photography, but there were a hundred and one places where she could have done it. It was Lisa that had brought her to this place. Even so she had resisted doing anything until she was in California, determined to start her search where nobody knew her. What did Lisa look like? What sort of woman had she become? Sally imagined her daughter in her own image, but without what she saw as her own faults and weaknesses. She pictured her daughter as the person she would like to have been. Strong-minded, courageous, ambitious. But how would that young woman react to the appearance of a mother who had given her away at birth? Joyful acceptance and welcome? Fierce anger and rejection? She could not bid for the former without risking the latter.

Perhaps she wasn't quite ready to phone. Tomorrow she would get the train into the city, walk up to Russian Hill, have a look at the house. Pick up the vibes, Isabel would say, and Grace would shrug, discomfited by the words. Why had she never told them about Lisa? A friend who had gone to San Francisco, she had said. It was totally misleading and when Robin asked her if she had managed to track down her friend, she had flushed deeply and said she was still trying to trace her. She had isolated this from the rest of her life; if she was going to crack open the memories, the hopes, the fears and the shame, she would do that in isolation too.

Nancy's feet clattered down the steep wooden staircase at the side of the house and Sally heard the rattle of silver bracelets as she appeared at the screen door. 'Come on in,' Sally called. 'I'm just making some coffee.'

'Gee, that's beautiful,' said Nancy, nodding towards the landscape on the easel. 'You sure captured that view. I wish I could paint, always wanted to. Always too busy teaching politics to students who think they're gonna change the world.'

Sally laughed and filled the kettle. 'And did any of them change the world?'

'Uh-uh,' Nancy smiled, shaking her head. 'But I did hear from one who's working in the White House. Mind you, that's nothing to boast about. Thanks, I'd love some coffee. You got those eucalyptus trees just perfect, but then I guess you'd have a lot of those back home.'

Sally nodded. 'Somehow they look different here, though, the effect of the landscape is that the same things seem totally different. Oh, look!' A grey squirrel darted along a branch and leapt off onto the top of the fence.

'Those darned squirrels don't even have the manners to be shy.' Nancy laughed. 'Sally, I don't know if this'll appeal to you, but Chuck has to go away next week and we have tickets for a concert on Thursday. It's the San Francisco Symphony. Nice program – some Beethoven, Haydn, and I can't remember what else. You're welcome to Chuck's ticket if you'd like to come along.'

'I'd love it, Nancy. Thanks. There's such a huge choice of concerts and theatre here, but I haven't managed to get to anything yet.'

They settled opposite each other on the two big cream couches. Nancy, small and supple as a teenager, kicked off her shoes and sat cross-legged, leaning back on the cushions. 'I always wanted to sit like that but my legs won't do it,' Sally said with envy.

'Yoga.'

'I've been doing yoga for years but I still can't sit in that position for more than a minute or two.'

Nancy shrugged. 'Some people can't. Being weirdly under-sized helps. You'd be welcome at our yoga class, y'know. It's only a couple of blocks away. Walking distance. I go on Wednesday evenings but there's a whole stack of classes. I've got a timetable upstairs. Look, honey, are you okay down here? Warm enough? Got enough saucepans, blankets . . .?'

'Nancy, it's great. It feels like a five-star hotel. I can't believe how comfortable you've made it.'

'Well, I'm glad. We're so happy to have you here. We only bought this house a year ago, and this is the first time we've leased the apartment. Our son Ross lived in it for a few months, but you're our first real tenant.' She reached out to pick up a framed photograph sitting on the side table, the Gang of Four taken at a party at Isabel's house a couple of days before she left for Portugal.

'My friends in Australia.'

'They look so nice,' Nancy said. 'You must miss those women. My friends are so precious to me. You know how it is – no secrets because they don't make judgments. Women friends are so special. When I was young I was so closed and secretive, but my women friends shook me out of it.'

Sally felt a deep flush creep up her neck. 'I do miss them,' she said. 'Very much. Although I do have a few secrets, even from them.'

The early morning fog had lifted, replacing the damp chill with glorious sunshine and a clear blue sky. Ahead of her the famous zigzag of Lombard Street rose steeply towards the junction with Hyde Street. Sally made her way up the steps forcing herself to breathe deeply. There was nothing to worry about, she was just going to walk along the street and take a look at the house. Maybe she would see someone coming out, maybe – but she pushed the thought away and walked on between the borders of blue and white hydrangeas, and up the steep sidewalk. Pausing at the top she caught her breath at the view of the city spread around her, the pastel buildings scattered over the hillsides as though by the hand of some amiable giant. Across the bay a ferry loaded with tourists ploughed a trail of white foam towards Alcatraz. How often had Lisa looked out on this view?

This was one of the city's most desirable districts. The large elegant houses bordering Hyde Street gave it an air of solid wealth. With property prices being forced through the roof by the youthful entrepreneurs of Silicon Valley, these homes were worth millions. The Mendelsons' was an old and beautifully restored, double-fronted, three-storey house, its walls painted a light cream picked out with touches of charcoal grey. A wrought-iron gate opened from the sidewalk onto a paved courtyard where orange and lemon trees grew in massive earthenware pots and water trickled from the mouth of a stone fish into a shallow limestone bowl. From the courtyard a short flight of stone steps led up to the front door. This was where Lisa lived or had lived, where she had spent her childhood and her adolescence. This was the gate she had walked through to go to school, returned through from her first date, perhaps walked out of to be married. An elderly couple, cameras around their necks and guidebook in hand, stopped nearby to photograph the view. Sally thought they must have been able to hear her heart pounding, or feel the intense heat that flooded her body. But they just smiled pleasantly and walked on.

She strolled a few yards up the street to a wooden bench and sat down, glancing uncomfortably around her. The street was clear and she drew her camera from the leather shoulder bag, focused and rapidly took several shots of the house. She wondered why she felt so guilty, as though she had no right to be there on the street, and certainly no right to be photographing the Mendelsons' home. The nervous anticipation that had driven her there had evaporated, leaving a strange and painful emptiness. She had expected to feel excited, fearful, but most of all connected. Instead she felt bereft. Her energy had deserted her and her limbs felt like lead weights. Perhaps it was the onset of flu. Her skin, which had been flushed with heat a few moments earlier, now prickled with the chill dampness of a cold sweat, and she shivered despite the warmth of the sun.

She dropped her head forward and sat for a while, hoping the feeling would pass, then she straightened up, took some deep breaths and tried to focus on the distant hills of Marin County across the bay. Tears ran down her face, and the light breeze that ruffled the waters of the bay seemed to cut into her flesh like ice. Why had she come here? What had she expected? A cable car lumbered noisily up the street, rattling past her on its way to the city centre. She stood up, her legs so unsteady she thought she might faint. A yellow cab was heading up the street and she hailed it, sinking with relief into the back seat.

'Embarcadero – the BART station please,' she said, and as the driver swung the cab into a U-turn she took a final look at the house.

'I think our seats are just over there,' Nancy said, striding ahead between less confident concertgoers down the shallow carpeted steps of the circle. Sally followed her and they picked their way along the front row, avoiding the feet of those already seated.

'Great seats,' Sally said. 'So this is the Davie Concert Hall – those organ pipes are pretty spectacular.'

'Nine thousand of them,' Nancy said with some pride. 'It's a Ruffalin.'

'I'm sorry?'

'Ruffalin – it's the name of the organ. Not that I know anything about organs, but I try to remember it because I feel I should know something about the main concert hall in my home town. Just don't ask me any questions about it, though.'

'That's okay, I'm sufficiently impressed already.'

'Good girl, you're supposed to be. Have you been to the Sydney Opera House?'

Sally nodded. 'A couple of times, when I lived in the eastern states.' She rummaged in her bag. 'Damn, I forgot my reading glasses – now I can't see the program.'

'It's the Beethoven first, the fourth piano concerto,' Nancy said. 'Want my glasses for the program notes?'

Sally shook her head as the lights in the auditorium dimmed. 'It's okay, I'll just sit back and enjoy it.'

To a gentle burst of applause the orchestra members filed on stage and settled down to tune their instruments. Then the conductor entered to a round of applause. As it died away he stretched a welcoming arm towards the wings and the pianist made his entry. A slight, wiry man with thinning hair and round steel-rimmed glasses, he bowed briefly to the audience and shook hands with the conductor and the leader. A hush fell over the audience as the conductor tapped his baton on the music stand and the first familiar notes filled the hall.

Sally sighed with the joy of anticipation, knowing that the music would temporarily free her from the anxiety that had settled on her since her visit to Hyde Street. She had thought that seeing the house where Lisa lived, walking the streets she walked, would take her closer to the act of making contact. But it had the opposite effect. The solid wealth of the house and the lifestyle it represented seemed like another world. She had imagined the Mendelsons as an ordinary middle-aged, middle-class couple in a pleasant, rather ordinary house, living the sort of life that she and her friends lived in Australia, maybe worrying about money, hoping they could afford to retire early. But theirs was obviously a very different lifestyle. She had caught the train to Berkeley and walked slowly back to the apartment, her legs still shaking, her head spinning. For years she had refused to think too much about Lisa. She had curbed her dreams, reined in her fantasies, and forced herself to concentrate on other things. Lisa had a family who loved her. That was all she knew, all she could bear to know. Why did she have to stir up the feelings again, revive the sense of loss, fuel once more the longing to know her daughter?

She had tried several times to compose a letter to Estelle Mendelson but each time she failed to progress beyond the first line. How could she explain herself? What would the Mendelsons think of her turning up after so many years? She felt small, powerless and frightened, as though her identity had evaporated. The Mendelsons had assumed huge and frightening proportions in her imagination. She missed everything about home, even her interfering sister, even Harry's stifling dependency, but most of all she missed Grace's fierce, frenetic energy, Robin's reliably calm and thoughtful presence, and Isabel's comforting warmth and understanding. She desperately wanted to run away and go home.

'There's a great view from the balcony,' Nancy said as the lights came up for the first intermission. 'Want to take a look?' They walked together along the wide corridor to where the glass-enclosed balcony revealed a spectacular view of the San Francisco City Hall.

'So what do you think of our symphony orchestra?' asked Nancy, fanning herself with the program. 'We're rather proud of it.'

Sally smiled. 'It's magnificent. The pianist especially, he's superb. Who is he? He looks just like Woody Allen.'

'Doesn't he just,' Nancy grinned. 'The music writers always refer to it – New York has Woody, San Francisco has Oliver Mendelson.'

'I'm sorry?'

'Oliver Mendelson, the pianist, that's his name. New York has Woody Allen, San Francisco has Oliver Mendelson. I think that's the bell, shall we go back? Sally, are you okay? You look awfully pale.'

'But, honey, what I don't understand is why it's any different that the Mendelsons are celebrities, as you put it.' Nancy walked across to where Sally was sitting on the settee and handed her a large brandy. 'Drink it all, you need it.'

Sally took the glass with suspicion. 'I don't usually drink alcohol.'

'You do tonight. It's medicine.'

Sally caught her breath as the fumes drifted up from the glass, and she sipped the brandy tentatively. It was better than she expected, smooth and warming. 'It makes them more remote; inaccessible, somehow.'

'But they're not inaccessible. You've walked right up to the house. Their number is listed in the directory just like anyone else's. They're the same people who adopted your baby all those years ago, just the same as if they'd been hard up and living on welfare in West Oakland. Sure, they're quite well known in San Francisco, particularly Oliver. He does have a bit of an international following. She gave up the opera years ago. They don't jet set around the world. Whatever it is, Sally, it's in your head.'

Sally stared at the brandy in the glass and then out across the vast expanse of twinkling lights and moonlit water that separated them from the city of San Francisco.

'Whenever I've thought about trying to get in touch with Lisa's parents I felt like I did when I left the hospital after she was born – a failure. Small, worthless and powerless to change anything, and so ashamed of what I'd done. It's as though I become that teenager again. The Mendelsons being important, successful people makes it worse.'

Nancy shrugged. 'Y'know, if you'd talked about this years ago I think you might have got rid of some of those feelings by now. I'm just so amazed that you never told your friends in Australia.'

'I hid it for so long it seemed set in concrete. It was years before I made the sort of friends I could have told and by that time the secrecy had become a way of life. I'm almost as shaken by the fact that I've told you about Lisa as I was by discovering that I'd been sitting for an hour watching Oliver Mendelson play the piano. I used to feel that telling the truth would change everything. But I've told you and the sky hasn't fallen in.'

'And you think the sky would have fallen in or you'd have been struck by lightning if you'd told your three best friends?'

Sally smiled ruefully. 'Sounds stupid now, doesn't it? Part of me knew they wouldn't think any less of me, but I couldn't make myself really feel that.'

'Well,' Nancy began, pausing to savour the brandy. 'Will you tell them now?'

'You'll think this is stupid but I still don't know. You see, in a way it feels okay to tell you because you're separate from the rest of my life. If you're shocked I can run away back home and still feel safe. Same as if Lisa and the Mendelsons reject me – no one else need ever know. I can go back home to Australia and keep my secret. Go on pretending that learning photography was the only reason I came to California.'

94

Nancy swallowed her brandy and stood up. 'It's not stupid. You took a big step coming here, visiting the street, looking at the house, and now telling me. It took courage to do that. The rest will come in time.' She patted Sally's hand and got to her feet, smiling down at her. 'I think you need something to eat and I certainly do – we have to soak up the brandy. Stay there and I'll make us a sandwich.'

'I'm sorry about the second half of the concert,' Sally said. 'I really appreciate you bringing me home.'

'Hey, what's half a concert between friends? Besides, I love a good story and yours is the best I've heard in a long time.'

Sally raised her eyebrows. 'You're not shocked?'

Nancy stood, her hand on the fridge door, her short cropped silver hair gleaming under the kitchen spotlights. She threw her head back with a noisy laugh. 'Sally, are you shocked if I tell you I had an abortion in the fifties? I got pregnant, but I took the other solution. So . . . are you shocked?'

Sally grinned. 'Of course not, just surprised.'

'Well, then, where's the difference? It's the story of so many women, but you seem to feel you have to be alone with it. It's like you're stuck in the sixties, thinking everyone would react like your mom and pop would've done if you'd run home from London and told them you were pregnant. And, Sally, honey, how do you know you were right about that? Maybe you figured that all wrong and they would've stood by you. So much of this is in your head, where it's been locked up all these years. Anyhow – end of lecture. What d'you want in your sandwich? I've got cheese, cheese or cheese.'

'I'll have cheese, please,' said Sally. 'The middle one!'

'Good girl. We'll have that sense of humour back real soon. Have some more brandy.'

'In her work during the war Lee Miller was aiming for the same journalistic standards she admired in Ed Morrow,' said the lecturer, flashing another image onto the screen. 'This is the body of a German soldier she photographed at Cologne in 1945.' The students gazed in uneasy silence, unnerved by the power and intensity of the image and the feelings it produced. 'Miller believed that Morrow assembled his stories entirely differently from anyone else and never tried to fool anyone. In her reports and photographs she was emulating Morrow, aiming for his honesty and acuity.' The projector was switched off and the lights of the lecture theatre flickered back to life. Sally pressed her hands against her eyes and blinked as the lecturer nodded in acknowledgement of the smattering of applause.

'She was some woman, that Lee Miller,' said Steve, leaning across to her. 'She did what she wanted to do and damn the conventions.' He was packing up his notebook, zipping the side pocket on his bag. 'You walking back my way, Sally?'

She nodded and stood up. 'Yes, it's too good a day for the bus.'

Following the crush of students leaving the hall they walked side by side out into the clear afternoon sunlight, down the broad steps and along the path that lead them through the famous Sather Gate off the campus and onto the street.

'How're you finding it here? Feel at home yet?' Steve asked. 'Not too homesick for Australia?' He was the only other mature student in the photojournalism course. He had begun life as a music teacher but had drifted into journalism and was now attempting to add a photographic dimension to his work. Sally liked his gentle, easygoing manner and quirky sense of humour.

'Not for Australia,' she said. 'I miss my friends but I suppose that's only natural. I love it here, it's a beautiful place, and I'm really enjoying the course.'

'Good – just wondered because you're looking a bit down in the mouth today.'

She smiled. 'A bit of family stuff on my mind,' she said. 'Do you have family here, Steve?'

He shook his head. 'My ex is in Vermont with her new husband. My daughter's working in London, and my son is a sound engineer with a band, spends a lot of his time on the road, crashes at my place when he's passing through San Francisco and beats the hell out of my computer and my piano.'

'I don't suppose you know a pianist called Oliver Mendelson?' she asked.

'Oliver Mendelson? Gee, Sally, he's way out of my league. He's a San Francisco tourist attraction, and he's pretty big on the international concert circuit. I'm just a dilettante music teacher with delusions about the fourth estate. Why?'

'Oh, nothing, just wondered. I heard him play at the Davie Hall last week. D'you know anything about him, about his family?'

Steve shook his head and ran his hand through his thinning fair hair. 'Can't say I do, although, come to think of it, I believe his wife used to be an opera singer. No idea if they have children.' He laughed and nudged Sally's arm. 'If you're that interested, why not go ask him. We have to do this Cartier-Bresson style portrait. Take your camera along and get some pictures of the maestro – do a Lee Miller on him.' They paused together at the corner of the street. 'Catch you later in the week, Sally,' Steve said, and he ducked off down the side street towards his home.

Sally walked on, turning into Telegraph Avenue where the sidewalks were crowded with shoppers browsing the tightly packed curbside stalls. An army greatcoat hanging on a dress rail packed with old clothes caught her eye, reminding her of the last photograph of the lecture. Stopping briefly to buy a bottle of water she wondered how it was that a woman like Lee Miller had so much courage and confidence. She wished she had grown up knowing the stories of women like that, women who seemed fearless, who grabbed life by the throat and shook it, the ones who ignored the rules.

Along the sidewalk some young men were playing chess, their boards perched on top of the tall plastic garbage bins. As Sally drew closer a lean dark man with heavy dreadlocks threw his arms up in exasperation, deliberately toppling the board and pieces to the ground.

'Hey man, cut that out!' yelled his opponent, pushing him in the chest. Sally stopped in her tracks, feeling a chill of fear at the prospect of the conflict but reaching instinctively for her camera.

The man with the dreadlocks straightened up and lunged at his opponent, who reached out to grab the matted hair with both hands. Sally moved closer. Bending forward and focusing rapidly, she took a dozen or more shots as the two men fell to the ground grappling among the rickety trestles of a flower stall and sending several buckets of dahlias and carnations crashing to the gutter. She finished the roll of film and moved back out of the way as a cruising police car drew alongside. Slipping the camera back into her bag she watched the two officers drag the chess players to their feet and then walked on, turning into the comparative quiet of a side street.

A couple of months ago she knew she would have ducked away as quickly as possible, but having the camera had made it different. Her first thought had been to get the pictures, not to get out of the way and pretend it wasn't happening. She felt strangely different, pleased with herself about something she knew she could not explain to anyone else. Photography made you see things in a different way, she thought, heading up the steep hill back to the apartment. It actually made you look closely, look in rather than look away. The eye of the photographer demanded the courage to step into the moment and capture it.

She opened her front door, dropped her bag on the armchair, threw open the window and turned to stare at the telephone. Then, taking a huge breath, she picked it up and for the first time she dialled the number she knew by heart. It rang four times and she was anticipating an answering service when the phone was picked up and a man's voice said, 'Hello.'

Sally paused, a hairsbreadth from slamming down the receiver in a panic.

'Hello?' he said again, and she thought she would faint with terror.

'I wonder . . . I . . . could I speak to Estelle Mendelson, please?'

'I'm sorry, Estelle's not here right now. This is Oliver Mendelson. Can I help you?'

SEVEN

'It's very simple,' said Robin. 'Just a little weatherboard place on a bit of land that sticks out above the beach. Apparently it's about a kilometre from the town site and the town's tiny.' She handed Grace a sheet of paper with a photocopied picture of the house and a brief description.

'Sounds frightful,' said Grace pursing her lips and looking with dismay at the half-filled packing cases spread across Robin's lounge. 'You, too, are out of your mind. Of course you were right to give Jim the ultimatum, but giving up work and moving out of here – don't you think you're cramming too much change into your life all at once?'

Robin picked up a deep amber glass vase, wrapped it in three sheets of butcher's paper and put it in one of the boxes marked for storage. 'I can't stay around here, Grace. I have to get away.'

'You're risking your career and leaving your lovely house to go and live in a little rat hole in the back of beyond. Don't let this business with Jim drive you away. It seems like you're punishing yourself.'

Robin shrugged. 'Who knows, maybe I am, but it feels right. It's only a year. I can come back when I've got myself together. It's not as though I'm selling the house. I really wanted to go south and now I'm going.'

Looking at Robin knee-deep in packing cases, thinner than ever in a pair of faded jeans and an old grey sweatshirt, Grace noticed that the shadows under her eyes were more deeply etched, and her skin had acquired a new pallor. 'But what will you do with yourself all alone down there?'

'Run, walk, get fit, rest, read, maybe write – I don't know. I quite fancy a lot of doing nothing.'

Grace started packing books into one of the smaller cartons destined for Robin's retreat. 'Look, I'll come down with you and stay a couple of days, help you unpack and settle in. We can work out what else you might need and I'll pop down again –'

'No, Grace, thanks for offering but it's not like that.' Robin sealed a box and straightened up to face her. 'I need to do it alone. Just like Isabel and Sally.'

'But it's not the same,' Grace protested, feeling herself flush with annoyance. 'You're doing this because of Jim, because it didn't work out. You're in a very fragile emotional state.'

'Jim was the catalyst but I'm not doing this because of him, I'm doing it *for* myself, because I want to. I wanted it from the day Isabel first told us what she was going to do. Now I'm actually doing it and I have to go alone, no visits, no food parcels, no mercy dashes, Grace. Remember Leslie Kenton – did you read the book?'

Grace realised she might burst into tears. It was a totally unfamiliar feeling to her and she was determined not to succumb to it. 'Yeah, I read it! But we were just getting to know each other,' she said, turning away to study the spines of the books. 'I've loved having this time with you.'

Robin put down the roll of tape and scissors and went over to her. 'So have I. And honestly, I don't know how I'd have got through this without you. Grace . . .' She paused until Grace turned to look at her. 'Grace, don't take this personally. It's not about you, it's about me, my retreat, what I have to do for myself.'

Grace nodded and, not trusting herself to speak, turned back to the books. 'So which day are you going?' she asked eventually, wondering if she could face another departure.

Robin took a final look around the house. Stripped bare of books and ornaments, with only the larger furniture remaining, it had an air of elegant minimalism. She walked around the room running her hands over the backs of chairs, across the smooth and creamy marble bench tops, the olive wool of the couches, and gazed out into the courtyard. Someone else would watch the roses bloom, the herbs thicken and spread, someone else would sit out on the deck on hot nights and hose the plants this summer. What would she be doing? A lump rose in her throat and she sank down into the big cane armchair trying to hold back the tears. Something hard was lodged between the cushion and the cane, and slipping her hand into the space she pulled out a pair of glasses – Jim's glasses. He had searched everywhere for them. She stared at them in shock, turning them over, opening and closing them again, feeling crushed by the weight of memory and grief.

He had begged her to wait, promised he would sort things out as soon as possible, but still did nothing. Finally she told him: 'I'm going away, down south. I don't want to hear from you, not until I come back.'

'But I'll call,' he said. 'I'll visit you. We can email.'

'No. A year.'

'And if I tell Monica and move out?'

'I don't want to hear from you until I come back. Sort out your life or keep it as it is; either way, I'm going to do this for myself. You must do what's right for you. We'll talk when I come back.'

She sighed at the memory of it, the pain and shock in his face, the slope of his shoulders as he walked away, the grinding emptiness she felt as he looked back at her as he stooped to get into the car, and the way the sun turned the tears on his face to pinpoints of light. Maurice rubbed around her legs and she bent to stroke him as he inspected his travel basket, which stood in the middle of the kitchen floor.

The phone rang and she jumped in surprise. She considered leaving it but it kept on ringing, so she blew her nose and picked up the receiver. Isabel's voice sounded as though it was coming from a tunnel under the sea.

'I thought international lines were supposed to be the latest technology,' Robin shouted above the rushing noises.

'Not this one, apparently,' Isabel yelled.

'Are you okay? Why are you calling? I mean, it's fantastic to hear from you but you said no calls.'

'I know, I know.' Isabel sounded hesitant, a little strange. 'I just . . . just wanted to talk something over, but this line's so bad.'

Robin changed ears. 'I can hear you okay above the noises. Listen, I need to tell you – I'm going away, I'm retreating! I'm leaving tomorrow morning, going down south, the remote cabin by the beach, running, the whole Leslie Kenton thing, except I don't have a novel about Beethoven or anyone else. I was going to write to you when I got there.'

'What about Jim?' Isabel yelled, her voice suddenly coming through loud and clear.

'To cut a long story short he promised he'd leave Monica and then didn't, and I was at the end of my rope. He still says he's leaving, but I don't know . . . all I know is, I'm getting away for a year. Just like you, just like in the book.'

The silence at the other end seemed longer than usual. 'Are you sure it's the right thing?'

'Positive. I'm going to make it the right thing. I'll send you all the details. It's so strange talking like this, trying to say everything quickly – I promise to write.'

'Yes,' said Isabel. 'Good, well . . . I don't know what to say. Suppose Jim leaves Monica now?'

'He'll just have to wait and see how I feel next year.'

'That's very brave, Rob. You'll take care of yourself?'

'Of course, that's what it's all about.'

'I see.'

Robin felt a strange sense of unease at Isabel's tone. 'Are you okay, Isabel?'

'Of course.'

'Is it wonderful there? Do you love it? What did you want to talk about?'

'Oh, it doesn't matter really. Just felt the need to make contact. It wasn't anything important. How's Grace?'

Robin pushed her hair back from her forehead.

'June died and Tim and Angela have gone to Japan for two

years. She's struggling, but you know Grace, there's not much one can do. She's been wonderful over this, we've got a lot closer. We haven't heard much from Sally, only a postcard. Have you?'

'Not a word. But that's probably a good sign,' Isabel said. 'It most likely means she's really happy and caught up in things there. Give Grace my love. Write and tell me more about what's happened. Are you okay about this Jim thing?'

'I haven't been, but I think I will be. It feels terrible but right, if you know what I mean.'

'I know what you mean. Well, take care and write soon.'

'I will. Isabel, are you sure you're okay? You wanted to talk –'

'No, no, I'm fine, it's great to hear your voice. Better go. I'm in a call box at the station. I have to get a train to Madrid.'

'Take care,' Robin called. 'I miss you.'

'You too. Look after yourself. Give my love to Grace.'

Robin dropped the phone back into its cradle and stared out at the darkening garden. Then she picked it up again and dialled.

'It's Robin.'

'Hi!' said Grace in an unfamiliar tone.

'I just got a call from Isabel. She sounded weird.'

'How d'you mean?'

'I'm not sure, just different.'

'Perhaps it was the line.'

'No; well, yes, it wasn't a good line but there was something else. She said she called to talk but then she seemed to change her mind. But it was just so nice to hear her.'

'Did she say anything else?'

'She sent her love to you, and she hadn't heard from Sally either.'

There was silence on the other end of the line.

'I feel I may have cut across her by jumping in with my stuff. Should I call back, do you – shit, I can't. She was in a call box.'

There was a pause and then Grace said, 'I think she'll call again if she wants to talk. She probably just wanted to make contact.'

'Are you okay, Grace?' Robin said, unnerved by the unfamiliar smallness of Grace's voice.

'I'm fine. A bit tired. What time are you going?'

'I want to leave about five in the morning, six at the latest.'

'Take care,' said Grace. 'I'll be thinking of you. Let me know if there's anything I can do.'

'Thanks,' said Robin, 'I will. Look after yourself and, Grace – thanks for everything.'

Not a word from Sally for weeks. Robin picked up her diary and flicked through the previous year's pages. This day a year ago the four of them had spent the evening together at Sally's place with a meal from the Thai takeaway and their favourite movie, *Enchanted April*. 'Well, aren't we predictable?' Sally had said as she dished out the food. 'Who wants to bet that we'll be doing exactly the same thing this time next year?'

'So what do you want me to do about the wheelchair?' Denise asked, putting the coffee down on Grace's desk.

'Huh?'

'The wheelchair for your dad.'

'Oh,' said Grace, 'just leave me the brochures. I'll talk to the nursing home at the weekend and see what they recommend. Next week we have to do some work on that training schedule. Can you mark us out some time in the diary?'

Denise picked up a bundle of files from Grace's desk. 'I won't be here next week, Grace, remember? I'm on holiday. Two weeks in glorious Bali and then two weeks in Cairns with my less than glorious mother-in-law. Actually, at the moment even that sounds pretty good.'

Grace looked up in surprise. 'But it can't be due yet. Did you change the dates?'

'No.' Denise shook her head. 'No, it's always been Saturday the thirty-first. I guess you've just been very caught up with your friends going off and then Tim and Angela. The temp is coming in tomorrow for a briefing. It's Leah, who you had last time. You said you liked her.'

'Yes,' said Grace quietly. 'Yes, I did. Sorry I forgot your holiday. I think it's because I always hate it when you're away, and going away seems to be what everyone's doing at the moment.'

Denise closed the office door, and Grace put her feet in the drawer and stared out across the river, where a cluster of sailing boats was assembling for a race. For a long time she felt nothing, just sat there watching the water and humming snatches of something from *Carmen* that she couldn't name. It was as though she had moved out of her body, like in a dream she often had as a child when she was floating high against the bedroom ceiling looking down at herself asleep in the bed and wondering what would happen next.

A strange detachment bordering on calm had settled on her after the conflicting emotions of the last couple of months. She had felt consumed by loss, first Sally and Isabel, then June's death and the sudden departure of Tim, Angela and Emily for Japan. All the people to whom she was connected had disconnected themselves from her. She had felt herself to be an anchor but they seemed no longer to need anchoring, and then Robin had needed her through those first few weeks of separating from Jim, and Grace had snapped back again into what she knew best. But Robin didn't need anchoring either. Quite suddenly she too was gone in a cut as clean and decisive as all the others.

'Love doesn't die just because you're miles away, Gracie,' Ron had said all those years ago when the company sent him to check out a rig on the northwest shelf. She had known he was right but she had grown accustomed to the proximity of those she loved; and now they had left her, starting with Ron, then her mother had died and now this sudden intense exodus over the last couple of months. Only her father remained and much of the time he wasn't really there at all. What had she done to end up alone like this?

Denise stuck her head around the door again. 'It's almost six, so I'm off. See you tomorrow.'

Outside, the streetlights were coming on and the traffic on the freeway had slowed to a crawl. Thursday, late-night shopping. She needed a new top to go with the black skirt she'd bought at the weekend. She could run into the city and see if she could find anything in David Jones. The guilt was fleeting. She'd just have to make up the super contributions next month. Right now Grace needed retail therapy, because for the first time in her life, she was afraid of going home alone.

EIGHT

As the train pulled out of Lisbon, Isabel stared, as though mesmerised, as the city lights faded into the distance. Tomorrow she would be in Madrid, another city, another country, another chance to start again but she knew that what had begun in Portugal was not yet finished. Tears rolled down her cheeks uncontrollably and she rummaged in her bag for tissues, thankful that she had the compartment to herself. Resting her head on the back of the seat she began piecing together, once again, the events of the last few weeks.

It began at dinner, that first night in Monsaraz on that magical terrace, the flames of the thick white candles flickering in the evening breeze, the pinpoint lights of the next village twinkling in the distance. The images, now so clear, unfolded like the opening steps of a complex dance; Klaus handing her a glass of wine, Antonia calling a welcome from the kitchen, her own anticipation prickling her skin, the photograph of the house and another of Eunice a burning presence in the pocket of her shirt.

'Antonia and I have known each other since we are young,' Klaus, her fellow guest, explained as they took their seats at the table. 'We are old friends. I come every year to Monsaraz to become sane again for a little while.'

Antonia ladled chilled cucumber soup from a blue and white tureen into matching bowls. 'The sanity does not last long,' she said. 'The Prussian work ethic takes over again when he gets back to Nuremberg. I hope you will like this soup, Isabel.'

Isabel slowed her breathing, reined in the questions that jostled for attention, and joined the subtle exchange of information that Klaus began by revealing himself as a historian. 'It is the pirates that are my passion,' he said, pouring more wine. 'Much of my serious work has been devoted to the navigators. Now that I am old I can indulge my fascination with the pirates.'

'Age has its advantages,' Antonia agreed, putting her napkin aside as she finished her soup. 'It offers new interests to replace those that are no longer available.'

'Are you a historian too, Antonia?' Isabel asked.

She shook her head. 'A translator. I translate from English into Portuguese and German. Sometimes very boring books, sometimes quite wonderful.'

Klaus piled butter onto his bread. 'But this book you like, yes? This one you work on now, about the Royal Ballet?'

Isabel thought her heart turned a somersault. 'You're interested in ballet?'

'Oh, in all dance,' Antonia said. 'When I was younger I was a dancer, so to work on a book like this is pure pleasure.'

Isabel took the plunge. 'My mother was a dancer. After the war she was in Europe, touring with a dance company. That's why I'm making this journey.'

'You're retracing your mother's footsteps?' Antonia asked.

'I'm visiting some of the places that were really special to her. Lisbon was her favourite. She said she had her happiest time in Portugal.'

'She was in the ballet?' Klaus asked.

'No, with a modern dance company from France. They were quite avant-garde, I believe. The director was a contemporary of Isadora Duncan.'

Antonia looked up sharply.

'Compagnie Fluide?'

'Yes,' Isabel said, her excitement rising. 'In fact, Antonia, I came here to Monsaraz to find you. You see, I think you may have known my mother.'

Antonia's face froze. 'I don't think so. Fluide was very

popular, and . . . yes . . . avant-garde. But I did not know any of the dancers.'

'Are you sure? You see . . .'.

Antonia stood up to collect the plates and Isabel took out the photograph. 'I found this picture of a house.' She held it out to Antonia, who took it without a word. Isabel looked across at Klaus. 'It's a photograph my mother had. On the back she's written "Antonia's house", so I found the house. And the baker next door told me I'd find you here.'

'This house belonged to my family,' Antonia said stonily. 'I did stay there for some time but my aunt lived there. She was also called Antonia, I was named for her. Perhaps she knew your mother, but she died almost twenty years ago.'

Isabel knew her disappointment was obvious. She looked down again at the photograph. 'I was hoping so much that you'd known her. It must sound silly but once I found the house and the baker told me about you, I had this idea that you might have been friends.' She held out the photograph of Eunice. 'This is my mother, taken in 1953. Her name was Eunice Pearson and she was a soloist. Are you quite sure you never met her? Maybe you saw her dance?'

Antonia hesitated slightly at the sight of the photograph and then turned away. 'It's a long time ago. I really can't remember,' she said as she carried the soup plates to the kitchen.

A slight breeze extinguished one of the candles, casting a shadow across the table. Isabel shivered, chilled by Antonia's lack of interest. Klaus reached out for the matches and relit the candle.

'So this is a quest, Isabel? ' Klaus asked awkwardly, turning the matchbox in his hands. 'Your mother, is she still alive?'

'She died last year. There's so much I wished I'd asked her and now it's too late. I guess that's why I'm here now, visiting the places she loved.'

'Of course,' Klaus said gently.

'I don't know why I felt so sure they had met. Wishful thinking, I suppose.'

Klaus shrugged. 'Was your mother also in Germany?'

'Yes, in Berlin, Nuremberg and Munich.'

'Then you must make it a part of your journey.' He smiled, refilling her wineglass.

'I plan to. I want to be in Germany in winter, to see the snow, to have a northern Christmas. It's something I've always dreamed of.'

Klaus laughed. 'You may regret it – the cold is really cold, not like your Australian Snowy Mountains. But you must permit me to show you Nuremberg. It is a magnificent city.'

'Klaus will make you walk for miles while he tells you the history of every building,' Antonia said, returning from the kitchen carrying a goat's cheese tart, a bright, hard energy in her voice. 'By the time he has finished, you will know the history of Nuremberg inside out.'

It was after eleven when Isabel pulled back her bedroom curtains, flooding the room with moonlight. Her early excitement and curiosity had evaporated, and she was left with disappointment and unease. It had been a bad start. Antonia had been totally uninterested in the pictures of Eunice and the house, and Isabel wondered if she had offended her with her questions. She was exhausted by the journey and her own nervous energy, but Monsaraz had its own magic, and despite Antonia's chilly response to her questions Isabel liked her and she liked Klaus too. She would stay on for a while at least. Eventually she fell asleep in the moonlight with the barely detectable sounds of a Mozart violin concerto drifting up from the garden studio.

Waking early the next morning, she showered and dressed, and then wandered down to the kitchen, helping herself to coffee from the percolator. She had been allocated her own space in the fridge and the pantry, and that morning Antonia would take her shopping for provisions. Klaus was sitting on the terrace, his long brown feet resting on the lower struts of the table, a book propped against a jar of peach preserve, as he tucked into a pale gold croissant.

'Good morning. Do you mind if I join you?' Isabel asked.

He jumped at the sound of her voice and got to his feet

immediately, the slight inclination of his body towards her marking him as distinctly German. 'Forgive me.' He smiled, whisking croissant crumbs from his beard with his napkin. 'Good morning . . . please, yes.' He indicated the chair at the other end of the table and Isabel settled herself with her coffee.

'I usually like to eat out here. Did Antonia tell you she takes her breakfast upstairs?' He offered her a basket of croissants still warm from the bakery. The smell was tantalising.

'I'd love one, thank you.'

He was gone in a flash to the kitchen, returning immediately with a plate and knife, pushing the butter and jam towards her. 'You're very kind,' she said, helping herself to a croissant. 'But I think the rules are that I look after myself.'

'*Ja, ja!* Of course, but it is your first morning, it's the least I can do as I am what I think you call already a sitting tenant.' He was a fine looking man with thinning hair, a closely cropped grey beard and a whimsical smile that brought his otherwise rather stern face to life.

Breakfast was punctuated by desultory, companionable conversation, and Isabel was loading the plates and cups onto a tray when Antonia appeared and suggested that it was time Isabel got her bearings, and was introduced to the supermarket.

'Ha!' Klaus laughed as Antonia picked up a shopping basket. 'Supermarket – this you will see, Isabel, is a somewhat extravagant description.'

They left him to his book and set off to tour the village. Antonia, obviously well known, exchanged greetings with a couple of young women whose children were playing together by the fountain in the square, and waved to a man who swerved and rattled across the cobblestones on a motor scooter. Elderly women dressed entirely in black sat knitting in their doorways on the sunlit pavement, and an occasional car crawled cautiously along. Antonia was a perfect guide, giving no hint of her short-lived coldness of the previous evening. Isabel's disappointment and confusion soon evaporated and she gave her attention to the task of learning her way around.

By the end of the week she was shopping with confidence. In the cool early mornings she took long walks beyond the village, through the ruins of the old castle, under the brazen gaze of the goats that wandered the hillside. She browsed Antonia's bookshelves for information on Spain and Portugal, and found books in English in which she could read about the places she planned to visit. She sat in the cool darkness of the church, listening to the organist at his daily practice and rested on the balcony gazing out to the misty lavender shadows of the distant hills. She watched the lacemakers who sat on the pavement, their intricate designs growing as the bobbins flew. And she discovered the local potter working at his wheel while others painted and glazed the bowls, dishes and vases and sold them from the adjacent shop.

Isabel wrote letters home filled with the details of her time in Lisbon and Cascais, and now the long, luxurious days of Monsaraz. They were easy letters to write, filled with small events and impressions, letters Doug would pass on to the children and his parents. She had expected to prepare her meals alone but the atmosphere was so relaxed that the three of them took it in turns to cook. A friend of Antonia's ate with them one evening, a robust Portuguese lawyer who had a practice in Lisbon and was visiting some clients in nearby Elvas. German friends of Klaus turned up one day on a trip from Évora. They came to dinner and stayed the night in the other guest room before heading off in the morning.

Isabel put her photographs away with the other papers from Eunice's past and turned her attention to the present. She relished the peace and quiet, and thought of her family with the affection of one removed from the wearing emotional peaks and troughs of normal life. She thought of her friends, Robin and Grace still at home, Sally on the other side of the world, and felt comfortably distant. She knew she was changing, growing – perhaps to match her new appearance – more relaxed and open. She lost a little weight and her pale skin turned from tender pink to light gold, for here she could tolerate the sun, which was less brutal than back home.

'I am planning an outing,' Klaus said one evening. 'I must take the bus to Évora and go to the bank. I may stay overnight.'

Antonia stretched her arms above her head, lifting her hair off the back of her neck. 'Perhaps I will come with you. I need to order some new spectacles and do some business at the town hall. Have you seen Évora, Isabel?'

'No, I just got off the train there and straight onto the Monsaraz bus.'

'Why don't we all go?' Klaus suggested, pouring the last of the wine. 'We can stay in the wonderful Monfalim, Antonia, and take Isabel to the Capela dos Ossos.'

Isabel raised her eyebrows. 'The Chapel of Bones?'

Antonia smiled. 'It's remarkable. Built from the bones of more than five thousand monks and nuns. It sounds gruesome but it's really incredibly beautiful.'

'Let's go,' said Isabel. 'Do let's go. Do you have time, Antonia?'

Antonia nodded and smiled. 'Certainly, I'd love it, if Klaus doesn't mind us interfering with his excursion.'

'I should like nothing better,' Klaus said, standing up and collecting the dishes. 'How often does a man of my great age have the opportunity to escort two beautiful women. Now I think it is my turn for doing the dishes.'

And so two days later they took the early bus to Évora and by mid morning were signing the register at Solar de Monfalim. The former summer palace of the dukes of Monfalim was converted now into an elegant and rustic hotel of narrow passages with whitewashed walls opening into simply furnished rooms, each with its own elegant bathroom. The high-ceilinged dining room panelled in dark wood and the cosy bar were lined with old paintings of dukes, their wives, their children and animals. The Monfalim was almost full, with only two rooms free. Klaus offered to stay elsewhere but the women insisted they could share one room and he could take the other.

While Klaus and Antonia did their errands Isabel wandered through the town, browsing in the elegant little shops and walking to the Roman Temple of Diana. When they met up again later in the day they went to the Capela dos Ossos, where the tibias, fibulas, pelvises, vertebrae and skulls of the religious departed created the interior of the Romanesque chapel. When they emerged, the afternoon sun had lost its heat and the shops were reopening after siesta.

'We have time to see the cathedral before the light goes,' Klaus said. 'I think I must prove to myself that I can still climb the tower.' He loped off ahead of them across the square.

Isabel and Antonia strolled silently, side by side through the cool and dusky cloisters. Isabel imagined she could hear the swish of the monks' habits on the paving, the creak of leather sandals, the rattle of rosary beads. Lost in her thoughts she cried out in shock when a large crow took off from a high ledge under the cloister, cawing and flapping its wings. Missing her step against the raised edge of the paving she staggered sideways and was only saved from falling by Antonia, who caught her. A chill brought her out in goose bumps but as she regained her balance and steadied herself, she felt the reassuring warmth of Antonia's body against hers, and her arm around her waist.

They faced each other, suddenly each within the other's space. Isabel felt Antonia's breath on her face, was mesmerised by the intensity of her gaze. Fleetingly Isabel felt Antonia was moving even closer but then she leaned back slightly and Isabel felt dizzy. A flush crept up her neck to her cheeks and, confused and embarrassed, she broke the gaze. For a fraction of a second Antonia increased her grip on Isabel's waist and then she dropped her hand.

'Are you hurt, Isabel?'

'No, no, not at all, just shaken. Thank you . . . you stopped me falling.' Their former ease and intimacy had turned to awkwardness.

'Perhaps we should walk to the base of the tower,' said Antonia. 'Klaus must be on his way down by now.'

Isabel nodded, feeling a strange mix of danger and excitement. Her heart lurched and she reached out to touch Antonia's shoulder, but the other woman had moved away and Isabel withdrew her hand, turning the gesture into a casual attempt to smooth her hair. 'Yes, of course. It's getting late, we should get back . . .' and her voice faded as she remembered the shared room and the intimacy it would impose on them.

The evening seemed interminable. Klaus, making his way enthusiastically through a bottle of wine, embarked on a long story about the reunification of Germany and seemed unaware of the new tension between the two women. It was after ten-thirty when, with his usual courteous bow, he bade them goodnight and wandered off up one of the passages to his distant room. Isabel's heart thumped nervously and she was relieved when Antonia stood up and announced that she would take a short walk before going to bed. With a small, distracted smile she picked up her light woollen wrap and went down the steps from the terrace and into the street.

Isabel stood for a while gazing at herself in front of the bathroom mirror. She looked so different from the woman who had stared back at her from the mirror in her bathroom at home. She touched her face, ran her fingers through her hair, then, after brushing her teeth and splashing some water onto her face, slipped quickly into bed and switched out the lights, wondering what would happen when Antonia came back. Should she say something? How could she name this feeling? Should she pretend that strange disturbing moment had never happened, that nothing had changed, that the devastating surge of emotional and physical chemistry had been an aberration? But Antonia's face was burned into her mind, as clear and unforgettable as the flood of desire she had felt at the other woman's touch.

Isabel punched her pillows, recalling the night she and Doug had lain on either side of the chasm created by her plans. She felt the enormity of the tension that had divided them and then the gentleness with which he took her hand. The slightest gesture could bridge estrangement, banish awkwardness, restore connection. But the wrong gesture could cause irreparable damage. She felt the sudden rejection as Antonia turned away, and saw the tense smile when she looked to see if Isabel was following. Had she imagined it or had they both been stricken by something that had taken them beyond friendship?

It was after midnight when Isabel fell asleep, and much later she heard Antonia let herself quietly into the room. She tensed again, listening to the sound of water running in the bathroom, the soft footfalls in the bedroom. Would she speak? Would she perhaps just touch her? The other bed creaked and there was silence. With a mixture of relief and disappointment, Isabel drifted back to sleep hoping that when she woke the next morning she would find that it had all been a figment of her imagination.

But it was not to be so easy. The tension between them was acute. Normal conversation seemed impossible as they made their way back to Monsaraz and settled again in the house. Isabel's confusion hardened to anxiety about what had passed between them and what it meant. Klaus was due to leave the following day, and she wondered what would happen once they were alone. Antonia was expecting new guests for the studio and the second room to arrive on the morning following Klaus's departure. Before then, surely, something would be resolved between them.

'It has been an exceptionally good visit,' Klaus said to Antonia the next morning, taking her arm as they walked to the bus. 'I wish I could stay longer.' He hugged her, kissing her on both cheeks, and drew her aside to say something softly to her just as the village priest, who was also on his way to catch the bus, greeted Isabel and took the opportunity to practise his English.

The bus lumbered under the archway and rattled to a halt in the square. 'And my dear Isabel,' Klaus said, taking both her hands in his. 'Do you promise you will contact me when you arrive in Germany? No – before that. I shall find somewhere for you to stay and I will show you the best of Christmas in Germany.' He leaned forward to kiss her on both cheeks and Isabel resisted the urge to hang on to him.

'Of course I'll be in touch,' she said. 'You don't escape that easily. I shall see you in the winter.'

He picked up his bag and followed the priest onto the bus. The driver started the engine and Klaus appeared again in the doorway. He blew a kiss to Isabel and stood for a moment looking at Antonia. '*Vergiss nicht, Antonia, verweile doch du bist so schön,*' he called and turned slowly back into the bus waving his hand in farewell.

Antonia's face was straight and a slight flush crept up her neck. They waited until the bus was out of sight before turning to walk back up the hill in silence. Isabel thought Antonia must have been able to hear her heart beating. The tension was driving her crazy. What had Klaus called from the bus? What would happen now?

They climbed the stone steps and walked along the high terrace into the shadowy coolness of the house. As Antonia turned towards the kitchen, Isabel reached out and put a hand on her arm. Antonia jumped as though burned, and as she turned to face her, Isabel saw in her eyes all the confusion and anxiety that she herself felt. But she also saw something else. She saw that Antonia was closed off from her. The intelligent, open gaze was gone and the striking eyes shone with a harsh, defensive light.

'Antonia, we need to talk.'

'Of course. We must decide what to eat tonight. Perhaps you would prefer to dine alone?'

Isabel followed her through to the kitchen, watching her open the fridge and contemplate the contents. 'Not about food, Antonia. We need to talk about us, you and me, what's changed between us.'

'There is some soup left and I shall buy some fresh bread,' Antonia said, ignoring her.

'Antonia, please!' Isabel heard the break in her own voice and Antonia must have heard it too, for she turned to face her. 'I felt so wonderful here, so peaceful, it was such a joy to be here. Your company, the house, everything, until . . . well, until two days ago in the cloister, and then . . . well, when I looked at you everything changed. I felt –'

Antonia raised a hand to stop her. 'No, Isabel, no! Please stop. It was a misunderstanding. You imagined something, I think. Perhaps I misled you. I don't know. Nothing changed, nothing, everything is just as it always was. You are my guest, we have become friends, that's all.'

Isabel stared at her, taking in the lines of tension etched across her face, the sheltered eyes, the uncharacteristically nervous way she twisted her hands. There was a long moment of silence. 'What did Klaus say?' Isabel asked.

'Klaus?'

'When he called to you from the bus?'

Antonia shrugged and began putting coffee into the percolator. 'Oh! Just a quotation.'

'A quotation?'

'Yes, yes. From Faust,' she said, her attention fixed on the water level in the jug.

'And what does it mean?' Isabel persisted, ignoring the feeling that she was being rudely inquisitive.

Antonia sighed and pretended to be studying the small print on a packet of coffee. 'Faust makes a pact with the devil . . .'

'Yes, yes, I know the story.'

'They agree that if the devil is able to produce a moment of pleasure so incredible that Faust exclaims *"verweile doch du bist so schön"*, the devil would have won Faust's soul . . .' She paused.

'But what does it mean, that phrase?' Isabel persisted.

Antonia raised her eyes and looked at her long and hard. 'It means, "please stay, thou art so beautiful".'

Isabel felt dizzy with the flush of heat that overwhelmed her. She put her hand on the table to steady herself. 'Why would Klaus say that?' she asked, a tremor in her voice.

Antonia kept looking at her for a moment and then turned away. 'Who knows?' She shrugged dismissively. 'Klaus, ha! He has a quotation for every occasion.'

That night was long and hot and Isabel spent most of it sitting on her bed, her knees drawn up under her chin, staring out across the moonlit hillside. How could it strike so suddenly? Was it love, or desire, or both? How could one accidental moment transform everything? How could it be that she was now supposed to pretend that it had never happened? It seemed that something like this should happen slowly, not in a sudden, sharp, disturbing moment. She and Doug had grown into love. As teenagers they had moved gently and tenderly around each other as if in a ritual dance. They were shy, tentative, nervous of taking risks, each feeling their way until it was clear to both of them that something had bloomed and was continuing to grow. But this was different.

It wasn't that she had never been attracted to anyone else. There had been times in the last thirty-four years when the chemistry crackled into life, and always she had resisted. But she had never before been attracted to a woman, and while it was certainly sexual, it was also something more, a sense that she suddenly knew Antonia in another way, that in that moment, each had captured and taken hostage something of the other.

Antonia resisted any attempt to open up a dialogue. Was she afraid, offended, shocked? Love between women had never shocked Isabel, nor had it ever really interested her. She had friends – women who had been in relationships or marriages with men – who in later life fell in love with women, and others who had always been unquestionably lesbian. It was part of life's diversity, not something that set people apart. But perhaps it was different for Antonia. Her Portuguese background might not be so tolerant.

When Isabel closed her eyes she saw Antonia, the tilt of her head, her slim brown hands lighting the candles, the sway of her hips as she walked down the street, the luminous sheen of her hair in the moonlight. Something precious and thrilling stood just beyond Isabel's reach, and each time she tried to grasp it, it slipped away.

By the end of the following day she was emotionally exhausted. Each subtle attempt to communicate with Antonia at anything more than the level of polite acquaintance had been rebuffed. At midday the new guests arrived, a retired science teacher from Lisbon who had stayed with Antonia before, and a Swedish student. Their presence in the house made the situation less awkward but it also reduced the chances of communication.

On the Friday morning that Isabel departed, Antonia walked with her to the bus, her face a mask, composed to keep intimacy at bay, but in the square she took Isabel's hands and they hugged each other. 'We will meet again,' Antonia said quietly, and Isabel couldn't tell if it was a statement or a question.

'I hope so,' she said, swallowing the lump in her throat. 'Before I leave Europe.'

Antonia's eyes flickered. 'Yes,' she said decisively, and her face softened. 'Definitely before then.'

Isabel picked up her bag and stepped onto the lowest step of the bus. She reached out her hand again, and Antonia took it. They stood there until the driver slammed the bus into first gear and Isabel turned to take her seat.

Tired and confused, Isabel made her way back to Cascais, where Sara's company proved a mild antidote to her mood. On the first day there she began a letter to Antonia thanking her for her hospitality. She would, she said, return to Portugal for a final visit before returning to Australia, and she gave Sara's address and telephone number. The letter went through many drafts over several days before she finally bought a stamp and mailed it. Something about those last moments at the bus stop had given her hope that Antonia might write or call. But as the days passed without any contact, she became convinced that what had happened between them had been more than Antonia could cope with – too powerful, too dangerous and challenging.

It was time to move on. She should be thankful that Antonia had saved her from the consequences of acting on her feelings. She was a woman – a very ordinary woman in her fifties, with a husband and children who loved her. The last thing she needed was to risk acting on a passionate impulse. Suddenly the enormity of her departure from home on such a contentious journey overwhelmed her, and she wondered if it had been some sort of madness that had driven her to turn her back on everything she knew and loved. She sank into guilt about leaving Doug alone, about not being around to help Debra with the children. Desperately needing to talk to someone, she called Robin. But Robin was caught up in the excitement of her move south and it seemed selfish to dampen that with her own problems.

She called Doug – her second call home since she had left Australia almost three months earlier. He was delighted to hear from her but also pressing to know when she would be back. A year, she reminded him. Well – nine months now. The children and grandchildren were well, they were getting her letters, even Debra was reading them and seemed to have let go of her anger. Isabel promised to call again in a few weeks and hung up feeling strangely empty. Life, it seemed, went on perfectly well without her, the people to whom she was indispensable obviously finding themselves perfectly able to manage in her absence. It was, of course, what she had wanted, but it seemed less gratifying in reality than it had in anticipation. And so she booked her train ticket to Madrid, and on a humid evening in early August, Sara went with her to the station.

'You look so different from the day I first met you,' she said with approval. 'You see how much easier it all is with fewer possessions?'

Isabel nodded. 'Absolutely. I'm sorry your spare room is still full of my stuff.'

'It's fine, I like it,' Sara said. 'It means you have to come back.'

'In the spring,' Isabel said, feeling once again the sadness of parting. She climbed into the carriage, closed the door and pushed down the window.

Sara stepped back onto the platform as the train jolted into movement. 'Have a wonderful time.'

'I will, and thanks, Sara, for everything, your hospitality . . . the transformation . . .' But it was too noisy now for Sara to hear and so Isabel blew a kiss to the rapidly disappearing figure on the platform.

The sadness enveloped her as the train rattled through the darkened suburbs. She had a flash of panic and then regret that she was leaving Portugal too soon, that her own emotional state had prevented her from fully experiencing the place she had so often dreamed of from the other side of the world. She was angry with herself for being too self-obsessed to appreciate where she was. And after all, maybe it was her imagination. Perhaps Antonia was just an intelligent and beautiful woman who had been a perfect hostess, and Isabel, out of her comfort zone and pushing the boundaries of her newfound freedom from responsibilities, had simply lost touch with reality. But as dawn broke over the landscape of Spain, she wept for the promise of passion and intensity of which she had had such a tantalising glimpse, and its loss weighed heavily on her.

NINE

'What do you think then? The purple or the green?' Sally asked, standing nervously in front of the mirror, an outfit in each hand.

'I really don't think it matters, honey,' Nancy replied. 'They both look great, so it's just a question of which you feel best in . . . most confident.'

'Right.' Sally nodded. 'In that case it's the purple, with the lime shirt,' and she stepped into the skirt and pulled on the silk shirt that lay on the bed.

'Sure you wouldn't like me to drive you there?'

'No thanks. It's really good of you but I think I need the walk and the train ride. I need to be on my own, get my head together.'

Nancy nodded. 'Sure. Well, you've got plenty of time. Take it easy. It's just the two of them, just a friendly meeting. Nothing to worry about.'

Sally pulled on her jacket and picked up her bag. 'It doesn't feel like that, it feels terrifying, as though I'm going for some exam and if I fail I'll have completely stuffed up the rest of my life.'

'And don't you think they're feeling just the same?' Nancy asked. 'Lisa's mother coming to check them out, after all these years. Will she approve of us? What will she think of the way we brought up her baby? What does she want from us after all this time?'

Sally paused, her hand on the doorknob. 'You think so?'

'You betcha! I'd rather be in your shoes. Think about it. And good luck.'

Sally walked to the station light-headed and nauseated; she had been too nervous to eat. When the train drew in she took a seat by a window and watched the hazy outline of the cranes on the Oakland waterfront. It was two weeks since the day she picked up the telephone to dial the Mendelsons and froze at the sound of Oliver's voice.

'Estelle is away for a couple of days,' he'd said. 'Can I help or will I have her call you?'

She had taken a huge breath and closed her eyes.

'May I say who called?' he asked again, as though trying not to sound irritated by her failure to answer.

'Sally Erskine,' she blurted out.

'Sally,' he said slowly, obviously writing down the message for Estelle. 'Irwin, did you say?'

'Erskine,' she repeated. 'E-r-s-k-i-n-e.'

'Right, Sally Erskine, and you'd like Estelle to call. Does she have your –' He stopped in mid sentence. 'Sally Erskine? You're not . . . do you mean –'

'Yes, Lisa's . . .' Mother? Should she say "mother"? Biological mother? It sounded ridiculous. Why hadn't she thought about how to introduce herself? 'Lisa's, er –'

'Oh my god, I'm so sorry,' he cut in. 'Of course you're Lisa's mother. Please forgive me, how stupid. Now . . . well, now I don't know what to say. Are you calling from England?'

'I'm in Berkeley,' she said.

'I see. And you . . .'

'I wanted to make contact.'

'Yes,' he said obviously at a loss. 'Yes, of course. It's a long time. I don't know what to say. I wish Estelle was here, she's away . . .'

She felt for him. She had taken him by surprise and he was disconcerted, wary but not hostile. 'I was hoping I might be able to meet you both,' she said. 'To talk, the three of us.'

'Not see Lisa?'

'That depends . . . Look, I don't want to cause any problems but I wanted to make contact, to find out about my . . . about Lisa. I'd like to see her but . . . well, that's really up to you. Maybe we could discuss it?'

She could hear his relief. Yes, he said, the three of them should meet and talk. As soon as Estelle got back they would phone and arrange a time and place to meet. Estelle's call had come three days later. And so on this bright July day Sally found herself walking up to the house in Hyde Street in her purple suit and lime-green shirt. She opened the iron gate and walked between the citrus trees up the steps to the front door.

What strange tricks the imagination can play. She'd expected a tall, elegant woman with strong features and thick dark hair, dramatic clothes, expensive jewellery. In her imagination Estelle Mendelson was Anne Bancroft, rangy, imposing, former opera singer still playing the diva. In reality only the eyes were as she had imagined, large, dark and searching, but they were set in a round, almost cherubic face framed by white hair pinned into a loose pleat from which a few wavy strands were escaping. Estelle was short, curvy to plump, and wearing jeans and a blue and white check shirt with a navy sweater thrown across her shoulders. Her only jewellery was gold hoop earrings and a wedding ring. 'Sally,' she said, smiling. 'It's good to meet you. I can see the likeness.'

Oliver was not a shock, although minus the white tie and the piano, and dressed in chinos and an olive green sweatshirt, he looked smaller and even more like Woody Allen than he had in the concert hall. They were older than Sally, both probably in their early sixties, gentle, softly spoken, and obviously anxious, just as Nancy had said they would be. She had a brief flash of insight into how this meeting might seem to them, and sensed, for the first time, that she was in a position of some power. They were feeling as vulnerable as she was, perhaps more.

They led her to a huge lounge room with mellow oak panelling, soft pale carpet, large comfortable furniture in muted tones, shelves crammed with books, and a few well-chosen artworks. A grand piano stood in front of the glass doors to the terrace, where scarlet geraniums bloomed in huge pots, and pink and white clematis draped itself over the sturdy posts of a pergola.

'Would you like a glass of wine, or perhaps some tea or coffee?' Estelle asked, gesturing Sally towards a chair.

She accepted the offer of tea and perched awkwardly on the edge of an armchair covered in amber velvet. The Mendelsons were equally ill at ease and the three struggled to negotiate their way through the pleasantries: Sally's appreciation of the house, Estelle's enquiries about her work, Oliver's more general questions about Australia. It was like unwrapping a parcel, each exchange slowly removing a layer of tissue until eventually the contents would be revealed. Which one of them would have the courage to remove the final layer? There was an awkward pause as they all sipped their tea, groping for the next line.

'You want to know about Lisa,' said Estelle finally, and as the last layer floated away Sally felt tears in her eyes. She had been prepared for hostility at worst, distance and mistrust at best. Having armed herself for some sort of struggle, the Mendelsons' warmth and openness disarmed her. She fumbled for a handkerchief and, as Estelle pushed a box of tissues towards her, she looked up to see that she too was crying.

'I don't know why I'm doing this. Crying, I mean,' Sally said, reaching for the tissues.

'Me neither,' said Estelle. 'Except that I'm so nervous of meeting you, and I guess you feel just the same.'

Oliver cleared his throat, put his cup down on the glass-topped coffee table, got up and walked over to the window.

'We didn't know what to expect,' Estelle said. 'We don't know what you want or why, and why now.'

Sally nodded, wiping her eyes, then rolling the tissues between her hands. 'I'm sorry. I should have written. For years I didn't want to know anything, couldn't bear to, but that changed. The last few years I've been haunted by the need to know about Lisa, how she is, what sort of person she is.' She shrugged. 'It's entirely selfish and I do realise how hard this must be for you.'

Oliver turned away from the window. 'We always knew it was possible you might want to meet Lisa,' he said. 'But as time passed and it seemed less and less likely, we felt safer. You see, all those years ago, writing to you seemed the right thing to do, but later we realised we'd left ourselves wide open.'

He paced back and forth across the room. 'You must know that what we did was illegal. Contacting you, I mean. I had a friend who was quite high in social services. I pulled some strings. We did it thinking we were doing the right thing for Lisa. Later we realised the risk we'd taken, not just legally, but in creating a situation that meant you could turn up at any time and take her away.'

Sally looked at him in amazement. 'Take her away? How could I? You adopted Lisa. As far as the law is concerned, you're her parents.'

Oliver and Estelle exchanged glances. 'Of course,' Oliver said. 'But the law really means nothing as a child gets older. Lisa always knew she was adopted and she accepted us as her parents. But if you turned up we could have lost her emotionally. Do you see what I mean?'

Sally felt the full extent of their anxiety. 'Yes. Of course. But Lisa's an adult now, independent. She may not even want to see me. You haven't told her yet?'

Oliver shook his head. 'We wanted to meet with you first. You see, the situation is more complicated than you think.'

'Look,' said Sally, starting to feel more confident, 'I know this may take a while. You need to tell Lisa and she needs time to think about it. Maybe she has her own family to consider, a husband, children?' She looked first at Oliver and then at Estelle, but both avoided her eyes. 'Lisa's not married? So she has a career, a place of her own. Honestly – I don't want to interfere in her life, I don't want to create problems.'

Silence hung heavily and Sally's confidence began to evaporate. 'What is it?' she asked. 'Oh, of course, she doesn't live in California. How stupid of me – I just never thought of it, just assumed . . . where does she live?'

Oliver took off his glasses and rubbed his eyes. 'It's not that, Sally,' he said, cleaning the glasses with a tissue before he put them back on to look straight at her. 'Lisa lives in California, she lives here in San Francisco, in this house with us, but no, she doesn't have a job and she's not independent.' He sat down beside Estelle and took her hand, drawing it through his arm so

127

that they were facing her, holding on to each other. Sally looked at their clasped hands, Oliver's slim and smooth, Estelle's pale and heavily marked by scars.

'Lisa is far from independent,' he went on. 'You see, there was an accident . . .'

The moment she woke she felt stifled, as though a blanket, one of those coarse, grey army blankets with a single blue stripe and blanket stitch along the edge, had been thrown over her face. Sally remembered those blankets, the itchy texture, the musty smell. She must have been about six when the fires threatened the town, and with a group of neighbours they had driven forty miles through dense smoke to the next town, where she and her family were huddled together on camp beds in the church hall. 'Try to get some sleep, love,' her mother had said, pulling the blanket up to Sally's chin. 'We're all safe now.'

'Not Ratso,' she had whimpered, wanting the big felt and gingham mouse who had somehow been forgotten in the last-minute rush. 'Not Ratso, he might get burned.'

'But you're safe, Sal, and Poppa and me and Tricia. We can always find another Ratso.' But Sally knew there would never be another Ratso and she pulled the blanket over her head to hide herself from the harsh light in the hall.

This morning, she was smothered with the same scratchy weight of greyness, the same stale and musty sense of loss and confusion she had felt that night. It seemed entirely appropriate that when she got out of bed and opened the blinds, Berkeley was bathed in brilliant sunlight, while the city of San Francisco was invisible under its blanket of summer fog. She barely had the energy to dress, let alone face the long walk she had agreed to take with Steve. But he had become a friend, practical and supportive once he had wrung from her the cause of her malaise.

He was right about the walk. For almost a month she had struggled along doing the minimum necessary to keep herself going in the photography course. Anything more was beyond her. She was isolated in her misery, unable to talk or to write letters home, her senses frozen. Her limbs felt leaden, the slightest physical exertion exhausted her. Each time she looked in the mirror she saw that her eyes and skin were dull, and there were downward lines at the corners of her mouth which she hadn't noticed before. She looked sick and she felt sick, as though she was being eaten away from the inside.

'You need some air, some exercise. Get out of your head, Sally, and into your body – do something physical,' Steve said, and she knew it made sense. She took a brief shower, hoping to clear her head, and pulled on jeans and a cotton shirt topped with a fleece vest to combat the chill of the San Francisco fog. And at the sound of the car horn she picked up her backpack, locked the apartment behind her and ran down the path to the gate where Steve was waiting in his old olive green Jaguar.

The traffic was moving fast on the Bay Bridge and they were soon heading along the final section from the wooded heart of Treasure Island through the city of San Francisco to the Golden Gate Bridge, Marin County and Mount Tamalpais. It was the first time in a month that Sally had crossed the Bay Bridge into the city. The first time since the terrible day of her second visit to the Mendelsons, when she had walked out of the Hyde Street house trembling with rage. She shivered at the memory of it as she stared across to Marin County through the rising fog.

The meeting Sally had so often dreamed of had taken place in Golden Gate Park. The movie that had always run through her head was of a sparkling young woman walking towards her. Their eyes met, there was recognition, understanding and finally tears of joy as they hugged each other. Despite what she knew, despite the Mendelsons' warnings, Sally hadn't let go of the dream even as she saw them there on the far side of the lake, Estelle and Oliver, the wheelchair between them. Even as she crossed the little wooden bridge she still had that vibrant Lisa with her, until Oliver turned the wheelchair towards her and she looked into her daughter's eyes for the first time.

The car, they said, had been doing eighty miles an hour when it drifted across two lanes, mounted the central strip and rolled upside down into the path of the oncoming traffic, ending up on the passenger side. As the leaking petrol burst into flames Lisa, unconscious in the passenger seat, was trapped in their path. Estelle freed herself from the seat belt and struggled to release her. Behind her other drivers attempted to haul her from the wreckage, and the flames licked up her arms and across her chest as she dragged Lisa from the burning car.

Estelle's burns were serious but Lisa's were savage, scarring and distorting her face and body so that even the most experienced plastic surgeon could do little to repair the damage. And there was brain and spinal damage too, the full extent of which only became clear as the days and weeks following the accident slowly unwound in an agony of grief-stricken discovery. Lisa would never walk again; the fluttering movement she could make with her hands indicated that one day she might be able to hold a plastic cup of liquid between them. For months she lay in a pressure suit, connected to a range of drips and monitors, hovering between life and death, until eventually she began to regain some strength. She had a repertoire of sounds from which her parents and carers could interpret her needs. Strangers disturbed her but she showed a childlike affection for those she knew well. No one knew quite how much or how little she could see, hear, or understand.

It was Oliver who told the story. He was away on tour, he explained, Estelle was sleeping after a heavy dose of new antihistamine tablets to cope with an allergy. Lisa was watching a movie when a boy from school called at the house and invited her to take a ride in his brother's car. Estelle and Oliver had already warned her away from him but Lisa, knowing that if she woke Estelle she would be forbidden to go, simply grabbed her coat and ducked out, thinking she'd be back home long before her mother woke. But shortly after midnight, when she found herself in a sleazy bar with the boy and two older friends being plied with drinks, Lisa's own alarm bells began to ring. Scared of getting back into the car she ducked into a phone booth and called home. Estelle got up, dressed, drank several glasses of water and drove the forty miles out of town to the bar in Sunnyvale. It was on the way home, with a repentant Lisa in the front seat and the relief of a mission accomplished, that she switched on the heater and began to relax. The adrenaline that had gotten her this far burned out, the drug took over and her eyes began to close.

On her first visit Sally had listened in horror as Oliver described Lisa's disabilities, and the special extension at the back of the house designed to accommodate her and a resident carer. Estelle had shrunk back into the couch as Oliver was talking, but Sally was scarcely aware of anything but shock and numbing disappointment. She wanted to get out of the house, get away on her own to find out how she really felt. She asked a few questions, though later she could not remember the answers, and she asked to see a photograph of Lisa before the accident.

Estelle got up, went to the bureau and picked up a stiff white envelope. 'I got some copied for you,' she said quietly. 'I thought perhaps you'd want to look at them alone, to keep them . . .' She should let them know what she wanted to do, they said. They would be happy for her to come to the house again to see Lisa, but it might be best if they met first somewhere else. Lisa seemed less disturbed by meeting people outside the house. They suggested the park, and then if Lisa was calm they could take a walk together and Sally could come back with them to Hyde Street.

She felt and thought nothing on the way home, aware only of white noise in her head. Back again in the peaceful familiarity of the apartment she began to thaw and carefully drew the photographs from their envelope. Slowly, one by one, she studied the pictures of Lisa as a baby, a toddler, a little girl in her first school uniform and the bright-eyed, glossy-haired teenager receiving an award at a school prize-giving. Even then a part of her held back, not accepting reality, keeping in her mind's eye the final picture, Lisa's dazzling smile on her sixteenth birthday, a couple of months before the accident.

That smile was still in her mind as two weeks later she stood in the park and looked into her daughter's eyes, searching the small pale face with its lattice of tight and shiny crimson scars. She could see nothing of herself, nothing even of what she could remember of Simon, and nothing of the beautiful sixte-year-old in the photograph.

'Lisa,' she said, taking a deep breath and leaning forward slightly to let the girl see her face. 'My name's Sally. I've heard a lot about you, it's so nice to meet you.' And she reached out to take one of the cool fluttering hands that slipped from her grasp almost immediately.

They strolled around the lake and Lisa cooed at the sight of children feeding a crowd of noisy brown and white ducks. The conversation was strained. Eventually Estelle bent to explain to Lisa that Sally was going home with them, and they wheeled her onto the electronic ramp of a specially adapted Volkswagen; Oliver drove them back to Hyde Street in silence. Seated at an angle in the back seat from where she could watch the girl in the chair, Sally felt her heart beating with a strange new urgency. It made her light-headed, inducing a sense of frenetic energy. Anger and resentment were building within her. She tried to make eye contact with Lisa but the nervous jerks of the girl's head always broke the connection. As they turned the corner into the steep climb up Hyde Street she took Lisa's hand again. This time it did not slip but was pulled away to the sound of a short inward breath. Sally felt a shaft of pain so acute that she wanted to howl. Instead she swallowed hard and turned her gaze once more to the street.

It was Estelle who suggested that Sally might like to see Lisa's room. She pushed the chair down a glass-sided passageway that ran along the terrace connecting the extension to the main house.

'Why doesn't she stay in the main house?' Sally asked. 'Why is she shut away out here?'

Estelle turned her head sharply. 'This is hardly shut away, Sally. Lisa has her own place where she can see the garden and isn't disturbed by strangers coming to the house. She gets very agitated by noise, and by people coming and going. We thought this would be peaceful for her. She can listen to music and watch television without getting distressed.'

The sunlit room at the end of the passage opened onto the garden and swimming pool through a wall made almost entirely of glass. There were colourful armchairs, an array of large soft toys, and an exotic mobile of sparkling fish hung from the ceiling.

On the walls mounted posters of Michael Jackson and Madonna were reminders that Lisa's life had effectively stopped thirteen years earlier. At the far end was a double-width hospital bed flanked by hoists and a drip stand; in the far corner, a second wheelchair and an oxygen cylinder.

'The carer's suite is through there,' Estelle gestured. 'And these doors open to the garden.' She opened one of the glass doors as Sally looked around the room with a growing sense of hostility.

'What a beautiful room, Lisa,' she managed, knowing she sounded hopelessly artificial. Lisa made a noise that seemed to indicate agreement. She nodded her head, in the same jerky way she had done on meeting Sally.

'Oliver takes Lisa into the pool most days during the summer, and sometimes Tessa, the carer, takes her,' Estelle said, opening the terrace doors.

'And you, Estelle?' Sally asked, hearing the aggression in her own voice. 'Do you take her swimming?'

Estelle looked at her in obvious surprise. 'No, Sally, I don't go in the pool,' she replied quietly, smiling across at Lisa and reaching down to straighten the girl's skirt. 'I'm not a good enough swimmer, am I, Lisa?' And she stroked a lock of pale blonde hair back from her daughter's forehead. 'Lisa's exercise is pretty important, you see. We have to keep her flexible for her own comfort, and that's pretty hard physically. Oliver does a lot of that, he and Tessa.'

There was a silence heavy with something new and painful.

'So you don't have to do anything?' Sally asked at last.

'Excuse me?'

'You, Estelle, you don't have to do anything. You have other people to look after Lisa. The staff do it all – how fortunate you are to be able to afford all this.' A part of Sally was amazed at what she was saying but her anger had developed a life of its own.

Estelle gave her another long look. Lisa's hands began to wave in agitation and her face contorted as though she sensed the tension. 'Yes, we are fortunate and we try to ensure that Lisa gets the best care we can afford.'

'It must make it a lot easier for you.'

'Of course,' said Estelle. 'She needs twenty-four-hour care. Oliver and I do all we can.'

'And when you feel like it you can shut the door on her, shut her out of your lives, like . . . like Rochester's wife. Where she won't embarrass you and your guests.'

Estelle looked at her long and hard, and then, without saying a word, walked over to tap on the door of the carer's apartment. A smiling young woman in a white overall opened the door, dragging her long hair up into a ponytail. 'Sorry, Estelle, I didn't realise you were back. Hi, Lisa – nice outing?'

Lisa made a sound of greeting and seemed to smile. The young woman said hello to Sally and took the wheelchair from Estelle. 'C'mon, Lisa, I'll take you to the bathroom and then you can watch TV.'

'I realise that this has come as a terrible shock, Sally,' Estelle said as they walked back up the passage to the house. 'But we have tried to do everything possible to make sure that Lisa is comfortable and happy and has the best possible care and treatment.'

Sally was a stranger to herself. A seething mass of emotions raged in her, foremost among them pure hatred for Estelle, who should have cared for Lisa and whose irresponsibility had turned her from a sparkling teenager to a scarred and hopeless wreck. Now she was trying to pass off neglect and unconcern as the best of care. For the first time in her life Sally knew she was capable of physical violence. She wanted to grab Estelle by the neck and hurl her against the wall, to smash the gleaming glass wall of the passage and kick over the great earthenware pot with the tall ficus that stood in the corner. She could barely trust herself to move and she tightened her grip on her bag in an effort to control her body, her nails biting into the soft leather.

'It seems to me, Estelle, that the best of care is the least Lisa deserves from you. It's your fault, your reckless driving destroyed her life.' The voice was not her own. It came from a raw, tight throat in a body in which every nerve ending seemed to have gathered on the surface of her skin.

Estelle turned to Sally, her face twisted with grief. 'I don't . . .' she began. But Oliver, who had been waiting for them in the

134

lounge room, moved quickly to his wife's side and took her arm.

'All this has naturally been a terrible shock to you, Sally,' he said, with an authority that she had not heard before. 'I think you should leave before you say something you may regret, although you already seem to have exceeded the limits of reasonable behaviour. You know your way to the door.' And he led the weeping Estelle out onto the sunlit terrace.

'I think you're being very unfair,' Nancy said as Sally told her the story. 'Look, honey, this is terrible for you, but it's terrible for them too, and they've been living with it for a long time. Sounds like they're doing the best they can. It's fortunate that they can afford to give her that care and a lovely place of her own where she's safe and quiet. You can't say they neglect her simply because they have some paid help. Would it be better if they were struggling in a tiny flat trying to cope with her, and getting worn to a frazzle in the process?'

But Sally's rage was as limitless as it was irrational, and it devoured her energy and her spirit. 'Why don't you go see a therapist?' Nancy suggested. 'There's a terrific woman in Oakland. You need professional help to sort this out.' But Sally would have none of it and Nancy came less often down the steps, less often called over the balcony to tell her that there was fresh coffee in the jug and peanut butter cookies on the table.

Unable to sleep Sally walked the apartment at night, her arms clasped like a straightjacket around her body. Other nights she surfed the television channels, searching among the assortment of old movies, soaps and exhortations to worship, in the hope of finding something to hold her attention and lift her out of her feelings. She tried to write what she felt, but after the first few words she ripped the pages from her notebook and crumpled them into the bin. She stared at her unfinished paintings in disgust, and the camera, which a few weeks earlier offered a new sort of vision, seemed to taunt her, its lens like a great reproachful eye. Now she felt blind and crippled, powerless, trapped. She felt like Lisa.

*

Side by side they toiled in companionable silence up the rough timber steps of the path leading along the edge of the ravine. The early fog had lifted and as the ground levelled out and the trees thinned, they were surrounded by hills scattered with poppies and cornflowers, stretching into the distance and dropping away to reveal the bay and the city tinged with hazy afternoon light.

'Looks like it's in soft focus,' Steve murmured into the stillness. 'Want to take a rest?' She nodded and they made for a cluster of flat rocks rising above the grass. Sally took off her vest and sank exhausted onto the grass.

Steve opened his pack and pulled out a package of sandwiches and a bottle of water. 'Turkey or pastrami, both on rye,' he said, offering her the package. 'How're you feeling?'

She shrugged, looking into the distance. 'Confused, angry, impotent,' she said. 'But the walk was a good idea. Thanks for bringing me, for taking the trouble.'

'No trouble, I like company when I walk. Know something? I'm worried about you.'

'Don't be,' Sally snapped, realising that she sounded just like Grace. 'I'll work things out eventually.' She picked up a turkey sandwich and bit into it.

Steve took a swig of water from the bottle and screwed the cap back on. 'Not this way you won't,' he said. 'Not until you either get some help or start asking yourself why you're feeling this way.'

Sally's anger rose again. 'You sound like Nancy. She's trying to send me off to a therapist.'

He shrugged and picked up a sandwich. 'She wants to help, so do I. But you sure make it hard and I don't want to see it get worse.'

Sally threw down her sandwich. 'Hard! I make it hard! How do you think this feels for me? For Christ's sake, Steve, it can't get much worse than it is. For years I dream of finding my daughter and when I do, not only is she a grotesque cripple thanks to her adoptive parents, but she's kept locked away in some specially constructed facility in the back yard. How much worse can it get?'

'Sally! Listen to what you're saying. From everything you told me it sounds like the Mendelsons adore Lisa. This must be their worst nightmare and they live with it every day. They love her – how d'you think this feels for them? They're doing the best they can, a beautiful suite, someone to look after her, exercise in the pool. A lot of people would've put her in a home years ago. Christ, Sally, what do you want them to do, crawl around in sackcloth and ashes? This could have happened to anyone. It was an accident, not neglect. Wanna know what I think?'

'Oh, yes please, do let me have your unprofessional opinion,' she said, her tone heavy with sarcasm.

Steve took off his sunglasses and looked straight at her, narrowing his blue eyes against the glare. 'This is not about finding Lisa, or about the Mendelsons and the accident. You're an intelligent woman and none of that makes sense. This is about a terrified teenager alone and pregnant and thousands of miles away from home. You've been bottling up all this anger and grief for decades. It's about you and that bastard who abandoned you. You were desperate and you gave away your baby. You abandoned Lisa, that's what you think, and you've never forgiven yourself. This is not about the Mendelsons, it's about you, your disgust at yourself, the anger and hurt that you've never come to terms with.'

The strength of her slap across his face took Steve by surprise, catching him off balance. He teetered precariously on the edge of the rock before falling backwards across the other rocks and rolling down the grassy slope one leg twisting underneath him.

Sally grabbed up her vest and camera. 'Thanks for the advice,' she called, turning away. 'I won't be asking for it again. I'll make my own way home.'

And she set off down the track at a fast pace until she reached the main road, where she hailed a passing car.

TEN

The cottage was perched on the highest point of the cliff and was larger and more comfortable than Robin had anticipated. It had broad verandahs with uninterrupted views of the ocean and the town in one direction, and of the surrounding countryside on the other. Each morning as she pounded back home down the track, her heart thudding with exertion, her breath floating in a cloud on the cold early morning air, she marvelled at her luck in finding it.

It was late morning when she arrived, tired and stiff after the four-hour drive from Perth in heavy rain. The first thing she had done after unloading the car was to grab some logs from the pile on the back verandah, scrunch up some old newspapers and light the small wood stove. Then she knelt back to watch as the flames devoured the paper, bit into the few bits of kindling and wrapped themselves around the logs. 'Good riddance,' she murmured, scrunching up the remains of the paper and tossing it into the log basket.

She had brought some of her own things for comfort. The purple and turquoise Indian cotton cushions from her bedroom were now scattered on the big faded couch. A couple of Sally's paintings replaced the watery old prints on the walls, and her books, ornaments and CDs filled the broad shelves. The floorboards, once polished to a high sheen, had dulled to a mellow glow and were scattered with heavy cream rugs. A courageous choice for a rental property by the sea, but just what she would have chosen.

She had found a place for her wok, rice cooker and vegetable steamer in the neatly fitted kitchen alongside its already adequate supply of cooking pots, and loaded her supplies into the pantry. The rest of her things she had dragged into the larger of the two bedrooms, dumping some bags on the brass and iron bedstead, and the top of the pine chest of drawers that doubled as a dressing table. By the time the stove needed a second load of logs Maurice had found a prime spot on the window seat; and Robin had set up the laptop on the desk at the far end of the lounge and stacked her files and papers alongside it. It would, she thought, do very well, and as she turned to survey her handiwork the sun broke through the clouds and cast a shaft of brilliant light across the ocean and in through the window. Sinking onto the couch among her cushions, watching the distant waves crashing on the beach, Robin thought, before she dozed off to sleep, that it might do more than just very well – it might very well be perfect.

The next morning she discovered the track: a long, narrow footpath that ran up the hill from the town, past the cottage and stretched northwards rising, falling and bending with the land for more than ten kilometres to the next settlement, a small cluster of holiday units and a couple of shops behind a popular surfing beach. She could hardly believe her luck. She had chosen it, the house and the location, sight unseen, the first property suggested by the agent in response to her call. Only in the last few days did she really stop to consider that she might have taken more time with the search. But luck, or some sort of divine guidance, had brought her to the right place.

As Robin dragged on her old tracksuit and running shoes that first morning, she was craving the cold, damp air in her lungs and the satisfying ache of hard-worked muscles. With the sea on one side and the brush-covered hillside on the other, she set off, slowly at first, checking out the surface and soon building to a faster pace. The only hazard appeared to be rabbit holes. That first day she ran just three kilometres, recognising that she had not run for several weeks and needed to break herself in. But she returned to the house longing for more, longing to push herself to the limit. And each day she built up the speed and the distance, able to measure her increasing stamina and fitness by time and how far she had gone.

For the first three weeks she spoke to no one. She had filled her car with food – vegetables, fruit, cheese, eggs, long-life milk and plenty of bread, which she had stowed in the freezer. She avoided the little town and encountered no one on her dawn runs. Before leaving Perth she had changed her mobile phone number. The only person who had the new number was Alec Seaborn, her partner, and she had told no one that there was a phone at the cottage. Even so, she had unplugged it, deciding only to connect it to the laptop when she eventually wanted to check her email. In time she would have to deal with contacts from work and home, but she was determined to allow herself to feel her way without disturbance. There was nothing that could not wait. She was out of touch and the feeling settled on her like a blessing.

For three weeks she ran, rested, cried a lot and slept, some-times for several hours in the middle of the day. She read some of the books she had owned for years but not found time to read, and lay on the couch listening to CDs she had forgotten she owned. The logic and intensity of Bach, the romance of Schubert, gave her a feeling of inner strength; she sang aloud with Peggy Lee and Billie Holiday, and danced alone around the house muddling the mindless lyrics on her Abba albums. On the few occasions when she experienced a stab of guilt about doing nothing, she reminded herself that she had not had a holiday for more than ten years and she actually did need a rest.

She could feel herself getting calmer, healthier; a sense of well-being grew within her. She had expected to feel lonely, geared herself for the possibility of depression or panic, warned herself that the reality of what she had done would suddenly send her crashing. But each day she woke with the feeling that she had saved her own life. Jim's absence was painful, but she had fought through her initial grief and fear before she left Perth. Now the undercurrent of sadness rippled through each day and strangely enriched it. She thought of him with love, but could reflect on their relationship without anxiety, without the temptation to pick up the phone and try to swing everything back to the way it used to be. She wondered about him, how he was feeling, wondered whether he too had moved to a place of peace within himself or whether he was still trying to work out what he wanted, and what was possible.

In a thick spiral-bound notebook with a pattern of sepia script on the cover, she wrote a journal for the first time in her life. Initially self-conscious, she soon found that with every passing day the process of recording her spiritual and emotional life became less inhibited. The writing was helping her to heal and to discover what it was she was supposed to learn from this radical change. She wondered when she would start to get bored and how she would handle it when it happened. For now, though, her life was opening like a flower. She could rest in its bloom, take time to examine each petal.

When her supplies eventually dwindled she ventured for the first time to the local shop, which also doubled as the post office. 'Wondered when we'd see you,' said the slight, grey-haired woman behind the counter. 'I'm Dorothy. I see you're a bit of a runner.'

Robin wandered around the little supermarket filling a rickety trolley from Dorothy's surprisingly comprehensive stock. 'You've got a terrific selection here,' she said, examining the vegetables, which looked as though they had come straight from some local garden, as well as some out-of-season strawberries and rockmelon. She piled her shopping onto the checkout counter. 'You must be very popular.'

'Aye, it's not so bad,' Dorothy said, starting to key the prices into the till. 'I carry as much as I can and I buy quality, that way people shop here rather than trekking into Margaret River or Augusta. They're a fussy lot around here. Fancy themselves a bit when it comes to cooking. Somebody says you're a lawyer.'

Robin pulled a face. 'News travels fast. Is that a Glasgow accent?'

Dorothy drew her breath in sharply. 'It's Edinburgh, if you don't mind. And I think there's a bit of south London in yours.' She grinned and paused, holding an earthy bunch of radishes. 'But we won't have any border wars here, and we'll leave you

alone if that's what you want. Got any problems, you give my Ted
a ring. Plumbing, carpentry, any odd jobs, he'll fix it for you. Now,
if you'll just come over to the post office counter I'll give you the
key to your mailbox.'

Robin put the shopping in the car and wandered unenthusi-
astically towards the bank of mailboxes. Slipping the key into the
lock seemed like taking a step back into her old life. Gingerly she
sorted the letters from the junk mail and tucked them into her coat
pocket, and when she got back up the hill and had parked the car
and unloaded the shopping, she slipped off her jacket and left it
on the chair on the verandah with the envelopes still sticking out
of the pocket.

The jacket stayed there overnight. In the morning she brought
it in and looked at the envelopes, hoping they would not shatter
the peace she had created for herself. The white and manila
envelopes from the office, the heavy cream one addressed in
Grace's distinctive handwriting and the flimsy airmail envelope
with the Spanish stamp demanded her attention, but she already
knew – absolutely, unequivocally – that she was never going back
to her old life.

She opened her work mail first and saw that she would have
to put in some time to sort out a few loose ends and start preparing an opinion she had not been able to offload. For a while she
stared at the other two envelopes, aware of the irony that letters
from two of her closest friends seemed strangely threatening and
intrusive. She opened the airmail envelope first.

Dearest Rob

*The idea of minimal contact seemed so much better in the
planning stages than it does in reality! I am battling the urge
to talk to a sympathetic listener – yes, you of course! And the
desire to know every detail of what's happened with you, and
how you're coping with the separation from Jim and work, and
the first weeks of your retreat.*

*I hope so much that it will work well for you. At the very
least you must feel the positive sense of having made some sort*

*of change, taken control of the situation. Now, perhaps, the
distance will give Jim time to sort himself out and you the
chance to reflect on what you want.*

*I called you that day to unburden a few things. At the time
I was on the point of running away, or rather running back
home – a few words of sympathy would have been the trigger.
Your news stopped me in my tracks and over the last week or
so I seemed to have edged a little closer to rationality.*

*I guess making changes in my life was about the need to
learn something, and as I am still not sure what that
something is, I guess I'd better keep going until I find out. I so
look forward to the day when we'll all sit down together and
relive our adventures. These changes throw us some emotional
and spiritual challenges. I think I am surviving the first round.
Being grown up is sooooooo hard.*

*I think of you being incredibly grown up and also being as
vulnerable as me, and send you my love in both. I miss your
company, your conversation, the Gang of Four, Australia –
heavens, I even miss the council.*

*My love
Isabel*

Robin put the letter down on the desk and sat for a while,
staring out of the window. Then she opened the one addressed in
Grace's neat sloping hand.

Dearest Robin

*I hope you are taking care of yourself and that the place is not
too bleak and uncomfortable. It's strange being here alone –
well, I mean without you, Sally and Isabel. Very lonely. I
suppose the kids being gone as well doesn't help. Last weekend
I went to visit Dad and he didn't recognise me. It's the first
time it's happened. Other times he has confused me with Mum,
or Ron's mother June, but he always knew that he knew me.
Last Saturday he looked at me as though I was a complete*

143

stranger. It was the most awful feeling. They say he may not recognise me again, or that next time I go he might be his old self again. It's all so unpredictable.

Robin, the other day I got a call from Jim. He asked if I could give him your postal address. He said he had sent you several emails but you hadn't replied. I said that I wasn't free to give out your address but that I would write and ask you if you would like me to give it to him, or if he should send a letter to me to forward to you. Let me know what you'd like me to do.

I haven't had anything other than postcards from Isabel and Sally. I have this picture in my mind of us all locked in different little punishment cells in different parts of the world. Me, of course, stuck in the same cell I've been in for years.

Robin, I loved the time we spent together. I hope we'll do it again. Let me know how you are and what you want me to do.

Love, Grace

Robin read the letters again and thought carefully about what they did not say. Having the mail in the house, opening it and reading it, had disturbed her. She resented having to deal with any of it. Reading Isabel's letter her friend's distress was apparent, despite her effort to hide it under the guise of getting it together. But Robin's own survival instinct told her that at present she had nothing to offer anyone else. She was creating something precious for herself and could not afford to, as it were, share the building materials. She would write, but not yet, not until she felt ready.

For the first time since she had arrived, she switched on her laptop. There were seven messages from Jim, one from Grace, several from work and some junk mail that she immediately deleted. Then she opened and read the messages from the office and printed out the essentials. Grace's message said much the same as her letter had done. She might be able to leave Isabel's letter for a while but she had to respond to Grace and do something about Jim. The alternative was the very real possibility that one of them would decide to pay her a visit to see if she was okay. Robin clicked on reply.

Hi Gracie

Thanks for your letter and email. Sorry for the delay. Thanks for letting me know about Jim and for not passing on the PO box number. I will send him a message to let him know I'm okay. Which of course I am. This place is heaven and I feel wonderful. It is the best thing I could have done for myself.

So sorry about your dad. It must be a very hard thing to cope with. I guess it's a bit weird being the only one there – 'everyone's gone to the moon' sort of feeling. I loved spending time with you too and of course we'll be doing it again! I had a strange little letter from Isabel. I think she's finding it all rather hard. She even said she had gone through a stage of wanting to run away. Thinking of you, Grace, take care and thanks again.

Love, Rob

Only Jim's messages remained in the inbox and Robin created a new folder called 'JM', highlighted the messages and moved them to it in bulk without opening them. Then she opened a new message template.

Dearest Jimbo

This is the first time I have opened email since I left Perth and I found your seven messages. I also got a message from Grace that you were worried about me. Jim, I haven't read your messages but I haven't destroyed them either. I really want to have this time for myself and not to worry daily about what emotional firecrackers may lie in wait in my email, so please don't write again.

I do understand that you would want to know that I am okay, safe, well, etc – all that stuff. So this is to tell you that

I am fine. I'm in a beautiful place and am enjoying solitude,
peace, quiet, lots of running, and time for reflection.

I think of you a lot and, in case you're wondering, yes, I do
love you and miss you, but it doesn't hurt so much now. As
you left the house that last day, you said you would let me
know if the time comes that you feel able to leave Monica. Jim,
please don't let me know. Just do or don't do whatever you
have to. I haven't left in order to force your hand. I left for lots
of reasons, just one of them being that I could no longer cope
with our situation. I've promised myself a year. If, in that time,
you make changes to your life it doesn't mean that I will rush
back.

Take care of yourself. Rest is very good for the soul, I'm
discovering. Remember that love doesn't just disappear when
the other person is not close by, it's tougher than that. This is
really all I can say for the time being.

Always with love
R.

She read it twice, clicked the send button and, with great
relief, closed the email program and turned off the computer. She
had done the essentials to protect her space, and she walked out
onto the verandah and stared down at the beach where a few
valiant surfers were hurling themselves into the waves. She
thought of Isabel, miles away in a strange place battling her
demons; about Grace, seemingly destined for some sort of
physical or emotional breakdown. She wondered about Sally and
what her silence meant. And Jim, his conflicting loves and loyal-
ties festering like a wound, contaminating everything. She loved
him as much as ever but his centrality in her life had changed. She
had become the centre of her own life, placed herself there by
making this change and she liked the feeling. She was never going
to let go of that position again.

Crossing to the bookshelf she took down Leslie Kenton's story
of her retreat to the Welsh coast. Flicking through the pages she
recalled how, six months earlier, she had identified with the anger,

despair and frustration. Now it had evaporated or transformed itself into this calm, which felt increasingly powerful. Was she doing it all wrong? Was she supposed to be suffering now? Surely it wasn't supposed to be as quick and easy as this? Kenton had immersed herself in the frenetic activity of writing, something she felt she *had* to do, that, together with the physical exercise, had brought her to her knees. To Robin it felt just the reverse. Six months ago she had felt herself on her knees. In the last month she had been raised, lightly, gently, tenderly almost, to her feet. She had a vision now of a life no longer constrained by her legal career or by the frustration of fitting in with others, with her friends, her partners, her clients and, most of all, with Jim. From now on she would direct the action. She picked a vivid pink Post-it note from the desk and in a thick felt pen wrote 'Authenticity!' And she stuck it on the door of the fridge and went out to the back verandah to get some logs for the stove.

ELEVEN

'So, tell me all about it,' Grace said, staring with distaste at the canteen's minestrone soup. 'Was it wonderful?'

'Heaven,' Denise said. 'Absolute heaven! Honestly, Grace, Bali was just what I needed. Even a couple of weeks with my mother-in-law seemed like fun after that. I'm a new woman.'

'I rather liked the old one.' Grace grinned. 'You certainly look well. The tan is very flattering.'

'I know, but the extra kilos aren't. Too much Balinese ice cream and Mum-in-law's carrot cake! But honestly, Grace, you should take a break too.'

'I'm going to,' Grace said, starting on the soup with caution. 'Oh, this minestrone is actually not too bad.'

'Ah! Do I see a couple of weeks in Kyoto coming up?'

'Uh-uh! No! I'm heading for your old stomping ground.'

'Not England?'

Grace nodded.

'Where?'

'East Grinstead. D'you know it?'

'East Grinstead? Of course I do, I grew up near there. Whatever would you go there for? It's not a holiday place, you know; just a country town, and not a very exciting one.'

'Actually, it has three martyrs, executed by the infamous Judge Jeffries, after whom Judge's Terrace off the High Street is named – but I expect you know all that.'

'Yes, I do actually,' said Denise, who had dropped her spoon.

'East Grinstead certainly has its own charm but not enough to justify taking a holiday there. Whatever is this about?'

Grace reached into her bag, pulled out a leaflet and held it up. 'The International Society of Quilters and Embroiderers is having its first-ever exhibition of patchwork quilts from sixteen different countries.' She picked up her glasses and began to read aloud from the brochure. '"Patchwork and quilting enthusiasts from around the world will gather for a seven-day working retreat to assemble a quilt to symbolise international friendship and understanding. This quilt will be hung in the main auditorium of the United Nations Human Rights and Equal Opportunity Commission in Geneva." Your soup's getting cold.'

'In East Grinstead?'

'Mmm. Well, nearby – a place called Copthorne. There's some great hotel and conference centre there.'

'I know where you mean,' said Denise in amazement. 'Well, good for you. I never thought I'd see you take a real holiday. Of course, you're very interested in all that quilting and stuff. So you're going to do the seven days? I suppose that means you'll be away a couple of weeks at least?'

'Three months!'

'Three months,' Denise repeated. 'You've never taken more than two weeks off in all the time I've worked for you, and then you said it was too long.'

'Times change,' Grace said, patting her lips with her napkin and pushing the empty soup bowl aside. 'I think I need a break.'

'I'm sure you do. It's just so amazing, though. And is this the right thing, Grace? I mean, East Grinstead is not the most riveting place. Why don't you go and visit Tim and Angela – don't you want to see Emily?'

Grace leaned back in her chair and crossed her legs. 'Of course, but they haven't been there long and, anyway, who wants a visit from their mother-in-law? You weren't all that enthusiastic about visiting yours. I think I should give them time to settle down. After East Grinstead I'm going to Brighton. That's where my mum and dad met. He'd been sent to work in a parish in England for a year and he met Mum on the pier where she was selling souvenirs. I've never seen it, never been to England. Now I'm going.'

'Brighton is noisy, crowded and has a terrible stony beach. There are some lovely antique shops and some good restaurants, but you won't like it.'

'I don't have to like it.' Grace smiled carefully. 'I just have to go.'

Grace wished she felt as confident as she thought she sounded. It had been a hasty decision, taken in a state of panic and she secretly felt it was a rather shabby effort. It lacked the elements of risk and drama inherent in Isabel's European marathon; the planned, provident and artistic virtue of Sally's sabbatical to study in California; and the simple, practical and healing purpose of Robin's retreat into solitude in the southwest. Indeed, it had no deep sense of purpose at all, no hero's journey, no element of the search for meaning. It was just an extended holiday. But to Grace, who thought a long weekend in Margaret River was stretching the boundaries, it also seemed dangerously long and self-indulgent.

Other people had always been able to get up and go with ease, Ron to work up north, her brother to do a spell of government service in the Antarctic, and even her father had gone away from time to time to work on a remote mission or station. Nurses with whom she had worked had come and gone over the years – her peers had trekked to London in the sixties, and in the eighties they went on short- or long-term health consultant contracts to Vietnam, PNG and Indonesia. Grace had had many opportunities but had always declined. She was needed here at home, she had responsibilities. She must keep the network of needy relatives, emotionally dependent friends and essential work contacts alive and throbbing. To say that Grace saw herself as a leader of the pack would imply a hubris that was not part of her nature. But she did see herself as a life-support system. Now, in a matter of months, the patients had all unhooked themselves from the system and discharged themselves from her care and, to cap it all, the midwifery training, her favourite project, had been removed from her jurisdiction.

The brochure had arrived in the mail the same day as the

email from Robin. Grace had been waiting for her call for help, the call she was sure would come when Robin, with only the seagulls for company, would need her. She had anticipated taking some time off to prop Robin up and build on the fledgling relationship that had developed over the last three months. A remote cottage on a windy headland was not her ideal choice of location but she was ready, willing and eager to respond to the call. Robin's affectionate but detached message with its tone of self-containment had stunned her.

The pictures in the brochure were seductive. It was the obsessive, meticulous orderliness of the patchwork that she loved, so predictable and reassuring. And the quilts lasted through generations, telling stories, holding secrets; the tradition of a group of women working together was a symbol of connectedness that appealed to her. She stared at the brochure, at the pictures of the quilts, at the pleasant-looking conference centre and the pale chintzes in the hotel rooms. She read about the nearest town and its history and, when she looked on a map of southeast England, she noticed its proximity to Brighton. She called a couple of other society members in other states and discovered that two women were going from Australia but no one else from the west. She could make a Western Australian section for the quilt and take it with her.

It was the money that was the problem. She checked her bank and credit card statements on the Internet and broke into a sweat at the figures, wondering how she could have spent so much in the last month, trying to remember what those sums were, several at David Jones, one at Oroton, two at Laura Ashley and a couple she didn't even recognise until she had stared at them for a while. So much for savings. She'd never been good at it and neither had Ron. They'd both gone blithely on enjoying life, spending what they earned, not worrying about the future. Then he'd become ill and stopped earning, and she'd taken a year off. It had all taken its toll. She printed off the statements and stared at them again and then at the retreat brochure. Then she tore up the statements, picked up the phone and by the end of the day it was booked. The people in human resources breathed sighs of relief that Grace was finally going to use some of her accrued leave.

'You know, Brighton's not that far from Southampton,' Denise said as they made their way back to the office. 'You could pop on a ferry and go see your friend Isabel. Isn't she in Spain or France right now?'

Grace flushed, as though she had been discovered planning a crime. Isabel's proximity had not escaped her attention. Robin's mention of the call and the letter from Isabel indicated that she might be glad of a bit of support, although the suggestion would have to come from her. 'Yes, but she's on a sort of lone journey, you know. I don't think she'll want visitors.'

'Hmm. She's probably getting pretty sick of it by now. You two could live it up on red wine and shellfish, and the French make the best coffee and croissants in the world,' Denise said, slipping out of her jacket. 'Wouldn't she think it a bit odd if you were so near and didn't pop over to see her?'

Grace shrugged. 'We'll see,' she said. 'And it depends what the dollar's doing. France is so expensive.' And she thought guiltily of the French francs she had ordered from the bank that morning – just in case Isabel needed her.

Leaving Australia was difficult, but the prospect of staying put was worse. Being scared and alone among strangers in another country suddenly seemed a lesser evil than feeling scared and alone at home surrounded by people she knew. By day she burned her nervous energy putting everything in the office into the most meticulous order. Colour-coded labels indicated the crucial sections of reports and projects, and every file had a brief status report or résumé attached to it. Denise's desk was piled with instructions and reminder messages. Grace's itinerary, which listed her movements down to the finest detail, with every possible telephone number and map reference, was fixed to the office whiteboard.

At night she worked a section for the quilt and made a master plan for her luggage. She knew exactly how many pairs of knickers she had packed, what colour they were and in which corner of which bag. She assembled a travelling medicine kit equipped to meet every possible eventuality, as though such simple over-the-counter remedies might not be available in

England. As she packed the herbal tea bags she did realise that chamomile and peppermint could probably be found in East Grinstead and Brighton, but it seemed a good idea to have them – just in case. And the cleaning cloths and scourers? Well, the furnished flat she had rented for ten weeks in Brighton might just not be spotless. One thing Grace couldn't stand was a dirty sink or dishcloth, and this way she wouldn't have to tolerate even five minutes of an unsavoury sink. Everything was meticulously organised – only her financial situation and her emotions were in chaos.

'Take some Valium or something, for goodness' sake,' Denise said as she walked with her to the departure gate. 'One won't hurt you, then you can relax on the flight. I can't believe this is the first time you've been abroad, Grace. You're such a sophisticated person.'

Grace thought she might throw up in the potted palm that stood in a stainless steel cylinder near the entrance to the coffee shop. 'The first time and probably the last,' she murmured, grasping Denise's arm. 'Are you sure you're clear about everything? The nurse practitioner program is the most important –'

'Grace, it's all right. If there's anything I'm in doubt about I'll call you. Now get through that gate and relax. Have a wonderful time. You're supposed to be enjoying this. It's a holiday, not an assault course.'

The hotel was a single-storey sandstone building, cunningly designed in a series of semicircles incorporating small courtyards filled with tubs of white geraniums, yellow pansies and blue lobelia. Alongside it the conference centre contained a pleasant main auditorium with, to Grace's relief, plenty of natural light and windows that could actually be opened, and a grand piano. Beyond it a small, elegantly designed gallery, carefully lit and with long narrow windows set into the slope of the ceiling, stood awaiting the arrival of the next exhibition.

Grace stood at the window of her room looking out at the tubs of flowers, and feeling an intense sense of relief that it all appeared so ordinary and familiar. She had made an overnight stop in Hong Kong, taking Denise's advice to break the long journey, and had immediately called the office to check that everything was okay. Denise had gently pointed out that she had only been gone for twelve hours and everything was just as she had left it.

She gazed at the geraniums wondering about this word 'retreat'; what it really meant. The book that Robin had lent her implied it meant being alone in order to make some sort of spiritual journey. But here she was about to spend a seven-day retreat with a crowd of strangers. Grace was not really sure what a spiritual journey was. She was a minister's daughter, so Bible readings, daily prayers and regular church attendance were part of her childhood and adolescence, but talk of spirituality confused her. Religion had always seemed to be about rules, morality and paying homage to a rather vengeful God. How did you build a spiritual life based on that, or indeed totally divorced from it as some people claimed? What was spirituality, anyway? What did people mean by having an inner life? She wished there was someone she could ask without feeling ridiculous. She'd almost asked Sally that last time after yoga, but then she'd chickened out. Did other women her age have this sort of spiritual black hole or was she just out of touch, locked in her old cautious, conservative, unquestioning ways?

Sighing, she slid open the glass door and stepped outside. It was September and the air was mild and soft. In the distance, beyond the boundaries of the hotel complex, cows grazed peacefully in a field full of daises, somewhere a clock chimed four, and Grace was enchanted with the idea that she was in England and it was four o'clock and time for afternoon tea. Closing the door she set off in search of the lounge, where she thought she might be able to order scones with jam and cream, send a postcard to Isabel and organise a rental car. The anxiety of the journey was lifting and she began to feel the first little quiver of enjoyment, even an unfamiliar sense of adventure.

It was on that first afternoon in England, as she sat in a sunlit corner of the hotel lounge with a pot of tea on the low table beside her, that Grace first laid eyes on Vivienne Hart. The lounge was an open area off the hotel foyer and as she looked up from her map of the area she saw an imposing woman with thick grey hair wound into a bun at the nape of her neck. 'I'd like them all taken through to the exhibition room now!' the woman said, leaning on the reception desk and waving her aluminium walking stick towards a pile of canvas containers. 'And we'll need to check the temperature in that room, and the light, before they're unpacked. Some of these exhibits are very old and valuable.'

Clearly the exhibition and its curator had arrived, and Grace watched as the hotel's two porters lifted the flat packs onto a large two-tier trolley. 'Over here, Gary, over here,' the woman called, and a slim young man dressed entirely in black and with one gold earring materialised beside her.

'Okay, Viv, okay,' he said, stroking her arm. 'Everything's under control. Nothing will be unpacked until we've checked the environment. I've got all the hanging arrangements in hand, so don't get your knickers in a twist.'

Vivienne was wearing black silk pants and a loose, flowing silk top in a dramatic pattern of scarlet and black, and on both wrists she wore chunky silver bracelets. She moved awkwardly, as though in pain and unaccustomed to the stick. Occasionally she seemed to forget she needed it and when she gesticulated with it, she swayed perilously.

'I think we'd better get you off your feet,' Gary said, tucking his hand under the elbow of her stick-free arm. 'Once we get through there I'll find you a seat and you can sit and give orders like the Queen Mum!'

'Pity I forgot my ostrich plumes and white gloves,' Vivienne responded with a laugh. 'It shouldn't be a problem to roll up a bottle of gin, though!' They disappeared together down the walkway, the three-pronged base of Vivienne's stick hitting the paving with uneven thuds.

Grace took the exhibition brochure from her bag and checked the small print on the back.

Vivienne Hart is the founder and immediate past president of
the International Society of Quilters and Embroiderers, and the

curator of this unique exhibition. Ms Hart is a textile designer and preservation consultant who has worked with museums and other fabric collections worldwide. Now retired, Vivienne Hart lives in Sussex and is involved in the organisation of many patchwork and quilting projects.

The exhibition will be hung by Gary Ducasse, of Ducasse, Hart Designs of 32 Emerald Square, Pimlico, London.

Grace took off her glasses and put the brochure back in her bag. Then she spent a careful few minutes composing a postcard to Isabel, at the Madrid address Doug had given her. She told her about the retreat, and gave her the address and the dates she would be in Brighton. Hopefully Isabel would jump at the chance for them to get together. She slipped it into the box at reception and set about the process of finding the best deal for a hire car.

There was no sign of Vivienne the next day, although as Grace drove out of the car park, she glimpsed Gary Ducasse directing deliveries to the gallery and looking rather harassed. Armed with a local map and some notes that Denise had given her, Grace drove to East Grinstead and stopped for coffee in a tiny café–bookshop along the Judge's Terrace. The atmosphere was redolent of the forties and fifties. The small space enclosed by stained oak beams and low ceilings was stuffed with books, old prints and photographs of the town over the decades. Two women in twin-sets and tweed skirts whispered to each other behind the counter about various orders and discrepancies in the takings, and customers asked in hushed voices if they might be allowed to buy a book. Grace sipped her coffee, served in fine china with a small jug of cream at a wobbly table, and half expected Margaret Lockwood or Celia Johnson to appear from behind a bookshelf in a high-shouldered, tight-waisted suit, with a felt hat tilted on the side of her head at a jaunty angle. She sat for a long while by the mullioned window, gazing out at the stone engraved to the memory of the martyrs.

What would she do when the quilt was done? A few days sightseeing in London, and then Brighton? She must have been mad to book that apartment for ten weeks. It was too expensive and the exchange rate was ridiculous. The time stretched ahead like a great void. Was it just that she wanted to be away while everyone else was away? Well, they would still be away when she got back, all of them. Around her, customers bought their books and drank their coffee, no voice rising above a whisper. The town looked much as it did in the photographs taken fifty years earlier. There was something calming about the pace of the shoppers passing the window and the hushed atmosphere of the shop. Perhaps it didn't matter after all, perhaps none of it mattered. She realised that she hadn't even thought about work since she had phoned Denise the previous morning and she had no sense that she ought to race off and do something else. A tight wire that normally bound her had loosened and she didn't have the energy or the inclination to worry about anything.

'I think we'll just about make it,' said Vivienne at breakfast on the morning of the fifth day. 'We're not as far advanced as I'd hoped but I think we'll get it done in time.'

'We're all having too good a time, Viv,' said Orinda, tucking into her scrambled eggs. 'Too much talk and fun and not enough work.' She reached out for the coffee pot and topped up her cup. An African American woman in her seventies, she had travelled from New Orleans with a group of eight other American women from five different states. 'I've been to the last ten quilting retreats,' she said, 'and this one is the best yet.'

'It's wonderful, Orinda. I hate the thought of it ending,' Grace said.

'This your first time?'

Grace nodded. 'But I can promise you it won't be the last.'

'Enjoying it then, Grace?' Vivienne smiled across the table.

'Tremendously, meeting the other women, working on the quilt – I just never imagined it would be like this.'

'Quilting's always brought women together in a very special sort of way,' Vivienne said, buttering her third slice of toast.

Orinda gave Grace a nudge. 'This dame don't only know about quilts, y'know, Grace. She once took me round the Pavilion in Brighton – those gowns and the drapes and embroideries she's worked on. I ain't never seen nothin' like it. You still into all that stuff, Vivienne?'

Vivienne nodded. 'I am and I'm planning to show Grace the Patchwork Project!'

Orinda clapped her hands and hooted with laughter. 'Oh lord, Grace, she's got plans for you. You gonna have a hard job escaping from this one. You wait till you see it.' She folded her napkin and pushed her thick spectacles further up onto her nose. 'I just love finding out ways the quilting sorta gets people together. Y'know when I started to make quilts?'

Grace shook her head.

'Back in the sixties, in the civil rights movement. There were four little girls burned to death in a church by white racists. Well, me and my friends, we didn't know what to do with ourselves. We had children the same age and we were all organising, demonstrating, marching, putting out leaflets, but somehow it didn't seem enough. We wanted to do something for those children. Something so's people wouldn't forget. So we got together and made us a quilt. Five of us, we got fabric from the girls' own dresses and from all their friends and we worked together on that quilt just like we're working on this one, all together. We embroidered their names, and dates. You know, that quilt is still hanging in the church to this day.'

'You're a legend, Orinda.' Vivienne grinned. 'How many quilts have you worked on?'

'Lord, girl, I don' know, lost count years ago. Anyhow, I was a latecomer to it. My momma was nearly blind so she didn't do no sewing when I was a kid or I would'a been doing the quilts twenty-five years earlier. But y'know, it was a real wonderful thing to discover, and all the women I've met doing this over the years, well, you'd never believe it. I got friends all over the world now.'

Grace sat back listening to Orinda and watching the other women. Five days ago they had been strangers, now they were connected by a common purpose and tradition. She had been the first one through the gallery door when the exhibition was hung.

Gary Ducasse had done an outstanding job. The colours and textures of the fabrics glowed in the gentle golden light enhanced by the subtle display backings of cream, peach and old rose. Grace had sat alone in the gallery enjoying the feeling of being surrounded by the work of women.

She wondered why it was classed as craft and not as art, for each quilt was a work of art that had survived decades of practical use. It was as beautiful as any painting or sculpture. Each stitch had been made by some woman's hand, some in hardship or servitude, some in loneliness, some in cooperation with others, mothers and daughters, friends and neighbours, sisters, aunts, grandmothers, going back more than two hundred years. Was it called craft simply because it was the work of women? Gazing at the tiny, even stitches, wondering what other uses the fabrics had had in those women's lives, gave her a sense of connection to the past. The growing sense of calm she had felt since arriving in England seemed to settle over her; that hard, safe feeling behind her ribs which had been so reassuring had slowly evaporated and, strangely, it no longer seemed important to get it back.

Within hours of the start of the retreat the cool sterility of the conference centre was transformed into a mass of colour and activity. The expanding tables, designed to accommodate the quilt as it grew, were surrounded by women who had travelled from around the world, bringing patches from their own quilting guilds, and from others. Forty-six women were working on this, taking it in turns to join and quilt the contributions from fourteen countries. Although most spoke some English, the room was filled with a mix of different languages. In addition to those from Australia, America and England, there were women from Germany, France, Holland, Austria, Hungary and Bosnia. There was a group of four women from Russia, two from India and others from South Africa, Zimbabwe and Sierra Leone.

As well as the sound of voices, the room was often filled with music. Grace had barely noticed that the brochure carried an invitation to bring musical instruments and national costumes. She didn't play an instrument and came from a country that had no national costume, but others were wearing theirs. The African and

Indian women were gorgeous butterflies in their long robes and saris; the Europeans were less dramatic but equally colourful. And they had brought along their music, songs and poetry. While some worked, others made music, several taking turns at the piano.

There were a couple of guitarists, a flautist from Holland, an accordion player from Austria, a woman from Zimbabwe with a zither, two violinists from Germany, and one of the South African women had small drums and some reed and cane pipes. Grace had anticipated a hushed, semi-formal conference atmosphere and the warmth and vitality delighted her. The women's stories, told in stumbling English helped along with gestures and dictionaries, had been deeply moving. They came from sophisticated cities and remote villages. They brought tales of rape and torture, luxury and privilege, babies who had died, wars that had robbed them of their homes and loved ones. There were stories of ease and struggle, joy, misery and, most of all, courage. Beside them Grace felt naive; her life seemed bland and shallow. She had read such stories, seen them on television news, registered them at a distance while worrying about what to cook for the next day's dinner party, or organising her papers for a meeting. She was intelligent and compassionate but she had more information than she could confront – her sensitivity had been dulled and her ability to make the leap of imagination into the emotional space of the people on the screen was crippled. Face to face the stories had a personal intensity that moved and challenged her.

It was Vivienne who started the singing. They had agreed to do an extra two hours' work after dinner to stay on schedule and as they settled on the benches, stretching the fabric, examining the stitching, selecting the next sections, she hobbled over to the piano and began to play a few old hymns and folk songs. Some of the women began to sing along with her. Grace, working alongside Orinda, kept sewing and singing softly. It was when Vivienne changed rhythm and played 'Cheek to Cheek' that, without looking up from her stitching, Grace began to sing a little louder. Orinda sang with her, and it was just as they got to the last bars of the song that Grace realised she and Orinda were the only ones left singing.

Without a pause, Vivienne swung into 'The Lady Is a Tramp' and Orinda grabbed Grace's hand and pulled her over to the piano. They were singing and moving together as though they'd rehearsed it a thousand times. Orinda's gutsy voice sounded as if it should have come from someone twice her size and she moved with the rhythm and agility of a woman thirty years younger. And Grace could hear that her own voice was as strong and true as it had always been. When they finished, the room erupted in applause and shouts for more.

Orinda, in her rather prim little yellow suit and steel-rimmed glasses, reached up to Grace and hugged her. 'Honey, you sure got some voice there,' she cried. 'What'll we do next? D'you know "Night and Day"?' And before Grace could answer she began to feel the music inside her, moving through her, driving her. She was back with Ron and the band again, up on the stage, and behind her she could hear his saxophone, crooning the blue notes. Her skin prickled and a lump rose in her throat. It lasted only seconds but she was shocked by the sharpness of the memory.

It was another half-hour before the women finally let them go and even then it was only because Orinda went on strike. 'Now look here, y'all,' she grinned, waving her finger. 'This little ole black lady's had enough for one day.' And she hung on to Grace's hand as they collapsed together onto a deep couch.

'Come on now, Grace, own up,' said Vivienne, sinking down beside them, 'You said you'd been a nurse, you didn't say anything about being a jazz singer.'

Grace laughed, feeling light-headed. 'At the hospital where I did my training one of the medical students played in a band. A crowd of us went down to hear them one night and . . . well, it just sort of happened. I'd always enjoyed singing, and I had a few too many drinks and got up and joined them. That's how I met my husband, he was playing sax.'

'No training then?' Orinda asked, and Grace shook her head. 'Me neither. Started just like you – must be we just got natural talent, honey!' And she threw back her head and laughed until her glasses slipped down her nose. 'Makes you feel good, doesn't it? Don't sing much myself these days.'

Grace laughed. 'You'd never know it! I thought you must be wowing them every night in the New Orleans clubs. D'you know, Orinda, it must be almost thirty-five years since I did any singing.' And as she said it she felt very much as though she might cry.

She walked briskly in her sandshoes and grey tracksuit, leaving the hotel just before six as she had done every morning since she arrived. Staying away from the main road she took the path that wound through the fields, down past a small copse, along the side of a dry stream bed and back through the village to the hotel. A heavy dew sparkled on the grass and the air was deliciously cool. She wanted to sing while she walked, sing loud, filling her lungs with the sharp morning air and letting the notes float out across the fields and through the still sleeping village streets. Instead she sang softly to herself, and wondered just how long ago it was that Ron had put away his sax, and why they had stopped making music together. Last night had been like opening a trunk of treasures hidden for years in an attic; she wanted to rummage through and examine them, take them out, shake them, spread them in the light. She stretched her arms above her head, drawing the fresh air down into her lungs, and began to jog the last stretch back to the hotel. She felt excited, energised, as though she had stepped from somewhere else right back into her own body.

It was almost seven o'clock as she made her way through the revolving door and across the hotel foyer. The smell of breakfast wafted from the dining room. A shower, then food – she was hugely hungry. She was just heading for the shower in her room when she noticed the message light flashing on the phone. She sat on the side of the bed and called the operator, who gave her the message to call Tim in Tokyo.

Breakfast was finished and the morning session already under way when Vivienne found Grace sitting alone in a corner of the courtyard staring at a tub of yellow pansies. 'Everything okay, Grace?' Vivienne stumped awkwardly across the paving and sank heavily onto the seat beside her. 'Blasted new hip's more trouble than the old one.' And she leaned her stick against the edge of the seat. 'I wondered where you were, missed you at breakfast.'

Grace stared at her, silent for a moment. 'It's my daughter-in-law, she's had an accident,' she said, her voice tense.

Vivienne looked at her in concern. 'Oh, I'm so sorry. Is it very serious? What was it? A car?'

Grace shook her head. 'She fell down some steps outside their apartment in Kyoto. She's broken her collarbone and her right arm.'

'Oh, poor girl, that's nasty,' said Vivienne, rubbing her own robust knees with the palms of her hands.

'Yes, she's in plaster, of course. Otherwise she's okay, thank goodness. I'd better find out about flights and so on.'

'Flights? What for? I thought you were staying on.'

'I was, but they want me to go up there and help out. Angie needs help – my granddaughter is almost four and my son, well, of course he's at work all day.'

Vivienne inhaled noisily through her mouth and then exhaled even more noisily. 'So you're going to drop everything? Can't they get some local help?'

'Oh yes, of course they could,' Grace began, her voice sounding strangely shaky. 'Tim's company has been awfully good, they've offered to pay for full-time help. But it's not quite the same, is it? They're used to me being around. They said they'd rather have me there than . . .' she seemed to run out of words.

Vivienne shifted her weight and turned to face her. 'But you're on holiday. Do you want to change everything? D'you want to rush off there?'

'I always help out,' Grace said, wondering why she felt too exhausted to move.

'You go to Japan?'

'Well, they've never been in Japan before. They just moved up there.'

'Hmm. Exciting! New life!' Vivienne said. 'Shame this has happened, but it's hardly the end of the world.'

Grace looked at her as though searching for answers. 'Do you have children, Vivienne?'

'Two of my own and Gary, who's sort of unofficially adopted. And two grandchildren.'

'So you know how it feels.'

'How what feels?'

'Being responsible for them even though they're grown up. It never stops, does it, the responsibility? That feeling of having to be there when you're needed.'

'Ah!' said Vivienne slowly. '*That* feeling! Yes, I know that one, Grace, but I strive to ignore it. Sometimes I leap to attention when summoned, but mostly I don't. Mostly I stop, draw breath and try to hold back from being the solution. It's surprising how admirably they manage their own lives given half a chance.'

They sat in silence. Grace crossed and uncrossed her legs and drummed her fingers on the arm of the wooden seat, searching for that nice hard feeling of control that had deserted her. Rising up in her chest and throat in its place was a great well of words and a lump that felt as though it might choke her. 'This has been so wonderful, meeting these women, being part of it, the quilt, everything. I was running away, you know.'

Vivienne looked up in surprise as Grace raced on, words spilling out punctuated by gasps that sounded like strangled sobs. 'Yes, running away, not forever, nothing like that, just running away from being alone. My three best friends all went away. They're all doing some sort of midlife retreat, giving up their jobs, doing their own thing in different places. Then the kids went to Japan. And my mother-in-law died and my father, who has Alzheimer's, stopped recognising me. I felt completely alone and useless. I'm used to being surrounded by people who need me. So I was running away from being all on my own, from not being needed.'

Vivienne leaned back, stretching her arms up and running her hands through her hair. 'Well, there you are, now you're needed again. Does that make you feel better?'

Grace was silent with shock at the unfamiliar sensation of tears running down her cheeks. 'It feels strange,' she said. 'I've only been here a few days but it felt so wonderful. When I got here I thought I must have been stupid taking all this time off, planning to stay in Brighton, on my own. I was scared about what I'd do with all that time. But meeting you and the other women, working on the quilt, what that means . . . and then last night, the singing and . . . well, something's changed. I changed, I felt totally different, as though I was on some marvellous adventure. Oh god, this must sound so stupid.'

Vivienne dropped her arms, leaned forward and took Grace's hand. 'It doesn't sound stupid at all. You decided to do something for yourself and you're enjoying it. It *is* an adventure.'

'I don't know why I'm talking to you like this,' Grace cut in. 'I never talk about how I feel, and now look at me, blurting all this out. And I'm crying. I never cry. I'm so sorry. But you see, it was all so different. As though I was different, as though I'd let go of a whole lot of things. I mean, I haven't phoned my office for six days, not since the morning I arrived. You don't know what that means for me.'

'I think I'm starting to get the picture,' Vivienne said.

'And now it's all gone, I have to pick everything up again. It seems . . . well, it seems so hard. I feel disappointed and . . . and . . .'

'And angry?'

Grace looked at her in surprise. 'Angry? No . . . I don't think . . . actually, yes. Angry, resentful . . . sort of put upon, if you know what I mean.'

'I know what you mean.' Vivienne paused. 'So have you thought about not going?'

'I did, for a moment, but it seems so . . . well, neglectful. I mean it wouldn't be a very nice thing to do, would it?'

Vivienne shifted her weight on the seat. 'Actually, Grace, I think it would be very nice. Very nice for you, and possibly only just a little awkward for your son and daughter-in-law. After all, they can manage, they can get help, you've said so. They're not going to fall apart without you.' She picked up her stick and struggled to her feet. 'I don't *need* you to stay, Grace, but I *hope* you will. I'd like to sew and to sing with you some more. Of course, you must do what feels right – actually, I hope you do what feels good, what feels good in your heart and your gut, not your head.'

She put her hand on Grace's shoulder. 'Imagine all those years without a song?'

And she hobbled off across the courtyard, back to the conference centre, from where the sound of African drums floated out into the morning sunlight.

TWELVE

'Okay,' said Linda, standing on the edge of the pool wrapped in one of the hotel's white towelling robes. 'Here's the deal. We've paid the day rate. That means we can use the pool, the spa and the sauna whenever we want. And, we each get to select three of the beauty treatments, that's all included in the price. If you want more than that then you pay the rate on the tariff card. Coffee and mineral water are free, and there's a running buffet that's included, so you just help yourself.'

Nancy pulled her robe closer at the neck and leaned across to Sally. 'I'm not sure my body can stand three beauty treatments in one day – it may go into shock.'

Sally smiled. 'I know what you mean, although at the moment I feel so revolting, not even the whole list could make an impression.'

'So how do we organise what we want, Lin?' Nancy called out to her daughter.

'Okay, Mom! Don't hassle me, I was just coming to that.' Linda started handing out cards for them to tick their selections. Sally stared at hers in dismay, feeling incapable of deciding anything. She wanted to close her eyes, lie back on the recliner, not move all day, not speak to anyone.

'Oh, and don't forget, folks, champagne and birthday cake at four o'clock! It's not just my birthday but Sally's too, that's Mom's friend over there. So try to fix your salon treatments so you can be out here by the pool at four.'

Sally was finding Linda incredibly annoying with her long, singsong Californian vowels. This whole tedious birthday with Linda and her friends at the smart Orchard Hotel Spa was the last thing she wanted. She had been talked into it by Nancy, who had discovered that Sally and Linda shared a birthday. 'Oh, c'mon,' Nancy had said pleadingly. 'Be a pal, Sally. It's good to do something different on your birthday. Besides, if you don't go I'll be on my own with six smart thirty-something lawyers. Come and keep me company.'

Sally sighed, ticked off her card for a massage, facial and manicure, and handed it back to Linda feeling churlish. Linda was a really nice person, interesting, intelligent, thoughtful and hugely energetic, but Sally just wasn't in the mood. She'd done this once before with the Gang of Four, in a little less luxury. They'd gone to a day spa in Perth. Isabel had been given two guest passes, so they had split the cost of the other two between the four of them. They had been almost hysterical by the time they got there, joking about how they needed beauty treatments before they braved the atmosphere of a place that dispensed them. 'It's okay for you, Grace,' Isabel had said. 'You always look as though you just came from some gorgeous salon. I feel like the *before* of all the before pictures ever taken. You know: "Look! We can even work with beached whales."'

'And I feel like some aged vegetable that's been left in the bottom of the fridge too long,' Robin had declared. 'An eggplant that's half slimy, half dried up.'

'You lot are disgusting,' Sally had said. 'Shaggy's what I feel, like some old, unkempt hippie.'

'Hmmph!' Grace had retorted, getting out of the car and straightening her immaculate cream pants and black T-shirt. 'Well, for your information, I feel like a wrinkled old prune.'

And they had bowled into the salon smothering their laughter and attempting to look as though they were accustomed to lazing around in expensive spas. What would they say if they could see Sally here now? What would they say if they knew what she was doing in California? She missed them desperately but felt, at the same time, totally cut off from them, unable to communicate with anything more than occasional postcards that revealed nothing. She had no idea how to bridge the gap created more by her own secrecy than by geographical distance.

'Well,' said Nancy, 'I'm booked for that mud bath thing in five minutes time, so I'll mosey on in there now, I think.' She picked up her bag and glasses and got to her feet. 'I'm so glad you came, Sally. You need to relax, make a fuss of yourself.'

Sally smiled up at her without speaking. Just a few weeks ago Nancy's generous support had been a gift, now it seemed like an intrusion.

'I haven't seen Steve around recently,' Nancy went on. 'Did he go away or something?'

'Just busy, I guess,' Sally said, flushing slightly and looking out over the pool. 'I haven't seen him. I haven't been to classes the last couple of weeks.'

Nancy folded her glasses and slipped them into their case. 'I realised that,' she said. 'Are you going to go back?'

Sally nodded. 'Yes, on Monday. I just couldn't quite cope the last week or so.'

Nancy nodded. 'Well, okay, a massage'll do you a heap of good. I'll catch up with you later, when I emerge from the mud.'

Sally made her way to the manicurist and was relieved to find she was Japanese with limited English. Smiles, nods and noises of appreciation could replace conversation. She sat, her hand on the pink cushion, watching the transformation of her neglected nails, thinking about Steve. He had, after all, only been trying to help and she had behaved appallingly – slapped his face and stomped off in fury. When she reached the main highway an elderly couple heading back into San Francisco had picked her up. They were tourists, on holiday from Boston, and they took her to the station in their rental car. From there she took the train to Berkeley, back to the precious seclusion of her apartment, back to the self-imposed prison of her anger.

She stretched out her fingers, the manicure had felt nice and suddenly she was sorry it was finished – maybe Nancy was right about a bit of pampering. She wandered through to the spa and, thankful to find it empty, slipped out of her robe. The warm bubbling water enclosed and supported her, and she closed her eyes and rested her head on the curved edge of the bath. The hum of the motor and the bubbling water were soothing, and she began to relax. She was almost asleep when Linda and a friend climbed in alongside her, with news of the excellence of the masseuse, and a guy in the hair salon who was a great cutter.

Sally was torn between her desire to stay in the spa and her need to escape the chatter, but two more women arrived and it was clear that the peaceful interlude was over. She climbed out, took a hot shower and wandered out to the pool again to kill some time before her massage and facial. The Orchard Hotel was located high in the Berkeley hills and from the pool terrace the view to San Francisco was spectacular. Sally traced the landscape along the sleek lines of the Bay Bridge until it reached the city, past the Coit Tower and the slim pyramid of the Trans America building to the high ground of Russian Hill. She stared motionless, feeling nothing but emptiness and the brooding depression that had accompanied her each day.

Linda was right. Hilda, the masseuse, was excellent, a tall, muscular woman with strong square hands. It was months since Sally had had a massage and she felt the knots crunching under Hilda's fingers in a relief that bordered on pain.

'You have a lot of tension here,' Hilda said, working vigorously around her shoulderblades. 'I can't fix it all in one day. Can you come back again?'

Sally nodded, the tension breaking up with every knot that Hilda ground out of her back. A couple of hours later, her face covered with a fresh scented cucumber mask and cool, damp cotton pads over her eyes, she felt lighter and freer than she had for weeks. In the warm semi-darkened room, with a background of rainforest sounds on the CD player, she began to think that some day, sometime, she might feel normal again.

There was no way to avoid the Monday morning lecture and the tutorial that followed it. She had missed two weeks and although she was keeping pace she knew she simply couldn't afford any more absences. The lecture hall was crowded and she slipped into a seat high up in the back row, with just a couple of minutes to spare. As the lecturer organised his slides and overheads she looked around for Steve but there was no sign of him. The lecturer lowered the lights and the first slide lit up the screen. In the half-light Sally caught her breath as Steve struggled in through the ground-floor side entrance on crutches, his right leg in plaster to the knee.

The slides flickered on and off the screen, the lecturer's commentary drawing murmurs of interest and the occasional ripple of laughter from the students, but Sally heard nothing. Her eyes were fixed on the front row of seats where Steve sat, his leg extended in front of him, crutches resting alongside him. She could see him facing her in the sunlight, swaying precariously as he struggled to regain his balance on the rock and then crashing heavily to the ground, his leg buckling under him as he rolled down the slope.

As soon as the lights went up she slipped out of her seat to make her way to the front, but a crush of students blocked the stairway down the side of the lecture theatre, so she ducked out of the back door and took the long path around the building, hoping to make it in time to catch Steve coming out. But the path was partially blocked by building works and she had to run a wide circle across the lawns to reach the other side of the building.

When she saw him he was moving quite fast on his crutches, talking with another man who was carrying his bag. 'Steve!' she called, gulping for breath. 'Steve, wait – please wait.'

He turned as she reached him. 'Sally, hi!'

'Steve, your leg,' she said, gasping for breath. 'I didn't know . . . What did . . . was it . . . ' She stopped, at a loss for something to say.

Steve glanced at the man alongside him and then back at Sally. 'I was walking on Mount Tam, tripped and fell,' he said straight-faced. 'Broke my leg.'

Sally stared at him in horror as a deep flush crept up her neck. 'Oh god, I'm so sorry. I didn't know. I . . . well, I haven't been to classes since, well since . . . '

171

'I noticed you weren't around,' he said coolly, turning away. 'Look, I can't stop to talk. Tony here's come to pick me up. It's the only way I can get about right now. See you around.' And the two of them headed off towards the car park.

Despair engulfed her as she watched him manoeuvre himself into the car. She wandered away across the grass and sat down, leaning back against a tree. She must have been overtaken by some madness – first the Mendelsons, then Steve.

She remembered how he had called for her that day, his thoughtfulness, and the courage it must have taken to confront her, the courage and the honesty of a real friend. Now Sally sat, knees drawn up, arms wrapped around them, and as the lump welled in her throat she sank her head onto her arms and began to sob. The clock in the tower struck five, the sun retreated and the air grew cooler but still she sat there weeping, unaware of passers-by who stopped to stare, ignoring the young woman who crouched beside her with an offer of help. For two hours she stayed there until the light had gone and she began to shiver with cold. Then she struggled stiffly to her feet, brushed the grass from her skirt and made her way off the campus onto Bancroft Avenue, where she caught a bus to the cross street nearest to Steve's apartment. Then she walked the last four blocks to the brown shingle house with the purple rhododendrons out the front and stopped in the driveway, giving herself time to muster her courage before she went up to the door of the ground-floor apartment.

'The door's unlocked, Tony, c'mon in,' Steve called, and Sally opened it and stepped inside. He was sitting in an old leather armchair, his plastered leg resting on a low footstool, crutches on the floor beside him. Half a dozen books were stacked on the floor near him, and lying across the chair arms his laptop rested on a short wooden plank. He continued typing, not looking up. 'Just finishing this last sentence,' he said. 'Be with you in a flash. Wanna stick the groceries in the kitchen?'

'It's not Tony,' she said nervously, and he looked up immediately, whipping his glasses off and staring at her in surprise.

'Sally!'

She stood in the dark of the doorway momentarily unable to move or speak.

'Well, I can't get up so you'd better come in,' he said, taking off his glasses. 'D'you want to sit down?' He nodded towards the leather couch.

Sally crossed blindly to the couch but couldn't bring herself to sit. 'Steve, I don't know what to say,' she began, unable to look him in the eye, her voice trailing away.

'Nothing to say, really,' he replied stiffly. 'Hey, Sally, what's the matter? Look at me, will you?'

She shook her head, once again unable to control her tears. 'I can't, Steve, I can't . . . I'm so ashamed. I'm so sorry . . .'

'Sally, don't cry, please don't. I'm just being a miserable bastard, trying to make you feel bad. Please don't cry.'

'I can't seem to stop,' she mumbled through the tears, shaking her head again. 'I've been crying for hours.'

'I can see that. Look, it's okay. I was pissed off, but now I'm so pleased to see you. C'mon over here – please, I can't get up.' And he reached out his hand and she stumbled over to him.

'Steve, I feel so terrible. I slapped your face, broke your leg and then I just walked off and left you.'

'Look, Sally, it was my fault. I had no right to say those things. It was none of my business.' He squeezed her hand and tilted his head to look into her face. 'It was just my typical male arrogance and I was way out of line. I deserved it.'

She grabbed a handful of tissues from a box on the floor. 'No! No! You were right, absolutely right. You were trying to help me and everything you said was right, about the past, about my shame and my anger at everything and everybody.' She sank onto the floor stifling more sobs. 'Ever since that terrible day at the Mendelsons I've been living through it all again, the fear, and the shame, and the pain of parting with Lisa. And the worse I feel the more I turn it into anger and try to blame the Mendelsons. Oh, Steve, when I think of how terrible I was to Estelle, that poor woman. I'm so ashamed. It could have been me in that car, but I was too weak and selfish to look after Lisa myself. And now look what I've done to you.'

Steve lifted the laptop onto the table beside him, pushed his plank over the side of the chair and pulled her towards him. 'I know,' he said. 'I know and Nancy knows too, we just didn't know how to get through to you.'

'You talked to Nancy?'

'Sure, she stopped me one day as I went out the gate. Before the Mount Tam drama, this was. She and Chuck don't know what to do. They want to help and so do I.'

'I don't deserve any help,' she said bitterly, holding on to both his hands. 'Look at you, you must be in so much pain, and I've messed up your studying. How are you coping like this?'

'Very little pain, but quite a lot of inconvenience. As I said, I was really angry for a while, but it's been wearing off, and now you're here, well . . . come and give me a hug.'

She hugged him hard, burying her face in the shoulder of his sweatshirt. 'I don't know why you're even talking to me, let alone hugging me,' she mumbled.

'I'm a masochist,' he said. 'I like getting beaten up. Look, why don't you stick the jug on and make us some coffee.'

'How long will you be in plaster?' she asked when she came back from the kitchen with the cups. She had washed her face and combed her hair in the bathroom while the kettle boiled, and she was starting to feel a little steadier.

'Another six weeks. And then another four with it strapped. It's a long job. But you tell me what've you done. Have you contacted the Mendelsons again?'

She shook her head. 'I've done nothing, Steve. Nothing except sit at home in my misery and put out miserable stay-away vibes to anyone who comes near me. For some reason Nancy and Chuck are still speaking to me. They must be saints. I just don't know what to do. I might've been able to make some sort of connection with Lisa but I ruined it all. The Mendelsons'll never let me see her again now. They were so good to me. Estelle even organised the photos for me. They trusted me and all I did was abuse them. Last night I thought perhaps I should just go back to Australia, pretend none of this ever happened. I could tell everyone that the course didn't work out, or it was too expensive to live here or something.'

'And start all the secrecy again?' Steve cut in. 'Lock it all up again so that it can come back and knock you flat some other time – only then it'll be twice as hard. Look, Sally, you've let the monster out of the closet and it's bitten you real bad, but you've got to make use of that. It was a terrible thing that happened to you, and you were all alone. Well, now you've got friends who know the truth. You don't have to be alone with it this time. If you run away you'll regret it. Anyway,' he grinned, 'I'm just beginning to get to like you – always had this fantasy about masterful dames!'

Sally smiled. 'Any of my friends would tell you I'm the least masterful dame around. I'm a wimp, a pushover. Usually I don't even speak up for myself when I should. I'm sorry, Steve, really sorry. I never hit anyone in my life before.'

'Well, I'm honoured to be the first victim of your latent violence.'

'I don't know what I can do to apologise.'

'I'm sure I'll think of some way to turn the situation to my advantage.' He smiled and reached out for her hand again.

'Well, what do you think?' said Nancy, putting a sliced baguette, a cheese platter and some pastrami and German salami on the table.

'I think I should open a bottle of wine,' Chuck said, getting up and going to the kitchen. 'Or would you guys prefer a beer?' They opted for beer and he returned to the big oval dining table with four frosty bottles, an opener and glasses. 'Want something to put your foot on, Steve?'

'I wouldn't mind that stool, Chuck, please,' he said, and Chuck pulled the stool over to him.

'So, she socked it to you, did she, pal?'

'She sure did, Chuck. That's one tough Aussie over there.' Steve grinned, lifting his leg onto the stool. 'Don't mess with her or she'll send you flying off the balcony.' Sally groaned in embarrassment.

'Hey, Sally.' Chuck smiled, pouring her a beer. 'Don't be shy. We're impressed, aren't we, Nance?'

'We sure are, Sally. I'm speechless with admiration!'

Sally looked around at them, smiling at her, sitting there ready for this round-table conference to help her decide what to do next.

'What are the options for Sally?' Chuck asked, inspecting his beer.

'Running away seems like a good one,' Sally volunteered.

'No way,' Steve cut in. 'You've come this far. Look, you're positively *almost* normal. Don't give up on it. You gotta try the Mendelsons one more time.'

'And if they tell me, as they have every right to, to jump off the Golden Gate Bridge?'

'So, there's nothing lost,' Steve went on. 'At least you gave it a shot.'

'Steve's right, Sally,' said Nancy. 'I know it's going to be hard for you to make contact after what happened, but I think you have to try.'

'Hear hear!' said Chuck, putting a thick chunk of cheese onto a piece of bread. 'You can't walk away now. Besides, you haven't had Thanksgiving in America yet.'

Nancy leaned over to Sally and took her hand. 'Honey, y'know I'm perfectly willing to call the Mendelsons, or go talk to them for you if you like. If you think a third party would help.'

Near to tears Sally stared around the table, profoundly moved by the support of these three people whom she had known only a few months. She longed to accept Nancy's offer, let her do the hard part of making the initial contact, sounding out the Mendelsons, putting her case, but she knew that if there was going to be any move at all, it had to come from her. 'Nancy, that's so good of you, but I think I have to do it myself.'

'I agree,' said Steve. 'It'll be hard, but you're right, I think the move has to come from you.'

'So what then?' said Nancy. 'Sally can't just turn up at the door. Should she call, or write? What?'

'Write,' said Steve. 'Write to Estelle. Tell her everything, about the past and about how you were feeling. From what you told me about the Mendelsons, I think they'll understand.'

'I think so too,' Nancy nodded.

Chuck shrugged and opened another beer. 'Sounds good to me.'

It was after ten when she drove Steve home in his own car. It was the deal they had made the day she had gone to his flat the previous week. She would drive his car and take him to and from university, and do his errands for him, until his leg was out of plaster. The challenge for Sally was to drive the big old Jaguar on the right side of the road. She negotiated the busy intersection and turned into his street.

'You'll do fine,' Steve said. 'I kinda like this, having a glamorous lady chauffeur. It'll do a lot for my image with the younger guys in the class!'

'Only so long as you don't admit that the chauffeur broke your leg.' She smiled.

'Mmm. That wouldn't be so good. Have to save that story for the dinner-party set.'

She stopped the car in the drive, as close to Steve's porch as she could get, and started to open the car door, but he grabbed her wrist to stop her. In the dark of the car he was silhouetted against the porch light. 'You will do it, won't you? You won't give up?'

She nodded. 'I'll do it. I dread the thought of writing that letter and, worse still, facing them again. But you're right, I'll never forgive myself if I don't. And the other thing is that if I ran away to Australia now, I think I'd have to keep the secret and I can't cope with that anymore. At least if I give it my best shot, whichever way it goes, I think I'll be able to come clean to my friends.'

She got out of the car and walked around to Steve's side to hand him his crutches. 'You've been a wonderful friend, Steve.'

'Yuk! Past tense?'

'Just a figure of speech.'

'I hope so. Definitely present, hopefully future! You'd be surprised how long I can spin this leg out if I have to.'

It was a difficult letter to write and it felt as though each sentence drained her energy as she told the story of her pregnancy, Lisa's birth and the decision to stay on in London. She wrote too about her eventual return to Australia, and her dismay on receiving Estelle's letter. She described not only the events themselves but also the impact they had had on her, the way she had felt. For three days the letter lay unfinished while she tried to summon the strength to explain to Estelle and Oliver Mendelson how those feelings from the past had crept up on her and turned to anger at them, how her shame and grief had interfered with her sense of reality. Once complete it lay waiting to be mailed, stalled this time by her realisation that once it was gone the final die would be cast. She had reached some level of peace, and while she wanted to see Lisa and also to put right the wrong, she wasn't sure how she would handle either rejection or forgiveness. Finally, on a mild October morning on her way back from doing Steve's shopping, she slipped it into the mailbox with a sigh, knowing that she had done the best she could. There was nothing to do now but wait.

'Any news yet?' Steve asked ten days later when she picked him up.

'No. I keep telling myself they'd want time to think about it. I mean, it's not going to be something they're going to throw themselves into straight away, is it?'

'I suppose not. Well, I have great news. Stacey, my daughter, is coming back from London. She's gonna be home for Thanksgiving.' Sally took Steve's crutches as he settled himself into the front seat. 'It's two years since I last saw her. I want you to meet her, Sally. I hope you two will get along.'

Sally felt a twinge of something that felt rather like jealousy as she walked around to the driver's door. 'That's great, Steve. When does she arrive?'

'Two weeks time and, Sally, this is where I have to grovel. Would you drive me to the airport to meet her?'

She didn't know why she wanted to refuse, and in any case she couldn't. If it weren't for her own stupidity, Steve would be driving himself to the airport.

'Of course,' she said, trying to inject some enthusiasm into her voice. 'Where's she going to stay?'

'With me initially, probably for a couple of weeks till she finds somewhere to rent.'

'So she's staying in California?'

'Yep. Got a job with the *Chronicle*.'

'I thought she was enjoying London,' said Sally, thinking that she sounded what Isabel used to call 'snarty' – critical and tight-lipped – and not really knowing why.

'So did I, but I think something fell through with some guy there. She may be running away from that.'

Sally turned into the car park and slipped into a vacant space. 'Well, you'll have a live-in housekeeper for a while.'

Steve laughed. 'Hardly. Stacey isn't really a housekeeping sort of person. But it'll be so great to see her again.'

Sally sat through the lecture thinking how strange it was that you could be feeling fairly peaceful and then something could happen to change your mood and you couldn't really put your finger on what it was. After the lecture they made their way over to the café, Steve, now quite agile on his crutches, keeping pace with the crowd as they crossed the street. He swung down into a seat while Sally joined the queue to collect their cappuccinos. 'Thanks,' he said as she put the coffee in front of him. 'Won't be long now before I can get the coffee and you can hold the table.'

'I thought you were going to spin it out as long as you could so you could get waited on hand and foot.'

'That's all very well but it's so darned inconvenient, and it slows everything down so much. Sort of takes the spontaneity out of life. Oh, don't get me wrong, Sally, I really appreciate every-thing you're doing, the shopping, the chauffeuring, keeping me company. But I guess I'm getting restless and it must be a real drag for you.'

She shrugged, looking down into her coffee. 'I've been enjoying it, really, even the cooking. I don't mind driving you, it's just that I still find the traffic a bit intimidating. But we had some good evenings watching old movies, didn't we?'

'But we can still do all those things when I'm out of plaster, of course . . . well, that is, if you want to. *I* can cook *you* a meal some-times, and we could go see a movie in the cinema!' He reached across the table and took her hand. 'You're a terrific woman, Sally. I don't think I told you how much I admire you and, well . . . care for you.'

She flushed. 'That's just because you think I'm tough and masterful.'

'Yeah, that too,' he grinned. 'You gotta admit that's pretty sexy.'

'Oh, come on,' she said. 'Finish your coffee and then let's get your jacket from the drycleaner's.' She watched him drain his cup, thinking how much she liked his square face that could change in an instant from a genial smile to intense concentration. As he put down the cup and looked across at her, she felt a lump in her throat and had to make an effort to pull herself together. She had lived the last few months at such a level of emotional intensity that she was on the verge of tears most of the time now. She'd have to get a grip on herself.

'Okay,' said Steve, 'let's go.' He hauled himself onto the crutches and they made their way back to the car.

'Before the weekend,' he said as she dropped him and his jacket at the apartment.

'Huh?'

'Before the weekend you'll hear from the Mendelsons. I feel it in my bones – the unbroken ones!'

'You'll be reading my palm next.'

'You better believe it. Gotta do something to keep myself occupied. But no, I feel it strongly. Wanna bet?'

'Okay,' she said. 'Five bucks.'

'Hey, big spender! You're on, five bucks it is. If you don't get something by Saturday I'll be very surprised.'

As it was she didn't have to wait until Saturday. When she got home it was waiting for her. Tucked in behind the phone bill and a letter from her mother was a long cream envelope with the Hyde Street address on the back.

'You won, Steve,' she murmured to herself. 'Five bucks it is.'

THIRTEEN

The harsh bite in the wind from the sea began to ease, the mornings dawned pink and gold, the evenings lingered pearl and lilac, the days were clear and gentle. Robin wandered the beach collecting tiny polished pink and white shells and pieces of barnacle-encrusted driftwood. The first spring holidaymakers began to arrive, and at dawn and dusk a few hopeful people stood on the firm sand casting their lines into the water. She thought she could stay like this forever, but she knew she must consider the future.

The house she had struggled to buy, lovingly decorated and filled with carefully chosen furnishings and artwork, no longer felt like a place to which she wanted to return. And the work that had been her driving force seemed like quicksand ready to drag her into its depths if she ventured too close. She knew she was finished with the law. But the gap it would leave remained a challenge.

'I thought I might take a little trip down the coast for a few days,' she said. Dorothy, stacking packets of biscuits onto a shelf, stopped work and looked up, pushing a strand of neatly permed grey hair back off her forehead. 'Augusta, Denmark, Albany – you know, the general southwest corner.'

'Nice,' said Dorothy. 'Best time for it. Before the uni term finishes, and you'll be able to take your pick of places to stay.'

Robin put a packet of brown rice and some soy milk into her trolley. 'D'you think Ted would keep an eye on the place and feed Maurice? I thought I'd take a week, ten days at the most.'

'Of course he will, no worries. You must be getting a bit bored up there by now.'

'Not bored. Just a bit concerned about the future, what I'm going to do and when. I know I don't want to go back to the rat-race but I'm not sure what I want to do instead.'

'I read your book – well, some of it.'

'The Leslie Kenton one? You did?'

'Aye. Very interesting.'

'You really thought so?'

'I did. Twenty years too late for me, of course, but it made a lot of sense. And I always like to read a book that has someone else's underlinings in it. I read those passages more carefully with the person in mind. Takes a bit of courage to do what you're doing.'

'It didn't feel like that. Once my friend Isabel started talking about it I really couldn't ignore it. Now I've got away, I seem to have smashed the mould. I have no idea what I want, only that I don't want to go back to my house, the law and all the rest of it.'

'Want me to the read the cards for you?'

'The cards?'

'Tarot.'

Robin laughed. 'You do tarot readings, Dorothy?'

Dorothy, looking mildly offended, stacked the empty biscuit box onto a pile of cartons on a nearby trolley. 'I certainly do and I'm quite well respected for it. I've got people who come to me on a regular basis.'

'Oh look, I'm sorry.' Robin blushed. 'I didn't mean to be rude. It's just that I thought . . .'

'You thought tarot readers sat in a tent at the fair wearing gipsy skirts and a shawl fringed with gold coins.'

'Something like that.'

'Well, now you know. Some tarot readers are elderly shop-keepers wearing tracksuit pants and a jumper from Target. Ever had a reading done?'

'Never.'

'Why don't you go through to the kitchen and put the kettle on. I'll get Ted to take over for half an hour and I'll do one for you now.'

'Really?'

'Why not?'

'How much do you charge?'

'Your first reading is a gift from me, Robin. A challenge to your scepticism. If you come back for more, it's twenty dollars for half an hour.'

The late afternoon sun cast a shaft of light through the window of Dorothy's crowded but spotless kitchen. Bundles of herbs hung on a fine rope above the range, drying in its warmth. Robin filled the old-fashioned kettle and put it on the hotplate. It reminded her of her mother's old kitchen in Battersea, a kitchen whose owner clearly refused to fully join the march of domestic progress. The shelves of the dresser were packed with jars of Dorothy's homemade jam and on the checked cloth that covered the kitchen table stood a small basket of eggs that Ted had collected from his chickens that morning. Dorothy came briskly through from the shop just as the kettle began to sing. Her glasses swung on a chain around her neck tangling with a purple cord that held a special thick-grip pen for arthritic hands.

'How do you do all this – the preserves, the herbs, read tarot and run the shop?' Robin asked. 'With . . . well, with your arthritis and . . .'

'And at my age, you were going to say! I don't know. I just jog along, and Ted does his share and more. I'm best when I keep moving. If I sit around I seize up. Here's the tea. You make it and I'll get the cards.'

Robin poured the boiling water into the teapot, took three mugs down from the dresser and then poured the tea and took one to Ted in the shop. Meanwhile, Dorothy fetched a small folding table, opened it and covered it with a deep purple velvet cloth trimmed with gold braid. 'This is as near as we get to the gipsy.' She smiled and Robin had the grace to blush.

'You have a seat there.' And motioning Robin to sit down, she set a well-worn pack of tarot cards on the table and, on top of them, a large chunk of unpolished rose quartz. 'Now,' she said. 'Because I've been running around I just have to sit quiet for a minute or two, centre myself. You should too. Just close your eyes and think about yourself.' And she rested her right hand on top of the rose quartz and closed her eyes.

Robin sat back, letting her eyes close, trying to stem her embarrassment. Grace would really have a laugh at this, but Isabel would be fascinated, Sally too. She felt a pang of longing for their company, their laughter, the chance to talk. What were they doing right now? What was Grace up to on this sudden and uncharacteristic holiday? She forced her thoughts back to herself.

'Right,' said Dorothy softly, opening her eyes. 'Now we can start.' She picked up the cards and handed them to Robin. 'Shuffle them, please, and while you do so, try to keep thinking what you want to find out.'

Robin was useless at shuffling the cards. They slipped and then clumped together, and as she fumbled with them she tried to gather her thoughts. Her scepticism and self-consciousness made it difficult to focus. She tapped the cards together and placed them back on the table in front of Dorothy, who deftly spread them face down on the velvet in a wide semicircle.

'Now, Robin, I need you to focus and suspend your disbelief for a while. I can read for three aspects of your life. What will you choose?'

Robin paused, embarrassed but intrigued. Dorothy seemed different, the brisk, busy shopkeeper had transformed into someone larger, more authoritative, the holder of mysterious knowledge and power. 'I'd like to know something about the present, what I'm doing now, like, what this retreat means for my life, where it's supposed to lead me,' she said. 'Then I'd like to know about a relationship. And, I suppose, last of all about work. I've moved out of something and don't know what to do next.'

'Okay, now you understand that the cards are not going to give you specific answers, they just throw light on the past and present – illuminate it, so to speak – and they can suggest, but not predict, the future.'

'Yes, I understand that.'

'Good. With your left hand pick ten cards, without looking at them, and put them face down in the middle of the table.'

Robin stretched out her left hand. What was she supposed to

do? Pick six in a row, or from different places? She wanted to make it look right for Dorothy, look as though she was trying. But as she reached out to touch a card she knew instinctively that it was the wrong one, and she withdrew her hand and paused until she was sure. She picked the first card from the other side of the circle, and the rest followed in natural, unforced progression.

Dorothy picked up the cards and laid them in a cross face up on the table, six on the vertical, the remaining four making the horizontal. 'Mmm,' she said, her hand on the quartz, her glasses perched halfway up her nose. 'This is a very interesting spread. Very interesting indeed.'

In over three months Robin had ventured only back and forth between the cottage and the town or along the cliff path for her daily runs. She had mapped out her own small territory with the cottage at its centre. Driving away from it made her uneasy. She paused at the junction with the main highway. She had planned to turn right and wander south down the coast but now she changed her mind and, without really knowing why, headed north. She would start with Busselton, buy some new running shoes, maybe a pair of shorts, and then head south on the inland road to Margaret River tonight, then maybe Nannup on Thursday, Pemberton on Friday.

Once on the highway her uneasiness began to lift, to be replaced by anticipation. She had all the time in the world, no one else to consider, total freedom to plan her journey, change it, abandon it, prolong it. Busselton was busy with morning shoppers. In the sports shop she bought a new pair of Reeboks and a couple of pairs of running shorts, and then, drawn by the smell of coffee in the mall, she drifted in to a small café and sat for a while at an outside table, sipping a café latte. Drifting was new to her. Before she left Perth she had always been heading from one destination to another. Time and solitude had worked their magic. She had learned to observe the changing elements, the twists of the wind in the trees, the shuffling clouds, the subtle shades of the light and the daily dramas of the sea. She had learned to live in the present. The race from A to B, the pressure of the next appointment, the next case, the next day or the next week had disappeared.

She wandered into a craft shop crammed with scented candles, herb-filled cushions and terracotta cherubs. Robin had never been an enthusiastic shopper. She bought what she needed and was willing to pay for quality, but she was not a browser or an impulse buyer. So back in the car she was surprised to find herself with six tablets of handmade lavender soap, an eye pillow which she was sure she would never use, several candles and a beautiful velvet patchwork cushion as a gift for Grace. She negotiated the traffic out of Busselton, turned south and drove slowly, determined to enjoy the journey. They had always planned to do this, she and Jim, wander around the southwest, visiting the galleries and wineries, buying pottery, walking in the karri forests and on the wild, lonely beaches. This was the trip they should have taken together. There ought to have been regrets, resentment and grief, but instead there was a peace borne of the melding of sadness and acceptance. The need to try to control what would happen, the longing for change and for resolution, had gone. Her preoccupation had always been with outcomes, but now she had a new awareness of process, a fascination with each new day and its value in the journey.

'I can recommend the bacon,' said the elderly priest sitting across the table. 'They get it sliced into very thin rashers and grill it until it's crispy. Not many places take so much care, and I can't stand thick, greasy bacon that tastes of pig. Father Patrick Shanahan, delighted to meet you.' He smiled and extended a hand.

'Robin Percy. I rarely eat meat but you make it sound very tempting.'

'Bacon here is a delicacy. I refuse to accept it as meat – it is in a food class of its own. I always stay here when I'm in the area. The ladies know how to look after their guests. Isn't that right, Dawn?' he said, smiling up at the woman who had materialised at his side with a coffee pot. 'I'm just telling Robin about the splendid service here.'

186

'You're a great advertisement for us, Father Pat,' she said. 'And we're always delighted to see you. Can I give you some fresh coffee?' The priest pushed his cup towards her and she filled it and left the pot beside him. 'Robin, good morning. Have you decided what you'd like for breakfast?'

'Father Patrick has convinced me about the bacon,' Robin said. 'With a poached egg and some wholemeal toast.'

Dawn had been working in the tiny office the previous evening when Robin appeared at the desk on the off-chance of finding a room for the night. 'You're in luck,' she said, untangling a strand of carrot-coloured hair from her huge turquoise and silver earrings. 'I've got one facing the lavender garden.'

Robin filled in the registration form and handed over her credit card. 'What a beautiful place,' she said, following Dawn through into the large ground-floor lounge of the A-frame building. The floor was scattered with rose and magenta kilims, and big cane chairs with cream cotton cushions were grouped around a huge fireplace where flames were just taking hold on some huge logs.

'Thanks. We like it,' Dawn said. 'We're still lighting the fire for the evenings. The spring days are lovely, but it gets a bit cold in here when the sun's gone.'

At the end of the room an open wooden staircase led up to a central landing with what appeared to be a gallery of rooms on either side. 'The breakfast room's through there,' Dawn said, pointing beyond the staircase. 'We serve breakfast between seven and ten. I'm afraid we don't do any other meals but, as you'll see, there's a kitchen up here for guests – fridge, microwave, a kettle and other bits and pieces, so you can heat something if you want.'

Robin's room was at the end of the building and the slope of the A-frame gave it an attic feel. A white quilt patterned with sprigs of green ivy covered the bed and alongside it was a small night table with an old oil lamp converted to electricity. In the corner stood a writing table and chair. Dawn opened a door to show her the bathroom and explained the hot water system.

'Here for the anniversary?' Dawn asked, handing Robin her room key.

'Anniversary?'

'The town's anniversary, day after tomorrow. The premier's coming to open a new bush trail and launch the forests policy. Some of the media people have been arriving today, and there's a whole contingent of protesters about the forests plan. You're lucky we've got a room. I only got the cancellation about an hour ago.'

Robin shrugged. 'I didn't realise. I'm just taking a bit of a tour of the southwest and I thought I'd take a look around Pemberton. It's years since I was here.'

Dawn laughed. 'You picked the wrong weekend! It'll be crowded.'

'I want to take a ride on that little steam train, the one that goes up into the forest. Does it still run?'

'From the old station.' Dawn nodded. 'I'll find you a leaflet on it. Now, do you have everything you need?'

The breakfast room was long and narrow with a rectangular table down the centre and upholstered benches on either side. Robin had been for her run, had a shower and glanced through the paper. It was nine-thirty and most of the guests appeared to have finished their breakfast and left by the time she made her way to the table.

'I'm here to do the blessing tomorrow,' Father Patrick explained. 'The bishop has honoured me with the task of standing in for him to bless the new forest trail; it comes after the opening and the policy speech. I sneaked in an extra day because I like staying here. And you – from the media or part of the official party?'

'Neither, I'm afraid. A tourist – but a local one.'

'Smells like your bacon is on its way,' he whispered conspiratorially. 'Now just you see if this isn't the best you've ever eaten.'

The kitchen door swung open and a small woman in chef's whites backed out with a steaming plate in one hand and a rack of toast in the other.

Robin drew in her breath in surprise. 'Josie Fletcher!'

'Well, Jesus, Mary and Joseph, it's Robin Percy,' Josie said. 'Oh for chrissakes, Father Pat, I'm sorry –'

'Seems like you two know each other,' the priest said with a smile. 'Don't worry, Josie, if the Lord can handle your language, I'm sure I can.'

'Josie, it's years – ten years at least. How are you? You look splendid.'

'Robin, Jesus, Robin, it's great to see you. Here, sit down, have your breakfast. I'll come and join you. I've finished the breakfasts now.'

She sat down, wiping her hands on the tea towel that was tucked into her belt. 'This woman saved my life, Father Pat. Y'know when I came to your parish to do my community service, I told you I would've gone to jail if it hadn't been for my lawyer? This is her! The woman who got me a deal to do rehab and community service instead of prison.' She turned back to Robin. 'Y'know, you saved my life, and then Father Pat saved my soul. I did my community service cooking meals for the old blokes who came to the church flophouse. Without you two I'd have had a couple of years in prison and then been out on the streets, back on the game and the drugs again. It's so good to see you.'

'You'd have beaten it in the end, Josie,' Robin said, starting on her breakfast. 'You're a fighter – you weren't ready to slide down that last slope. But what are you doing here? Apart from cooking bacon to die for – you were right, Father.'

'I'm a part-owner, Robin. And not through immoral earnings or drug dealing. Dawn! Dawnie, have you got a minute?' she called. And Dawn strolled in from the direction of the office. 'This is my partner, Dawn Lockyer. I gave up bad men and fell in love with a good woman. Remember that lawyer I told you about, darl? This is her, Robin Percy.'

Dawn joined them at the table and Robin glanced at Father Pat. He raised his eyebrows and grinned. 'I know, I know, not respectable company for a priest, but I'm here to save their souls – the bacon has nothing at all to do with it. You see, I even have to take responsibility for introducing them.'

Josie laughed and punched him on the upper arm. 'You love it, Father Pat, you know you do. Two hundred hours of community service and he had me enrolled in the flock.'

'You, Josie,' Robin spluttered, nearly choking on a piece of toast. 'You became a Catholic?'

Josie smiled proudly. 'A fully paid-up member, so to speak. Well, goodness, what would you expect? It had to be something dramatic to turn me around.'

Robin turned to Dawn, who was sitting back in her chair twisting the fringe on her crimson shawl. 'And Dawn?'

'Well, I like to think I saved Josie's heart,' she said slowly. 'But she and Father Pat haven't yet succeeded in saving my soul.'

'Not for lack of trying, I might say.' Father Pat laughed. 'Josie was a pushover. Dawn's proving rather intransigent!'

'It's eleven years, you know, Robin,' Josie said. 'I've grown up a bit since then.'

'You still look about sixteen. The hair's great – makes you look even younger.'

Josie gave a noisy hoot of laughter and ran her hand through her spiked, bleached hair. 'I'll be forty in a couple of months.'

'Sickening, isn't it?' said Dawn, looking affectionately at Josie before turning to Robin. 'All that shit she did to herself, the drugs, the tricks, she should have terrible skin, bad teeth, bloodshot eyes, and be overweight. You'd think she'd at least have the decency to look a little puffy. She's got no right to look like that.'

'I've got good genes,' Josie said, 'like Joan Collins. I read it in *New Idea*.'

Dawn and Robin exchanged glances and Robin rolled her eyes. 'Joan Collins also gets her photos taken in soft focus and probably spends a thousand bucks a week on beauty treatments,' Dawn said.

'Too right!' said Robin. 'Which reminds me, is it likely I could get a massage here today – before I move on – at such short notice? It's months since I had one.'

'Camilla!' said Dawn, and Josie nodded vigorously. 'A friend, the other end of town. The best massage in the southwest. Want me to call her for you?'

'Please! Later this morning would be great, then I can get in a train ride and get going this afternoon.'

'But you can't leave so soon,' Josie cried as Dawn walked out to the office. 'Can't you stay a bit longer?'

Robin hesitated. She had felt the old pressure to move on. 'Well . . . I was going to head on down to Albany.'

'Can't you delay that a bit? Stay another night. I want to find out what you're doing. How come this hotshot lawyer is trailing round the southwest on her own?'

'But the room . . .'

'That was a cancellation. It's free till Sunday. You can stay a couple more nights if you want.'

'Camilla can do an hour and a half but not until four o'clock,' Dawn said, standing in the doorway, phone in hand.

'There you are!' Josie smiled. 'You have to stay. Can't start off on that drive at that time of day, specially not after a massage!'

Robin nodded agreement to Dawn. Father Pat folded his napkin and stood up. 'Ah, the pleasures of the flesh. Time I was away, ladies, excuse me. I have a meeting with my Anglican colleague down at the church. But could I invite you all to have dinner with me tonight?' He looked at Robin. 'They do a very good meal at the pub, but I'll need to book a table as the whole world is in town.'

Father Pat was right again. The bar was crammed with locals, tourists and media people, and they had to push their way through the crowd to get to the restaurant. The political affairs reporter from *The West Australian* waved to Robin above the crowd. He lifted his glass to her, his expression forming a question mark. She smiled, shaking her head, indicating that she was with friends. He gave her a thumbs-up and turned back to his conversation. Then she felt a hand on her shoulder. 'Robin Percy! What're you doing here?'

She didn't recognise him immediately, and grappled for his name. 'John Jackson,' he said, 'ABC Radio. We met at Isabel's place, and at the law courts a few times.'

She apologised, remembering that he had been a court reporter before moving to the political round. The others were already at the table and, as she slipped into her seat, Robin thought how nice it would be to be alone in her room with a book. She was thrilled to see Josie with a new life, a business and with Dawn. But she had lost the habit of being with people every day, and the company and constant conversation had exhausted her. Josie had decided to join Robin on the train ride through the forest, so what might have been a reflective interlude was a noisy, energetic three hours of conversation and reminiscence. Robin had intended to say as little as possible about her private life, but Josie's openness had loosened her reserve. She ended up describing her retreat to the south coast, right back to Isabel's decision to go to Europe, and Sally to California.

'And your other friend?' Josie persisted as the little train clattered and clanged through the narrow tunnel of branches that overhung the line. 'Grace, is it? Did she do it too?'

Robin shook her head. 'I'm not sure what's happening with Grace. She was very hostile to the whole idea at first but she had softened up by the time I left. I got a letter from her about a month ago. She seems to have gone on a longish holiday to England. Most unlike her, so perhaps the whole idea got through to her just a little.'

Josie was delighted. 'You have to tell Dawn about this,' she insisted, ducking her head to avoid a branch that pushed through the open side of the train. 'It's a bit like what she's done. She's older than me you know, ten years. Used to be a real estate agent, but her marriage broke up. Around the time we met, her kids had left home and she'd made up her mind to get out of the business and disappear into the countryside.'

'And so you disappeared with her?'

'More or less. It took a bit of time. You see, we were friends first, and neither of us had ever dreamed we'd have a relationship with another woman, although I was attracted the first time I saw her. I didn't know it was the same for her. I thought it was just me going through some funny phase and I'd get over it, so I was pushing it away all the time. Then we went out with a crowd of friends one night and everyone went back to Dawn's place for coffee, and when all the others had left I was still there and – well, to cut a long and intimate story short, we realised we both felt the same.'

'And you never looked back!'

'Not for one single moment,' Josie said in a tone suddenly loaded with emotion. 'Every day I wake up and thank God for having Dawn in my life.' She swallowed and looked out the window. 'So you see,' she said, bouncing back into her usual ebullience. 'It's the perfect marriage – respectable middle-class divorcee and disreputable Irish hooker elope to the southwest forests.'

'With the blessing of the church, no less!' Robin smiled.

Josie sighed. 'Well, with the blessing of one friendly priest, at least. Dear old Father Pat, we don't see a lot of him but he's like part of the family. I told you, he was the priest in charge of the parish when I did my community service. But he upset some of the less enlightened stalwarts of the parish with his tolerance of various dropouts like me, and he was pretty vocal in support of gay Catholics. So it all got a bit difficult and the bishop moved him on. The bishop is actually quite tolerant himself, so he made Father Pat into his travelling diplomat. Sends him off to sort out problems and to fill in at various functions, hence the blessing of the trail.'

They had got out of the train at the turning point and wandered, with the meandering trail of other visitors, down the steep path to a clearing where the river boiled and churned over a steep fall of rock. 'So now,' said Josie, crouching at the water's edge and trailing her fingers in the sparkling river, 'you have to tell me your darkest secrets too.'

'I told you.' Robin grinned, avoiding eye contact. 'The retreat is my dark secret.'

'Not good enough! There's more. There has to have been more than three terrific women friends and the law.'

The silence hung between them while sightseers wandered around taking photographs and struggling to keep their children from attempting to paddle in the treacherous surge of the river. 'Sorry,' said Josie, standing up. 'I shouldn't be so pushy.' She dried her hands on the seat of her jeans.

'No, it's okay,' Robin said. 'It's just that it's difficult, not something I can really talk about. There was someone . . . still is, but . . .'

'Married?'

Robin nodded. 'Married, high profile, teenage kids. And that's part of what I'm working out by being here. It's not the reason for making this retreat, but it is a major thing I have to sort out for myself in the process.'

The hoot of the train siren called them back on board and they rattled down into town. Robin drove Josie back to the guesthouse and then took a stroll around the town before following Dawn's instructions for getting to Camilla's house for her massage.

'The local trout is usually good,' said Father Pat as they examined the menu that evening in the pub restaurant. 'You see, Robin, I find my way around the state by the gastronomic signposts! Only trouble here is, the portions are usually too large.'

'Absolutely,' said Robin. 'Portions everywhere are too large for me. How do you feel about sharing?'

They ended up ordering two portions of grilled trout between the four of them, and supplementing them with a large mixed salad and French fries.

'We should have a toast,' said Father Pat, who had ordered a local chenin blanc and filled their glasses. 'To old friends and chance encounters.'

'To old friends and chance encounters,' they chorused, and started on the food.

'You know,' said Robin, helping herself to salad, 'this is so strange. I was told that I was due for a chance encounter.'

'Who by?' Dawn asked.

'Before I left on this trip a friend read the tarot cards –'

Josie, who had just swallowed some wine, almost choked. 'You had someone read the cards? Ms Rationality herself consulting the tarot?'

'Not really,' Robin said, blushing. 'Never before, in fact. It was just that I was talking to this woman and she offered, and so I went along with it.'

'Wonders will never cease. So what did she say?'

'Actually, she made a lot of sense, about quite a few things,'

Robin said. 'But just at the end she said something about there being a chance encounter and she wasn't quite sure, but she said I should take care.'

'Good advice considering the company you've fallen into,' Father Pat said.

'As a matter of fact, the chance encounter she said I needed to be strong for was with a man.'

'Ha! She meant you, Father Pat.' Josie laughed. 'They're even issuing warnings about you now!'

'I love the tarot,' said Dawn. 'It's the way it makes you think about things in different ways. I mean, I know it's only what you choose to make it but I've often found it helped me to clarify things. Could you pass the wine, please, Robin.'

It was as she leaned across to hand Dawn the bottle that Robin glanced up and found herself looking straight at Jim, who was heading into the restaurant with Monica and another couple. Robin froze as Dawn took the bottle from her hand. She saw the shock and indecision on Jim's face as his eyes met hers, the slow turn of Monica's head and her instant recognition. It all seemed to happen in slow motion. She saw John Jackson watching with obvious interest, and the guy from *The West Australian* raising his eyebrows.

At that moment Robin realised that Monica knew. They had run into each other in a restaurant or at a function before. Jim would stop to speak to her, and she and Monica would exchange a polite greeting. This time it was different. Monica, her hand on Jim's arm, turned to the table they were being shown to and paused to choose a seat that would place her with her back to Robin. Jim's eyes flickered warily and he gave Robin a polite but almost imperceptible nod of recognition. She stared down at her plate feeling physically sick. They were accustomed to maintaining distance; she didn't want him to come to the table, but the fact that he had not, and the look on Monica's face, spoke volumes.

'You okay, Robin?' Josie asked. 'You're looking a bit flushed.'

'Must be the wine.'

'You've hardly tasted it,' said Dawn.

195

They were still trying to sort out the seating at Jim's table as she took deep breaths to calm herself. She would just have to sit it out, she thought, thankful that they would not actually have to meet and speak. But it was not going to be so easy. As Jim moved around the table he and Father Pat saw each other, and Father Pat raised his hand in greeting and beckoned him over. Jim hesitated and then, excusing himself from his party, he walked across the room.

Father Pat stood up, holding his napkin, hand outstretched. 'Your Honour,' he laughed. 'Good to see you, Jim, it's been a long time.'

'Your Holiness! How are you? I heard you'd be acting bishop this weekend.'

'You're here for the celebrations tomorrow, Jim?'

'We ... I am,' Jim said, looking carefully at Robin. 'The premier's opening the trail and launching the policy. I'm unveiling the plaque at the courthouse.'

'Let me introduce you to my companions,' said Father Pat, turning back to the table. 'This is Justice Jim McEwan. Josie Fletcher and Dawn Lockyer, who run the Lavender Hill Guest House, which you are sadly missing out on by staying at some fancy hotel. And Josie's friend Robin Percy.'

Jim smiled and shook hands with Josie and Dawn. 'Robin and I know each other already,' he said, looking straight at her. 'Haven't seen you around for some time, Robin.'

She looked up, trying to keep her voice steady. 'I'm taking a bit of time off,' she said.

'Not everyone wants to spend their life in a courtroom, in a funny wig,' said Father Pat, suddenly seeming flustered and trying to cover it.

'Indeed not. And you'll have your best dress on tomorrow, I hope. The little white and gold number?'

'I certainly shall,' said Father Pat, looking increasingly uncomfortable. 'Well, this is a nice surprise.'

'Yes, but I mustn't keep you from your meal.'

'No, no,' said Father Pat with some relief. 'You must get back to your friends. Good to see you, Jim.'

At the end of the restaurant the small bush band suddenly struck up 'Click Go the Shears' and Jim, ostensibly giving the band his full attention, made his way back to his table.

'A judge, eh?' said Josie, helping herself to the last few fries. 'You two have friends in high places.'

'Yes,' said Robin and Father Pat in unison, and as she met his eyes across the table, Robin saw that he knew exactly what the score was. She stumbled on through the rest of the meal, the plates were cleared, desserts refused and coffee ordered. The added noise of the band, and a few people who had decided to turn the minute uncarpeted space in front of it into a dance floor, helped to mask her discomfort.

Josie, resplendent in tight black jeans and T-shirt, a black leather belt with studs, her platinum spikes shining under the warm lights, was trying to urge Dawn to dance. 'C'mon, darl, when do we ever get the chance?' she pleaded. And Dawn shrugged off her fringed shawl and stepped onto the floor with her, like a redheaded gipsy in her black T-shirt and scarlet skirt.

Alone at the table with Father Pat, Robin felt her embarrassment mounting and started to shred a paper napkin between her fingers until the priest's hand settled on hers to still it. 'I'm sorry, Robin. That was my fault.'

She looked at him in surprise.

'I beckoned Jim over, I didn't realise . . .'

'How did you know?' she asked, swallowing hard.

'I've known Jim for years. We've served on committees together, we're both members of the Irish Club. I'd heard the talk about him and a prominent lawyer. Frankly, I'd forgotten the name until I went to introduce you to him.'

She leaned back in her chair sighing. 'I've taken time out,' she said. 'But I suspect that tonight is an indication that things have changed for him in my absence.'

'Would you like to leave?' Father Pat asked. 'We could walk back to the guesthouse together and leave the girls to their dancing.'

'I was thinking of going –' she said.

'It's best if we go together. They'll worry about you walking home alone. I'll let Josie know.' He edged his way through the

197

dancers and spoke to Dawn and Josie, who turned to her and waved goodnight and went on with their dancing.

Robin took her jacket from the back of her chair and walked with him to the bar, deliberately avoiding eye contact with John Jackson while she waited for Father Pat to pay the bill.

'You must find this very difficult,' she said as they walked side by side up the hill in the clear, cool moonlight.

'Why is that?'

'You must disapprove of me . . . the other woman . . . breaking up the good Catholic marriage.'

'Aha! I see! I should have a scarlet letter 'A' tattooed across your forehead, and then start the stoning. Breaking up a good Catholic marriage, is that how you see it?'

'It's how I think others would see it,' Robin said. 'I suppose it would have been easier if Jim weren't so well known, and if Perth weren't such a small, parochial city. I'm starting to realise how naive I was, thinking we had kept it quiet. My friends all seemed to know, you knew, and in the pub there were a couple of reporters . . .'

'I doubt that it's ever easy,' said Father Pat, gazing up at the perfectly clear sky to locate the Southern Cross. 'Every community is small in some way, especially when it comes to extramarital affairs.'

'I thought you'd be giving me a sermon on the way home.'

'Is that what you'd like? Would it help to assuage your guilt?'

'You think I should feel guilty?' she snapped.

'I think you *do* feel guilty, that's different.'

'I should roll up to your confessional and you could tell me to say three Hail Marys, give me absolution and tell me to go forth and sin no more.'

His laughter rang sharply in the still air. 'Dear me, how very old-fashioned and cynical you are, Robin. I think nothing of the sort.'

'I'm sorry,' she said. 'That was very rude of me.' She jumped as a rabbit darted from the scrub across the path in front of them.

'There's so many of them these days,' Father Pat said.

'Extramarital affairs?'

'Rabbits.'

They walked on in silence.

'So what are *you* thinking about all this, then?' she asked as they reached the door of the guesthouse.

Father Pat turned from trying to fit his key into the look and looked at her. 'My dear Robin,' he said, leaning back against the door. 'I think the world is full of basically good men and women who find themselves in exceedingly complex situations, of which this is one. You're projecting your assessment of the situation onto me. Your dilemma is nothing to do with what I may or may not think.'

'What do you mean?'

He unlocked the door and turned back to her. 'I mean, Robin, that there are many ways of living a life of integrity, and they do not necessarily fit into neat categories. The determining factor, surely, is where we feel our own integrity lies.'

FOURTEEN

Isabel stood in line at the post office waiting to collect her mail. There were still three people in front of her and the clerk was moving increasingly slowly as the minutes of the hot September afternoon ticked away. At last the American backpacker at the desk retrieved his letters and the queue moved up. The Alicante post office was in a narrow street of tall buildings a couple of blocks back from the spectacular Ramblas, and just a few minutes' walk from the small hotel where she had been staying for the last three weeks. Isabel pushed damp strands of hair back from her forehead and craned her neck to see over the shoulder of the man in front of her. The desk clerk was checking every conceivable piece of identification belonging to a young woman who spoke rapidly to him in Spanish and rapped the desk angrily with her fist. The clerk's pace did not change. Isabel checked for the third time that she had her passport and international driver's licence. Her irritation was mounting. Doug had told her on the phone that he needed her signature on some papers for the bank. He would mail them to her and she should sign them and send them straight back. The post office arrangement had seemed a safer solution than sending them to the cosy but chaotic hotel, where everything seemed to happen by accident rather than design. The woman moved away from the desk and the man in front of Isabel stepped swiftly forward, slamming his passport onto the counter.

Isabel breathed a sigh of relief and moved up, her turn next, and now there were five people behind her. Overhead a dark wooden fan clunked rhythmically as it moved the heavy air around, and outside a couple of bare-chested young men in shorts, boots and hard hats started up a drill to cut through the concrete paving. She had been waiting for almost twenty minutes and was longing to be outside again, sitting at a café on the esplanade to catch the cool breeze from the sea. The old gentleman wandered away from the desk clutching a parcel and muttering under his breath and Isabel was at the counter in seconds, pushing her passport towards the silent young man behind the glass screen. 'There should be one large package,' she said carefully.

'*Qué?*'

'*Uno!*' she said, holding up one finger. '*Carta.*' She mimed opening an envelope.

'*Sí, sí, señora – una carta. Un momento, por favor.*' He noted down the details from her passport and then gave her a form to complete with the details of her address in Alicante, while he searched the pigeonholes and returned with Doug's package and another letter.

'*Señora Carter, dos cartas!* Two letters,' he said with the flicker of a lazy smile. 'Sign here, please.'

She signed and picked up Doug's heavy padded envelope, gazing inquisitively at the second, unable to recognise the stamp or the handwriting. She moved away from the counter, rummaging for her glasses, and stopped by the door to put them on. It was a Portuguese stamp. Her stomach lurched at the prospect of a letter from Antonia, but the postmark was Cascais, and the sender's name on the back of the envelope was Sara Oakwood. The instant of excitement had been too fleeting for her to feel any great sense of disappointment. She had not heard from Antonia since she left Monsaraz two months earlier.

Isabel smiled to herself at the thought of a letter from Sara and, putting away her glasses, she walked thankfully out of the post office and headed for her favourite café. The streets were stirring to life after siesta as she strolled over the cream and maroon tiles set alternately in sweeping waves between the palms. She loved this street – it was what had made her decide to stay in Alicante for a few weeks before heading north up the Mediterranean coast. She was tired of moving around and needed to stop, to be somewhere impersonal, somewhere only pleasantries between guest and hotel staff were required.

After leaving Lisbon at the beginning of August she had spent a week in Madrid and then made her way south by train to Córdoba, Seville and across to Granada. She was enchanted by the mystery and beauty of southern Spain, and fascinated by its history. In each place she found accommodation with women in the network, the basic two nights with some, a week or more with others. In Córdoba, Rafaela, a retired teacher in her late seventies who had had a wartime fling with an Australian soldier, had been thrilled to have an Australian in her home. Isabel had stayed there for three weeks until Rafaela's son arrived on a visit from Barcelona and needed the room. The Australian boyfriend had been a Perth boy and it hadn't been difficult for Isabel to persuade Rafaela that it was not too late in life for her to make a trip to Australia and see his home town. Rafaela agreed. She would come, she said, when Isabel was home again and had recovered from her travels.

In Seville and Granada and places in between she had stayed in other homes, exploring the cities and villages and reading about their history. It was after her first two nights in Alicante that she felt the need to stop moving for a while and to be somewhere free of the intensity and intimacy of staying in private homes. She found a small fourth-floor room with a bathroom in an old-fashioned family hotel where they gave her a weekly rate that seemed almost too good to be true. Two weeks later she had called home and Doug asked her to stay on for a few days so he could express mail the papers to her. Now she was restless, ready to move on, for she had identified the strange niggling feeling that had followed her since she left Madrid. Eunice's life in Europe had suddenly taken on a higher priority. She was still wishing she had made time to go through Eunice's things before she left, but she would get some of those letters and diaries now if Doug kept the promise he had grudgingly made over the phone.

'Where d'you think you'll be at Christmas?' he had asked, and she told him she was aiming for Germany. 'I could get a couple of weeks off at the beginning of January. It's usually a quiet time. You said I was allowed one visit.'

'You make it sound like prison,' Isabel had laughed.

'Sorry! Not at all. You'd be surprised how well I'm managing. I'm very self-sufficient these days. But you did promise . . .'

'Yes,' she said. 'Of course, it would be lovely to meet in Germany.'

'We could spend New Year together. I think I should stay here at Christmas. For the family, I mean, keep it all going as normal.'

Isabel felt a burst of affection for his stoic adherence to the way things had always been done. 'Are you planning to cook Christmas dinner, darling?'

'Hey, steady on! I'm not that domesticated. No, I thought Mum would come and do it and we could all have Christmas here, same as usual, except that you wouldn't be there, of course. So it won't be the same unless . . . well, unless you thought about coming back early . . .'

'No!' she said, almost too quickly. 'No, I won't be back early. You come to Germany in January, it would be lovely to have New Year together. I'm aiming for Nuremberg and you'll fly in to Frankfurt. I'd like you to meet Klaus, I know you and he will get along.'

'That's the fellow you met in Portugal?'

'Yes.'

'Okay. Well, I'll get on to Qantas and see what the flights are like. I'll do it this week, it's bound to be busy then. And you'll stay on in Alicante until these papers arrive?'

'Yes, of course. Oh, and Doug, could you have a look in that box of Mum's old letters and stuff. It's in the cupboard under the stairs. I'd like you to send me some things.'

He let out the familiar sigh he always gave when she asked him to do something he found tedious. It was a little-boy trick designed to make her withdraw the request. Isabel didn't withdraw it, she ignored the sigh, noticing how much easier it was to ignore it over the phone than face to face.

'The box is easy to find, it's right near the front.'

'You don't want all of it, surely!'

'No, of course not, just anything that relates to the south of France, Paris, Germany and Lisbon. Places I'm planning to go to.'

'But you've already been to Lisbon.'

'Yes,' she said, 'but I'll go back, I think – not till after you've gone, but I will.'

'Why? What's in Lisbon? Some cute Portuguese toyboy?' There was an edge to his voice but she wasn't sure what it was. Not jealousy, but perhaps fear of not being part of her plans?

'Not just one, darling, a whole bevy of them. Seriously, I loved it and it feels unfinished for me, I want to go back.'

'Oh well, you know best, but it seems a bit of a waste to go back. You could go somewhere else instead, or come home sooner.'

She ignored it. 'So you'll find those things for me? Letters, postcards – anything about those places – and send them with the papers?'

'Why don't I get Deb to sort them out for you and I'll bring them in December?'

'Look, Doug, I want them before then. It won't take long.'

'But I want to get these papers off to you tomorrow.'

She took a deep breath. 'I'm asking you to do something that will take an hour at the most. The stuff is in quite good order. And it will need a rather larger package than you were going to send. Surely you could find time to do that for me.'

'Okay, okay, she who must be obeyed has spoken. I'll get right onto it.' His tone was curt now. He hated inconvenience, hated having to do for himself the things she or his secretary usually did for him, hated the service tasks of other peoples' lives. For so long it had seemed natural to her, now it irritated her.

'Thanks, darling.'

'Yeah-yeah.'

There was an awkward silence. 'Well,' she said, 'I must be running out of time on this phone card. How about I call again when I've put the papers in the mail?'

'Yes, please do. And I better get a move on. I'm off to Deb's for a meal.'

204

'Okay, give them all my love.'

'Of course.'

'Bye then. Love you.'

'Yes, you too – bye. Let me know when you've mailed back the papers.'

She sat in a cane chair outside the café, ordered a cappuccino and tore open the bulky padded envelope. The sheaf of papers from the bank were stapled together and her mother's things had been carefully wrapped in a piece of calico and tied with tape. A small sealed envelope was tucked under the knot. She was impressed – how did he know to wrap the letters in cloth not plastic? He really could be so sweet and thoughtful when he tried. He must have sorted them out the same evening of their telephone conversation, for the package had been posted the following day. She glanced at the bank papers first, and the yellow Post-it note on the first page.

Izzy

Make sure you read this lot through and feel happy about it.

Then sign and date in the places marked. You'll need to get the signatures witnessed.

Whiz it back soon as poss and give me a ring to let me know.

Ta and love
Doug

She put the papers back into the manila envelope and turned to the package, smiling with affection at the image of him wrapping her mother's papers. She slipped out the small envelope and opened it.

Hi Mum

Wonder where you'll be when you read this. Dad's been fussing around over this stuff of Grandma's. He brought the box over when he came for dinner last night and asked me to sort out the things you wanted. He's left the bank papers with me to send to you as well.

I hope this is what you need. Isn't it fascinating! I could have spent hours on it. I never knew you had all this. I hope you won't mind but I'm going to hang on to the box and have a look at some more of it. I'll be really careful. I loved the old programs from Grandma's dancing days. All my life I saw her in the wheelchair so the dancing was never quite real, but now there are the programs and pictures and things. It brought me out in goose bumps.

I think I can organise it a bit better. I know you said one should never keep old papers or fabrics in plastic, so I'll wrap them all in cloth like this one. Hope you have a fab time going to those places, you are soooooo lucky. Still, you deserve it if anyone does. Everything's fine here. We all miss you, of course. Honestly, isn't Dad hopeless!! I can't believe it, he's got us all running round after him, me, Mac, Luke, Nana and Grandad Carter, AND did you know he's got someone in to clean once a week! Lucky old Kate being in Sydney, but now he's got her on the run too, looking for flights to Germany on the Internet. I mean, he's the CEO of a huge government department and he can't even organise his own life. I think it's a learned helplessness, though, so it's good he's had a chance to notice what's normally done for him. Of course, if we had any sense we'd all tell him to get on with it but he's so lovely we all get sucked in!

Luke has a gorgeous new girlfriend – her name is Cecilia and is she exotic! He's such a dag, how does he get these amazing women? She's really nice too. I know he's emailing you from time to time so you'll have his news.

Thanks for your lovely letters. Have I grovelled enough about my appalling behaviour before you left? Just in case, I'll say it one more time – I'm really, really sorry for being such a selfish brat (if one can be a brat past thirty), I was just scared of you going away and everything changing. Mac and the kids are fine, Danny and Ruth have started kindy two mornings a

*week and love it – thank goodness, I was dreading it. They've
done these paintings for you – something else for you to carry
around! Hope your new streamlined travelling self is surviving
the journeys. I loved the pictures you sent – your new hairdo
looks great and you look so much YOUNGER!*

*Everyone here sends their love, specially me – and I send
heaps. I miss you.*

Deb

*PS Ran into Denise (Grace's sec) last week. She says Grace
hasn't phoned the office once since the first day she arrived in
England! Just sent a couple of postcards and one – only ONE
– email about work!!*

Isabel smiled to herself at the postscript. Dear Grace – so she
really had taken the plunge. In Cascais she had got a letter from
Grace posted in Australia before she left for the quilt retreat, and
later, while she was in Córdoba, Sara had forwarded a card that
Grace had posted on her arrival in England. Since then it seemed
Grace was very busy enjoying her own adventure. Isabel
wondered briefly how Sally was getting on in San Francisco.
Robin had emailed with more information about her retreat to the
southwest, and said she had had an aerogram from Sally, who
seemed to be having fun, loving California and enjoying the
course. No word, though, of the friend she had hoped to find.

Isabel stroked the calico wrapping of her mother's papers and
sipped her coffee. So Doug had got Deb to organise the package,
and he had everyone else looking after him, including someone to
do the housework. She felt strangely ambivalent. Her love for him
was as solid as ever, but she was irked by his manner. 'Learned
helplessness' was a good description, and she knew she was the
one who had taught him, encouraged it over more than three
decades. He was a wonderful husband and father, but she sensed
that in leaving she had let go of the part of herself that always put
the needs of Doug and the children first. Kate, Luke and Deb were
obviously adapting to the change but it seemed Doug was playing

the same old role, even though she was gone. She sighed and slipped his papers and the calico package back into the envelope. A strong breeze was whipping in from the sea. She would open her mother's things back at the hotel.

She picked up Sara's envelope and tore open the flap, taking out a one-page note wrapped around another envelope.

Dear Isabel

Hope you are fine and still travelling light! Remember, backpack and one small grip – don't break the rules or you'll regret it. So glad you liked Córdoba. I adore it, and Rafaela – what a character.

Speaking of characters, I got a call from Antonia Peralta. She was in Lisbon last week and rang to know if you were here. When I said I didn't know where you were she asked me to forward a letter when I heard from you. So I met her in Lisbon, we had a lovely lunch at a café in the Baxia. What a stunning woman. She seemed really keen to get this letter to you, so when I got home I rang your husband in Oz. He said you'd be in Alicante for another week or two.

My sister's on her way out here for a couple of weeks from her ghastly job in Manchester, I'm so looking forward to seeing her.

Let me know how you're going and if you really do plan to come back again in the new year.

All good wishes and love
Sara

Isabel stared at the long cream envelope with her name on the front written in Antonia's controlled and distinctive script, and took several deep breaths. She turned the envelope over slowly trying to anticipate what it might contain, but was too shaken by its presence to think straight. She had left Portugal with the heavy ache of longing that she had felt since the moment in the Évora cloisters, and the emotional chaos that it sparked for her. In the intervening weeks she had managed to let some of it go, along with her confusion at the strength of her attraction to another woman, and Antonia's enigmatic reaction. But she still felt that something precious had slipped away from her.

She slit open the envelope and took out a sheet of cream notepaper and an old, slightly discoloured theatre program.

My dear Isabel

I must first apologise for not responding sooner to your letter. I have been busy, but it was not only that. I have been coming to terms with a rather difficult personal crisis relating to the past, which arose during your visit, and it has devoured all my emotional and physical energy. Forgive me for being rather withdrawn, a fact I think you attributed to something you had done. Not at all. It was entirely my problem and I trust it did not spoil your last days in Monsaraz.

It was such a great joy to have you here as a guest. I hope that you will return as you suggested, before you go back to Australia. I should so much like to see you again. You mentioned that your mother was with Compagnie Fluide in the fifties, and as I sorted through some of my old personal papers I found this program, which I think you would like to have. It reminds me that I did in fact see your mother dance on a visit to Monaco, an occasion which, with the discovery of the program, I now remember quite clearly. She was a dancer of great grace and elegance. The night I saw her she was wearing a floating chiffon gown in eau de nil, and she took the audience by storm. I hope you will be happy to have this to add to your collected memories of your mother.

I have a letter from Klaus in which he mentions how much he looks forward to seeing you in Germany before too long.

For myself I look forward to your next visit to Monsaraz and I send you my warmest wishes for the remainder of your travels.

Antonia

Isabel's hands were trembling, her skin prickling, as she read the letter again with a mixture of fascination and disbelief. If Antonia had indeed been experiencing a personal crisis relating to the past, then why had it so instantly and dramatically changed things between them that day in the cloisters? And why had she refused to talk about it? And the program? When Isabel had mentioned Compagnie Fluide, Antonia had been abrupt, uninterested, yet now not only did she have a program for one of their performances, she could remember seeing Eunice dance and even what she had been wearing when she danced that night. Isabel turned to the fading gloss of the program, which was for a performance at the Théâtre des Beaux-Arts, Monaco, on 14 April 1953. Eunice's name as the soloist was on the front.

Isabel's heart beat faster as she turned back to the letter. Antonia was sixty-five now, which would have made her around twenty in 1953. Why did she have a theatre program for that year? None of it made sense. She was tempted to go straight to a phone booth, call Antonia and demand an explanation, but something warned her to hold back. She would spend a day or two looking through Eunice's letters and diaries before taking the bus north. She picked up her mail, paid for her coffee and made her way through the now busy streets to the hotel.

Back in her room she spread the papers in order across her bed and over the floor. Deb had organised them chronologically. There were letters from Eunice to her mother and father, and theirs to her. Among them were letters written in Isabel's own round, childish hand, and there were photographs they'd sent each other. Eunice in a ruched satin bathing costume on the beach in front of a hotel in Nice; rugged up with scarves and mittens against a background of snow; in a halter-necked evening dress leaning against Eric with a dangerously tilted champagne glass. Isabel recalled the long-forgotten thrill of their arrival in Australia and the time spent staring deeply into the tiny images of Eunice's face, waiting for it to deliver to her some tangible sense of the mother she could barely remember. And then there was Isabel herself playing under the hose in Grandpa Pearson's garden, sitting on the old hammock leaning shyly against her grandmother, embarrassed by the camera; dressed as an angel in the school nativity play, and standing bolt upright with pride displaying a cup and certificate won for swimming.

Isabel felt what she had not felt for so long, that complete sense of aloneness that she had known as a child. The feeling that she was waiting for the waiting to be over and to have her mother there, just like all the other girls, and her mother would be hers and hers alone. She sat cross-legged on the floor among the letters gazing at a picture of Eunice, laden with packages, outside a department store in Berlin, and remembered that there was a message on the back.

Darling Isabel

This is me shopping for your Christmas present. I wish I could be there when you open it but I know you'll have a lovely Christmas with Grandma and Grandad.

All my love, sweetness,
Mumma
2 December 1952

Isabel flicked away the tear that was threatening to drip onto the picture, remembering Christmas Day 1952 when she opened the card attached to her present and found the photograph inside. She stared at it now as she had stared at it then, recalling how carefully she had read the message aloud and asked, 'Will Mumma be back for next Christmas, Grandma?'

'Oh, baby, I'm sure she will. She promised. And you and she can go Christmas shopping together.'

'And will it be snowing like in Germany?'

'Not here,' Grandad laughed, stuffing tobacco into his pipe. 'Not in Australia, Izzy, you know it doesn't snow here, and it's always hot at Christmas.'

She had taken the card, the photograph and presents – a white blouse with big puffed sleeves, embroidered with little blue flowers, and a pink-cheeked doll with long fair plaits dressed in

German national costume – over to her favourite rose velvet chair. To the background of the voice of the new Queen coming from the radio she dreamed of Christmas shopping next year in a Perth that was strangely covered in snow and where children with sledges slithered happily back and forth across the pavements. But by the next Christmas, Eunice was married and recovering in a Monte Carlo hospital while Eric sat beside her reading her the cards and letters from home; and Isabel was opening another gift on the promise that Eunice and the new daddy really would be home in February.

She slipped the picture back into place and stared in frustration at Eunice's diary for 1953. The entries were scrappy but consistent, three or four brief entries a week, special performances, parties, trips along the coast, exhausting rehearsals, dreadful dressing rooms, appreciative audiences, and the search for new dance shoes. Piecing together the evidence, she discovered that the company had left Germany in January 1953 and after a short stay in Paris, where they had a two-week booking, they travelled on by rail to Nice for a long series of performances that would last until the latter part of the year. It was all there, the whole journey, the arrival, the problems with the hotel suites shared with other dancers, the glamour of the Riviera, meeting Eric at a cocktail party and falling in love, even the performance that matched Antonia's program, all tying in with the letters home from the time, but a month later there was nothing. From mid May the pages of the diary had been torn out leaving a gap until the beginning of October, and although the diary entries commenced once again on the Riviera, the letters from those missing months came from Lisbon.

Isabel sighed and slid her finger down the yellowing strip of Sellotape that had been used to secure the pages each side of the torn-out gap. Why had Eunice suddenly gone to Lisbon while the company stayed on in France? Why had she torn out the pages, and what about Eric? He was a feature of the narrative until the middle of May and then again in October, but there was no mention of him in the letters from Lisbon.

She picked up the theatre programs Deb had mailed and

found the twin of the one that Antonia had sent, the only difference being a seven-digit number pencilled onto the corner of Antonia's. Isabel began to gather up the papers. She was determined now; she would go straight on to the Riviera. She would take the bus up the Spanish coast and into France and stop there for a while. She rewrapped Eunice's papers in the calico and then sat at the table to read the papers from the bank, signed them and put them into the envelope. Then she went out into the cool evening and walked down to the bus terminal to find out the timetable of the buses travelling north.

As she sat on the bus the following day, gazing vaguely at the warm-toned buildings and purple bougainvillea starting to drop its blossom, the spooky feeling returned. What had happened to make Antonia suddenly remember so clearly that she had once seen Eunice dance? She was lying, or at least she was holding something back. What did she know about Eunice, and was it related in some way to the incident in the cloister? Isabel closed her eyes and leaned her head back against the seat. She would go to the theatre, the Théâtre des Beaux-Arts in Monaco, see what she could discover there. But it was probably a fool's errand. It was all so strange, so confusing – the gap in the diary, the program, Antonia. She was annoyed by it, frustrated by Antonia's duplicity. Probably the only way she would find out was by going back to Monsaraz. In the meantime, though, she felt herself hardening with a determination to get to the bottom of it.

FIFTEEN

The flat was on the top floor of a seven-storey building, three blocks back from the sea, on the border of Brighton and Hove. It had two bedrooms, a lounge, kitchen and bathroom, and everything one could possibly need in the way of kitchen utensils, towels and linen. The windows of the lounge and the main bedroom looked out to the sea, and off the bedroom there was a balcony large enough for a couple of canvas chairs. The lounge window took up the whole of the wall; Grace had learned not to look straight down at the sheer drop, which made her feel she might just walk through the window and fall off the building. She had moved the black wrought-iron dining table with the glass top across in front of the window to make it feel safe. Because the flat was on the top floor the view of the sea was unbroken. On clear, sunny days, even when the wind was cold, the flat was flooded with golden light and on wild, wet days, the wind whistled and roared around the building and the rain lashed horizontally against the windows. As it was England and early November, the latter weather was more common. It felt, she thought, rather like living at the top of a lighthouse.

Grace stood at the bedroom window looking out over the clay-tiled rooftops and windswept trees to the distant sea, barely visible through the haze of rain. What struck her, as she thought of the other members of the Gang of Four, was that three of them had all ended up near water. Sally's card told her she could see the San Francisco Bay, Robin could see the Indian Ocean and here she was looking out at the English Channel. Even Isabel's cards indicated that she had spent much of her time first on the Atlantic coast of Portugal and now by the Mediterranean. Grace had heard something once about water being healing, and she wondered if they had all unconsciously been driven to place themselves near large expanses of it.

There was a tap on her bedroom door and Orinda popped her head around it. 'I'm ready when you are, honey.'

Grace turned with a smile. 'Okay, I'm ready too. I wish you weren't going, I'm going to miss you so much.'

Orinda, wearing a white raincoat over a pair of navy trousers and a yellow jumper, perched on the edge of the bed. Her face seemed darker than ever above the white waterpoof mac. 'I'm gonna miss you too, Grace, but I gotta get back. I've already been here five weeks longer than I planned. And I can't stand any more of this English weather.'

Grace sat down beside her. 'I know, isn't it frightful! How do people manage to live here and be sane?'

'Well, they're not, are they?' Orinda grinned. 'They don't have to be sane. They're English, that's different, they get to be eccentric.'

Grace laughed and put her arm through Orinda's. 'It's been wonderful being with you. And with Vivienne. You two have been just what I needed.'

Orinda smiled and put her hand over Grace's, where it rested on her arm. 'Well, Grace, you can't have enjoyed it more than I have. Y'know, I meant to go straight home with the others after the quilt was done, but I stayed because I wanted to be with you folks. And it's been real good of you to let me stay here with you.'

'It's not going to be the same without you.'

'No, but you and Viv will still have a good time together. Y'know, she's waiting for me to go so she can get you in on this scheme of hers. Don't let her bully you, you gotta have a holiday.'

'I know, but I feel like a different person since I got here. Like I discovered a part of me that's been shut up for years.'

Orinda patted her hand. 'I know. It's so easy to get stuck in a rut, 'specially when it's a nice comfortable one. Promise me you'll keep singing?'

'I promise.'

'Promise me you're gonna come visit me in New Orleans? I'll take you down to the Three Coins Club and we'll sing together and wow 'em.'

'Just try and stop me.'

Orinda stood up. 'Well then, let's get going. I gotta plane to catch and you're my chauffeur.'

They hugged each other with tears in their eyes.

'Don't start crying yet,' said Orinda. 'We ain't even got to the airport. For a dame who hadn't cried for years, you sure got good at it now!'

Grace picked up Orinda's suitcase, opened the door, and they went out to the protected rear landing of the block and pressed the button for the lift. 'You take care of yourself, honey,' Orinda said to Grace with a final look back at the flat. 'Think about taking a bit more time away. Wouldn't do you any harm to stay on till the New Year.'

'I can't say it hasn't crossed my mind,' Grace said as the lift doors slid open.

Grace had to pull off the road three times driving back from Gatwick Airport because she couldn't stop crying. She cried almost every day now – Orinda was right, she surely had got good at it. Sometimes she would wake up crying without even knowing why, without even feeling sad. She would lie still in her bed letting the tears flow. 'Sometimes,' she had said to Vivienne, 'I feel that all this crying is healing me, isn't that stupid?'

Vivienne had let out a noisy hoot of laughter. 'Grace, it's not stupid at all, that is just what's happening. These are the tears that you haven't shed for decades, the ones you didn't shed when your mum died, when your husband got cancer and died, when your kids left home, when your granddaughter was born. They're the sadness and grief and joy tears. Of course they're healing. Honestly, Grace, for a really smart woman you some-times say the dumbest things.'

But the tears left her weak and exhausted. She couldn't believe how much she had slowed down. Back home she was always up between five and six, doing yoga, taking a shower, doing the housework, and after work she was out, having dinner with someone, going to a meeting, a concert or a movie, babysitting Emily. Even when she was at home she was reading minutes and agendas, position papers or reports, making notes, working out how to solve problems. But these days she made coffee in the small white kitchen and took it back to bed. There she'd sit, propped against the pillows with the curtains pulled back so she could see the sea and the weather, reading magazines, novels and short stories.

Sometimes it was ten o'clock before she got up and then she'd discover Orinda just emerging from the small second bedroom with her book, watching morning television in the lounge or writing a letter to her daughter in Oregon. It felt to Grace like the greatest luxury she had ever known, and as though, at present, she was incapable of doing anything else. She had lost interest in shopping and spent her energy instead on walks along the seafront, occasional sightseeing to Arundel or Chichester, a brief drive with Orinda to Vivienne's place for lunch or dinner. And there, with Vivienne at the piano, she and Orinda would sing their way through everything they knew, laughing and dancing until they were both exhausted. Then back home for more books, more tears, more sleep.

On the day she had decided not to fly to Japan, she had phoned Tim and told him she would be happy to help out, but not for a few more days. She would stay until the quilt was finished and then take a flight to Tokyo. It had taken a huge effort to overcome her guilt and indecision and make the call, but as she put down the receiver she felt overcome with anger and disappointment, anger that so much was always expected of her, disappointment that despite the fact that she was a mature single woman, she still felt trapped, still felt she had no freedom to do what she wanted. Later in the day, after contemplating her conversation with Vivienne, she called back and told them that she had changed her mind; she wanted to stay on in England. They would have to get some local help.

'But why?' Tim had asked, sounding hurt.

'Because I want to stay on here, do as I planned,' she'd said.

'We thought you'd love to come, and we really need you. I thought you'd want to see Em and help Angie a bit.'

'I would love to come, I'd love to see Em and help Angie, but it doesn't suit me to do it right now.'

'But we need you,' he said again, with just a hint of the wheedling ten-year-old asking her to wash the whole team's football gear.

'You need some help, darling,' Grace had said, and it had required an iron will to hold her ground. 'But, as you said, the company has offered to provide that. I know it's horrible for Angela, and awkward for you, but it's not as though she's seriously ill. The local help will probably be far more efficient than me.'

'Oh well, if you feel your holiday is more important –' he began.

'Actually, at the moment, Tim, that is exactly what I feel,' she cut in. They had hung up a few moments later, the tension humming down the line across the thousands of miles that separated them.

Well, Grace had thought, despite the fact that her whole body was shaking, that *is* what I feel – I was perfectly honest and Tim is just going to have to put up with it. And she had walked back into the conference room thinking about all the commitments that had seemed so intractable and important and now just seemed irritating.

'No good bitchin' about it,' Orinda had said to her a couple of weeks later when Grace started talking about how trapped she felt by all the things she'd have to return to. 'You set it up yourself, honey. Now you're the only one who can unpick it – it's like taking the papers outta the patchwork. Know what I mean? You make the templates, you stitch on the fabric, then you join all the pieces to make the quilt, but you can't move on to the quilting. The quilting is the best part because it gives the quilt texture, fullness, character. But you can't do it until you unpick the first part you set up; you gotta take out the tacking and remove all the papers. Those things worked for you for a while, Grace, now you're moving on to another stage. Gotta do the unpicking first.'

Beside her now on the car seat were five airmail envelopes, stamped and addressed to Australia. They were her resignations from five committees and Grace had written them before Orinda left, knowing that her presence in the flat would serve to strengthen her resolve. As she headed on through the rain down the A23, she slowed at the sign pointing to Hurstpierpoint and, pulling across into the inside lane, she decided to pay Vivienne a visit. There was a mailbox on the corner and she pulled over and picked up the letters. For a few moments she sat shuffling them, staring at the names and addresses on the envelopes. Then she opened the car door, and leaned out in the rain and slipped them into the red box. Orinda would never forgive her if she didn't mail them. More importantly, she might never forgive herself.

Vivienne was sitting by the fire, her feet on a stool, surrounded by lists and piles of fabric. 'So she got away all right?'

Grace nodded, feeling the tears start again.

'Sorry I couldn't come to the airport, but if I missed that hospital appointment, God knows when I'd get another.'

'I know, it was fine, Orinda understood, and I cried enough for you and me!'

Vivienne grinned. 'Cup of tea?'

'Please,' Grace said. 'But stay there, I can make it. What did the hospital say?'

'They said I'm as good as new – well, more or less. I don't have to go back unless I feel I need to. I can throw away the stick when I feel okay without it.' She cleared the papers from her lap and clasped her hands across her stomach watching as Grace poured water into the teapot. 'So what now?'

'Huh?' Grace looked up.

'What about you now? You've still got four weeks left, haven't you?'

'Yes,' said Grace, setting a mug of tea down in front of Vivienne. 'Until the first week of December.'

'And what will you do?'

'Well . . . I guess the things I came here to do.'

'Which are?'

Grace grimaced. 'Not really sure. I mean, I wanted to get to know Brighton a bit because it was Mum's home. It's where she and Dad met. I wanted to be away from home for a little while.'

'So are you happy about going back in four weeks?'

'At the moment I don't know how to. I can't even visualise it and it seems quite scary.' She paused. 'I feel I've changed quite a lot in a very short time but I'm still grasping at that change. It's as though I can be this new person here but I'm not sure if I can sustain it at home. You know, it feels so bad because I resent all the things that I was so committed to. I'm frightened that when I go back they'll swallow me up again, that this new feeling, this emerging, different self will get drowned.'

Vivienne put down her cup and stood up. She went over to the fireplace and threw a couple more logs onto the fire, jiggling them into position with the big iron poker. Grace noticed how much more easily she was moving, as though the clean bill of health from the hospital had given her the confidence to move more freely. Vivienne leaned against the shoulder-high mantelpiece for a while, looking down into the fire.

'I think you should honour that feeling. You felt you needed to be away for a while so you left. Then you nearly took off in the middle of everything in order to be the perfect mother, or mother-in-law, or grandmother, or all three. But you got through that. You've changed, Grace – dramatically. When I first saw you I thought you were the most uptight woman I'd ever met in my life, but each day you unravelled a little – in fact, sometimes it seemed like each hour. Have you ever seen those speeded-up films of a caterpillar turning into a chrysalis and then a butterfly emerging? It's been like that. So fast. You have to give yourself time to adjust, to feel confident in it. You trusted the feeling that told you to get away, I think you have to trust the feeling that says it's too early to go back.'

Grace carried her cup to the window and stared out through the diamond-shaped leadlights at Vivienne's sodden garden, which a month earlier had still been colourful with the last of the roses and wisteria. 'I told you, when I left Australia I was running away, I just wanted a holiday.'

'I know that. And there was no way you wanted the inner journey stuff that your friends were interested in. But now?'

'Now it feels different. I don't really understand it . . .'

'It feels different because you've started on the journey, a retreat sort of journey. Just being out of your space, working with the other women on the quilt, has jolted you. Without realising it you put yourself in a situation that was bound to have an effect on you. It cut through all that superficial manic energy and dumped you somewhere else – on a journey. On the sort of journey your friends are making. Without knowing it, Grace, you kick-started the same process for yourself.'

Grace turned to look at her. 'But all the things that happened to me happened because of you, you and Orinda.'

'Bullshit,' said Vivienne unceremoniously, tossing her tea-leaves into the fire and walking over to the teapot to refill her cup. 'The only person who could make the change was you. Sure, you saw and felt things here because you were in a different environment with different people. But you were ripe and ready for it, Grace, however much you tried to convince your friends and yourself that you weren't. The way you're feeling now is proof of that.'

Grace shook her head. 'I don't understand it. What the others saw in it was an inner journey. They kept talking about spirituality, about having a spiritual life. I didn't really know what they were talking about.' She paused. 'Now I wonder . . . What do you think a spiritual life is, Viv?'

'I think,' said Vivienne, 'that a spiritual life means different things to different people and that rather than knowing what it means for me, maybe you should work out what it's going to mean for you.'

'I always thought it was something about religion, about being a Christian or a Buddhist or something else. You know, my father was a minister but I never inherited his faith.'

'But you inherited a role: your mother's, probably.'

Grace looked at her in surprise. 'I'm not at all like my mother. What do you mean?'

Vivienne smiled. 'Now I'm in hot water – don't we all hate that feeling that we might have turned out like our mothers! I think I'd better shut up.'

'But I know I'm not like my mother,' Grace protested. 'And you can't know differently because you didn't ever meet her.'

'True. But I have known lots of minister's wives – Anglicans, Baptists, Methodists – and mostly they follow the mould.'

'What mould?'

'Running the parish. Organising everyone, being indispensable, putting everyone else first, making sure everyone is supported, that things run smoothly. Thinking everything will fall apart if they relax their vigilance for a moment. It's inevitable, I guess – or, at least, it would be very hard to fight the expectations.'

Grace seemed fixed to the spot. She saw her mother setting out around the town in her neat belted suit and trim little hat, a basket on one arm. She saw herself following behind as they went from one house to the next, then on to the church to check the flowers and the cleaning rosters, then to the village hall to a meeting about the Christmas concert, or the Easter Bilby party. She saw herself standing silent and polite and playing quietly alongside her mother's chair at CWA meetings. She remembered the pressure of being the vicar's daughter, the need always to be clean and tidy, to be quiet and polite, an example to other children.

Instantly she was suffused with the loneliness, the hurt and frustration she had felt as her mother's attention focused always on other people. She felt the same weight on her chest that she always felt when her mother came to kiss her goodnight on her way to do something else, look after someone else. She teetered on the edge of the great black hole that had haunted so many of her childhood dreams, and that had threatened to draw her into its darkness the day Tim and Angela broke their news. She saw the teenage Grace helping to run the Sunday School, reading the paper to old Mr Barns who was nearly blind, collecting odd balls of wool for the CWA and magazines for the hospital, organising the little kids to sing Christmas carols at the old people's home. She grasped for the free spirit she saw in Emily, that she remembered in her own children, and she knew that it had not been part of her own childhood.

Vivienne put a hand on her arm. 'Good God, Grace, I'm so sorry. Whatever have I said? You look terrible. You look as though you've seen a ghost.'

Grace turned to her, a mass of confusion. 'I think I have,' she said. 'I think a ghost is exactly what I've seen.'

SIXTEEN

'I think I'm gonna put you here, Sally, next to Chuck. Then perhaps Linda and Craig over there and Steve down the end here next to me.' Nancy paused, hands on hips, surveying the table, which was set for thirteen.

Sally put the place cards in front of each setting. She had painted them, as Nancy had requested, on cream card with borders of autumn leaves. How long was it since she had been anywhere for dinner where there were place cards? What had seemed quaint when Nancy had first suggested it now seemed delightful.

'So then we'll have Dick here, please, and then Barbara over there just where you're standing, and Steve's daughter – what's her name again?'

'Stacey.'

'Yes, Stacey – she can go here. What's she like, anyway? D'you think you two'll get along okay?'

Sally put the cards in place and stepped back from the table with a shrug. 'She's okay, I think. I haven't really had a chance to get to know her yet, but I'm sure it'll be okay.'

'Well, honey, don't fall over yourself with enthusiasm, will you?' Nancy laughed. 'It doesn't sound like she's going to be a bosom pal.'

'No, but she doesn't have to be, does she?' said Sally with a wry smile. 'Steve and I are just friends, after all.'

'Yeah, sure,' Nancy said with a grin. 'And I can check her out myself this afternoon. Doesn't the table look terrific?' She walked over to Sally and hugged her. 'I'm real glad you're here for Thanksgiving. It's such a special time for us.'

'My first ever Thanksgiving – it's so good of you and Chuck to include me.'

'Include you? You're part of the family now. How about we try out Chuck's punch before we go get ready?'

Back in her apartment Sally surveyed herself critically in the bedroom mirror and decided she looked considerably better than she had done a few weeks earlier. The shadows under her eyes had faded and her skin had regained some of its freshness. The deep sea green of the dress highlighted the colour of her eyes. She hung her head forward, vigorously brushing her hair up from the roots, then straightened up, letting it settle before fixing it back from her face with the tortoiseshell combs. Satisfied with her appearance she wandered through the living room to the window and fixed her gaze on the San Francisco skyline. What would the Mendelsons be doing? How would they spend Thanksgiving? Surrounded by family and friends probably, a log fire burning in the grate, wintry sunlight pouring through the windows from the courtyard, warmth and laughter, shared memories weaving through the conversation. And Lisa? Where would she be? In the midst of it, or perhaps more likely with her carer in the quiet of her own suite. Sally sighed and turned away from the window, picking up Estelle Mendelson's letter. Despite the countless times she had read it in the last three weeks, she unfolded the soft hand-made paper and read it again.

Dear Sally

Thank you for your letter. Oliver and I have read it many times, and talked at length about what happened.

We appreciate your honesty, and know it must have been a difficult letter to write. The first time we met we both felt most warmly towards you. We felt we could share our love and concern for Lisa. After you left that day much of our anxiety had lifted.

You obviously realize how devastating your second visit

*was for us but your letter has helped us to understand the
circumstances in which you gave up your baby, and the pain
and remorse that you've lived with so long. We can understand
how the shock led you to react as you did. I too have blamed
myself just as you blamed me. Over time the sharpness has
eased, but there is not a day in my life when I don't wake to
guilt and sadness; rather, I suspect, as you have woken each
day with the guilt and sadness of your loss.*

*So where does this leave us? Well, we feel we must put
what happened behind us and move on but we both feel we
need a little longer for the dust to settle. Thanksgiving is
nearly here, and Oliver has a three-week concert tour between
Thanksgiving and Christmas. Our suggestion is that we meet
on the first of January. We have always spent that day at home
here with Oliver's parents, it's a family tradition. So why don't
you join us for lunch on that day? Perhaps you would like to
bring a friend along.*

*Just send me a line to let me know if you accept our
invitation and then we can all look forward to the start of a
new and different year.*

*Oliver and I send you our warmest wishes for
Thanksgiving.*

Estelle

Sally sighed and folded the letter back into its envelope. She
knew she was incredibly fortunate to have a second chance but
the weeks until New Year's Day seemed to stretch interminably
ahead. 'But they're right,' she said to herself, taking her coat from
the wardrobe. 'Of course they're right.' And picking up Steve's
car keys, she let herself out, and went up the steps to the street in
fading light to collect Steve and Stacey for the Thanksgiving
dinner.

At the far end of the table Nancy was explaining to Steve that the
incredible tenderness of the turkey was due to a method she had

discovered the previous week in the cookery pages of *The San Francisco Chronicle*. 'Before you cook it you soak it for twenty-four hours in a mix of cold water and rock salt. Lord knows how it works, but I must say I'm really happy with the way it turned out.'

'Definitely your best ever, Mom,' Linda called across the table. 'A culinary triumph!'

'Great turkey, but I hope it's not the best the *Chronicle* can do,' said Stacey through a mouthful of food, her rather loud voice shocking the rest of the table into silence. 'Aw, shit, guys. No, Nancy, I don't mean that, it's the best ever turkey. I mean, I just hope there's more interesting things to do at the *Chronicle* than cookery features.' She leaned back in her chair, looking around the table. 'Cookery writing isn't really my scene.'

'Ah yes, Stacey, you're going to work at the *Chronicle*,' Chuck began in an attempt to relieve the awkwardness. 'When do you start?'

'Monday. It'll be cool, I reckon. I know a guy there who's on the international desk. We were in college together here in Berkeley.'

Linda helped herself to roast potatoes and passed the spoon over to Craig, her boyfriend, who was dissecting the remains of a drumstick. 'Why'd you leave London, Stacey?' she asked.

'Oh well, y'know, London . . . it's dark, it's cold and it's full of English people.' Stacey looked around in anticipation of a laugh, which didn't come. 'The English, y'know, they're so full of shit!'

Nancy raised her eyebrows at Barbara, her oldest friend, who had kept her distinctively English accent despite having lived in America for almost twenty years. 'Don't take it personally, Barb.' Nancy smiled.

'Oh gee, Barbara, you're English, of course. I'm sorry. There's a lot of good things in England, like . . . well, like the countryside, and the buildings, great old buildings, castles and stuff . . .'

Barbara gave her a long look and turned back to Chuck's brother to resume their stalled conversation.

Nancy pushed back her chair, moving to clear the plates, and Sally got up to clear from her end, watching as Stacey leaned over to engage Barbara's Texan husband, Dick, in a conversation about old cars. 'Take my dad here,' she was saying. 'He's driving around in this old Jag that just gobbles up the gas. Now, wouldn't he be better to change it for something more modern?'

Steve met Sally's glance and grinned. 'She means being driven,' he said. 'Only ten more days, then I throw away the strapping and the stick and drive again. But I'll be sorry to lose the chauffeur service.'

Sally smiled. 'Don't kid me, you're just itching to get back behind the wheel. I can feel it every time I start the engine. And you're constantly fighting the urge to tell me how to drive it.'

'That obvious, is it?'

''Fraid so. But it doesn't bother me in the least. I think it'd take me years to get used to driving here.'

While Nancy carried the desserts through to the table, Sally stacked the dirty plates in the dishwasher and stood for a moment watching Steve's daughter through the doorway. Stacey tucked her thick blonde hair behind one ear, the fingers of her other hand drumming impatiently on the table. She was wearing a lime-green T-shirt, black jeans and a broad silver belt. On one golden forearm was a small black stylised tattoo of a bull's head. Stacey was a Taurean, and appeared to delight in accentuating her bullish characteristics.

Sally had worked so long with teenagers that she had thought herself immune to the culture shock she experienced with younger generations, but Stacey was something else. From the moment they met at the airport, Sally had felt constantly on the wrong foot. Stacey's peremptory manner, her loud voice and her habit of crossing personal boundaries, physical and otherwise, unnerved Sally. Stacey was, as the kids at school in Perth used to say, 'full on'. Sally recalled reprimanding Dani, a quiet, awkward girl, for losing her temper and yelling at a good-natured but irritating newcomer to the class. 'But she's always in ya face, Miss!' Dani had protested, wandering off to sit hunched and brooding in her usual corner spot. It was a good description of Stacey, Sally thought – always in ya face. And with Stacey behaving like a disruptive twenty-seven-year-old teenager, Sally felt uncomfortably like Dani.

'It's a combination, you see,' Stacey was saying, leaning so close to Dick that he actually shifted his chair slightly. 'My dad is Steven and my mom is called Tracey, so they called me Stacey. Cute, they thought. I think it's a bit sick.'

Steve rolled his eyes at Nancy, who was handing him a portion of apple pie. 'Okay, Stace, give it rest, will you? It was your mother's idea.'

It was midnight by the time they had watched the fireworks from the balcony, and the party began to break up. Steve was hugging Nancy in the hallway, and Chuck was thumping Craig on the shoulder with promises of a game of golf. Pulling on her coat Sally waited as Steve released Nancy, shook hands with Dick and Barbara, and turned to say goodnight to Chuck.

'We don't need you driving anymore, Sally,' Stacey said, leaning in front of her to pick up the Jaguar keys from the hall table. 'I'll drive home.'

Steve swung around on his crutches. 'C'mon, Dad,' Stacey said, urging him towards the door. 'Sally doesn't like the traffic and I need the car anyway – now, let's get going. Thanks, you guys.'

Steve's eyes met Sally's across the hall. 'Sally? What d'you, er . . .?' He looked at her, wanting help, but she had none to give. His discomfort was obvious.

She shrugged. 'It's up to you,' she said. 'Your car, your daughter . . .'

He seemed frozen. 'Okay, then. Okay, if that's all right with you.' He leant awkwardly forward to kiss her on the cheek. 'I'll call you.'

'Sure,' she replied, swallowing the tremor in her voice. 'Take care. Goodnight, Stacey.'

But Stacey was by now halfway along the path, calling to Steve to get a move on and to mind the steps.

It wasn't about the car Sally told herself the next morning as she walked to the little market near the station. She really preferred to walk, she needed the exercise. No – it was the feeling of being pushed aside. She had enjoyed being chauffeur, which had involved a great deal more than just driving. She had cooked meals and they had shared takeaways, watched old movies on video and she'd introduced him to some Australian films. The movies had crystallised her homesickness, left her feeling uncomfortably disconnected. While the US might dominate the news back home, in America Australia might just as well not have existed. She hadn't seen one item of Australian news in the papers or on the TV bulletins. As far as Americans were concerned, Australia was a big zero, and some people really did believe that there were kangaroos on the streets of Sydney. Most of the people she talked to had never heard of Perth and didn't even know there was a state of Western Australia, but Steve was really interested. So interested that they had raided the library and his coffee table was stacked with books about Australia and a couple of Australian novels.

Standing in the queue to pay for her vegetables Sally felt a great stab of homesickness. The young Mexican guy at the checkout packed her food and handed it to her with a greeting in Spanish. She left the market and found a table outside the coffee shop. The front of the café was already decorated for Christmas and across the street the shop windows sparkled with rows of gold angels and silver snowflakes. Sipping her coffee in the winter sunshine Sally was overwhelmed with longing for the company of her friends, for their conversation, their laughter, and the sense of being understood. She smiled to herself, thinking how Grace would have taken Stacey on with a few biting remarks, how well Isabel would get along with Nancy and how Robin and Steve would have enjoyed talking politics.

It was the twenty-sixth of November, and they had promised to exchange news at Christmas. A detailed warts-and-all record, photocopied and sent to each of the other three. She would reveal the real reason behind her trip to California. Warts-and-all it would be, although she was not sure she needed to reveal the full extent of her attack on the Mendelsons. It would be a long, hard letter to write. Isabel's card had told her to send the letter to Doug, who was meeting her in Germany. Grace seemed to be staying with a woman in Sussex, and Robin's would go to the post office box down south.

Pushing her cup aside, Sally picked up her shopping and set off for the walk home. Stacey wouldn't be around all that long, she supposed. Eventually she'd find a place of her own, buy a car and move out. But maybe it wouldn't be the same then, anyway; perhaps the times she'd enjoyed with Steve were simply a product of his reliance on her. She was annoyed by his mild acceptance of Stacey's command-and-control style and the way he had allowed her to be displaced by it. It was so typical of a man to take the line of least resistance as long as it didn't inconvenience him. Harry had been like that, deeply involved one day, offhand – even cold – the next, always picking the easy option. Anyway, it wasn't as though she was having a relationship with Steve. He was just a friend, and he hadn't seen his daughter for a couple of years. Perhaps she should be more understanding. But by the time she reached the apartment she was still annoyed and Steve's message on the answering machine asking her to call him added to her irritation. She didn't feel like talking to him.

She unpacked the shopping, made herself a sandwich and sat down to work on an assignment that was due on Monday. By five o'clock the work was finished, and she got up to put on some music and flex her muscles before starting the letter. She rarely closed the blinds as the view was always so engaging – in the next-door garden and along the street the tiny white pinpoints of the Christmas lights grew brighter as evening closed in. The phone rang and she let the answering machine pick it up. It was Steve again, saying that he hoped she was okay, he guessed she must be busy. He asked her to call back. When he hung up she took a deep breath and got out a thick pad of ruled paper. Switching on the desk lamp she sat down again and with a last look out of the window, she began to write.

Dearest Isabel, Grace and Robin

What wouldn't I give for a round-table conference right now! I've missed you all so much and, as I start this letter, I'm realising just how much. Where will I begin? I've heaps to tell you and I'm not sure how you're going to feel about it all, but I suppose the best place to start is at the beginning, the very beginning . . .

*

When Sally walked into the lecture hall on Monday afternoon, Steve beckoned her to the seat beside him just as the lights dimmed and the lecturer began his critique of the images on the screen. For the next forty-five minutes they sat side by side in tense silence.

'I was getting worried, Sally,' Steve said, turning awkwardly towards her as the lights went up to a trickle of applause. 'I left a couple of messages.'

'I know. Sorry I didn't get back to you. I had to finish the assignment and there was other stuff I needed to do.'

There was a tightness around his mouth that she hadn't seen before. 'I guess you must have been glad not to have to run around after me for a change.'

When she had seen him sitting there an hour ago her annoyance had changed to pleasure and then to a mix of confusion and anxiety. Now the annoyance returned in force. He was playing the victim, throwing out self-deprecating remarks to make her reassure him. It felt like Harry, trying to manipulate her into saying that she wasn't really hurt by the hateful things he'd said when he was drunk the night before. She was sick of that game. Sick of picking up emotional baggage. She looked him straight in the eye. 'No, I was really pissed off about Stacey's behaviour and what happened the other night. I needed time to get over it.'

He held her gaze. 'I know,' he said. 'It was totally unacceptable and I shouldn't have let Stacey get away with it. I'm really sorry. That's why I called, to apologise.'

She had expected the mind games, the ego and the manipulation that would somehow make it her fault, and his straightforward apology took her by surprise. She opened her mouth to protest and shut it again. 'I'm sorry I didn't call you back,' she said eventually. 'Actually, I was sulking!'

The corner of Steve's mouth twitched. 'Not without good reason,' he said.

She shrugged. 'I think I'm a bit oversensitive at present.'

'Sally, don't,' he said, taking her hand. 'This was not oversensitivity on your part, it was insensitivity on mine. That and

Stacey being her normal bullish self. Do you have time for a coffee?'

They walked together to the café. 'Is Stacey picking you up?' Sally asked.

He shook his head. 'No, no, she started at the *Chronicle* today. God knows when she'll be home. I took a cab.'

She brought the coffee back to the table, and squeezed into the narrow space between the table and bench. 'So how're you getting back?'

'Cab again, I guess – since I was fool enough to upset the chauffeur.'

'Isn't Stacey using the car?'

'She used it over the weekend, but she's buying some little car off a friend, and she used the train to get to work. You know what the commuter traffic is like on the Bay Bridge.'

Sally nodded. 'Well . . .' she hesitated. 'If you want, I could . . .'

'Yes!' Steve said. 'Yes please, I want!'

She laughed. 'Okay, should I go home with you and get the car, then I can pick you up for the tute tomorrow?'

'I don't just love you for you driving, you know,' Steve said, and she blushed, looking away in embarrassment, gazing unseeingly towards a group of students unchaining their bikes from the coffee shop fence.

'Oh yes?' She smiled without meeting his eyes. 'I bet that's what you tell all your chauffeurs.'

The tension from the lecture theatre was gone, replaced by a new awareness of the warmth of his arm almost touching hers, his good leg close to hers below the table. 'No,' he said. 'But then I never had a chauffeur before, and I've never been interested in anyone else's.'

She sipped her coffee, unable to look at him, unsure how to react to the chemistry that had suddenly materialised between them.

Steve's hand moved to cover hers. 'Sally,' he said quietly, and she looked up. He lifted her hand to his lips and kissed it. 'Come home with me now?'

*

'The strapping is a bit of a handicap,' Steve said almost three hours later, pulling himself into a sitting position and leaning back against the bedhead.

Sally trailed her fingers down the length of his good leg. 'I didn't notice it impeding your performance.'

'That's very kind of you, ma'am, but you don't have other performances to judge against.'

She sat up too. 'No, but I anticipate the forthcoming ones.'

He leaned forward smiling, kissing her lightly on the lips, and then reached for a packet of cigarettes that were on the night table.

'Cigarettes! You don't smoke!'

'My secret vice. One a day, or usually night, in bed.'

'But you can't smoke – this is California, nobody smokes. I mean, well, it's like Western Australia, virtually smoke free.'

'Virtually, not entirely!'

'It's a terrible habit.'

'Aha – I detect the fanaticism of a reformed smoker.'

'Exactly!'

'I shouldn't even have one?'

'Not one!'

'You'd never make love to me again if I smoked a cigarette now?'

'Never.'

'And if I threw them away you'd have wild, passionate sex with me every day of the week?'

'Absolutely – weekends too!'

He threw the packet across the room.

'Well, almost every day . . .'

'Aha! You made a promise.' He drew her towards him, sliding down the bed on his back. 'Be gentle with me. I was recently beaten up by some ferocious woman on a mountain trail.'

'You probably deserved it,' she murmured.

Neither of them heard the sound of the front door, nor the bedroom door. It was instinct that made Sally stiffen and turn and when she did, there was Stacey standing in the doorway. Sally pulled up the rumpled duvet and Steve dragged himself back into a sitting position. 'Stacey, c'mon now! You could've knocked. This is my bedroom, for God's sake.'

Stacey turned and flung herself out of the room, slamming the door behind her. The noise of the television blasted up from her room and another door slammed.

Steve grimaced. 'Sorry, Sally. Seems like some kids never grow up,' he said with a wry smile. 'You know you can't leave now, don't you? I mean, if you get up and leave now she'll think she's embarrassed you into going. You are forced to lie here with me for at least another hour, then it won't look like we got up because of her.'

'I think I can put up with you for another hour,' she said, kissing his shoulder. 'Was Stacey always like this?'

'Christ, no. She used to be much worse!'

The television must have been too loud even for Stacey, for now it was turned down to a low murmur of voices and music. They lay side by side, drowsy in the warmth of the bed. Sally's body was heavy with pleasure and satisfaction. She pressed her face against Steve's chest, loving the smell of him, the roughness of the gingery hair against her cheek. 'I might need to stay longer than an hour,' she whispered, her eyelids drooping with sudden exhaustion.

He stroked her hair. 'Hey,' he murmured. 'I was only talking minimums.'

'Sounds like someone crying – is that Stacey?'

'Doubt it. The iron woman doesn't cry, she only bellows. Must be the TV.'

'I never did this before.'

'I see – you're a virgin!'

'Very funny! I mean, I never went to bed with a friend.'

'You slept with your enemies?'

'What I mean is that things always started with instant lust and burned out just as quickly.'

'And this is different?'

'Well,' she said, 'I thought we were friends, not . . .'

'Not what?'

'I didn't know the chemistry was there.'

He laughed. 'You mean all these weeks I was having erotic fantasies about you, you weren't having them about me?'

She shook her head. 'I will now, though. I promise.'

'Promises, promises. So are we still friends?'

'Uh-huh!'

'And lovers too? I just want to get this clear.'

'And lovers too. Stop talking.'

'And do what instead?'

'Sleep would be nice.'

'Ah,' he sighed, sliding down beside her, his face so close she could breathe his breath. 'Yes, that might be a good idea.'

SEVENTEEN

The bookshop was halfway along Albany's main street between the clock tower and the waterfront. Robin noticed it as she came out of the church on the other side of the road. Church was unfamiliar territory, and as she sat in a rear pew enjoying the stillness, she wondered what had led her there. 'You must have put a spell on me, Father Pat,' she whispered into the silence. 'Where do I go from here?'

Disconnected thoughts seemed to circle and dive like seagulls, failing to produce any answers or even clearly to define the questions. Jim, her job, her home, her future, what was she to do? She had set out from the cottage at peace but the previous night's encounter with Jim in the pub had damaged her equilibrium.

She had left Pemberton straight after breakfast despite Josie's urgings to stay on until Sunday. The last thing she wanted was to bump into Jim and Monica again. Exchanging phone numbers and email addresses, promising to stay in touch, she had hugged Josie and Dawn, who stood outside the door of the guesthouse ready to wave her away.

Father Pat had gone to early mass but came hurrying back as she slammed down the lid of the boot. 'I thought I might've missed you, Robin.' He smiled. 'I'm glad I made it in time.' He took both her hands in his.

'I didn't want to leave without seeing you, Father, and thanking you for last night.'

'My dear girl, you only ate half a dinner but it was a pleasure.'

'Not the dinner – well, yes, that of course, which was lovely. I mean, when we got back here. Our conversation. It was very . . .' She paused. 'Challenging, I suppose. Thank you.'

'I'm glad. We made the most of the remains of that lovely fire and had the place to ourselves. What better than a drop of malt whisky and some intelligent conversation? You don't want a blessing, I'm sure, but it comes with the package, I'm afraid. God bless you, Robin.'

'You'll call in and see me if you're anywhere near?' she asked. 'You know where I'm staying.'

'I do indeed. I expect to be this way again in a couple of months. I shall come and interrupt your solitude.'

'I'll look forward to it. And you won't . . .'

'I won't disclose your whereabouts to anyone at all.'

Robin felt better once she was on the road, although she despised herself for running away from the chance of another encounter with Jim and Monica. Consoling herself with the thought that she had already stayed longer than planned in Pemberton, she had driven straight on to Albany.

Too cold now to stay longer in the church, she went outside again, blinking in the sunlight. On the opposite side of the street she saw the Irish café whose bacon Father Pat had recommended, and threaded her way through the crawl of the traffic. It was then that she saw the bookshop: a long, narrow old building, its original façade still intact and tastefully painted in heritage green. The main window was devoted to Ian McEwan and right in the middle, with the brown binding and the etching of a balloon on the front cover, was *Enduring Love*, the only McEwan she hadn't read. She went inside, picked up a copy of the book and took it to the counter where a woman sat studying book catalogues.

'I'll have this one, please,' Robin said. 'But I'll have a look around first.'

The woman tucked an escaping strand of grey hair into the loose knot at the back of her head and smiled. 'Please, go ahead.

That's an excellent book. My husband reckons it's McEwan's best, but I prefer *The Child in Time*.'

Robin, who had failed to convert any of her friends to McEwan's books, was delighted to find a fellow fan. 'That's my favourite too! That and *Amsterdam*.'

The woman nodded. 'I really think he's my favourite author. I'm so disappointed when I get to the end of his books, I feel quite lost. Anita Brookner's another one. There's something about those English authors.'

Robin nodded. 'I've enjoyed a lot of her books but recently I got a bit sick of her suppressed, well-behaved females.'

'Yes, I know what you mean, but I still love her – the ordinariness, the attention to detail. Anyway, I mustn't keep you, you wanted to look around.'

Robin liked the layout of the shop, the golden glow of the old pine shelves, the librarian's steps, the small armchairs in bright colours placed at vantage points, and the cone-shaped shelf stand with a circular upholstered bench seat beneath it. Two-thirds of the shop was devoted to new books and classics, the remainder to a selection of old and rare books, chosen by someone who obviously knew the trade. Robin had a reasonable collection of old law books and on these shelves she found a couple of volumes she'd wanted for some time.

'You obviously know your books,' the woman said as Robin put them on the counter.

'Not as well as whoever buys in your stock.'

'That's my husband,' the woman said. 'He's been in the trade for years. Credit, cheque or savings?'

'Credit, thanks. I love the way you've organised the shop. It's very inviting.'

'Thank you. We like it, we'll be sorry to leave it. We're moving in the New Year. Going to Tasmania.'

Robin looked around the shop. 'It'll be a wrench for you to leave this. Who's taking over?'

The woman put the books into a paper carrier bag with the name 'Booklovers' printed on the front in dark green. 'Don't know yet. We're still trying to make up our minds whether to advertise it now or leave it till after Christmas. November's not a very good time to sell.' She pushed the credit card slip across the counter and handed Robin a pen.

Robin signed, her heart pumping furiously, as if she had just done an eight-kilometre run. 'What's the trade like?'

'Very good, really, especially considering there's three other bookshops in town. We do well out of it, there's just the two of us. The tourist trade is very good in the summer.' She handed Robin back her Visa card and the bag of books. 'Enjoy those. You're not local, are you?'

Robin shook her head. 'No – Perth. I'm just taking a break.'

'Well, it's nice to meet you. Enjoy the rest of your time in Albany.'

Robin stood on the pavement looking around in confusion, her excitement so great that she couldn't remember where she'd parked the car. 'Calm down, calm down,' she told herself. 'Get your act together and get back to the car.' There it was, parked in one of the bays on the crest of the hill.

She ran up the street and fell into the front seat, started the engine and slowly drove back down the hill past the shop, turned at the end and drove back up and down past it again. She was supposed to be finding somewhere to stay. She had to find a place quickly and then think what to do. She had to calm down before she did something very silly. After all, how could you be totally confused about the future one minute and then walk into a bookshop and want to buy it the next? It was mad!

'Calm down,' she told herself aloud. 'Find a room and then you can concentrate.' She rummaged among the maps on the passenger seat for the paper on which she had written the name of the place Dawn had recommended. Glancing down at the address, she turned left into Grey Street and began searching for the guesthouse.

It was midday on Tuesday before Robin went back to the bookshop. She had forced herself to stay away for three days, to think the idea through, to make sure she hadn't gone completely off her rocker. She wasn't really sure that three days was long enough to test the latter, but at least she had forced a decent interlude upon herself. She was good at decisions. Her history was one of letting things lie, and then quite suddenly taking a surprising decision and acting on it. That, she thought wryly, was how it had been with Jim and the decision to get out of his life and into a new life of her own. A fast decision and a sound one; painful, scary, challenging but infinitely liberating and, she was convinced, the best course of action she could have taken in the circumstances.

Her parents had always agonised over decisions, her father being the ultimate procrastinator, so much so that the night that he checked his football pools and announced that he'd won, no one in the family took much notice. They were all so sure that even if he had picked the right teams he would, as usual, have left it until the last minute to mail the coupon in case he wanted to change his mind, and then missed the last post. Robin thought her own firm and spontaneous decision-making had probably developed as a reaction against her parents, but whatever its origins it had served her well in the past. The decisions to study law, to come to Australia, to buy in to the practice, to buy her first house and then the present one, had all been taken quickly and based on gut feeling. Why should this one be any different?

On the previous Sunday she walked for hours along Middleton Beach, watching her own footprints in the pale sand, considering her situation. If it hadn't been for the chance encounter with Jim she might have felt more cautious, but clearly Monica now knew about her and, despite that, Jim had stayed put. That shed new light on the past as well as the future. There had been so many times when his leaving would have been the sensible, honest and obvious thing to do. Now, by her own leaving she had forced the situation and it seemed that it was all over. 'I think I'm exhausted by the paradox,' she had told Father Pat as they sat by the dying fire back at Dawn and Josie's guesthouse. 'Always being told that I'm the most important person in his life, that I keep him sane, that it's me he really loves, and yet always finding that I take second place, to Monica, his children, his work – everything. That probably sounds unreasonable but I just seem to have run out of steam.'

'It sounds entirely reasonable to me,' the priest had said, pouring her a second whisky.

'I mean, if I really loved him, surely I ought to be prepared to take second place, to understand his commitments – after all, on one level I respect him for not being able to turn his back on his responsibilities. So there's paradox there, too.'

Father Pat stabbed at the fire with a long iron poker, and added a couple of logs. A shower of sparks flew up the chimney and the flames flickered to life. 'Life and emotions are very different from the law, Robin.' He smiled. 'The law is wonderfully logical. We know – you and Jim know especially well – what the boundaries are. You take a situation, you look at the options and how you can work with them. It's probably very clear what's right and what's wrong. Of course there are subtleties of analysis and interpretation, but basically it's all pretty clear. Life and love, well, they're just chaos. The rules are all over the place, subjective, always up for grabs. You can't be sure what you're dealing with.' He sipped his drink and leaned back, crossing his legs. 'The law is like the Catholic church, the rules are clear and that's why we cling to them. It feels safe. The church, or in your case the law, provides a framework, but life doesn't always fit into the framework and that's what makes it so hard.'

'But what's wrong with me?' she began, struggling briefly against tears. 'How can I love him passionately but then be prepared to let it all go? What about all those great romantic liaisons? That actress Juliette Drouet, she waited fifteen years for, um . . . Who was it? Well, whoever it was, she wrote him seventeen thousand letters and he never left his wife.'

'It was Victor Hugo, and I think it was twelve years, and look what happened to her. If I remember my history correctly, Hugo removed her from a very active social and professional life, set her up in a small apartment and virtually forbade her to have any sort of social connection. She submerged her identity into a creative man. The great love stories of the past, Robin, often have a very dark side for the women. But then you don't need a Catholic priest giving you the feminist analysis – you already know that.'

Robin swallowed her whisky. 'I can't actually believe that I'm talking to a priest about all this anyway,' she said, getting up to pace back and forth across the room. 'No offence, Father, my

242

apostasy goes back a long way and I'm known for keeping my cards close to my chest.'

'Well, your cards are safe with me. Coincidence has brought us together. Perhaps it helps that I know Jim. He's a good man. You're both good people caught in a timeless and rather tragic situation, but you decided, wisely it seems to me, that if Jim wouldn't or couldn't put you first, you'd put yourself first. A decision of integrity and some strength and not without its difficulties. You're not a Juliette Drouet, Robin, you're an independent woman and this is a different world. You're a successful lawyer, you've struggled to get to this stage of life – why would you be prepared to disappear into purdah and write seventeen thousand letters, or emails, or whatever lovers do these days?'

Robin laughed and blew her nose. 'How come you know so much about love?'

'You think because I'm a priest I've never been in love? My dear Robin, falling in love with all the wrong people at all the wrong times has been the story of my life. Without it I might well be a bishop myself instead of His Grace's troubleshooter who's too big a risk to be left alone in any particular parish.' He picked up the empty glasses and slipped the silver flask of whisky back into the pocket of his jacket. 'Time for bed, I think. Sleep, like prayer, is wonderfully soothing to the savage breast.'

Four days later Robin stood on the opposite side of the road looking at the bookshop through half-closed eyes. What was it worth? Was it freehold or a lease? Was that storage space on the first floor, or maybe accommodation? She opened her eyes fully and took a deep breath. She would never find out standing here.

'Well, hello there, you're back again,' said the woman as Robin walked into the shop. 'How're you enjoying *Enduring Love*?' She put down the armload of books she had been passing two at a time to a tall, thickset man perched at the top of a ladder.

'Actually, I haven't had a chance to start it yet,' Robin admitted. 'I've had rather a lot on my mind.'

The woman nodded. 'So, can I find something for you or are you just browsing?'

'As a matter of fact, I came to talk to you about the shop,' Robin said.

The woman raised her eyebrows. 'The shop?'

'You mentioned that you were considering selling it?'

'Well, yes,' she said, glancing up at the man on the ladder. 'Not just considering, we're definite about it. It's really a matter of when we do it.'

Robin paused, swallowing hard, her heart beating fast with the excitement she was trying to contain. 'I might be interested in buying – depending, of course, on all sorts of things . . . I don't even know what you have in mind. I wondered if we could discuss it, or perhaps you'd prefer me to go to your agent?'

'We don't have an agent yet,' the man said, coming down the ladder. 'I'm David Tranter. I see you've already met my wife, Sue.'

'Robin Percy,' she said, shaking hands with them both. 'I hope I haven't come at a difficult time but I'm not here for long.'

'Not at all,' he said. 'It's fine, absolutely.'

They stood, the three of them, awkward for a moment in the silent shop, not sure what to do next.

'Why don't I put the kettle on and you can ask us what you want to know,' Sue said, and she hurried off to the back of the shop.

David Tranter wiped his hands on a soft duster. 'Good idea. We've had the place valued of course, Robin. There's the shop and an apartment upstairs. The accountant has all the books ready for inspection. It's just as Sue said, we've been debating about the best time to sell. Anyway, come and see the rest of the place. Are you in the book business yourself?'

Dorothy was shelving biscuits when Robin called in at the shop on her way back to the cottage. She straightened up, one arm full of Tim Tams. 'The wanderer returns. How was your trip?'

'Good,' Robin smiled. 'Very good, thanks. How many Tim Tams are there in a packet?'

'No idea, dear, I only sell the things.'

'The answer is: not enough.' Robin grinned.

'Well, you're clearly in good form and you're looking very perky. There's quite a bit of mail for you. Maurice has adopted us. I think he got lonely – he's spent a lot of time down here.'

Robin smiled. 'Thanks, Dorothy. I'll just pick up some bread and fruit and then I'll get the mail. You remember the cards, the reading you did?'

Dorothy nodded as she continued stacking biscuits.

'When you were talking about the future?'

'I don't predict the future, Robin, I just tell you what I see in the cards.'

'I know, I know. But there was something to do with my work, do you remember? Something you said about seeing words on paper being important?'

'I remember. And you said it must be about you having started a journal.'

'Yes, but could it be about books, do you think? About working with books?'

'You have to be the judge of that, Robin. The journal was your interpretation, but if you feel it means something different, well, that's what it is with the cards, really – whatever you choose to make of it.'

Robin looked at her thoughtfully. 'Yes, well, that's good, that's what I thought – that, and the part about making an important decision.'

'And the chance encounter –' Dorothy said.

'Yes!' Robin cut in. 'You were quite right about that.'

'I know, Pemberton. You ran in to an old friend in Pemberton last Friday.'

Robin's jaw dropped. 'How did you know that?'

Dorothy laughed. 'Don't look so shocked, he came here looking for you. Nice chap, very handsome. Monday, I think it was. Said he'd bumped into you in Pemberton and there hadn't been time to talk, and now he was on his way back to Perth with friends. They wanted to go to a winery for lunch but he wasn't keen so he popped over here to see you. Couldn't stop long, he said, because they all had to get back to Perth that night. I was surprised, really, because I thought you'd not told anyone where you were. But I suppose you must have told him when you met him. Anyway, he said he'd try again some other time.'

Robin stood motionless for a moment. 'I see,' she said eventually. 'No, I didn't tell him where I was. Someone else must've done that.'

She wandered around the shop in a daze, picking things up and putting them down again, unable to think straight, until she managed to organise a few apples, a loaf of bread, some milk and half a dozen eggs. She put the shopping in the car and unlocked her mailbox. There was a package from the office, cards from Grace and Sally, and a letter from her mother. At least there wasn't a letter from Jim, but how had he found out where she was? She was sure Father Pat wouldn't have broken his promise, and it certainly wouldn't have been Josie or Dawn. Grace and the others were all away. Jim must have found out that she had a post office box here and then just taken a chance that in such a small place he'd be able to locate her. Her confusion turned to anger. It must have been the office, and she had specifically told them that the address was confidential.

Dragging the shopping out of the car she ran up the verandah steps and dumped it by the door with the mail, but as she turned to go back for her bag she saw a narrow white envelope tucked between the door and the jamb. She pulled it out, her anger mounting. In the top right-hand corner was the address of the judges' chambers. So he had not only found the place, he had found the house – he had been here. Had she come straight home from Pemberton he would have walked in on her, a flying visit while Monica had lunch a few kilometres away. Once again he had slotted her in between his other commitments. Now, even though it was obviously over, he was still calling the shots, turning up on the doorstep when it suited him, ignoring her request not to contact her. For so long she had accepted the inequities of their situation: he could call her at home, she could not call him; his family and his work agenda came first, then she was fitted in between social commitments, golf, the health club. He had been the focal point of her life but she had been peripheral to his. Suddenly the fire of her anger was smothered under a pall of depression. She dropped the envelope, unopened, on top of the other mail and went slowly back to the car for her bag. If ever she needed a reminder that she had done the right thing, she would only have to remember this moment. Without Isabel and Sally to act as a catalyst, she might have gone on for years, always thinking that her life with Jim was just around the next corner, and always being disappointed.

She dialled the office, needing to take her anger out on someone. But the receptionist assured her that she didn't even have the post office box address. Mr Seaborn, she said, was the only person who knew how to contact her. Alec Seaborn was an old friend and the senior partner in the practice. They had known each other for almost twenty-five years and it was with his encouragement that Robin had migrated to Australia. She apologised to the receptionist and asked to be put through to Alec, whose obvious delight at her call fell on stony ground. No, she assured him, she wasn't ready to come back to the real world; she just wanted to know why he had given her address to Justice McEwan's office. But he had not. The address – location, even – had not been given to anyone; indeed, no one had asked for it.

Robin apologised again and they talked briefly about cases and the opinions Alec had sent her. He tried hard to get her to specify when she would be back and her resistance made him suspicious. 'Are you planning to come back at all – ever?' he asked suddenly, and she paused just a little too long. 'Look,' he cut into the silence, 'please don't make any final decisions yet. Let's talk about it. I'll come down there, or meet you halfway, whatever you like. We need to discuss this face to face.'

'I want a couple more weeks,' she said, pulling out her diary. 'How about next month – December? The week beginning the fifteenth, or do you want to wait until after Christmas?'

He didn't want to wait. They arranged to meet for lunch in Bunbury on the eighteenth. 'Don't make any decisions yet,' he said again. And she didn't mention that one major decision had already been made.

The late afternoon sun cast a mellow light in the lounge, and she opened the glass doors to the verandah and lay down on the couch. Maurice leapt up effortlessly alongside her, settling immediately at her feet. As she leaned over to stroke him a lump rose in her throat. She now saw not just that it was over with Jim, but how hard it had always been; how she had forced herself to rise above the hurt and resentment, to pretend that she could handle it. Not until those last days had she actually asked him to leave, but he had promised it constantly and she had colluded in his rationalisation that the time wasn't quite right. She had felt magnanimous in not pressuring him, enjoyed occupying the high moral ground of forbearance, especially as she had always assumed that, in the end, he would do as he had promised. She wondered briefly if Monica had been playing the same game. So many people seemed to have known. Had Monica also known but decided to stay silent, refusing to acknowledge the situation because it would force a confrontation?

Robin stared at the unopened envelope now propped on the dresser. What to do? Jim had told Dorothy he would be back, but Robin reasoned it was unlikely that he could set aside the minimum of a full day needed to make the round trip for at least a couple of weeks. She had time to think. Write? Email? Calling him was out of the question, as was seeing him face to face. She wished Isabel was there to talk to. She would even have called Grace had she still been in Perth. As it was she lay alone, watching the sun set and occasionally staring at the envelope, wondering whether she would open it.

It was after ten when she woke, shivering, for she had left the doors open and the nights were still cool by the sea. She closed the doors, made tea, had a hot shower and went to bed, reminding herself that it was the end of November and she needed to begin her Christmas letter. Next morning, when she got back from her run, she sat down at the table and started to write.

Isabel, Grace, Sally – my dear, dear friends

Why are you so far away? I need you here. Life is confusing me at the moment, or maybe I am just confusing myself. How I miss being able to talk through my latest crimes and misdemeanours. I feel if I could do so it would all start to make sense. Then I wonder if absence is important for this reason alone – the experience of working out difficult stuff without one's most trusted friends. As you said, Isabel, it's tough having to be so grown up! Don't expect this letter to sound logical or organised (hold your breath, Grace, and count to ten!!). Logic has drifted out to sea, organisation eludes me, but the first thing I should tell you is that I am planning to sell my house and buy a bookshop in Albany . . .

EIGHTEEN

Isabel had agonised and procrastinated over the Christmas letter, starting it, tearing it up, starting again and then stalling, eventually mailing it at the end of the second week in December, the day she left the Riviera for Germany. She longed for the company of her women friends and held back the tears as she slipped the letters into the mailbox. In Alicante and in Monaco she had constantly pictured the Gang of Four together, walking along the beach in the windy winter sunshine, shopping in the crowded weekend markets, visiting the perfumeries in Grasse, and watching the rich and famous in the restaurants of Nice and Cannes.

Writing the letter added poignancy. She wanted to share the places she'd been, the things she'd seen, the people she had met, and it was with her friends, more than her family, that she wanted to share her experiences. Despite the complications of their own lives, Sally, Robin and Grace would empathise and understand what she was going through in a way that Doug and her children could not. Face to face it would be so easy, such a relief to talk it all through. But she hadn't found a way to express the subtlety of her feelings in writing, to describe her reaction to the light, to the sea, to the density of the human history that surrounded her. They knew what Portugal, Spain and the Riviera looked like. How could she tell them how it felt to be here, how it affected her, how it was changing her? And she had no idea how to begin writing about her confusion over and fascination with Antonia. It was as though a new map had been drawn and superimposed on her journey, a map that she couldn't quite read.

She had left Alicante in a rage, angry with Doug for dumping the job of Eunice's papers on Debra, angry most of all with herself for her collusion in his learned helplessness. Reflecting on more than three decades of marriage she saw that she had gone from caring to caretaking, and that the caretaking had been woven through with unexpressed resentment and frustration. Why was it not possible for him to remember his own mother's birthday? Why had he never had to wrap a gift? Even his gifts to her, the children had wrapped for him when they were old enough. Why did she always do for him what any adult should do for himself: take his clothes to the cleaners, make dental appointments and remind him to keep them, iron his shirts, book the car for service and deliver it? It wasn't even that she had more time. She too had always had a full-time job, only taking breaks to have the children. Her last full-time job, as mayor, had been endlessly demanding of her time and energy.

As she travelled north along the Mediterranean coast, her resentment irritated like a stone in her shoe. Liberated by distance from the minutiae of servicing other's lives, she had discovered a fresh ability to fully experience her own. It wasn't just that she had more time, she also had more creative space in her head, and that meant that she could better enjoy and appreciate her surroundings, works of art, wonderful buildings, the history and culture of new places. Curiosity and creativity had moved into the space previously occupied by the responsibility of looking after others. Life back home in Australia would have to be different, but as she rehearsed explaining it to Doug, she could picture his impatience and the fragmented attention that would indicate that he found it irksome. She would be asking him to change the habits of decades, and to do so without the motivation she felt, or the expectation of benefit.

Isabel's anger and frustration extended even further. The longing for Antonia that had plagued her was now overlaid with a confused mass of emotions. Antonia was playing some sort of game, and it made Isabel mistrust everything, including herself.

The day she left Alicante she had mailed a note thanking Antonia for the letter and the theatre program. She was moving on to the Riviera, she said, and then to Germany before Christmas. She would return to Portugal in the spring, and she hoped they could meet again. But since mailing the letter her resolve had hardened. Doug was arriving on New Year's Day, and would stay for two weeks in Germany. As soon as he left for Australia she would return to Portugal and to Monsaraz.

Throughout the journey to the Riviera she was infected with a curiosity sparked by the gap in Eunice's diary and her certainty that Antonia was keeping something from her. She headed for Monaco with a strength of purpose that implied arrival would bring resolution. It did not. It did, however, bring her to another place of the heart, very different from but almost as enchanting as Monsaraz. The woman she stayed with for the first two nights knew a family who had a small studio to let. By now it was October and the tourists were starting to leave the coast, the mild pine-scented air was just as Isabel had imagined it, and she knew she wanted a long stay.

'It is very simple,' Madame Velly explained, showing Isabel around. 'Sometimes we have let it to an artist, once to a writer. These people like it for the quiet, you see?'

Isabel saw. The studio was at the far end of the Vellys' walled garden, which rambled up the hillside. Fading bougainvillea and clumps of untamed geraniums pressed against the pink-washed walls, and the heavy scent of overripe fruit wafted in from the adjacent orchards. The windows looked out over the Vellys' taste-fully overgrown garden and the rooftops of Monaco, to occasional glimpses of the sea. It was an old building simply converted, a large room combining living and sleeping space, with a kitchen alcove and a small bathroom. Terracotta tiles and the minimum of furniture were appealing in their simplicity and Isabel was pleased to find it less expensive than she had anticipated. 'We leave you alone, madame, but you come to the house whenever you wish. If you need something, always you are welcome.' Madeline Velly smiled and pointed to a wooden gate set into the garden wall. 'You have privacy by using that entrance, if you wish. The bus to the *centre ville* takes five minutes – it goes down this street. If you walk, it is twenty minutes. If you have baggage my son will collect it for you.'

The next day Isabel was unpacking, grateful once again to Sara for streamlining her wardrobe. 'It's all so much easier without the baggage,' she told herself aloud as she stashed the lightweight grip on a high shelf. 'Now I just have to work on some of the other sort of baggage.'

After a trip to the supermarket to fill the small refrigerator, and a day of organising her new surroundings and writing some letters, she set out the following day in search of the Théâtre des Beaux-Arts, following an old street map of Monaco that she had found in one of Eunice's diaries. The theatre had figured large in her childhood imagination. Eunice's letters were full of stories of the dancers jostling for space in the dressing rooms, the elegant decor, a problem with the lighting. And the best story of all was the one in which Eunice was presented to Prince Rainier, after the performance. 'Fancy me meeting a real prince,' Eunice had written home. 'He's a bachelor, you know, the most eligible bachelor in the world, and so charming and handsome. I heard that Princess Margaret is rather keen on him.'

'What does that mean, Grandma?' Isabel had asked, staring at the photograph of Eunice curtseying to the prince. 'Illegible bachelor?'

'Eligible, darling, not illegible. It means that the prince is looking for a wife.'

'Does he want to marry Mumma?' she had asked, sick with fear that the prince would carry Eunice off to his castle, never to be seen again.

'I don't think so, darling, but that wouldn't be so bad, would it? You wouldn't mind living in a nice castle in the south of France, would you?'

'Could you and Grandad come too?'

'Just try and stop me.' Her grandmother smiled across at Grandad Pearson, who shook out his paper and gave a short dry laugh.

'Queen Mother would suit your grandma very well, Izzy,' he had said with a smile.

Sitting on a pavement seat under the palm trees, Isabel read the diary entry made a couple of days after Eunice had met Prince Rainier.

> *Heavens, a real prince who bowed when he shook hands, and I did my best curtsey, of course. Sylvia said he was making eyes at me – if only! What would it be like to marry a prince? I suppose every woman who meets him thinks about it. He's certainly a real dish. I think I could adapt to being royalty. Anyway, I mustn't keep going on about him. Eric's getting frightfully jealous. We've only known each other a few weeks, but he's awfully smitten, poor darling. And I must admit to being pretty smitten myself. I do like all the embassy stuff, the parties and receptions. In the absence of the possibility of royal status the prospect of being the wife of a diplomat comes a good second! Dear Eric, he has such adorable blue eyes and a noble profile. God, how superficial I am – he's actually a lovely man in every way and I think he might pop the question any day now.*

Just a couple of weeks after that, Eunice was dancing again at the Beaux-Arts, in a pale green chiffon dress, and somewhere in the audience Antonia was watching her.

Despite the warmth of the day, goose bumps crept along Isabel's arms and down her spine. Sitting there with the diary and the program was like stepping back into her mother's life. She wanted to be inside the theatre, to sit in the auditorium just as Antonia had done, to look around and see what Antonia had seen. At first she couldn't find the theatre. The changes in the streets since Eunice's map was printed had her walking around in circles until she realised that she had already passed it twice, only now it was called the Princess Grace Theatre. It was late afternoon by that time and, undeterred, Isabel headed for the box office to ask if she could take a look inside. It was not a normal request, the woman at the desk told her in a clipped Parisian accent. There was a rehearsal in progress, but she would consult the manager. Did madame have a special reason for wanting to visit the theatre outside of performance times? She nodded when Isabel, in awkward French, explained that her mother had danced there with Compagnie Fluide in 1953. The woman indicated a seat and asked Isabel to wait, the manager would be with her in a few moments. She roamed the foyer impatiently, studying the history of the theatre, which was told via a series of framed photographs and accompanying text. The Beaux-Arts had been completely refurbished in December 1981 under the direction of Princess Grace. She would not, after all, be able to look upon the scene as her mother and Antonia had done.

'Perhaps you'd like to see photographs of the theatre as it used to be,' the manager suggested in hushed tones as he led her to the back of the theatre where some dancers were in rehearsal. His English was excellent and he seemed genuinely delighted to meet the daughter of a past performer. 'It is beautiful now, of course, but you would like to see what it looked like in your mother's day?' He was too busy to spend time with her then and there was a ballet festival beginning the next day, but if she cared to return during the last week in October, the theatre archivist would be available. There would be photographs of the original theatre, performances and performers, perhaps even some of her mother. Isabel's heart leapt at the prospect, and she thanked him profusely and made an appointment for the last week in October.

In the days that followed she could think of little else, reading over and over again Eunice's jottings, the stories of dressing-room tantrums, good and bad audiences, parties with Eric, and drives along the steep coastal road to Antibes to an exhibition, Nice for an embassy reception, or Cannes for a jaunt on someone's yacht. She entered into another world, a world of diplomats and dancers, a glittering, cosmopolitan one that bore no relation to her own with her grandparents. She vacillated between jealousy and the feeling, one that had haunted her since childhood, that her mother was always beyond her reach. It was almost incomprehensible that her quiet upbringing in a Perth backwater had been so closely linked to this glamorous life on the other side of the world. Perhaps if her mother had returned triumphant from Europe, bringing with her the sparkling aura of performance, it might have been different. But Eunice had returned a grief-stricken invalid.

Isabel had been bitterly disappointed when Eunice and Eric returned from Europe. Her excitement had evaporated the moment she saw them. Her mother was neither the glamorous dancer of the photographs nor the vivacious mother who had lived in the pages of her letters, but a thin, pale woman whose face was lined with pain and whose wheelchair was carried down the gangplank onto the Fremantle wharf by two sailors. Isabel's jealousy was born in that moment, for as the chair was set down it was pushed to the terminal by a tall blond man in a Harris-tweed jacket, the bowl of a pipe sticking out the breast pocket. A stranger who talked like the men who read the news on the radio, and who seemed to have first claim on her mother. Poor Eric, he had shown such patience.

Years later he had told Isabel that the moment he saw her that day, in her blue coat with the velvet collar and her matching hat and white gloves, he had fallen in love with her. 'I felt as though you were my real daughter, as though I'd always known you. I'd no idea you were going to give me such a hard time. You looked like a little angel, but you really tested my patience.'

It took at least two years before her anger, disappointment and jealousy burned itself out, before she learned to live with Eunice and Eric as they were, devoted to and dependent on each other, a couple of which she could not be a part. She had grown to love Eric as if he had indeed been her own father. Only since her mother's death had Isabel realised how many questions she had left unasked.

Isabel spent long days in the old Monaco museum and the library, building up a picture of the life Eunice must have led. She scrolled through the newspaper archives on microfiche, strug-gling with the French headlines, to learn about the people who lived in and visited Monaco in the fifties: the cars they drove, the restaurants in which they ate, the clothes they wore. She walked for miles to drink tea in hotels where Eunice had drunk tea, to eat dinner in the restaurant where Eric had proposed, to search for a dress shop where Eunice had bought a wool stole, a leather shop where she had bought a handbag. She took train and bus rides exploring the coastal and inland towns, always referring where she could to something in Eunice's diaries. A visit to a *parfumerie* in Grasse, a picnic spot near Antibes, a favourite beach. She even managed to locate the place where Eric's embassy car had broken down and they had waited by the roadside for a breakdown truck to arrive from Cannes. Each time she rounded a corner to a new street or another magnificent view, she paused to wonder if it was still as Eunice would have seen it.

Within days of Isabel's visit to the theatre Eunice's life had become more real, more present, than her own. But still the absent months frustrated her, and she could see no way of finding out what had happened to take Eunice away from the company in Monaco for several months in 1953. By the last week in October she was in a fever of anticipation and she knew that whatever she might find at the Princess Grace Theatre would now fit into her understanding of those times.

'You are our most welcome guest,' the young manager told her with a smile, pressing tickets for the ballet into her hand. 'Please take your time and Lisette will help you with anything you need.'

Dressed entirely in black with dazzling crimson lipstick that matched her dyed crimson hair, Lisette was the theatre's part-time historian/archivist. Isabel thought she had never seen anyone look less like a theatre historian than this robust young woman whose breasts threatened to burst forth from the tight black fabric of her low-cut dress. 'So tell me, Madame Carter, where do you wish to begin?' Lisette asked, leading Isabel to what looked like a library reading room, the shelves packed with bound copies of old programs, file boxes full of photographs, and walls covered with photographs of performers, patrons and audiences.

And so they began with the arrival of the dance company in early February 1953. Isabel was giddy with excitement. She had to restrain herself, slow herself down to take notes and to apply the blue stickers that Lisette had given her to mark anything she wanted to copy. It was all there, the booking sheets, the performance listings, the costings, the names of the dancers, the audience numbers, the programs with Eunice's name, sometimes on the front cover, sometimes inside, on posters and handbills, and in newspaper and magazine reviews. The company would perform for a few weeks, then there would be a different company, and then they were back again with a new program. As she turned each page Isabel felt as though she was walking behind Eunice, a fly on the wall in the dressing room, in the front row of the stalls at a performance, a silent observer at rehearsals. Constantly on the verge of tears, she was intent on drawing from the documents whatever they could tell her. But in the middle of May, Eunice's name disappeared from the archives, only reappearing in mid October when she danced again for a few weeks before the accident cut her down.

'There is a file,' Lisette said thoughtfully, 'a correspondence file. Perhaps we find the answer there.' By now they were on first-name terms and Lisette, with the detective-like curiosity of the historian, was also anxious to fill the gaps. She scanned the correspondence archive, shaking her head as page after page revealed nothing of relevance. 'Ah! *Voilá!* I have it,' she exclaimed at last. 'A letter from the director of Compagnie Fluide to the director of Théâtre des Beaux-Arts. Mademoiselle Eunice Pearson is to take *congé* . . . how you say . . . ?'

'Leave of absence?' Isabel volunteered.

'Yes, that is right, leave of absence for reasons personal and of health. She goes to Lisbon for four weeks. But then, look, in this next letter here . . . it is made longer . . . extended, you say? Until *fin Septembre.*'

Isabel thought she might faint. 'Personal and health reasons . . . does it say anything else about those reasons?'

Lisette shook her head. '*Non.* Look, you can read for yourself – it is not a difficult letter for translating.'

'Is there anything in there when she comes back?'

'Perhaps,' Lisette shrugged. 'We will see.' And she worked her way on through the file. 'Just this,' she said a few minutes later. 'Just this letter advising that she is back a little early and then her name is on the programs again. You see she comes back and within two weeks is dancing again as a soloist. So whatever this health reason she must have stayed active while she was away, or she could not dance again so quickly when she comes back.'

The two women stared at each other in confusion across the vast table now piled with files and papers. 'You want we take a look at the photographs? I don't know, maybe she is there, your mother. Now I too want to see her! I must look at her, I will be desolate if she is not there.'

But Eunice was there, curtseying to Prince Rainier, in a photograph so familiar to Isabel that she gasped in recognition. She was there on the stage, moving like a leaf in the wind against background swathes of white fabric, entwined with other dancers on what appeared to be a glass lake, peering into a dressing-room mirror with three other dancers, their hair tied back as they applied their make-up. There were half a dozen pictures so stunningly and purely Eunice that Isabel could not contain her tears.

Lisette brought her a glass of water. 'We can stop, Isabel, if you want. You come again tomorrow?'

'No, no, let's continue. Unless you don't have time.'

They found their way through more images. 'Perhaps,' suggested Isabel in a shaky voice, 'we could look for the fourteenth of April. I know she danced on that night. Someone whom I met recently saw that performance.'

'Here,' Lisette said triumphantly lifting an envelope from the file. 'This is the night.'

So this was the dress of eau de nil chiffon, this was the performance that Antonia had seen and forgotten, but for which she had kept the program. The camera had captured Eunice in arabesque, her body in a graceful arc, her head thrown back, one arm behind her, the other arched above her, her shingled hair gleaming in the spotlight.

'*Elle est tellement belle,*' Lisette breathed in admiration.

'Beautiful, yes,' whispered Isabel, almost unable to believe what she was seeing. 'Are there any more for that date?'

Lisette delved into the envelope. 'Some, yes. You want to have these rephotographed, I think, for yourself. I can arrange it for you. These . . . well, no, she is not on the stage but, look, here is a party, I think after the performance, perhaps she is here.'

The shiny black and white prints were as sharp as the day they were taken, only the slightest yellowing at the corners proving that they were over forty years old. 'Such good photography then,' Lisette said, spreading the photographs on the table.

'There's my stepfather,' gasped Isabel, picking up a picture of a group of people in evening dress raising their champagne glasses to the camera. 'The fair man here, my mother married him later that year.'

Lisette turned over the photograph. 'Yes, it is as I thought. A party after the performance on the fourteenth of April. It is here in the theatre, it seems to celebrate the birthday of the founder of Compagnie Fluide.' She pushed the photographs across to Isabel. 'You look through these, Isabel, I go to fetch us some coffee, and then we look in October when your mother comes back.'

Isabel drew the photographs back across the table, slipping one after the other aside to see if Eunice or Eric would show up again. She was almost at the end when she found it, a photograph of the party. In the foreground was Eric, deep in conversation with an elderly man in a dinner jacket, and further back, almost hidden by other guests, Eunice, still in the chiffon dress, champagne glass in hand, conversed with a young woman in a halter-necked dress. She picked it up, entranced at first by the sophistication of Eric's stance, the manner in which he leaned forward to explain something to the other man, then by the long curve of Eunice's neck, the slim arm with the hand holding the champagne glass and a cigarette in a long holder. She was so captivated by the grace of Eunice's posture that she very nearly overlooked the other woman gazing intently into her mother's face. A woman whose face was undoubtedly the same one into which Isabel herself had gazed so intently in the cloister at Évora. Antonia.

It was the first time in her life that Isabel had seen snow and the delicate blanket that covered the rooftops and spires of Nuremberg enchanted her. 'You can see the pictures but nothing tells you how it feels,' she said. 'It's the stillness of it, even here in the city, the snow changes everything. And the light – it's so weird.'

'Ha! That is more snow up there, Isabel, that is what makes the light this way. You will like it less after a few more weeks,' Klaus said, gripping her elbow to guide her across the street. 'Everything slows down, everything is more trouble. But *ja*, I know, it's very beautiful. I can't believe you didn't see the snow before. Come, we go to a café in that street and I introduce you to good German hot chocolate.'

Isabel had fallen instantly in love with Nuremberg and with what she had seen of Germany, even before the snow started to fall, before she woke on that Christmas Eve morning. As the train had carried her from the south of France along the borders of Italy and Switzerland and into Germany, she wished she had left earlier and given herself more time, more stops along the way. Travelling north from the mild Mediterranean winter the temperature dropped rapidly, and from the window of the train she frequently caught sight of snow-clad mountain tops as the landscape changed to the dense forests of Switzerland and Germany, and to towns and villages that looked like a series of operatic sets. Klaus had met her at the station and driven her home to his apartment on the fourth floor of an elegant old building on the banks of the river.

'The apartment is ready for you in two days,' he explained. 'It's just ten minutes from here. It belongs to a friend from the university. He is leaving to go to England for a few months and he is happy to have someone stay there. Until then, please, be my guest.'

Since then she had moved into the apartment and started to find her own way around, shopping for food in the nearby supermarket, and even finding an Australian newspaper at the bookshop on the same street.

'So you like Germany with and without snow?' Klaus asked, steering her between the slow-moving traffic. 'And your husband? You think he will like it too?'

'He'll love it, I know he will. You know, Klaus, I never imagined it would be so beautiful, and the people are so friendly.'

'It is just because they see your Australian smile, Isabel. We are not very friendly to strangers, but if you ask us something or give us a task to do, then we will break our backs to answer the question or do the job.'

Isabel had left Monaco with a folder of photographs and photocopied documents from the Théâtre des Beaux-Arts, and she had held high hopes of Klaus as a source of information about Antonia. But in this respect he had disappointed her. Their families had been friends during their childhood and they had met again in the mid fifties when Klaus was doing some research in Portugal. They saw each other from time to time over the years, in Monsaraz or in Germany.

'It's strange,' he agreed when Isabel told him of Antonia's letter and showed him the photograph taken at the theatre. 'But then maybe she forgets. It is a long time ago, much of the river has flowed under the bridge. You will go back to Monsaraz, yes? The photographs are very good. You must be happy to find all these pictures, Isabel.' And he moved her on to other subjects, seemingly unaware of the tension that had dominated the days after their visit to Évora. Isabel almost began to doubt the intensity of her own memories, but she returned always to the fact that if Antonia had remembered the performance and found the program, she must also remember that she met Eunice at the party. Why hadn't she mentioned that in her letter?

But there was nothing more she could do until she returned to Portugal, and that she would do after Doug's departure. He was due on New Year's Day and would stay until mid January. All she could do until then was enjoy the fairytale beauty of Germany in winter, with Christmas trees twinkling and the shop windows decorated with all the trappings of a northern Christmas. This was what she had wanted, what she had yearned for last Christmas Day as she sat at the table in the early afternoon heat of a Perth summer, watching the dismay on everyone's face when she mentioned that she might not be around next year. Something, somewhere totally different was what she had wanted, and that was what she had got. Tomorrow they would all be seated around that same table, without her. She would call them and tell them how she loved them. Missing them would be a small price to pay for an experience so new and exciting, something she might never enjoy again. And the freedom from preparations delighted her. Christmas could happen without her working herself to exhaustion in the preceding weeks – this year she could sit back and let it happen around her.

The day after she arrived in Germany, Klaus had taken her to a department store in Nuremberg where she bought a couple of thick sweaters, a pair of boots, socks, some warm pants and a polar fleece jacket, which was light but incredibly warm. She thought Sara would have been proud of her, not only for the practical choices but for her restraint in buying only what she really thought she would need. She had considered buying something glamorous to wear for Klaus's Christmas dinner to be held on Christmas Eve, in true German fashion, but had held back, knowing that it would be another thing to carry with her when she left. But then, as they crossed the street, an olive-green velvet skirt caught her eye in the window of a shop. 'How far away is the hot chocolate, Klaus?' she asked.

'Here.' He indicated with a wave. 'Two more shops from here.'

'Look, just give me ten minutes, will you? I want to try on this skirt. Go to the café and I'll join you there.'

He wandered off to the coffee shop and she slipped inside the boutique. '*Das Rock bitte,*' she said to the smiling sales assistant, indicating the window display, and a few moments later she was unzipping her jacket in a fitting room.

The skirt came with a fitted, long-sleeved jacket with embroidered frog fastenings in a darker green, and she had bought a cream silk blouse to go with it. As she stood in front of the bedroom mirror that evening, Isabel was delighted that she had given way to the last-minute shopping impulse. It was the first time since leaving home that she had actually dressed up, and she couldn't remember the last time she'd worn a skirt. 'Forgive me this moment of madness, Sara,' she whispered to her reflection, 'but I think it was worth it.'

She picked her bag up from the dressing table and looked at the photograph of the Gang of Four propped against the mirror.

She picked it up, perching for a moment on the nearby stool. What were they doing now? Robin? Probably sleeping – it was the middle of the night in Australia – but was she all alone in her remote little cottage or would she have gone back to Perth for Christmas? And Grace, somewhere not so far away, perhaps also seeing her first-ever snow. And finally, Sally – no snow in California, what would she be doing this Christmas Eve in a country that was just waking as Isabel set out for the evening. She had hated writing her letter but longed for theirs. They had sent them to Doug, who would bring them to her in Germany, and she was impatient for their news.

She stood the photo against the mirror again. In a few days Doug would be here with her, in this apartment. She stared at the small photograph of him that she always carried with her. She had taken it one cool winter morning when he came back from playing golf. His fine grey hair was blown back from his face by the sea breeze, and she snapped him as he turned towards her with his characteristic half-smile. She moved the tips of her fingers lovingly across his face. She was ambivalent about his visit. Part of her longed to see him, hold him, talk to him, and another part wanted to be left to finish her European journey alone. There were the conversations they had to have about change, conversations best left for home, but she was not sure they could be postponed until then. She put Doug's photo back beside the Gang of Four and stood up, smoothing her skirt with a sigh. Then she switched off the lights, made her way down the stairs to the street and the nearby taxi rank.

'Isabel!' said Klaus, drawing her into the warm brightness of the hall. He had invited a dozen people to his Christmas dinner, which he had been organising for several days. '*Bitte, kommen Sie rein*. How beautiful this dress you bought. *Wunderschön*. Now everyone is here. And there is a surprise.'

He tossed Isabel's coat onto a bench seat in the hall and led her through into the living room, which was already full of people. Isabel straightened her jacket and pushed back her hair. She had forgotten to ask Klaus if anyone else spoke English, but she realised suddenly that she didn't care if she went through the whole evening unable to speak to anyone. To be here at this time was like being in one of Eunice's Christmas stories, which were always full of dinners the night before Christmas, cosy interiors and log fires, cities cloaked in snow, children throwing snowballs and sliding on the ice, and horse-drawn sleighs decked with bells and red ribbons.

Klaus shepherded her between the guests towards the sideboard, where a small silver tureen rested above a blue flame. He tilted it to fill a tall glass. 'Here, Isabel – *Gluwein*. It is what you call, I think, mulled wine – warm, very good, very strong.' He handed her the glass and she sipped it cautiously. It was certainly strong, spicy and delicious. She sipped again.

'*Gesundheit!*' She smiled.

'*Ja, Gesundheit!* Now the surprise, not just for you, Isabel, for me too! I come home after our chocolate-drinking this morning, and my telephone is ringing. Who is there when I pick it up? Well, come in the kitchen, see who it is!'

And as he pushed open the door Isabel found herself face to face with Antonia once again.

NINETEEN

Late in the afternoon of New Year's Eve, Grace lay on the couch in front of the fire in Vivienne's living room reading Sally's letter just one more time. It had arrived that morning bringing relief as well as news. Letters from Isabel and Robin had arrived the week before Christmas, but there had been nothing from Sally and as the days between Christmas and New Year unfolded, Grace had grown increasingly uneasy.

Isabel's letter was confusing: part travelogue, part detective work about her mother, and she constantly mentioned a woman she had met in Portugal who had once seen her mother dance. She sounded distant, confused about what she was doing and why. Six months ago a letter like this would have infuriated Grace, but now it was a relief to discover that at least one of her friends seemed as disorientated and confused as she was. Robin, by contrast, was clear and focused, although the fact that she made no mention of Jim McEwan spoke more of denial than resolution to Grace. She was selling her house and her partnership in the law firm and buying a bookshop in Albany. Grace's initial reaction was shock and fear at the decision to relinquish a brilliant career for a quiet life in a country bookshop. She had tossed and turned into the small hours, worrying about Robin's future, but next morning she admitted to herself that her anxiety was really about her own plans, which also involved radical and risky changes.

But now here was Sally's letter, a long, painful and passionate story, an apology, and an explanation of her real reasons for going to California. The tone was sad but hopeful, she loved the course and using the camera was helping her to see things in a different way. She felt more confident and she had met a man who seemed to be more than just a friend. The letter, photocopied and sent to the others, had a remarkable tone of maturity and self-knowledge. Folded inside it was another letter, a personal one to Grace. Two pages of flimsy airmail paper closely covered with Sally's small neat script, a letter with a story undisclosed to the others, a story that Sally needed to tell and which she thought Grace, more than anyone else, would understand.

She wrote about her anger that exploded in a devastating attack on Lisa's adoptive mother, about the black hole of depression into which she had fallen, and the way she had sent this new man flying so that he broke his leg. Grace laughed and cried and laughed again each time she read it. Finally she put the letter down, got up from the couch and checked the time. It was five o'clock, nine in the morning in California. She dialled the number on the letter and waited for the ringing tone, but the operator told her that lines to the US were busy and she should wait a while before trying again.

Freda, Vivienne's Labrador, barked at the kitchen door and Grace let her in and fed her from a tin of Chum. The cold, still air from the garden battled the heat from the Aga. The forecast snow had not fallen, although Grace had hoped for it all day. 'You won't be so keen once it arrives,' Vivienne had said, laughing, when she called from Oxford that afternoon. 'It looks wonderful at first but it soon deteriorates into loathsome slush.'

'It's okay for you,' Grace said, 'you're just blasé. I've never seen snow and I'm going to be so disappointed if it doesn't arrive soon.'

'Well, I hope you enjoy it, and I'm very grateful to you for staying in the house. I always worry about frozen pipes when I go away in winter.' She had left a couple of days before Christmas to spend the festive season with her daughter, who was married to a farmer and lived just outside Oxford. 'Come with me,' she had said. 'Jennie and Sam have heaps of space, and my other daughter and her family, and Gary and his boyfriend will be there. It'll be a real English family Christmas.'

But Grace had not been in the mood for meeting new people, let alone staying with them. Since the day that Vivienne had brought her face-to-face with herself, she had felt unable to concentrate on anything other than how she would restructure her life when she got back home. A week later she had called the office and told Denise that she would not be back until the end of February. And then, at Vivienne's suggestion, she had given up the Brighton flat and moved to the house in Hurstpierpoint. It was a financial relief as well as a pleasure, but there was no way she could cope with a full-scale family Christmas.

'Well, then, it's my good luck to have a house and dog-sitter over Christmas. Are you sure you won't be lonely and depressed on your own?' Vivienne had asked.

'I think a couple of weeks alone sounds like heaven,' Grace said. 'Total self-indulgence and no need to worry about any of the usual Christmas stuff.' And that was how it had been. Apart from sending presents and cards to Japan, and to her father in the nursing home, Grace had thankfully exempted herself from Christmas and spent the days taking brisk walks and drives through the wintry countryside, trying to understand the past and reconstruct the future. For a woman who, a few months earlier, had always been on the go and rarely alone, she had come to an abrupt and surprising halt.

Grace made herself a cup of tea and a chicken sandwich, carried them back to the lounge, picked up the phone and dialled California again.

'And you didn't mind being alone over Christmas?' Sally asked when she had overcome her delight at the surprise phone call. 'You didn't want to race off somewhere and organise something or look after someone?'

'Nothing was further from my mind.' Grace laughed. 'In fact, talking to people is the last thing I want to do at present, except that once I'd read your letter, I just had to talk to you, tell you how brave you are to do all this.'

'I thought you might be hurt or annoyed that I'd never told

you. We've been friends so long, but I'd locked myself into silence, you see . . .'

'Of course I see, and of course I'm not hurt or annoyed, but I'm so glad you've told me now. And when it comes to being locked into things, well, I'm the world champion at that. Is it today you're going to lunch with the Mendelsons?'

'Tomorrow. I was seriously panicking when you called but talking to you is making me feel better. I have to be very careful that I don't stuff it all up a second time. Be on my best behaviour.'

'Just be yourself, Sally,' Grace said. 'They liked you the first time or they wouldn't be giving you a second chance.'

'Being myself is more complicated since I uncovered bits of me that I didn't know existed. I keep discovering a stranger.'

'Me too. Can you imagine me lying around for hours reading books, watching movies and crying?'

'Sounds very un-Grace-like but also pretty healthy,' Sally said. 'Especially the crying.'

'Well, then, I should be the healthiest woman in England. I cry constantly about everything and nothing. This morning I cried for an hour because I saw a robin dragging a worm out of the ground.'

Sally laughed and paused for a moment. 'You do sound very different, Grace. Softer, more vulnerable, I suppose.'

'Vulnerable with a capital V. I only came here for a holiday, because I didn't want to be alone when you lot had gone. Now look what's happened! That Isabel has a lot to answer for.'

'When are you going home? When do you have to start work again?'

Grace took a deep breath – telling Sally of her decision would be a test of her own feelings. 'I'm not going back to work.'

'Sorry? What do you mean?'

'I'm not going back to work. I didn't put it in the letter because I didn't really decide until Christmas. I phoned Denise the day after Boxing Day, and then I phoned the dean's office. I'm taking early retirement.' The silence at the end of the line unnerved her. 'Are you still there, Sally?'

'Yes, yes – of course. I'm just taking it in. Early retirement, I see, okay, and you're sure about this?'

'I was hoping you'd help me be sure, now you're making me nervous.'

'Sorry! Don't be! I'm just so amazed. Tell me more, what are going to do?'

Grace took another deep breath, to steady herself. 'I'm staying on here for another month or so and then I really have to go back to tie up things at work, do a handover. Then, well . . . I'm not really sure yet. I'll take my time, smell a few roses, try to concentrate on just being instead of doing. But I'll have to find a part-time job. There might be a bit of consultancy work with the health department. That would suit me, as long as I mend my spending habits.' It sounded good, she thought, it sounded clear and confident. She breathed more freely. 'What do you reckon?'

'I reckon it's fantastic, Grace, really brilliant. But you were always worried about money. Will you manage okay?

'As I said, I'll have to pull my head in a bit and I thought I'd sell the flat. I could buy somewhere at half the price and still be very comfortable – scale down, you know what I mean.'

'Yes, yes, I know. I'm so pleased for you. I've been worried for so long –' She stopped suddenly.

'It's okay,' Grace said. 'It's okay, you're allowed to be worried now. I mean, I can now accept that in the spirit it's meant. I think it'll be okay, it's a bit scary, but one thing I'm sure about is that I can't live the way I did before. When are you coming back to Perth, Sally?'

'I'm not sure yet. I'm due back at school mid July, my visa expires at the end of May, so I'll have to leave then. A lot depends on what happens tomorrow, really. It seems to be all I can think about at the moment.'

'Of course. And this man, Steve, is he . . . well, is he . . .?'

Sally laughed. 'No he is *not* an alcoholic. Hard to believe, I know, but I seem to have broken the pattern. I'm so lucky. He may come back with me for a holiday. You'll like him, Grace, I know you will.'

'I'm sure I will, and he's the lucky one. Did you have Christmas together?'

'We did. It was a bit fraught, the daughter problem – his daughter. I mentioned her in the letter . . .'

'She sounds deadly.'

'She's pretty grim. I'm not sure how all that's going to pan out, but I guess it'll be okay in the end.'

'Sally . . .'

'Yes?'

'You're a wonderful woman, my most precious friend. I don't think I was ever really able to tell you that. Oh God, now I'm crying again. When will this ever stop?'

'You too, Grace. The crying's good, don't worry about it. I miss you. You'll take care, won't you? So many changes . . .'

'I will, I'll be fine, and you . . . tomorrow, especially . . . I'm thinking of you. Be strong, don't be ashamed. I'll see you in a few months.'

Grace sat in the darkness staring into the fading fire. This time last year she had been heading off to a New Year's Eve party, at Isabel's in-laws, surrounded by friends and acquaintances. Bright lights, laughter, conversation, good food and wine. At midnight they had sung 'Auld Lang Syne' and she had gone home to bed exhausted. Now, for the first time in her life, she would be alone as the year turned. She wondered why it had always seemed so important to be out celebrating, surrounded by people, when what now seemed to matter was solitude. She leaned back on the couch contemplating the evening stretching ahead of her: the news, a Cary Grant movie on television, and then perhaps she wouldn't even stay awake until midnight. Freda settled by the couch resting her head on Grace's knee. 'Just you and me tonight,' Grace said contentedly, stroking her golden head. 'Happy New Year, old girl.'

She woke early next morning to an unfamiliar pearly light between the curtains. Jumping out of bed she flung them back and gasped in delight: the garden, the trees, the village rooftops and fields as far as she could see were covered in snow, and it was still falling. Dragging on her tracksuit Grace ran down the stairs and through the kitchen. She thrust her feet into Vivienne's boots, which stood by the back door, and stepped out into the eerie stillness of the garden. The snow softened the stark winter landscape and muted every sound. It settled cool and delicate on her hair and eyelashes. Freda, who had followed her, sniffed the air and wagged her tail, hoping for a walk, as Grace stood there in the silence letting the snow settle on her, marvelling at the pristine whiteness of the paths and the rose beds, the delicate outlines of the trees and bushes. The snow smelled of damp linen and she inhaled deeply, drawing some snowflakes up her nose, making herself sneeze.

Alone in the white garden she stretched out her arms, turning around in circles as a sudden shaft of sunlight broke through the clouds and rendered the garden a dazzling, blinding white. Dizzy and breathless she scooped snow in her two hands and held the melting whiteness to her face, feeling the softness, tasting its bland metallic coolness on her tongue. Finally she rolled it into a ball and threw her first-ever snowball, delighting at the way the hardened snow fell apart in a powdery white shower when it hit the gate.

'All my life and I've never seen this before,' she whispered into the silence. 'And if Isabel hadn't decided to go away I might never have seen it.' It seemed suddenly that there was so much more to see, here and in other places, places she had never dreamed of going, places she had always thought herself too busy, too needed, to take the time to see. As she strolled around the garden listening with fascination to the crunch of her footsteps compacting the snow, she felt the tears begin again. They were the tears of wasted time and missed opportunity, the roads not taken because she had stuck so rigidly to what she knew and what she could control. Now, on this brilliant and beautiful English morning, the snow had transformed her view just as it had transformed the physical landscape. How could she have been so frightened? How could she have become such a control freak, keeping everything on such a tight rein to manage her fear? Where had it come from, that fear that had gripped her unacknowledged for decades, the fear that manifested as a hard, tight feeling which had in itself come to mean safety?

'Oh my god,' she said aloud. 'I'm fifty-six in a couple of weeks, and there's so much I still have to do.' She stopped in her tracks, remembering her last birthday, an evening picnic by the river with Robin, Sally and Isabel, and the feeling that had swamped her as they held up their glasses to drink to her and then sang 'Happy Birthday'. All the big, important things have happened, she had thought in that moment. Nothing changes from now on.

'Tomorrow is the first day of the rest of your life, Grace,' Sally had said that night. And secretly she had thought it a stupid remark but had smiled and nodded because she loved Sally and didn't want to be ungracious. Now she threw back her head and laughed aloud, the snow falling into her mouth. Then she sat down abruptly in the snow and rolled on her side, laughing again, rolling over and over in the snow while Freda bounded around her, barking in excitement.

Minutes later, her soaking tracksuit abandoned on the kitchen floor, Grace stood in her underwear in the lounge and stared at Vivienne's big untidy desk where she had sat a few days earlier to make the life-changing calls to Denise and the dean. On the floor alongside the desk was a pile of files that Vivienne had obligingly removed from the bottom drawer so that Grace could put her feet in it if she needed to. Smiling at the empty open drawer, Grace picked up the files and dumped them back in the drawer, closing it firmly with her bare foot. Then, drawing a deep breath of satisfaction and resolve, she headed upstairs for a shower and some dry clothes to wear on this, the first morning of the rest of her life.

'Well, either the snow or two weeks alone seem to have kicked you further along the road to change,' Vivienne said five days later as she parked the car in the forecourt of a community hall in south London. 'I'm having trouble keeping up with your evolving personality!'

Grace flung open the car door with a laugh. 'If you're having trouble, how do you think my kids and the others back home will cope?' She stepped out onto the ice, stamping her feet to warm them. 'Imagine how terrified they'll be when they hear about the early retirement. They'll all be thinking up ways to stop me trying to organise their lives for them! Meanwhile I'll just be revelling in my own life. Now, what's this scheme you and Orinda have been on about for so long?'

Vivienne locked the car and picked up the stick she had brought along for safety. 'All will be revealed in a few minutes,' she said. 'And you may wish you'd never asked.'

'It wouldn't have mattered if I hadn't asked,' Grace said, amused. 'You've been threatening me with it for weeks, but you've avoided actually telling me about it.'

'No point trying to get you excited while you were a weeping mass of confusion. Now you're a woman ready for anything, I can take advantage of you!' Vivienne retorted. She made her way carefully over the ice towards a set of double doors beneath a colourful sign that said 'The Patchwork Project'.

The previous day Grace had taken an early train to Victoria Station to meet Vivienne. They had done a lightning tour of the National Gallery and then wandered down into Trafalgar Square, and Grace, who had spent her life with her mother's terror of birds and other fluttering creatures, had bought a bag of birdseed. She gritted her teeth at the first touch of fluttering wings, but her fear soon faded along with the tight feeling in her chest as she stood still and confident with pigeons flapping around her head and settling on her outstretched arms. From the square they had gone to an organ recital in St Martin-in-the-Fields, and then eaten a thick bean soup with crusty bread at the restaurant in the crypt. Vivienne had booked them into a small hotel where the rooms were too hot and the water not hot enough, and they had collapsed on their beds for a couple of hours to recover before calling a taxi to take them to the theatre. Seeing *The Mousetrap*, now in its forty-fifth year, had been close to the top of Grace's list of must-dos while in England. As they drove out of London heading for home the next morning, Vivienne had suggested a detour to introduce Grace to her sewing scheme in south London.

'Okay.' Vivienne grinned, leaning heavily against the door that scraped noisily over the stoop. 'This is it, my baby that's grown into a monster. Ta-rah!'

Before she walked in, Grace could hear the music coming from a stereo system and the voices of women singing along, loud and flat, with Barry Manilow. It was a small hall with a floor of bare boards and a preponderance of ugly green paint. On the stage at one end cardboard boxes were stacked deep and high, and on the floor were piles of cotton dresses, skirts, blouses and curtains. In the middle of the hall a collection of tables set out in a square formed a work area and around them sat more than a dozen women, laughing, talking and singing as they worked. Some seemed to be cutting off buttons and stripping out zips, others were cutting the fabric into large squares and stacking it in piles. A couple of small children sat on the floor amid the piles of clothes, playing with a plastic truck and some coloured bricks.

'Whoa, look out, girls, the boss is here!' called a birdlike woman with pure white hair. 'Stop looking as though you're enjoying it.'

She dragged herself up with her walking frame and slowly made her way towards Vivienne while others called out greetings from the table.

''Bout time you paid us a visit, Viv, and I thought you'd've got rid of that stick by now,' she said with a grin as Vivienne enveloped her and the walking frame in a bear hug.

'I've only got it because of the ice, Florrie. Mostly I don't use it now, honest!'

'Well, I'm glad to hear it. Didn't have a stick meself until I got to eighty, so you're not allowed one in your sixties. Brought us another volunteer, have you?'

'A visitor rather than a volunteer,' Vivienne said, turning back to Grace. 'This is my friend Grace, she's from Australia and she stayed on after the quilting retreat.' She gave Florrie a nudge in the ribs. 'I'm hoping she might get involved, so make it look like fun.'

Florrie extended a bony hand that disguised a grip of steel. 'Pleased to meet you, Grace. You're a marked woman if Viv's got plans for you. Don't expect to get back to Australia without her drawing some promise of blood, sweat and tears.' She gripped Grace by the elbow and drew her closer to the table. 'What you see here is a sweatshop.'

'And Florrie's the tyrant who's worse than any Victorian employer,' called a plump young woman who was breastfeeding a baby at the far end of the table. 'Take a seat, come and join us.'

'What it is, you see, is not a sweatshop,' Vivienne explained as they sat at the table with mugs of tea made by a smartly dressed woman in her fifties who would have looked more at home at a charity lunch. 'It's a workshop. All this cotton clothing comes from the major charities. They get this stuff given to them for their op shops but half the clothes they can't sell, so instead of sending it to the rag merchants who only give them a few quid for it, they give it to us—just the cottons. It's all washed. There're a couple of big washers and driers out in the back kitchen. Then we bring it back in here and start work on it.'

'Too much talk, not enough action,' Florrie called, pushing a couple of pairs of scissors towards Grace and Vivienne. 'Talk and work at the same time. Get the buttons and the zips off that pile of stuff.'

Vivienne picked up the scissors and began snipping the buttons off a blue floral dress. Gathering them together, she slipped them into a small snap-lock plastic bag. 'It's a value-adding project, which means it adds value to the stuff that's given to us by the charities. When the cottons are clean they're brought in here, the buttons are taken off and sealed in bags, the zips come off and they're packed into bags of two, four or six. Then they go back to the op shops and get sold, and we get the money. You know how expensive buttons and zips and trimmings are, well, these are all in good condition, and sorted and packed they sell like hot cakes. We can get more for a pack of six or eight buttons than the op shop can get for the blouse they come from, or for a huge pile of clothes sold for rags.'

'And zips!' cut in the elegant tea-maker who was now sitting beside Grace. 'Think what you'd pay for six zips these days. But you can buy this pack of six secondhand zips for half the price and we get money for our running costs. I'm Zena, by the way. I've been coming here a couple of mornings a week for the last three years.'

'Then there's the exciting bit,' said Vivienne. 'That's what's

276

going on over the other side of the table. The hems and seams are cut off so there are just pieces of clean cotton fabric and it's packed into those boxes. Then we send the boxes to women's sewing circles in all sorts of places – Nigeria, Botswana, Sierra Leone, several others. You probably know that Oxfam and some of the other aid organisations have set up sewing groups for women in developing countries? They provide sewing machines and the women are taught to sew so they can earn their living. In fact, there's an Australian woman who set up a whole lot in East Timor a couple of years ago.'

Grace nodded. 'Yes, Mavis Taylor, I read about her, she lived in Melbourne. She's incredible, she's over eighty and she'd never done anything like it before.'

'Exactly, and this is similar. What we've started to do now is value-add to that. We send women – quilters and patchworkers, experienced women who know the techniques and are good at design – to other countries so the local women can learn patchwork and quilting design and techniques. As well as doing dressmaking and other types of sewing, the women can actually get into designing and making quilts and cushion covers. The patchworkers show them some of the old principles of patchwork and then discuss with them how they might develop patterns and designs using their own cultural symbols and stories.

'Some of the quilts are sold in the towns there – if the women can get them into the markets and shops they're sold to the tourist trade. But they're making such incredible quilts and hangings and cushions that we're encouraging them to make special pieces that can be sold around the world for a really high price. That's part of what Gary's doing now through our design company. He markets these special pieces for us. He has them on display in the showroom but he also travels overseas a lot so he takes them with him and sells them to buyers in New York, San Francisco, Paris, Brussels – all sorts of places. Each quilt has a card with its history – you know, stuff about the fabric being rescued from the rag merchants, prepared by volunteers, and then designed and made by the women's sewing circles. And if the women have a story to go with the design, that goes on the card too.'

'And the money goes back to the communities?' Grace asked.

'Yes, and now we've been going for four years, the money is rolling in. It's having that vehicle to get to the overseas buyers that has made the difference – the quilts are sold in some really spiffy locations. The retailers have to sign an agreement that they will only take ten per cent of the sale price, Gary recovers his costs and even so, about sixty per cent of the sale price goes back to the sewing circles. And we're actually getting special orders now – I mean, the sewing women are getting special orders.'

'C'mon over here, Grace,' Florrie said, beckoning Grace up the steps to the stage. 'Come and look at these. Gary's taking them to an exhibition in Rome next week.' From a wooden packing case she took a folded quilt that had been wrapped in calico. 'This one was designed and made by women in Sierra Leone. The first one they made was called "Fire" and it sold for more than three thousand US dollars in New York. It paid for a well to be sunk near the village, so now they've called this new one "Water".' Florrie held one end of the quilt, resting her arms on her frame, and Zena took the other end, unfurling a gorgeous light, thick quilt patterned in waves of blue and green with showers of tiny patterned fabric strips in blue, green and white cascading between. Grace caught her breath.

'Magnificent, isn't it?' said Vivienne, who had now joined them on the stage. 'You should have seen "Fire", it was just as spectacular, in red, orange and black. It's now hanging in the foyer of a women's hospital in New York.'

Florrie pulled two more quilts from the case, one made in Botswana, and another from Sierra Leone.

'And all the material is cleaned and sorted here?' Grace asked.

'No, we've got another workshop in Liverpool,' Vivienne said. 'But it's run just the same as this. A workspace donated by the local council. The fabrics come from local organisations, the work is all done by volunteers. The shipping costs are covered by donations and the money that comes from the buttons and zips. We've got about sixty volunteers here, haven't we, Florrie?'

'Seventy-one at the last count,' Florrie said. 'The workshop's open every day, ten till four, and Wednesday evening till nine. You come along when you can, there's always plenty here. Thing is, you see, it's company for the women. Some of the young mothers come and bring their kids, and the old dames like me come for someone to talk to, and then there's the posh tarts like Zena here who come along to bring a bit of class and see how the other half lives!'

'You're shocking, Florrie.' Zena laughed. 'I come for the company too, and to do something useful with my time.' She turned to Grace. 'It's a lot more fun than tennis and bridge.'

Grace looked around at the quilts that had been created from messy piles of fabric, at the women working, talking and laughing together in the big chilly hall, which was filled with the same energy and spirit that had been a part of the quilting retreat. 'Did you start all this, Viv? On your own?'

'More or less, with a little help from my friends! And now Orinda has the same deal going in the US. They're sending fabric down to women in Mexico and Brazil.'

Grace took a deep breath. 'It's incredible. Honestly, it's brilliant. I . . . I don't know what to say . . .'

'Say you'll think about it, Grace,' Vivienne said. 'Say you'll think about Indonesia, perhaps, or Vietnam. Say you'll think about fitting it into your new life.'

It was four-thirty and almost dark when Vivienne pulled onto the M23 and headed for home. They had spent several hours at the workshop, looking at the accounts, and the business and marketing plan that Vivienne and Gary had drawn up for the Patchwork Project.

'It's not exactly self-funding, is it?' Grace asked.

'No,' Vivienne admitted, negotiating her way into a faster-moving lane of traffic. 'We get donations from quite a few places now, especially since we've got some of the more spectacular stuff to show.'

'But I think you've topped it up a bit, haven't you?'

'From time to time, yes, I have,' she admitted. 'Certainly at the start, but not now. Gary's topped it up too, but not with money, with effort. He's been as good as gold. I don't think we could have got this far without him. We also had a seeding grant from the government at the start.'

'I could probably get something going back home,' Grace said as a truck roared past sending a shower of mud and slush onto the windscreen. 'I think I could.'

'Look, Grace, the most important thing is that you keep going strongly along your present path, looking after yourself, getting out of the rat-race. I'd love you to get involved in this, but I don't want to dump a lot of stuff on you when you're sorting out your life. Just keep it in mind and if it feels right, then it can be as much or as little as you like.'

'I have to organise earning a living first,' Grace said. 'But working part-time I could spend some time on this.'

Grace's love affair with the snow lasted until the whiteness melted to a dirty slush, worsened daily by freezing rain that turned the roads to dangerous rinks of black ice. 'I don't think I could cope with this weather for long,' she told Vivienne as they sat around the kitchen table looking at the information on women's aid projects in the Asia-Pacific region Grace had found on the Internet.

'Told you so.' Vivienne grinned with more than a slight air of triumph. 'But just wait a few weeks till the snowdrops start coming up. It's a pity you can't stay until Easter, see the spring.'

'Don't I wish. But I have to face the music back home. I can't tell you how much I'd like to stay on, despite the weather!'

'Well, you've got another four weeks so we must make the most of it. Why don't we go down to Brighton this afternoon? I can take you to the Pavilion and show you the costume collection and the fabric restoration we did.'

They cleared the papers off the table and struggled into their coats.

'Four weeks,' Grace sighed, pulling on a pair of Vivienne's boots. 'That should be long enough to feel confident about the new me before I go back.'

Vivienne grinned. 'Everything you've done indicates courage and determination. I don't think you'll fall in a heap when you get home, but I suppose a few weeks to consolidate it is a good thing.'

But it was just two days before Grace had the opportunity to test her new self on her home ground. When they got back from Brighton the message from the nursing home was waiting on the answering machine. Reverend Duckworth, her father, had had a stroke and a fall and he kept calling Grace's name. The doctor thought he would only last a few more days. Grace listened to the message several times and then called the nursing home.

'I wondered what I would do if this happened while I was away,' she told Vivienne. 'After all, half the time he doesn't know who I am, but . . .'

'But now he's asking for you and you can't ignore it?'

Grace nodded. 'I don't think this is just me thinking I'm indispensable. There simply isn't anyone else, not family or friends, I mean. They're all dead, or too old and frail themselves. There's no one else to be with him, and no one else to bury him. This time I really do have to go.'

Vivienne nodded. 'Of course you do. You may not make it in time, but you won't forgive yourself if you don't try. Go and find your ticket and I'll start dialling the airline. We'll see if we can get you on a flight tomorrow.'

TWENTY

'Now that we've got her into her underwear and skirt, we'll sit her up gently and put her sweater on, and then use the hoist to lift her into the chair,' Estelle said. 'C'mon, honey, that's it, pop your arm through here, and now the other one . . . well done. Can you smooth down the back of her dress, please, Sally. Good. Now, up we go, Lisa.'

Sally watched as the frail figure in the hoist was lowered into the wheelchair. She picked up Lisa's shoes and took them over to her, kneeling on the floor beside her, picking up the small bony feet and sliding them carefully into the soft red leather pumps.

'That's it!' Estelle said, smoothing down her own dress and pinning back a strand of white hair that had escaped the knot at the back of her neck. 'You're getting really good at this, Sally. Want to go out and sit by the pool now, Lisa? Daddy's making us some coffee.'

Estelle opened the glass doors and Sally wheeled Lisa out into the sunlight, parking the chair alongside the big table while Estelle adjusted the sunshade to protect Lisa's face, and draped a rug over her knees.

'The sun's beautiful this morning but it's not really all that warm, is it? How about you, Sally? March is more summer for you, isn't it? Don't you feel chilly?'

Sally shook her head. 'No, this suits me fine. I'm not keen on the very hot weather. I usually go into hiding in the summer.'

Oliver came out through the kitchen door carrying a tray laden with a coffee plunger, mugs, a jug of cream and a plate of chocolate-chip cookies. 'Hey, Lisa, you look great in that red sweater,' he called, setting the tray down on the table. 'Is that the one Sally brought you? Want some coffee?'

A slight flicker seemed to cross the girl's face and one hand began its characteristic fluttering wave.

'I think that means yes,' Oliver said, and he poured a little coffee and a lot of cream into a plastic mug with a spout. 'I'll leave it there a while to cool,' he said. 'Sally, coffee for you? Cream?'

Sally took the mug from him, watching as he poured Estelle's and then his own before sitting down. She was ill at ease but it was nothing to do with the Mendelsons' hospitality. It was twelve weeks since the New Year's Day lunch at which she had hoped to put things right, wipe clean her slate and start again. 'It'll be fine, Sally,' Steve had said as they drove across the Bay Bridge on New Year's Day. 'Whatever happens today can only make things better. The worst is over – all you have to do is stay cool, be strong and let them take the lead. It's just a friendly lunch. Okay?'

'Okay! But . . .'

'But what?'

'Well . . . I don't know, really . . . don't expect anything rational from me, Steve, I'm too scared to make sense.'

They were approaching the tollbooth and he slowed down, reaching out to take her hand. 'I know. But it's gonna be okay. Believe me.'

She squeezed his hand, thankful for his reassuring presence. And it was as he'd predicted, a low-key family occasion. Estelle and Oliver had welcomed her warmly, Estelle even reaching out to hug Sally and then taking her arm to lead her through into the lounge. Sally, dizzy with nerves, thought her tension must be obvious, and felt shamed by their generosity. Oliver drew Steve into the room and poured drinks while Estelle introduced them to Oliver's parents, Simon and Naomi. The senior Mendelsons were well into their eighties, with the same small, spare build as their son.

Naomi grabbed Sally's hand and patted the space beside her on the couch. 'My dear, I'm so happy to meet you. Estelle and Oliver told us all about you. It's so wonderful that you've come to see Lisa, our darling girl. You know, I can see the likeness, not strongly, but just there in the eyes and the shape of your face. Now, come and sit down here and tell me all about yourself. We're all family now, aren't we?'

Sally sat beside her, taking a deep breath. Clearly the parents had not been told the full story.

'This must all seem pretty strange to you, Sally,' Simon said, passing her a small dish of olives. 'But y'know, we're all delighted to see you here.' He patted her shoulder and wandered over to the window to join Oliver and Steve.

Naomi soon had Sally looking at photographs of her other children and grandchildren, Lisa's cousins, she said, who all loved her to bits. 'They all take their turns,' she confided, lowering her voice as Estelle went out to the kitchen. 'All of them come around and help out with Lisa. It's a lot of work for Estelle, you know, that's why she gave up the opera. She had a wonderful career but Lisa was more important.'

Sally's cheeks burned as Naomi talked about the hours Estelle spent exercising Lisa's limbs and trying to teach her to speak again. 'But in the end it just seemed it was going nowhere. That lovely girl, such a tragedy. I can't imagine how you must feel to get here and discover this, Sally. Now, did you say you've got some pictures of your mom and dad?'

By the time lunch was served Sally was feeling more relaxed, and as they went through to the dining room Tessa, Lisa's carer, wheeled her into the room and Naomi took Lisa's hands in hers and planted a kiss on the top of her head. 'Here you are then, darling girl,' she said, instinctively toning down a few decibels. 'And doesn't that necklace look lovely. Look, Sally, this was one of my Christmas gifts to Lisa. We have Christmas and Hanukkah, darling, don't we? Any opportunity for celebration!'

'It's her favourite now, Mrs Mendelson,' Tessa said. 'She wants to wear it every day.'

'My, and it suits her so well,' said Simon, coming over to Lisa. 'You got a kiss for your old granddad, sweetheart?'

Sally looked to Estelle for guidance. 'She'll probably remember you,' Estelle said. 'Take Steve and introduce him.'

It all seemed so simple but, even once the first hurdles were over, Sally saw that everyone, including Steve, was more at ease in dealing with Lisa than she was. 'But it's inevitable,' Steve had said later that evening as they walked through the San Francisco streets still festooned with Christmas decorations. 'It's easy for me because I don't have the hopes, the expectations, all the emotional investment that you have.'

But Sally was disappointed in herself, and she stayed that way. Even now, almost three months later and after visiting Lisa every week, she felt a hollowness as she learned to do things for and with her. Each visit was the same: the anticipatory tension, the disappointment on arrival, the sense of emptiness and futility while she was there. She was an outsider, and no amount of warmth and generosity on the part of the Mendelsons could change that. Whatever she had hoped for the day she made her first reconnoitring trip along Hyde Street was long forgotten. But what had she hoped for once the situation was clear? What had she expected once she had dealt with her anger and grief and made peace with Estelle and Oliver? Putting things right had been the most important thing and now there seemed little else left to do. Lisa's ability to relate to people was limited to those she had known all her life. It rested on the knowledge of a shared past, and the expectation of love and care. The people around her knew the person Lisa had been, but Sally had no foundations on which to build.

'What shocks me,' she said to Nancy later, 'is that I actually feel very little for her. I feel grief about the accident and a sort of peace that I've connected with them all, but I can't seem to feel real love for Lisa. I'm strangely detached. Do you think there's something wrong with me?'

Nancy shook her head and went on potting the seedlings that were spread out on the balcony. 'Nope, I don't think there's anything wrong with you at all. I don't think there's anything there that you can relate to. It's not as though Lisa can contribute anything, there can't be any real interaction. What exists between Lisa and the family exists because it's always been there. They work to keep that alive. I don't imagine it's possible for her to build something new.'

'Well, there's Tessa, the carer. She has a relationship with her.'

'But didn't you say that Lisa knew Tessa before the accident?'

'Yes, she's the daughter of Oliver's parents' housekeeper.'

'There you are then,' Nancy said, pressing a marigold into a pot. 'Same thing. Memory, familiarity and the effort by the others to maintain the relationship they had before the accident.'

'I feel like a complete moron,' Sally said. 'I launch myself over here, bounce along to the Mendelsons', throw a tantrum and upset them, upset you guys and Steve, break his leg and then, when I'm lucky enough to get a second chance, I can't really feel anything.'

Nancy stood up and took off her gardening gloves. 'Want my advice, Sally? Let go of it. You've done what you came here to do. You saw Lisa. Nothing went as planned, but you laid a ghost. She has a family who love her. Frankly, there's not really anything you can do, except visit from time to time, stay in touch. It can't go any further than this. It's time to move on.'

'That's exactly what I told her,' said Steve, coming out onto the balcony with more plants. 'Time to move on, Sally, for your sake and for theirs. They're real nice people and they adore Lisa. They'll accommodate you, but they don't need you. You can only complicate things for them and for yourself.'

'Sounds right to me,' said Nancy. 'Time to think about something else. Concentrate on the photography, finish your course. Stop going there every week, stop trying to be involved, just stay in touch.'

'You can be more involved with me if you like,' said Steve, putting his arm around her shoulders. 'Or do I have to break the other leg to get your undivided attention?'

Sally punched him lightly on the chest. 'You! Whatever did I do to deserve you?'

'I think you must have been very good in a former life. You can focus all your attention on me and my daughter problems. Don't you reckon, Nancy?'

Nancy set the new pots along the low wall and turned to him, raising her eyebrows. 'Steve, I reckon your daughter's more of a challenge than any sane woman would want to take on!' she said. 'Do you guys have time for a beer? Let's find Chuck and a bottle opener.'

In the end letting go was easier than she had anticipated. She was surprised that she felt no guilt, and no great sadness, just relief in moving away. And she could see that Estelle and Oliver were relieved too. Together they found a middle ground of respect and affection. Sally was part of the extended family, she would always be welcome, and Lisa was held at the heart of a family who loved her – Sally's presence was not really relevant.

Although the anxiety ended, the hollowness persisted. Sally wondered what it had all been about. For thirty years Lisa had been her dark secret. The pain, the loss and the shame had been the background music of her life, in recent years acquiring a discomforting pitch and tone. Now she was free. She threw herself into the final weeks of the course, catching up on assignments, attempting more challenging and creative work, grasping at the new vision and sense of herself that the camera helped her to discover. But time was slipping away and decisions had to be made.

It was almost Easter, her visa would soon expire and there were more painful separations ahead, for as she moved away from Lisa she was allowing herself to move closer to Steve. For the first time in her life she was in a relationship in which she received as much as she gave, and she didn't want to lose it. Earlier in the year Steve had suggested that he might return to Australia with her for a visit, but he had not mentioned it again. She wanted to talk to him about where they were heading, but was reluctant to raise the subject. As each day passed she grew increasingly uneasy, not even mentioning the inevitable departure, the need to book her return flight and make plans for home. She wasn't sure if the taboo was a joint creation or purely of her own making.

*

'I've had an invitation,' Steve said on Easter Sunday as they drove north through the vineyards of the Nappa Valley to Calistoga. 'Well, not an invitation, more an offer – an offer of work.'

Sally twisted in her seat to look at him. 'A good offer? What is it?'

'A good offer. The California Jazz Association wants me to do a book on jazz in California. A coffee-table-type book, you know, lots of pictures linked by a creative essay.' He glanced away from the road to look at her. 'It's good money, and of course it would be a terrific thing to do, a book like that . . .' He paused glancing at her again. 'What do you think?'

'What do I think? Well, it's wonderful,' she said, forcing herself to sound enthusiastic. 'Will you write the text and do the photographs as well?'

'Write the text, yes, and take some of the photographs. Some will come from archives, obviously. It's due to be released at the jazz festival in Berkeley at the end of next year.'

She was appalled at her own selfishness, fixing her smile as she looked ahead at the road. 'So you'll have to get on to it soon. I'm really pleased for you. It's just the sort of work you were wanting, isn't it? Have you signed a contract?'

He shook his head. 'Not yet. I have to go to Sacramento for a couple of days next week to fix up the deal – that is, if I decide to do it.'

'Why wouldn't you do it?' she said, watching the serried rows of vines stretched along the taut wires above the newly turned earth. 'It's a great opportunity, you'd be crazy to turn it down.'

There was a pause before he spoke. 'It's a lot of work, time-consuming . . .'

She felt him look at her again but kept her head turned away.

'Yes, but the course finishes in a couple of weeks. You'll have more time. You've been saying for weeks that you need to organise some work.'

He swung the car off the road and onto the verge, and switched off the engine. 'What's going on, Sally?'

She turned to face him, hoping the sunglasses hid more than just her eyes. 'What do you mean? Nothing –'

Steve struck the wheel with the heel of his hand. 'Don't give me that. We've been through this before – pretending there was nothing between us. All these months together and now in a few weeks you're leaving and not a word, not even a hint about what happens to us.'

She stared at him and swallowed hard, grasping her hands together in her lap. 'What do you want me to say? You know I have to leave, I don't have any choice.'

'I know that. And I know you've done what you came here to do. But is that all? I mean, am I just supposed to drive you to the airport, wave goodbye and pretend I'm happy about it?'

'Why are you angry with me, Steve? I don't have a choice. I won't have a visa, so I'm not allowed to work here. I have to earn my living too. Are we fighting about this?'

He looked away, stiff and angry, until his shoulders slumped and he ran a hand across his eyes. 'No,' he said, shaking his head. 'No, of course we're not fighting. It's just me . . . I don't know what to do. I can't bear it that you're leaving and you won't even talk about it. I feel . . . well, I just feel helpless.'

She reached out and took his hand. 'It's not just me, Steve. You haven't mentioned it either. I thought you didn't want to talk about it. I was frightened you'd think I was trying to pin you down.'

He looked at her and put his hand up to touch the tear that had sneaked from under the sunglasses. 'Oh, pin me down. Pin me wherever you like, just don't leave me wondering what to do.' He got out of the car, walked around to her side and opened the door. He drew her out of the car and pulled her close to him. 'I don't have fancy words for this. I love you, Sally, I don't want to lose you, and I don't know what to do.'

'I love you too, Steve,' she said, burying her face in his neck, loving the soft warmth of his skin and the way he held her. 'I don't know what to do either. I haven't known what to say to you. You did say you might come back with me, but you never mentioned it again and I thought you'd changed your mind. Then . . . when you told me about the job . . .'

He held her away from him, looking intently into her face. 'I didn't mention it again because you didn't. I thought maybe I was being too pushy, wanting to go with you, interfering in your life. But I love you. If you feel the same then we'll find a way to be together somehow.'

She gazed out across the vineyards. 'You know, this looks a lot like home, like the Swan Valley,' she said. 'Wine-growing country. I so want you to see it.'

'Then I will. But I'm not looking for an Australian holiday, Sally, I'm talking about a future, either here, or there, or somewhere else. But you and I together.'

'I want that too, Steve, but how? I need to earn a living and I don't have a green card, and I'm not likely to get one. And I don't know about the situation back home, whether you'd be able to work there, what the visa situation would be. It seems so hard, impossible almost.' Her tears were flowing freely now and he held her closer, stroking her hair, kissing the top of her head.

'It's not impossible,' he said. 'We'll find a way to do it. You're too precious to me, Sally, I'm not going to be beaten by bureaucracy – American or Australian.' He paused and reached into the car for a box of tissues, handing them to her, waiting while she dried her eyes. 'You know,' he said with a smile, 'it may be that the only way to do it would be to get married.'

'Are you serious?'

'Deadly serious. But I heard you tell Nancy that you're not the marrying kind.'

She stared at him, her body flooding with a sudden terrified heat, her heart seeming to beat so loudly that she felt he must have been able to hear it.

'No . . . no, I'm not . . . or at least, I haven't been. But I guess, well . . . I guess I could . . . I could change if that's what it took.'

Steve grinned. 'So is that some sort of acceptance of a proposal?'

She laughed and dabbed at her eyes again. 'Did you actually propose? I thought it was more of a bottom line, a fallback position if all else fails.'

'Would you like me to go down on one or two knees?'

'Neither.' She smiled. 'Definitely not. Look, I accept the proposal that we must be together. I love you – I want to be with you whatever it takes.'

'Even if it takes getting married?'

She paused again. 'It sounds so terrifying. I so much prefer the idea of just being together. It's not because I don't want to make a commitment to you, Steve, I do. It's just marriage and all the baggage that goes with it . . .'

'We're grown-up people, Sally – middle-aged. We can make it whatever we want it to be. It's just a piece of paper we may need to enable us to be together. The relationship we have will be the same, but we may have to be married in order to be together in the same country. To make it legal.'

She sighed, thinking how much she loved his square face, the crinkles around his eyes, and the way those eyes not only saw her but knew her. He made her feel strong, and beautiful, and loved in a way she had never known before. She put her hand up and touched his lips with her fingertips. 'Well, I guess I'll love you and want to be with you legally or illegally,' she said.

The phone was ringing as she unlocked the door to the apartment. She dumped her camera case and raced to grab the receiver, expecting it to be Steve. When she heard Stacey's voice she wished she had let the answering machine pick up the call. Stacey sounded uncharacteristically subdued.

'Is my dad there, please?'

Sally swung her shoulder bag onto the table and ran a hand through her hair. 'He's in Sacramento, Stacey. You could try his cellphone.'

'Yeah, I tried that but he's not answering. D'you know where he's staying?'

Sally put down the phone, collected the slip of paper with the hotel number from under the fridge magnet, and read out the name and the number of Steve's hotel. 'But I doubt he'll be back there till this evening,' she added. 'He was expecting to have some long meetings with the publisher and some people from the Jazz Association.'

There was silence at the other end of the line.

'Stacey, are you . . . is something wrong?'

'No, nothing. I'll leave a message if I don't get him. Thanks.' She hung up.

Sally stared at the receiver, shrugged and hung up with the familiar sense of irritation that she experienced each time she encountered Steve's daughter.

Clearing a space on the table she spread out the photographs she had just collected from the developer, and studied them with satisfaction. She had taken them at first light in the Mission District, and she knew she had captured the bleak chill of the dawn, the despair of the old man rolling up his thin mattress and stuffing it into the shopping trolley with his other meagre possessions. She had caught the hopelessness in the eyes of the teenage panhandler outside the Dolores Mission, and the brutal reality of the police officer shaking the mountainous woman from her blanket on the steps. She had set out to capture the darker side of the city, to portray the other life behind the affluent sunlit streets, and she knew she had achieved it. These would make up the portfolio for her final assessment and she was pleased with what she had done. She sat down to draft the accompanying legend, staring again at the photographs, satisfied with the honesty and the dramatic impact of her work. So absorbed was she, she didn't notice that a couple of hours had passed since she'd arrived home, then she heard a sharp rap on her door.

'Stacey!' she said, amazed to see her standing on the other side of the security screen. 'I told you, Steve's not here.' She unlocked the screen door. 'D'you want to come in?'

Stacey nodded.

'Did you call the hotel?' Sally asked.

'Yeah, I called, I left a message. I tried the cellphone again and called the operator – it's not working.' She stalked the room in jerky strides, avoiding eye contact. 'Great view,' she said quietly, stopping at the window briefly before pacing the room again. She noticed the photographs spread across the table. 'Did you take these?' she asked, not looking up.

'Yes, they're for my final assignment.'

'They're good,' Stacey said. 'Brilliant. You must be pleased.'

Her voice was thin and flat, several decibels lower than her normal tone. 'It must nearly be the end of semester.'

Sally hesitated. Stacey's eyes looked red, her skin dull, and her manner was unusually restrained. 'Just a few more weeks,' Sally said. 'Stacey, why are you here? Are you okay?'

'Oh, I dunno.' She shrugged, turning back to the window, her shoulders slumped. 'No. Not really.'

Sally stiffened, trying to dispel the feeling that this visit meant trouble. Stacey was the one black cloud in her relationship with Steve. However many times he assured her that Stacey had her own life and would not affect them, Sally still saw her as a disaster waiting to happen. She had spent several sleepless nights wondering how Stacey would react when faced with the fact that she was a permanent fixture in Steve's life. The silence was heavy and tense. Sally cleared her throat awkwardly. 'Would you like some coffee?'

Stacey shook her head and as she turned, Sally could see that she was crying. She hesitated, curbing an instinctive reaction to go to her and offer some sort of comfort, needing instead to protect herself.

Stacey dabbed her eyes with a handful of tissues and took a couple of deep breaths. 'I had an abortion,' she said with a sudden noisy sob. 'I don't have anywhere else to go.'

Sally's anxiety dissipated in the blinding relief that the situation was not about her. She guided Stacey to the sofa and sat down alongside her, taking her icy hand. 'Good heavens, Stacey, you're frozen. I'll get you a blanket.'

She fetched a blanket from the bedroom closet and wrapped it around Stacey, who drew it up to her chin. Sally lifted her legs onto the sofa and tucked the blanket under her feet. She was crying bitterly now, shaking uncontrollably and apologising with every breath.

Sally crouched down beside the sofa. 'It's okay, Stacey, don't apologise. You need to cry. Can you tell me what happened? When was the abortion?'

'This morning,' Stacey said through her sobs. 'I just came from the clinic.'

'All alone? Didn't you have someone with you?'

She shook her head. 'They said I had to but I told them someone was waiting for me outside.'

'And you drove here?'

'I drove to Dad's first, that's when I called you. Then when I couldn't find him I just drove around and around, and then I didn't know what to do, so I came here. I didn't want to go to my apartment, the guys I share with . . . I didn't want them to know. I had nowhere else to go. I'm sorry.'

'Don't, don't be sorry. I'm glad you came here. Now, what did the clinic tell you to do when you left?'

Stacey shook her head. 'I can't remember. They gave me some printed instructions but I don't know what I did with the paper. I shouldn't have come,' she said, starting to get up.

Sally pushed her firmly back onto the sofa. 'You just stay there, Stacey. You're not going anywhere. You did the right thing coming here, and there is no way you're leaving now. Tell me the name of the clinic and I'll call them for instructions, and then I'll try to get hold of Steve.'

Stacey shrank back into the cushions as Sally talked to the clinic staff. 'You just have to keep your feet up and rest,' she told her when she'd hung up. 'Keep warm, plenty of fluids and call them if you're in pain or if there's any heavy bleeding.'

Stacey nodded, the tears running silently down her cheeks. She was barely recognisable as the belligerent, outspoken woman who had upset everyone at the Thanksgiving dinner. She looked like a teenager, a broken child, and her eyes followed Sally as she paced the room, phone in hand, trying to reach Steve.

'The mobile's definitely not working,' Sally told her eventually. 'The operator says it's not responding, there must be something wrong with it. He'll call eventually, Stacey, then you can tell him.'

Stacey shook her head and blew her nose on a handful of tissues. 'I don't know how to tell him. I feel so ashamed. When he wasn't at his apartment I felt desperate because I had no one, but I was relieved too, relieved I didn't actually have to tell him.'

Sally sat down beside her again. 'There's nothing to be ashamed of, Stacey. Steve loves you, he'll understand.'

Stacey shook her head. 'I don't know. I've been so stupid. Dad thinks I can look after myself, that I'm independent and competent, all that stuff. This isn't me, as far as he's concerned. He's proud of me.'

'And he'll still be proud of you.' Sally smiled, taking her hand again. 'Look, I'm going to make you some tea, you need something warm to drink. Then, if you want, you can tell me how all this happened.'

'I was in love with him,' Stacey said eventually, clutching the warm mug in both hands. 'We worked together on the newspaper in London. He was so cool. His name's Andrew and he looks like Hugh Grant, he even has the same accent, and I was just head over heels. He thought I was something else – he said so, he liked me being tough and noisy. Ballsy, he called me, so I kept acting more tough. He told me he was separated from his wife and getting a divorce.' Sally shivered with a sense of déjà vu.

The affair had lasted several months until Stacey discovered that Andrew had moved back with his wife. 'So that was it. I was devastated. I chucked in my job. I couldn't go on working with him and I didn't want to be in England, so that's when I came back here. I thought I'd stay with Dad, he'd understand, I'd hang out with him for a while. But when I got here I felt so stupid, like a failure, you know. Running away from a married man, it's such a cliché, and Dad was really hung up on you and that just froze me up. So I decided to tough it out and not say anything. I kept on pretending I'd come back because I wanted to work at the *Chronicle*.'

'But that was November,' Sally cut in. 'You came back just before Thanksgiving. You weren't pregnant then.'

'Andrew came over here in February,' she said. 'He had to cover that climate change conference in LA and he came here first. I thought he'd come to tell me that he'd decided to leave his wife. But of course he hadn't.'

Sally shifted her position on the sofa, lifting Stacey's feet so that they rested on her lap. 'Have you told him about this? I mean, did you let him know you were pregnant?'

Stacey nodded. 'Oh yeah! I called him as soon as I realised. Last-chance thing, you know . . . maybe this will make him see that it's me he really loves. Well, no way. He was horrified, told me to get rid of it straight away. He wasn't a bit concerned about me, or about the baby, only that his wife might find out. That's when I really got the message. So I found the name of a clinic and . . . well, you know the rest. I'm really sorry to land on you, Sally. I've been a real dog . . . it was just that I came back looking for Dad, and when I found him he was missing – emotionally missing, if you know what I mean. I was jealous.'

Sally squeezed Stacey's foot through the blanket. 'It's okay. You could still have told him, you know. He would've wanted to know. I suppose that with the broken leg and what was happening with us, he just didn't pick up that you needed him.'

Stacey stared into her mug. 'What d'you think he'll say about it . . . the whole thing? He'll be so disappointed in me.'

'Stacey, you've known your father a lot longer than I have but my guess is that he'll say he loves you very much and –'

'But the abortion . . . will he be okay about that? He's pretty cool but men sometimes feel differently.'

'I think he'll be fine about it and anyway, Stacey, it's your decision to take, it's your life. You don't need his approval.'

'But I want it,' Stacey mumbled, the tears starting again. 'Desperately want it. I'm scared of him disapproving of me. Not being good enough.'

'Steve loves you, Stacey, he's a very open-minded person. Believe me, it'll be okay, he'll understand.'

'I feel such a failure. Here I am, almost thirty, and I've made such a mess of things. Lord knows what you must think of me. You know, I liked you straight away, Sally, but I treated you like shit, then got pregnant, now I end up on your doorstep. What you must think of me . . .'

'Stacey, I think you're very brave and very lonely. And I know how it feels, honestly I do, because I've been there. Look, I think it's time I told you a story . . .'

TWENTY-ONE

Robin was heading north towards Perth on the South Western Highway when the motorcyclist cut in front of her so sharply that the adrenaline pumped up her heartbeat and prickled her skin. She slipped off the road into the forecourt of a service station and went in to the shop to get a cup of coffee. It was a bitter, watery concoction in a polystyrene cup and she gagged on it, pouring it immediately onto the grass. Collecting her bottle of water from the car she wandered towards a shaded patch of ground where a few wooden seats and some scruffy grass claimed to be a picnic area. A huge truck pulled onto the forecourt, brakes screeching to a noisy halt, dark fumes belching from the exhaust. Robin turned away in distaste, watching the late morning sunshine glinting off the sleek chestnut coat of a horse grazing in a nearby paddock. Take some deep breaths and calm down, she thought. This is not about the motorcyclist.

She had left home that morning angry. It was an anger that she had manufactured for herself to avoid naming her fear. It was futile anger at her own body for interfering with her plans, for interrupting her peace. This trip to Perth was the last thing she needed. She wanted the test over and done with, to get back to the cottage. She gulped some of the water and took deep breaths, grinning suddenly at the realisation that she was behaving just as Grace used to do when things got in her way. She drained the bottle, wondering whether Grace was really as different as she had sounded on the phone. Well, she'd soon find out, she'd be there in a few hours time.

She was looking forward to seeing Grace, who had been home for almost three months. It was the day before Good Friday and Robin needed to stay in Perth for the test results until Tuesday. She was grateful for Grace's offer of a bed. Robin's own house had sold quickly and the deal on the bookshop had gone through with similar speed, though the Tranters had asked to stay on until June before leaving for Tasmania. It suited Robin because she had also bought the cottage – the thought of leaving it in a month or two had been too hard and the owners were more than willing to sell it to her.

So, she thought, here I am heading for Perth, where I have no home, no office, no law practice, no lover, for some stupid test – and it will probably turn out to be just a scare. In mid December she had met Alec Seaborn for lunch in Bunbury and, despite his earnest request that she reconsider, had told him that she wanted to sell her share of the practice. She would buy the bookshop and the cottage, and would find another woman to help her run the shop, someone who could be left in charge when Robin wanted to spend time at the cottage. The bookshop would produce income and satisfy the businesswoman in her, but the cottage meant creativity and peace of mind.

After the meeting with Alec she had gone home filled with energy and resolve, and finally opened the envelope that had sat above the fireplace for the last few weeks. Jim's note was dated the Monday after she had seen him in Pemberton.

Dearest Robin

Forgive me, but I've been desperate to contact you since Friday night. The people I'm with wanted to stop for lunch so I took the chance to duck out and try to see you to put things right.

I am so sorry about what happened at the pub. I was shocked to see you there and then when Father Pat waved me over I didn't know what to do. It all felt terrible. I so want to see you and talk to you. Please don't make me wait until this wretched year is up. By the way, I got your address from Doug Carter. I ran into him just before heading to Pemberton. So please don't tear strips off anyone else for this.

   I miss you so much, Robin. Please get in touch when you've read this and let's talk things over.

My love always,
Jim

Strengthened by her conversation with Alec, she felt she could handle a meeting without falling apart and she emailed Jim saying she was prepared to see him. But within seconds of sending the message she received an automated response telling her that Justice McEwan would be away from chambers on leave until the end of January. Any urgent enquiries should be directed to his assistant. A few days later she got a reply from Jim himself. He had taken Monica and the kids to Fiji for an extended holiday, he said, but he'd be back in Perth on the twelfth of January. If she told him when and where she wanted to meet, he would be there. Her vulnerability returned, ignited by the idea of the long family holiday in an exotic location, but she replied, suggesting they meet at ten on the morning of the sixteenth of January at a small café in the hills east of Perth where they had once stopped for breakfast. She would meet him, but she was still too vulnerable to invite him onto what she had made her territory.

And so she had driven this same route on a brilliant January morning, leaving before dawn to allow plenty of time, and arriving to find him already there, nursing the morning paper and his second cup of coffee at a corner table. She paused a moment in the doorway, watching as he scanned the paper, his half-glasses resting below the bridge of his nose, the open-necked shirt a vivid blue against his Fiji tan. He sensed her looking at him, glanced up and for a moment they remained frozen in tension before he cleared his throat, smiled and stood to greet her. She couldn't think what to do. A kiss on the cheek? A hug? Surely they weren't going to shake hands?

'You look wonderful,' he said, hugging her before taking her hand in his and leading her to the table. She saw that it was going to be a struggle. Since she left Perth she had felt she had some control of the situation. Now, within seconds, the balance had shifted and he had taken charge again. 'The southwest air suits you,' he said. 'You look younger, so relaxed.'

'You look pretty good yourself.' The words seemed to strangle themselves at the back of her throat as she faced him across the table. Her earlier confidence had evaporated. She was unsure whether what she felt was longing or panic.

Jim let go of her hand and picked up the menu. 'Coffee? And will you have some breakfast?'

'Just coffee, nothing to eat, thanks,' she said, swallowing hard and feeling a flicker of irritation as he ordered bacon and eggs. How could he eat at a time like this? She remembered Grace's story of the man who slept soundly the night his wife announced she was leaving. Men really were a different species.

They slithered cautiously across the black ice of preamble and pleasantries, the recent death of a mutual acquaintance, the new appointment of a woman to the High Court. The old intimacy taunted them with its inaccessibility.

'So you weren't annoyed with Doug?' Jim said, suddenly changing tack as he picked up his knife and fork. 'Telling me where you were, I mean.'

She watched as he moved a poached egg onto a piece of toast and speared it with his knife. 'Not with Doug, no,' she said. 'But I was angry with you.'

He looked up in surprise. 'But I explained how it was in the pub,' he said. 'What else could I do? Pat and I are old friends, I couldn't ignore him.'

'I don't mean the pub. I know there was nothing else you could do then. But before you made that trip to Pemberton you got my address. You didn't just turn up at my place to apologise for the situation in the pub. You planned to come there either during that trip or another time. Despite the fact that I made it absolutely clear I didn't want you to get in touch, not even by email, certainly not to turn up on my doorstep.'

He patted his lips with his napkin. 'Robin, I wanted to see you, needed to see you.'

'And you're used to getting what you want!'

'True. Except when it comes to you and me. I love you, Robin.'

'Do you, Jim? Did you? Really? And love conquers all, does it? Even respect for my wishes?'

He reached across the table to cover her hand with his. 'Robin . . . you're the most precious person in the world to me. I hadn't seen you for months.'

She moved her hand. He felt like a stranger, though so much of what was happening was intimately and instantly familiar. 'Let me explain something,' she said, her voice low, her fortitude returning. 'For four years I sat on the edge of your life, I respected your professional space and most of all I respected your family commitments. I never called you at home. I took exceptional care never to venture into the other areas of your life. I organised my time around your availability. I watched you and Monica being a couple at numerous functions and made sure I never crossed the boundaries. For four years, Jim, you called the tune on everything. When we would meet, where and for how long, where we could and couldn't go . . . everything. I went along with it because I loved you, I respected your situation. But when I set some boundaries for myself, you trampled all over them. You ignored my requests to let me be alone, you kept emailing, you ferreted around to find out where I was, and you even turned up on my doorstep. Does any of this register with you, Jim? Do you see what I'm saying?'

'Of course, of course,' he said, setting down his cutlery and pushing the plate aside. 'Of course I understand and I realise it was wrong of me. But doesn't it mean anything to you that I love you so much and needed so desperately to see you?'

Robin threw her head back and crossed her arms. 'Tell me this, Jim – if I had turned up to join you on the golf course one weekend, or rung your front doorbell one evening, or . . . or arrived at your hotel in Fiji because I loved you and wanted to see you, how do you think you would have felt? Do you not think you'd have felt that I had no respect for your wishes?'

He stared at her briefly and then dropped his gaze to the table, clasping and unclasping his hands.

'I think . . .' he began. 'Well, I think that . . . it feels different somehow, the sort of situation you describe. It's different, isn't it?'

She shook her head. 'No, Jim, not to me it isn't, it's not different at all. I can't tell you the number of times I wanted to see you, to be with you when you were with your family, or your golfing friends, or any of the other places that I couldn't go with you. I can't tell you the number of times that I wanted to walk up to you when you were with Monica, wanted to touch you or kiss you or just share a joke with you. Even just to call you when you were at home. I didn't do it because of you, Jim, not because of Monica or your children, because of you, because I loved and respected you. This situation to me is no different. You were totally insensitive to my feelings. It was *your* feelings you were thinking of, *your* love, *your* need. I don't think you gave a second thought to how I might feel.'

She pushed back her chair, got up and walked out onto the verandah. She needed fresh air to calm her frustration and sense of helplessness.

He followed her, placing his hands on her shoulders. 'Robin, I'm sorry –'

'Monica knows, doesn't she?' Robin cut in, swinging around to face him. 'She knows about us, I could see that in the pub.'

He dropped his hands. 'Yes, yes, she knows.'

'You told her?' she demanded, longing to hear him say that he had told Monica as a prelude to a decision to leave.

'She found out. Apparently someone whispered it to her at some function and I think she was already suspicious. So she confronted me with it.'

'And what did you say?'

'At first I tried to bluff it out and when it was clear that it wasn't working, I owned up. But I told her that it was over.'

'Over?'

'Yes.'

'When was this?'

'Oh, I don't remember exactly, a couple of weeks after you went south, I think.'

'And you told her our relationship was over?'

'Yes, yes, I did.'

302

'And was it over then, Jim? Was it over for you?'

'Well, no, of course not. You were just taking time out. I wouldn't see you for a while. It seemed the best thing to say.'

Robin sank onto the wooden bench, shaking with a mixture of hurt and anger. 'Do you remember telling me how much you wanted to leave but hadn't the heart to tell her?'

'Of course I do. Many times.'

'How we talked about what you'd do if somehow she found out? You'd be relieved, you said. You wanted it over. Even if it weren't for me, you didn't want to be with Monica. If she found out and you just had to admit it, it would be a gift, you said. You'd leave on the spot.'

He said nothing. Thrusting his hands into his pockets, he walked to the verandah rail to stare into the distance. 'I couldn't do it, Robin,' he said quietly, without turning around. 'When it came to it I just couldn't do it. I don't love Monica. We jog along okay but I don't love her – well, not in the way I love you. That day, the day she asked me, I stood there looking at her and I couldn't do it. Everyone thinks Monica's as tough as old boots, but in many ways she's quite fragile and dependent. We've been together for thirty years, and then there's the children and the whole life, the context into which it all fits. I stood there looking at Monica and I realised that I couldn't change anything – or perhaps I mean *wouldn't* change it. However much I wanted to, wanted to be with you, do all that we planned, I couldn't do it. It was too late. I was stuck and I didn't know how to be any different.'

He turned to face her and there were tears in his eyes. 'You'd made me feel I could be a different person with a different sort of life, but that day I knew I didn't have the courage. So I did the cowardly thing. I lied, and somehow, in some horrible way, it felt right although I knew it was wrong . . .' He pulled a handkerchief from his pocket and dabbed his eyes.

So that was how it was. For months she had argued with herself, one moment believing there was a future together, the next that there was none. One day believing that she preferred her life without him, the next hoping that time would bring them back together. So now she knew. She thought she should feel pain, or if not pain then panic or depression. What she felt was sadness, and relief that finally she knew what she was dealing with.

'I don't expect you to understand,' he began. 'I don't even know how to explain it to you properly. I know it's not fair to you . . .'

She put a hand on his arm. 'Don't, Jim,' she said. 'You don't need to explain any more. I understand. I really do understand now.' She took his handkerchief to dry her own tears. 'I just wish that you had told me years ago. It's all the dreams and expectations, you see, the promises, the plans that never materialised, that's what's made it all so hard. If I'd known from the beginning, I would have had a choice. I wish you'd told me before.'

'I couldn't tell you before because I didn't know. Believe me, Rob, I didn't know. I believed there would be a time when I could do it. I loved you so much, wanted what we'd planned. I still love you, I still want it, but . . .' His voice trailed away and he shrugged. 'But in the end I couldn't do it.'

Robin tossed her empty water bottle into the bin and wandered back to her car, remembering how they had woven their words to find a peaceful way to separate.

'Can we see each other?' he had asked, and she had paused, wondering how it would be.

'Is that what you want?'

He nodded. 'Of course, but you've made me see how different it is for you.'

'I can't go back, Jim,' she told him. 'I love you, maybe I always will. But it can't be as it was before. I think we can be friends, eventually, with a bit more time. Let's just take it gently.'

He lifted her hand to his lips and kissed her palm. 'However you want it, Robin. I mean it. However you want it.'

Now, just over three months later, Robin shivered at the memory. The anger was gone but the sadness remained. The pain in her chest tightened and she glanced at her watch. Time to get back on the road or she'd be late for the hospital.

'It's just a little lump,' she said. 'Probably a cyst, nothing to worry about, but the doctor said I had to have this done.'

'Quite right,' Grace said, looking at her intently. 'And they'll give you the results . . .?'

'Tuesday morning, they said, but they wanted me to stay up in town in case I have to go back. It's just a nuisance, it being Easter.'

'Not a nuisance for me,' Grace said. 'It's wonderful. Which breast is it, by the way?'

'Left,' said Robin, lifting her arm to indicate the side of her left breast. 'Just here. Found it in the shower – anyway, enough of that. They've done the biopsy and I just have to wait till Tuesday. But what about you, Grace? You look great, different somehow.'

Grace grinned. 'I *am* different, thankfully. You won't believe it when you've been around me for a while, Robin. I hardly believe it myself.'

'I'm so sorry about your father.'

Grace sat down on the couch, tucking her legs under her. 'Thanks. I'm glad I got back in time.'

'Did he recognise you?'

'Just at the very end, he did, I think. I've seen it happen before – the person seems to have gone and then in the last few moments they come back. There's just this moment of clarity and recognition. It was like that, very peaceful. So much changed for me in England and then Dad died and it seemed like that completed something. There's this very strange feeling that everyone who knew me as a child has gone. It's very odd, as though that part of me no longer exists because it has no living witness. It's a bit scary but it's quite liberating too, like getting permission to change. And you, Robin, your shop and the cottage, I so want to hear all about it.'

Robin blushed. 'I thought you might come down sometime over the next few weeks. You could come to the cottage for a few days and I'll take you down to Albany. If you've time, that is. If you've sorted out the work stuff.'

'I've heaps of time. I've done the handover and everything will be stitched up next week. After that I'm free, and I'd love to come down. I'm dying to tell you all about England and the women I met. I'm going to go back later in the year, but I'm going to New Orleans first. It's so exciting, Robin. I know I'm going to bore you silly with all this stuff but this patchwork project I told you about in the letter is such a wonderful thing, I'm going to try and get it going in Vietnam.'

There was a new gentleness about her, Robin thought, the old need to control had gone. She had been a woman of sharp chiselled outlines that now seemed rounded and softened. 'You even look different,' Robin said.

'Yes,' Grace smiled. 'Older.'

Robin paused.

'It's true,' Grace said. 'It's okay, you can say it.'

'Well, yes, you do look a little older, but better, more relaxed, healthier – more whole, I suppose.'

'I'll go for that – especially the "whole" bit. I've discovered bits of me that I never knew I had, and others that went missing years ago. Did I ever tell you that I used to sing a lot when I was younger, when I met Ron? I found my singing voice again, along with a whole lot of other things.' She leaned back against the cushions. 'And I lost some other bits.' She grinned. 'Some of the bits that were hardest to get along with, I think. And you've changed too. You don't look particularly well, Robin, but you do look content. Anyway, you must be hungry. Why don't we go out for a meal – somewhere we used to go.'

Robin dropped her bag in Grace's spare room and splashed cold water over her face. She suddenly felt relaxed and refreshed. She had dreaded an inquisition from Grace about the lump, about her health, about Jim, and none of it had materialised. She brushed her hair in front of the mirror, staring intently at her reflection. The anger of the morning had dissipated. She was looking forward to spending the Easter weekend with Grace, remembering the pleasure of her friends and realising how much she had missed them. She picked up her jacket and ran down the stairs. 'Okay,' she said, 'let's go.'

'I thought we might go to Fremantle for fish and chips,' Grace said.

'Fish and chips! You? You always grumbled about it. You like designer food and trendy coffee shops.'

'I do, but these days I like lots of things I usen't to. And this is the new me – I'm trying to economise. Have you heard from the others? You know Sally'll be back in a few weeks . . .'

On Tuesday morning Robin had coffee with Alec Seaborn and the woman who had bought her share of the partnership. Diana Hooper was in her mid thirties, plump, plain and bristling with energy that seemed to spark and crackle around her. She had an engaging manner and Robin suspected she was also tough and uncompromising. Diana, clearly fired up by her new business venture, could barely sit still long enough to drink her coffee.

'She's going to wear me out,' Alec said wryly when she left the table to take a call on her mobile. 'D'you remember when we were like that, Robin? When you first came here?'

'I was thinking of exactly that.' She smiled. 'And thinking that I'm glad all that ambition and drive are over for me.'

Alec shook his head and put more sugar in his coffee. 'I'm beginning to think it may be over for me too,' he said. 'It's all starting to seem a bit much. I'm thinking maybe you've got the right idea, Robin.'

She wandered back through the city shops and splashed out on new moisturiser and a pair of beautiful pyjamas in fine white Indian cotton. Grace was getting lunch and after that Robin thought she would call Dr Chin's rooms. All being well, she had planned to head back home this afternoon but Grace had persuaded her to stay another night and leave early the next morning.

Grace was on the phone when Robin got in. 'Oh look, don't hang up,' she said. 'Robin's just walked in.' She held the receiver out to her. 'Dr Chin for you. He called the mobile but you didn't answer.'

Robin's insides did a somersault. She took the phone from Grace and sank onto the nearby chair while Grace went out to the kitchen, filling the kettle and cutting thick slices of rye bread for their lunch.

'What news?' she asked, looking up as Robin's shadow fell across the kitchen doorway.

Robin stood white-faced. 'He wants to see me right away. Like now. He wouldn't say anything else.' She swallowed hard. 'It's bad, isn't it, or he'd have told me?'

Grace put down the bread knife. 'Well, it's probably not the best. You're going now?'

Robin nodded. 'I wondered if you'd come . . .'

'Of course,' Grace said, taking off her apron. 'I'll drive.' And she urged Robin towards the door. 'C'mon, Robin, bring your bag. We'll be there in fifteen minutes.'

She put her arm through Robin's and led her out of the apartment building to the car park, urging her gently into the front seat of the car.

TWENTY-TWO

When Isabel found herself face to face with Antonia in Klaus's kitchen on Christmas Eve, she was galvanised by the same intensity of feeling she had experienced in the cloisters at Évora. Antonia, elegant in a long-sleeved, long-skirted black wool dress, her silver hair knotted in a loose bun at the nape of her neck, was sitting on the edge of the kitchen table talking to a distinguished-looking man who leaned against the draining board. As Klaus ushered Isabel into the kitchen Antonia turned and slid from the table, setting down her glass. 'Isabel,' she said, moving towards her. 'I am so happy to see you again,' and she reached out both hands.

Isabel's mouth was dry, her face flushed with shock. 'Antonia,' she said. 'I'd no idea . . . Klaus didn't say . . .'

'Of course not, Isabel. As I tell you now, I didn't know until this afternoon,' Klaus said. 'But it's a wonderful surprise, is it not?'

Antonia put her hands on Isabel's arms and leaned forward to kiss her. Isabel's cheek burned at the kiss and she struggled to return it.

'It was a sudden decision, Isabel,' Antonia said. 'My brother José, he lives here, and he is going to visit our sister in America, she is very sick. I decided to meet him here in Nuremberg and travel with him. Please, let me introduce you,' and she drew Isabel across the kitchen. José bowed slightly and shook hands. He was older than Antonia and the likeness was unmistakable, but he had a coldness about him that made him seem totally different from his sister. Isabel felt strangely unnerved and intimidated – José was formally polite but not particularly friendly, and later he seemed to be deliberately ignoring her.

Isabel was tongue-tied. For months she had conducted an intimate imaginary life of the heart and mind with Antonia. She had so often rehearsed the conversations they would have when they met again, the way she would demand answers, the feelings she would try to express, but now she was awkward, embarrassed. She felt like she had as a teenager, when she'd had a crush on an older girl at school. The intense and intimate friendship she had nurtured in her imagination then suddenly seemed foolish and naive when she found herself alone with the object of her affection in a railway carriage. She had been gauche and awkward, and she felt the same way now.

Klaus and José herded them back into the dining room where, along with the other guests, they took their seats at the table. Isabel found herself on Klaus's right while Antonia sat on his left. Close enough for casual conversation, too far apart for anything significant. The young man on Isabel's right was a philosophy lecturer with perfect English who was fascinated by Australia. At the far end of the table, José was deep in conversation with Klaus's cousin, a doctor from Mannheim. Antonia's eye contact was steady, with no sign of the defensiveness of the last days in Monsaraz, but as the evening wore on, it was clear that this was not an occasion for intimate conversation.

'I must see you again. I need to talk to you – alone,' she told Antonia as they sat by the fire after dinner.

'Of course we must talk,' Antonia replied. 'But José and I fly to New York the day after tomorrow. I don't know . . . perhaps you are free tomorrow afternoon? It is Christmas Day, but –'

'Yes,' Isabel cut in. 'Tomorrow afternoon will be fine. Where shall we meet?'

'I know the apartment where you are staying,' Antonia said. 'If you wish, I can come there at four o'clock?'

'Please. That will be perfect. I need to ask you some questions, Antonia.'

'And I owe you an explanation and an apology. Tomorrow then.'

Back in her apartment Isabel, though exhausted by the mixture of excitement and anxiety, was too keyed up to sleep. She made tea and sat in her dressing gown in the darkened lounge watching the snow falling silently on the rooftops of Nuremberg. She finally fell into bed just after four – twelve hours to wait. She had nothing planned for Christmas Day and was relishing the idea of spending it alone. Perhaps she would walk to the cathedral to listen to the mass, wander the snowy streets, a silent observer enjoying her solitude. Antonia had not been part of the plan, but for Isabel there could have been no more perfect addition to Christmas Day.

It was the front doorbell that woke her and she sat up bleary-eyed in the strange, steely white light of a snow-filled sky slanting between the gap in the curtains. The bell rang again and, wondering who on earth could be visiting her at nine o'clock on Christmas morning, she swung her legs out of bed and pulled her dressing gown around her. '*Ja, ja, ich komme, ich komme,*' she called, making her way to the door and pressing her eye to the viewing hole. Doug was standing in the hallway.

'Surprise, surprise! Merry Christmas, darling!' he cried, dragging his suitcase across the threshold and wrapping her in a bear hug. 'It's bloody cold here, isn't it, but the snow's wonderful. Here I am, a gift from Father Christmas. I bet you didn't expect to see me this morning. I'm dying for a coffee and some breakfast. They feed you absolute crap on these flights.'

Isabel ran her hand through her hair and tightened the belt of her dressing gown. 'You're not due for another week,' she ventured, leading him through into the kitchen.

'Ah, but I thought I'd surprise you. Are you suitably surprised?'

'I'm gobsmacked,' she said. 'I thought you wanted to have Christmas the same as always for everyone.'

'Right! When I first booked I was going to spend Christmas at home, but Deb said that Mac's parents were coming over from England so they might just stay home at their place. Then Mum

311

and Dad decided they were going to Bali for Christmas, for a change.'

'What about the others?' she asked, busying herself with the coffee plunger as she tried to pull herself together.

'Well, Kate and Jason decided to go to his parents in Noosa and as for Luke, well, he didn't seem too bothered. He and this new girlfriend seemed quite happy to go off somewhere on their own.'

'So much for not being able to do anything different at Christmas,' Isabel said, instantly ashamed of the harshness of her tone, but it went unnoticed by Doug, who was high on his own arrival. She was a mass of conflicting emotions: delighted to see him, annoyed at the unexpected intrusion and the assumption that she would be thrilled to see him whenever he chose to turn up. Touched by his wish to please her, she was also angry that he took it for granted that he could walk in on her, surprise her in a way that turned her plans upside down. She had always suspected surprises were for the gratification of the surpriser rather than the surprisee, and now her suspicions were confirmed. Doug's ebullience bounced off the walls of the formerly peaceful apartment as he scattered the contents of his suitcase across the floor, searching for gifts from the family, photographs he had brought for her, a thicker pair of socks for his cold feet.

Isabel steeled herself, pulled eggs and thinly sliced German ham from the fridge and began to cook breakfast for the first time in months.

'You look fantastic, Iz,' he told her finally, mopping up egg from his plate with a piece of rye bread. 'Even in the dressing gown. You've lost weight, haven't you?'

She nodded, glad that he'd noticed, wanting suddenly to shower and dress and appear as her new remodelled self.

'I have, and I had my hair cut. Look, I'll go and have a shower and get dressed. Do you want to rest or what?'

'No, I slept for eight hours on the flight, I'm raring to go. I'll have a wash and you can show me the lie of the land. What'll we do today?'

She took a deep breath. 'Well, why don't we go for a walk in the snow? I'll show you a bit of Nuremberg and then . . . I have to meet someone this afternoon. She's coming here but I'll take her out for a coffee and you can have a sleep.'

'No,' he cried, slipping his arm around her waist. 'Put her off, tell her your husband just arrived, she'll understand; it's Christmas, after all. I don't want to sleep, I want to spend the day with you,' he said, kissing her.

'We'll see,' she said, moving away. 'I don't want to change it. You sort your stuff out, there's plenty of room in the wardrobe. I won't be long.'

She stood in the shower in a state of shock, scalding water streaming down her body, wondering how she would handle the rest of the day. She felt invaded, yet she knew that her reaction would seem small-minded and hurtful. She ought to be delighted to see him. In the past she would have been thrilled at his early return from a business trip. But something had changed. She had reclaimed some part of herself, some personal space that was clear to her and not to Doug; she needed him to understand it before he crashed through any more boundaries, but didn't know how to tell him so soon after his arrival without hurting him.

'Well!' he exclaimed as she went back into the kitchen dressed now in black pants and the deep purple sweater she had bought on arrival in Germany. 'You really have lost weight, and your hair looks terrific. So this is what happens when you get rid of the old man for a few months.' He got up from the floor where he was unpacking his case and put his arms around her. 'We could always spend the day in bed,' he whispered, rubbing his cheek against hers. 'It's been a very long time.'

Isabel froze. There were rivers to cross before she could return to the old intimacy. She feigned a laugh and pushed him gently away, running her hand through his hair. 'Nuremberg first,' she said. 'I could do with some fresh air. I had a very short night. Find your walking boots and we'll get going.'

They walked together through the lightly falling snow, across the bridge that spanned the glassy surface of the river, up the hill to the castle brooding snow-clad above the city. They stopped to listen to a busker playing Christmas carols on bagpipes, and ventured inside the door of the cathedral to hear the choir singing the Christmas mass. And as the time moved on, Isabel's resentment grew. Doug was revelling in every moment, talking constantly, telling her news of the past months in the department, a change of minister that had required him to brief and support the new arrival. There were problems with the plumbing in Deb and Mac's new house. His parents had won seven thousand dollars on the lottery, hence the trip to Bali. The grandchildren seemed to be growing fast.

'Did you bring my letters from Grace, Sally and Robin?' she asked as they stopped for hot chocolate where she had sat with Klaus.

'Yep,' he said. 'They're in my bag. By the way, I ran into Jim McEwan a few weeks ago. That rumour I told you about him and Robin was true – did you know that?'

'Yes,' she said. 'I knew.'

'Well, you didn't tell me. Anyway, I was at the opening of the new court building and he buttonholed me. Wanted to know if you would know where Robin was, so I told him she was down south. Couldn't remember where at the time, but when I got home I remembered you mentioned on the phone that she was in Danderup Bay, so I called him back to let him know. It's only a tiny place, it wouldn't have been too difficult for him to find her there.'

Isabel froze. 'You mean you told him where to find her?'

He nodded, draining his cup and pouring some more chocolate from the jug. 'Yes, he was very happy about that. I like Jim. Not keen on his wife, though, so I thought that was good about Robin and him.'

'She went away deliberately,' Isabel said, hearing the ice in her voice. 'She asked him not to get in touch. To leave her alone.'

Doug shrugged. 'Well, I wasn't to know that. She'll probably be delighted to see him. Did you cancel your friend, by the way?'

'I told you, I don't want to cancel her,' she said, unable to keep the edge from her voice. 'She's leaving for New York tomorrow.'

'It can't be so urgent it can't wait until she gets back. What is it – just a girls' chat on Christmas Day? Is that more important than your husband who you haven't seen for months?'

314

She felt herself about to snap. 'I can't suddenly change every-thing because you've arrived a week early, Doug,' she began. 'If you'd let me know –'

'If I'd let you know, Izzy, I couldn't have surprised you, could I? Surely you can sort out this woman so we can spend our first day together. After all, it's not work or anything impor-tant. Just give her a call when we get back and tell her not to come.'

Isabel couldn't trust herself to reply. They walked on, Doug still oblivious to her mood, still high on jet lag and the novelty of his surprise. Perhaps he would crash soon, she thought, the flight and the time difference catching up with him. But his energy level remained high as hers evaporated. She was short of sleep, and her desire to see Antonia and her anxiety over how she could get time alone with her was all-consuming. It was almost three-thirty as they let themselves back into the apartment.

'Can you let me have some marks, please,' he said. 'I'll change some traveller's cheques tomorrow. And we should give the kids a ring as it's Christmas Day. What time is it back home? I can't work it out. Should we call now or later? Is Bali on the same time as WA or is it different –'

'Doug,' she said, dropping her keys on the hall table, 'stop. Please stop. Back off, I can't take this.'

He looked at her in amazement. 'What do you mean?'

'This, this whole thing. You arriving out of the blue, walking in on me. Taking me over like this. You can't just turn up and expect everything to stop, and me to be like I was seven months ago. It's different now.'

He hung his coat on the hall stand and rubbed his hands together. She could see that she did not really have his attention. He was still too caught up in himself.

'Different? Why is it different?'

'Well,' she began, nervous now, unsure how to phrase it. 'I've been living a very different life, things have changed for me. I wasn't expecting you, I need time to adjust.'

'Isabel, we're married, you don't have to worry about adjust-ing to me. This is us, you and me. I've missed you, a hell of a lot.

If you went away to make me appreciate you, it worked, so you can come back now.'

He laughed affectionately, patting her bottom as he moved past her, and anger shot through her like a bullet. She wondered if he had always been this impenetrable, this immune to how she was feeling. She couldn't remember if she had felt like this before. She was tired, confused, the past was a blur. Perhaps the way he was acting was just a strange combination of months of separation and the buzz that some people get with air travel.

'I came away for myself, Doug, not to create anything for you, and I'll come back when I'm ready.'

He swung around to face her. 'And when will that be?' he asked, his tone changing. 'When will it suit you, Isabel, to return to your husband and family? This personal journey of yours, just how much longer is it going to take?' His voice was heavy with sarcasm.

'I told you I wanted a year,' she said. 'You agreed to that. I expect to be back by June.'

'I don't agree to it anymore,' he said, throwing himself into an armchair. 'I want you to come back with me in January. It's ridiculous, Isabel.'

She swallowed hard, took off her coat and scarf, and laid them over her arm. 'When I first talked to you about this, Doug, I told you I didn't need your agreement, and I don't need it now. I'll come back by June as I promised.'

Doug thumped the leather arm of the chair with his fist. 'Why, Isabel? Why, for God's sake? What's all this about?'

And she realised that he had never actually asked her this before. In all the conversations they had had before she left, they had talked about how he would manage without her, what arrangements she had made for him. Occasionally they had talked about the places she was going, but he had never tried to find out what she wanted from this trip, from twelve months of time out.

'I wanted time and space to myself without being at everyone else's beck and call,' she said now. 'I wanted to discover more about Mum's life, and to see places I've always wanted to see. But most of all I wanted to find out who I was in places where no one

316

knew me, where no one had any expectations of me, where I could be free to do what I wanted, to be whoever I chose to be.'

'Was it so bad being Isabel Carter, being married to me?'

She wasn't sure if he was being deliberately obtuse or if he really didn't understand. 'I can't begin to explain it to you in those terms, Doug,' she said. 'And I can't explain it like this, feeling as I do at this moment.'

'How do you feel at this moment, Isabel? I'd have thought you'd be feeling pretty happy that I turned up to surprise you on Christmas Day, travelled all this way to be with you. So how *do* you feel?'

She sank down into an armchair and put her face in her hands before finally looking up at him. 'Well, to be honest I feel you've invaded my space, that your intentions were good but the effect on me is devastating. I know you meant well, Doug, but I'm offended by the way you've walked in here and trampled over everything. You've assumed that it's okay to do this, you haven't considered how it might feel for me. You don't seem to understand or respect the fact that I have a life here and that I can't – I don't want to just switch it off because you've turned up –' The ring of the doorbell seemed unnaturally loud and she jumped as it interrupted her.

'Hadn't you better answer it?' Doug said as the bell rang again.

Antonia stood uncertainly in the doorway, clearly surprised to find that Isabel was not alone. 'I'm sorry,' she said. 'I think we said four o'clock, Isabel?'

'Yes, we did. Antonia, this is my husband, Doug. He arrived unexpectedly from Australia this morning. Doug, this is Antonia, who I stayed with in Portugal.'

They shook hands and Isabel watched as Doug greeted her, the consummate diplomat, charming, polite, interested. He spoke briefly to Antonia, mentioning Portugal, the snow, Nuremberg and her imminent visit to the US.

'My sister,' she explained. 'We think she does not have long to live. A stroke last year and now another. It seems important that we visit her, spend time with her now.'

'Yes, of course,' Doug said. 'Family things are so important. Antonia, it's wonderful to meet you but I'm sure you'll understand that Isabel and I would like to be alone together after all this time. Perhaps you two could meet up again when you get back from New York?' Isabel watched in disbelief as, ignoring her completely, he guided Antonia to the door. She had no words, no will, no energy to stop it happening. She felt like a child.

Antonia glanced uncomfortably from one to the other, raising her eyebrows at Isabel. 'Well, I . . . er . . . Isabel, will I see you again?'

The words seemed trapped in Isabel's throat. She wanted to hold on to Antonia, beg her not to leave. An elastic band was tightening in her head. She managed only to swallow the pain and ire, and force out a weak smile. 'Of course. When will you be home again?'

'Four weeks, perhaps,' Antonia said. 'Maybe a little longer. You will come to Monsaraz?'

Isabel nodded. 'Yes please, I'd like that. We have a lot to talk about.'

'Then I will write when I am back and I will see you again in Monsaraz,' Antonia said, and she put her arms around Isabel, holding her close for a brief moment, looking into her face. 'I will be thinking of you, Isabel, you are in my heart.' She smiled. 'So nice to meet you, Mr Carter, I hope you enjoy your holiday.'

Isabel watched her disappear around the corner to the staircase and turned back into the apartment in despair.

'There,' he said. 'That was okay, wasn't it? She didn't mind at all and you can catch up with her again in a few weeks, though heaven knows why you want to go back to Portugal.' He rummaged in his hand baggage, which lay beside the chair, and drew out a beautifully wrapped package. 'Here's your present – hope you like it. Deb picked it, of course. Well, you know I'm no good at that sort of thing.'

Isabel stared at the package. 'I guess Deb wrapped it too.'

He nodded with pride. 'Good at it, isn't she, the way she does the ribbons and stuff? Now, come and sit down here with me, Izzy, and let's sort this out. We can't have a row on Christmas Day.'

*

Isabel sat in darkness where she had sat the previous night, looking out across the city. On the CD player Yvonne Kenny sang the Handel arias, Isabel's Christmas gift from Luke; around her shoulders was a soft cream cashmere shawl from Deb; on the coffee table in front of her were the opal pendant, Deb's choice for Doug's gift, and the three letters from Grace, Sally and Robin. She was too overwrought to open them yet, and she sat there with a cup of coffee, allowing the beauty of the music to soothe her. Doug was fast asleep in the bedroom. Their conversation had swung back and forth for several hours, always dominated by his sense of surprise, and his own centrality. He seemed to have forgotten the anger and bitterness that had flashed between them prior to Antonia's arrival. He was Father Christmas again, dispenser of gifts and goodwill, creator of plans, bearer of tidings from afar. Isabel, shaken by the day's events, barely spoke, letting him talk, answering questions and trying to quell her growing panic and frustration. At seven she put together a simple meal of pasta – the fridge was not ready for Doug-sized meals. He ate it hungrily, washing it down with German beer, declaring himself ready for an evening walk. But in the short time it took her to wash the dishes he fell asleep on the sofa, and when he began to snore she nudged him gently and suggested he would sleep more comfortably in bed. Nodding and barely opening his eyes, he let her guide him to the bedroom. 'Love you, Iz,' he mumbled, hugging her. 'Great to be here.' And he dragged the duvet up to his chin.

The hardest thing to cope with was the recognition that in terms of the way things had always been between them, Doug had done nothing wrong. He was the same as ever. He had always maintained a good-natured dominance, as a loving and responsible father, deeply involved in a demanding job, pleased and proud of his home and family, taking pleasure in providing for them, getting his way in everything, the mundane organisation of life taken care of for him by his wife and children. This was the way she had loved him and lived with him. It was she who had changed, she who, through separation, had been forced to face the fact that the assertive, strong-minded woman she had been in public was not the person she had been at home. She had been two women, the public and private. She went out into the world and made decisions, fronted up to difficult people, fought for what she believed in and didn't give up. But at home she was another Isabel, a more traditional woman who rarely argued, who conceded most things to her husband, serviced his life and encouraged her children to do the same. He was the master of the house and the family, and, in a multitude of overt and subtle ways, he maintained a benign dictatorship enabled by her.

She despised herself for her spinelessness, for what seemed a lack of integrity in this double life. But she also knew that while she had gone along with it for decades, she had done so because, despite irritations and resentments, it had, on the whole, been good. Now, though, the shades had gone from her eyes. She was different and she could never go back to what had been. How could she cut through the habits and assumptions of thirty-four years? She knew she must begin to plant the seeds of change that would help him to understand that her decision to take this trip was the fork in the road. When she'd told him that she did not need his agreement to go away, it was the first time she had ever really confronted him and held her ground, the first time she had wanted something passionately enough to oppose him and take it for herself. On reflection his eventual acquiescence was more astounding than she had realised at the time. She remembered how they lay in bed the night she had told him she wanted to go away, how they were separated by the chasm of their emotions and how, in the end, it had been Doug who had reached out and conceded the ground. Even Isabel had not realised where it would lead them. All she knew now was that it had to be resolved, that it was something they had to do together, and that she had no idea how to begin.

Isabel's commitment to take it slowly and gently work towards change was sorely tried over the next two weeks. She was determined to try to get it right with Doug while still battling her frustration and disappointment over her lost opportunity with Antonia. On Boxing Day they made phone calls to the children and Doug's parents, and with them Isabel dutifully played the game of being thrilled by the wonderful surprise of his arrival. She took him to the famous toy museum where she knew he would love the huge and complex model railway. They ate lunch in a café off the square and walked by the river, and in the evening found a traditional German restaurant where Doug could have frankfurters and sauerkraut. She struggled to push away her resentment over things she had never before noticed, to reassure him of her love for him as a foundation for any sort of change. But it was in the bedroom that the cracks began to widen. Emotionally exhausted and still trying to live her other life, Isabel could not mask her feelings. She was accustomed to sleeping alone, and she was not ready to share her bed. She did not want to be held and kissed but she made an effort to respond; it was when Doug bent to take her nipple in his mouth and slipped his hand between her legs, she felt her skin grow cold and her muscles tense – and so did he.

She felt for his hurt and anger, but it was not something that she could suddenly change. The chasm widened dramatically. They became like polite strangers, careful not to brush against each other for fear of being misunderstood. Doug, now as vulnerable as Isabel had been since his arrival, grew quieter and withdrew. They did more sightseeing, more walking, more eating, and slept at the far edges of the king-size bed. Klaus had invited them for dinner and then back to his apartment for coffee. Isabel had hoped it might ease the tension but it only made things worse. As the evening wore on Doug became even more withdrawn, and when they finally said goodnight and Klaus helped Isabel with her coat and kissed her on both cheeks, Doug took his coat and walked out, barely acknowledging Klaus.

Back in their apartment he told her with icy calm that he now understood the reason for her frigidity. How long had she been having this affair with Klaus? How could she have taken him to dinner with her lover?

Isabel was dumbstruck. 'This is about us, Doug,' she told him. 'There's no one else, not Klaus, not anyone. It's about the way things are between us. The problem's not an outsider, nor is it lack of love. It's about the way we are, the way we've always been. I've changed in the last few months, I'm a different person, and my relationship with you needs to reflect that. I'm sorry – it must be hard for you to understand. I don't want to hurt you. I love you just as much as ever, but I need a new way to make this work.'

He shook his head wearily. 'It's worked for thirty-four years,' he said, his shoulders hunched, hands in his pockets. 'Why shouldn't it keep on the same way? I'm still the same person.'

'But I'm not! Look, please let me try to explain . . .'

The days were long, tense and painful but they did make some progress. Doug began to listen without always cutting her off, and he began to ask questions. She held him, stroked his hands, his face, his hair, kissed him, did everything she could to try to assure him of her love, but that was as far as she was able to go.

'Come back with me, Iz,' he asked her again the day before he left. 'Let's sort this out at home.'

She stroked his cheek, shaking her head, tears sharp in her eyes.

'I can't, Doug, not yet. I'm not ready. Please remember what we talked about, about how we can be different.'

He clung to her as the flight was called. 'I love you,' he said. 'I want it all back as it was before. You will come back, won't you?'

'I'll come back,' she told him. 'I love you, of course I'm coming back, but not to the way it was. We can make something new, I know we can.'

She stood in the airport lounge at Frankfurt watching as the steps were drawn back from the aircraft and it taxied slowly to the runway. Part of her wanted to go with him, to pretend that everything was as it had always been, but she knew it would not work. She had to finish what she had begun. Barely able to see through her tears she took the airport bus back to the city and then the train back to Nuremberg.

Waiting for her on the doormat was a brief note from Antonia in New York. Her sister was dying and she would stay with her until the end, another month, perhaps a little longer.

I was disappointed not to talk to you at Christmas, Isabel.
Perhaps you have gone back to Australia already, but I hope

*you stick to your plan to come to Portugal again. We have
much to talk about, things I cannot put in a letter. I am asking
that you have patience with me and believe that I will be in
touch again as soon as I am able to leave here.*

Isabel sighed, folding the letter and putting it back into the
envelope. She was caught in limbo. Exhausted by the emotional
tension of the last two weeks and weary of discovering new
places, she resolved to stay on in Nuremberg until news of
Antonia's return. Then she would slowly make her way back to
Portugal. She sank once more into her solitary life and the work
she had set herself of documenting Eunice's life in Europe in as
much detail as she could. The gentle silence of the snow-clad
German winter cocooned and soothed her until it was time to
move on once more.

TWENTY-THREE

'So how bad is it?' Sally asked as Grace pulled out of the airport car park and onto the main road back to Perth.

'Bad. The mastectomy itself was successful but there are complications. She has secondaries. It's not looking good at all. She keeps talking about that pain in her chest too. D'you remember she always said that everything she ate gave her indigestion? Well, that's come back. It's actually a problem with her heart, they're doing tests on that today.'

'And how's she coping?'

'She's okay – as okay as anyone could be after surgery and losing a breast, but she doesn't know the rest of it yet. I know her oncologist. He wants her to get some strength back before he breaks the news.'

Sally stared out of the window, slightly confused that she was back home but finding it unfamiliar.

'Is that a good idea? I mean, shouldn't she be told?'

Grace shrugged as she negotiated a lane change. 'Who knows what's best? I'm sure I don't. I wish he hadn't told me, though, because it makes it hard to act as though the worst is over.'

In the back seat Steve was half listening, half taking in the unfamiliar flatness of the landscape. Grace glanced at him in the rear-view mirror. She had been pleasantly surprised when he shook hands and hugged her at the arrivals gate. 'Sally told me about your needlework project,' he'd said, steering the luggage trolley through the crowds. 'And I'm so sorry about your dad, but it was good that you were home in time to be with him.' He wasn't handsome but there was something open and attractive about his face and his easy physical manner. He wore a soft old leather jacket, a dark green shirt and chinos, and seemed perfectly relaxed finding himself in a new country and under inspection by the first of what would be quite a number of Sally's friends.

Eyes still on the road Grace reached across and squeezed Sally's hand. 'It's great to see you. You were so brave to do what you did.'

'That's what Steve says,' Sally replied. 'It really doesn't feel that way. I was devious and selfish, and I caused a lot of hurt and disruption for everyone.'

'I see you haven't stopped being hard on yourself,' Grace said, and glanced up to see Steve grinning at her in the mirror. 'And you're the only woman I know who had to break a man's leg to catch him.'

'Yeah, and she didn't even need to.' Steve laughed. 'I was just standing there begging to be caught.'

Grace had been uneasy when Sally had called to tell her that Steve was coming home with her. 'What – for good?' Grace had asked.

'No, he's coming to see Australia. We haven't decided what we're doing really, but Steve has to write a book so he'll have to come back to Berkeley in August. This'll give us a chance to decide what we're going to do from then on.' Grace had been visited by the ghost of her former self, a voice that urged her to warn Sally to be cautious and not rush into anything. She had taken some pleasure in ignoring the voice but it was only when she met Steve and saw how he and Sally seemed to fit together that its last whispers evaporated.

'Everything's ready for you,' she said as she pulled in to the drive of Sally's townhouse. 'The cleaners went in the day after the tenants moved out, and I've put a few bits and pieces in the fridge and the pantry, so you'll be okay until you feel like going shopping.'

'Still the same old Grace?' Sally said, raising her eyebrows.

Grace shook her head. 'No way. The old Grace would've made up the beds, baked a cake, put a casserole in the freezer and Steve through an interrogation by now.' She laughed.

'I love the new one just as much as I loved the old one,' Sally said, hugging her. 'Thanks for everything.'

'Yeah, Grace,' Steve cut in. 'Specially for picking us up, it was real nice of you. But I was looking forward to the interrogation – I had some lies all ready.'

Grace backed out again into the street and started to head home, but at the next set of lights she changed her mind and turned left towards the hospital. She had called in early that morning to see Robin. Now it was almost five-thirty, and she thought Dr Chin might have broken the news to her that afternoon, in which case Robin would need someone to talk to. The city commuters were just hitting the freeway and the traffic had slowed to a crawl. Grace tuned the radio to Classic FM and the breathtaking purity of a Haydn trumpet concerto filled the car.

The road, the traffic, the surroundings were all so familiar but something was missing. She puzzled for a moment and then realised that it was that old hard feeling in her gut that had always felt so safe. That tightly controlled knot of tension, once so reassuring, had been gone for ages and a whole lot of other stuff with it, but while she had hung on to what she had learned in England once home again in Perth, familiarity constantly triggered her old habits. For four days she had sat at her father's bedside, holding his hand, talking to him as he slipped in and out of consciousness, wondering how much he understood in those waking moments. It had given her time for reflection, time to recognise how mechanical she had been, always taking control, looking after everyone, even those who didn't want or need it. She had felt trapped by the needs of other people, but it was her own need to be needed that had really imprisoned her. She wondered how she would be when she was with Tim, Angela and Emily again.

She decided to keep a journal, to write in it every day and record the triggers. She remembered a nurse on a psych ward talking to a patient who was about to be discharged after a long battle with drugs. 'Don't get too cold, too hungry or too tired,' the woman had said, looking intently into the young man's face. 'That's when it'll get you, the old habits, the reactions, the cravings, and that's when you're most vulnerable. Look after yourself.'

Grace's addictions were work, control and constant activity, and the gratification was the same as a drink or a hit. She had to learn to let go and to be alone with herself. Once she had dealt with her father's funeral and made arrangements to finalise her job, the time and space that had seemed so attractive when she was in England suddenly opened up the black hole again. She stood at the edge looking down into the darkness and saw that it was the same darkness she had faced when she made the decision to go to England. That decision had saved her. Now she must learn to save herself by staying put.

She mapped out a long-term plan. Her father's death had eased her financial situation. The legacy wasn't large but it was sufficient to take the edge off the financial anxiety, and strangely enough she no longer had any urge to shop – it seemed that she had all she needed and more. Later in the year she would visit Orinda in New Orleans and then go on to England to firm up plans with Vivienne. In the meantime she would have to think about a job. And then there was the short-term plan: structure her days to let herself stop *doing* and just *be*. She had made good progress, surprised herself by her ability to change pace, to pause, to let go of things, but Robin's illness had rocked her and she was struggling to hold her ground.

Grace had been delighted at the prospect of Robin staying with her over Easter and she had been only slightly concerned about the biopsy. It would turn out to be a cyst, she was sure, and Robin seemed relaxed about it. She looked thinner than ever. She was pale and often seemed breathless, but the weekend had been a delight and, once again, their friendship had deepened. Robin's diagnosis changed everything. She had initially refused surgery and bolted back to the cottage, then later she called Grace, who drove down and brought her back to Perth for the operation. Not so long ago Grace had longed for Robin to need her help. Now Robin *did* need it and Grace was scared. The irony was not lost on her. Getting through the mastectomy was manageable, but now she knew the worst about Robin's condition she was very concerned about the future. Sally clearly didn't understand the implications. When Robin was discharged she would need long-term care. Sally was deeply involved with Steve and would soon be back at work. Isabel was still in Europe and Jim McEwan out of the picture. Who else was there? Grace wondered how much she could do without letting it take over her life. Right now she was a lifeline for Robin, but for her Robin was the ultimate test.

She parked in the hospital car park, and wandered slowly up to the third floor and along the corridor to Robin's room. The door was closed and she tapped gently before pushing it open. The bed was turned back and empty, and sitting in a low armchair in the corner by the window was a small grey-haired man in a dog collar, his head resting on the chair back. He was fast asleep. Grace stood in the doorway wondering what to do. She had grown up with dog collars, priests did not bother her, but Robin was an atheist with little patience for the church. She thought she should wake the priest and get rid of him before Robin was brought back from wherever she was. Grace let the door swing closed behind her and cleared her throat. The man stirred, opened his eyes, paused to decide where he was and, seeing her, jumped to his feet, straightening his jacket and smoothing down his thinning hair. 'I'm so sorry. I must have fallen asleep.' He nodded towards the bed. 'I understand she'll be back any minute.'

Grace walked past him over to the other chair. 'Of course,' she said in the old authoritative Grace voice. 'Sorry to have to disturb you but you'd better not wait. She won't want to see you.'

'I'm sorry?' he said.

'She's not really interested, you know. Not a Christian. Probably best to get on and visit someone else.' Grace picked up a vase, tipped out the water, refilled it from the tap and put the flowers back.

'Oh, I think she'll be happy for me to wait,' he observed.

'I doubt it,' Grace said sharply, slipping past him to straighten the sheets on the bed.

'Once a nurse, always a nurse,' he said, sitting back in the low chair. 'You do those hospital corners like lightning.'

Grace straightened up and crossed her arms. 'Look, I don't want to be rude, Robin's not my patient but she is my friend and I don't want her bothered.'

He stood up again with a smile. 'You must be Grace,' he said. 'Robin told me a lot about you. Father Patrick Shanahan – not just a priest but also a friend. I'm delighted to meet you.'

Robin lay by the window in the darkened room watching the lights in the city's tall buildings. It was the first time in her life she had been in hospital and she was still shocked to find herself there. The painkillers made her drowsy and when she moved her head, her eyes seemed to take a while to follow. Her arms were leaden and her legs seemed to float. The pain relief was effective but it was the fear that was the worst thing to cope with. She was never ill, she did all the right things, ate sensibly, ran daily, slept well, gave up smoking years ago, drank very little alcohol. It didn't make sense that she could not just be sick, but dangerously ill. That afternoon Dr Chin had told her that the cancer was in her lungs, and that he was also arranging for her to see a cardiologist. How could this have happened to her? She was furious with her body for letting her down, frustrated by a condition she couldn't change, terrified of what was to come.

She'd spent half an hour talking with Dr Chin and now she could barely recall any of it. It was the feeling rather than the facts that had stayed with her, the feeling of everything being taken away, of being ripped off by some superhuman force against which there was no defence. She thought she could cope with losing a breast. It was quantifiable – the cancer was in her breast, the breast would be removed, the cancer gone, a new breast would be constructed and then she would be back to normal again. Life could go on as planned. But now . . .

She sighed and shifted her position against the pillows. 'It's like everything is up for grabs now,' she had told Father Pat that evening. 'My whole life has been put on hold and I don't know how long for – in fact, this may be my life from now on.'

'Take it slowly, Robin,' he'd said, sitting on the edge of the bed and holding her hand. 'You're going to feel a bit stronger as you recover from the operation. That's the time to start thinking about what you want to do.'

She had called him the previous evening, not wanting to hound Grace again but needing the sort of conversation in which the essentials were clearly stated and what was unsaid was clearly understood. He was in Geraldton and they had talked at length on the phone. The last thing she had expected was that he would immediately make the five-hour drive to Perth. As the nurse helped her into her room he was sitting in the low chair chatting with Grace.

'So you two have met, then?' she asked once the nurse had helped her back into bed and closed the door.

Grace nodded. 'We have. I tried to throw him out. Did my ward sister act!'

'And I was terrified, of course.' Father Pat grinned. 'But I managed to tough it out.'

Robin had waited until Grace left to tell him the crushing news that it was not all over as she had thought. She hadn't wanted to burden Grace with it just yet, for while Grace had been rock solid in her support, Robin could see her struggling to handle the crisis in a very different way.

'Grace is being fantastic,' she told Father Pat, 'but I don't want to dump all this on her – she's likely to feel that she's responsible for looking after me.'

'Well, you have to find a middle course, Robin,' he said. 'She'll want to help because she's your friend, she loves you. And you also have to ask for what you need.'

'I am going to ask her to see Dr Chin with me again. I can't cope with all the medical stuff. I need someone who understands it and who I can talk it through with afterwards. As for the rest of it, I just don't know. There's the cottage and the shop – all sorts of decisions I have to make.'

'A few more days,' he said. 'Give yourself a chance to recover from the operation.'

He got off the bed and walked to the window. 'Would you like me to let Jim know?' he asked.

Robin hesitated. She had been toying with the idea but had finally decided against it. 'It seems unfair to run to him when I'm in trouble,' she said. 'I'm the one who ended it and when we met in January we parted friends, but I felt I couldn't be too close to him, it was too hard.'

'And now?' he asked, turning to face her.

'Well, now I do feel I want to see him but I don't know how to ask.'

'Then let me talk to him,' Father Pat said. 'Leave it with me.'

It was half past eleven and she closed her eyes, longing for sleep. She had rejected the sleeping tablets because they left her so groggy. Alec Seaborn had called in to see her during the morning but she was still too confused to be able to decide what she wanted to do about the shop. He had called the Tranters, who had volunteered to stay on as long as necessary.

'I'm sorry to mention this, Robin,' he'd said. 'It's an awful thing to say at a time like this, but I'm concerned that you don't have a will.' He was right, of course, and how ridiculous it seemed now. A lawyer without a will – she must sort it out in the next few days. 'Just let me know what you want and I'll fix it,' Alec had said.

But what did she want? Where should it all go if anything happened to her? The cottage, the shop, her investments, the artworks and books she'd collected over the years. She sighed and pulled the pillows up behind her so she could see the night-time landscape in greater comfort. It had given her a strange flicker of pleasure to discover Grace and Father Pat chatting in her room, a feeling that she was part of something, her friends being together for her sake. Apart from the Gang of Four she had been a loner. Her family were all in England. Her mother was still alive and well placed, and her brothers and sisters were doing nicely. She had been away from her family for so long that they didn't really feel like family. It was her friends who had sustained her over the years and whose company she cherished now.

She thought of Grace, battling the habits of a lifetime, planning her visit to New Orleans and working on plans for Vietnam. She, like Robin, managed her life largely alone, even more so since the departure of Tim, Angela and Emily. Friends were replacement family. Sally wasn't alone anymore. She had Steve, who seemed to have passed Grace's initial inspection with honours. Would Sally stay here or go back to America with him? So much change – Grace's, Sally's, her own – seemed suddenly overwhelming. And then there was Isabel, from whom there had been only the occasional postcard since her Christmas letter. The letter was an enigma, obviously hiding so much more than it revealed. Something significant was happening for Isabel that she was not yet ready to share with them. She wished Isabel was here now. There was something calm and unchanging about her presence, something reassuring. Grace had said she was due back quite soon, and Robin fell asleep hoping that it would be very soon, wishing that she could open her eyes in the morning and see Isabel standing at the foot of her bed.

TWENTY-FOUR

Sally hung on to Steve's arm as they walked down the hospital corridor. The smell of hospitals reminded her of Lisa's birth – it meant pain and loss, and it always drained her energy. 'I can't believe how sick she looks, Steve. She's so thin.'

He put his hand over hers. 'She sure doesn't look good, but you said she was always pretty skinny.'

'But not like this. I suppose, yes, she was always thin, but she was fit, healthy. Now . . .' Her voice trailed away.

Steve had driven her to the hospital so she could spend some time alone with Robin, returning an hour later to collect her. Sally hoped she had managed to conceal the shock she felt on first seeing Robin. They had clung to each other in tears, until Robin reached for the box of tissues and patted a spot on the bed for Sally to sit.

'I've missed you,' Robin said. 'I was just stunned by the story in your letter. I had no idea.'

'Of course not. How could you?'

'I feel I let you down, *we* let you down. If I had been a better friend then you might have felt able to talk about it.'

Sally shook her head. 'No, no, it wasn't that. I was well into secrecy before I met any of you guys. It was cast in stone and you were – *are* the most wonderful friends. Honestly, it was about me, not about any of you.'

Robin reached out and took both her hands. 'And Lisa? How have you left it? Will you see her and the Mendelsons again?'

'That's the irony of it, really.' Sally sighed. 'I did all that and then I just found I felt so empty. It was as though there was nothing more there for me. I never did really connect with Lisa. Now that I've left I can see that Steve and Nancy were right in what they said. It was never really going to be possible to build a relationship with her. I feel enormous sadness and some frustration about it and, yes, I do want to see her again. I want to see Estelle and Oliver. They're such lovely people, I feel closer to them than to Lisa. But what about you, Robin? I'm so sorry to see you here.'

Robin smiled and shrugged. 'I certainly never thought something like this would happen to me. Remember how we all used to think that Grace would get some terrible illness or have a stroke? Well, now she's calm and fit, meditating and writing a journal, and here I am flat on my back and not at all sure about what the future holds.'

'And what about Jim?'

Robin laughed. 'Weird, isn't it? You and your secret, and me and mine! It's over, Sally. I mean, I do still love him, I guess that's not going to change, but I can't cope with the relationship anymore. I understand what happened for him, I believe he always meant what he said. He thought the day would come when he could leave Monica, but when it came to it he couldn't do it. So I have to move on and, frankly, I think I was doing that rather well until this happened. Anyway, when do I get to meet this man of yours? He must be pretty good if even Grace approves.'

Sally laughed. 'You can't take any notice of Grace these days, all the old benchmarks have gone. She's getting positively flaky. But isn't it great to see her like this? I can hardly believe it.'

'Too right. But I'm worried that this problem of mine is pushing some buttons for her.'

'Grace'll be okay,' Sally said. 'I know what you mean, but she'll handle it. She wants to do her best for you but look after herself as well. I think she'll get it right.'

'And Steve?'

'Ah, Steve. What can I say? Of course I think he's wonderful and I'm feeling like I've never felt before. The men I've been involved with have seemed very strong, but they've actually been quite dependent. It's so different with Steve. He takes responsibility for what he does, he can admit when he stuffs up and he puts so much into the relationship. He keeps surprising me because I expect him to behave like the others and he doesn't.'

'So what will you do? Will he stay here?'

'Just until August. He has some work to finish back in California.'

'And you?'

'I don't know, Robin. We're trying to work it out. The one thing we're both sure about is that we want to be together, but we have to decide where and how. I loved California but I'd prefer to stay here, so Steve needs to work out how he'd feel about that and we have to sort out where we are with the immigration laws. We're feeling our way at the moment.'

'And the dreadful daughter?'

'Stacey? Not so dreadful, after all. In fact, she turns out to be a perfectly normal, vulnerable human being. Nancy and I have both been amazed at the change in her. I'll tell you all about that later, though. I want to know about your cottage and the bookshop.'

When Steve put his head around the door, Sally and Robin were eating chocolate and speculating on what Isabel was up to in Europe and when exactly she might be back. 'Let me have a look at you, Steve,' Robin said, reaching out a hand to draw him closer to the bed. 'I want to see if you live up to your advance publicity.'

He took her hand, flushing slightly with embarrassment. 'All lies,' he said. 'I have feet of clay.'

Robin smiled. 'That's splendid,' she said. 'That makes you one of us. I'm so pleased to meet you at last. Are you surviving the inspections?'

'Everyone's been terrific to me so far.' He grinned. 'I feel real welcome.'

'And Perth?'

He turned to look out at the view across to the city. 'Looks good to me,' he said. 'But anywhere with Sally in it looks good to me!'

They walked on down the stairs and out to the car park. 'I have to find out more from Grace about what this means in the long term,' Sally said. 'It looks to me as though it might be a very long time before Robin is able to cope on her own.'

Steve nodded, unlocking the car door, and held up the keys to Sally. 'Are you driving or am I?'

'You, please,' she said. 'You seem to have taken to it rather well. Do you mind?'

He shook his head and slipped in behind the wheel. 'What about that guy she was involved with? A judge, wasn't he? Where's he in all this?'

'Out of it completely, it seems,' Sally said. 'It's over, they're friends, but it won't go any further.'

Steve started the car and they moved slowly into the traffic heading out of Perth south to Sally's place. 'What she said about the cottage,' Sally asked him, 'what do you think?'

'You mean when she offered it to us to stay in?'

'Yes. Would you like to go?'

'Honey, I'd love to but this is your call. You may not want to go away at the moment – you just got home. It'd be great to go down there, but you have to decide what feels right. I'm happy whatever I do, just so long as I'm with you.'

Sally hesitated, looking out of the window. 'She made out that it might just be nice for you to see that part of the state, but I got the feeling she *wanted* us to go there. It was almost vicarious. As though it brought it closer to her. What do you think?'

'I told you what I think.'

'Then let's go for a few days. Later in the week, perhaps, when we're over the jet lag and I've found out a bit more from Grace.'

'So what does it all mean, really?' Robin asked.

'It means, Robin, that the prognosis is not good,' said Dr Chin, making a steeple with his fingertips. 'A few months perhaps, a little more, a little less. Of course there are people who do recover, but it's unusual.'

'And there isn't anything you can do?' She was feeling stronger today, and having Grace there with her helped.

He shook his head. 'We can control the pain, and to some extent the other symptoms. But we can't cure it.'

Robin swallowed the lump in her throat. 'And in the meantime?'

'You're going to have your ups and downs. And they really will be up and down, times when you'll feel really good and others when it's rock bottom. In the main you'll feel pretty weak and you'll need help. You'll be very tired, no energy. You've had that heart condition for years. What you thought was indigestion was a lot more sinister and the cancer puts your whole system under stress. I think you should resign yourself to the fact that you won't be able to manage alone.' He looked across at Grace. 'You understand, Grace. I don't want to exaggerate, but Robin will need care.' Robin saw Grace nod and felt her squeeze her hand. 'Now the hospital can help you with arrangements. There are various solutions . . .'

Robin nodded, feeling the exhaustion take over. She had no stamina – she had been sitting there for about fifteen minutes and felt as though she had done an eight-kilometre run.

Dr Chin took her hand. 'One day at a time, Robin,' he said quietly. 'One day at a time. That's the only way to do it.'

'Of course you must come to my place,' Grace said once Robin was back in bed. 'We can plan from then on. We'll manage something . . . together.'

Robin looked at her and smiled. 'No, Grace, you don't want that and neither do I. You know it's not the answer. It's wonderful of you but it can't be that way. You have to have your new life and I don't want to be dependent on you –'

'But you have to have somewhere to go when they discharge you.'

'Maybe, but only temporarily. You must be clear about that. This is not a long-term arrangement. This is not what the last year has been about for you or for me. The other thing is, I don't want to be in Perth. It's too close to all the things I want to escape from. I want to go south again, that's my home now.'

'So how do you think you'll cope?'

Robin smiled again. She felt calm somehow, and was thinking more clearly. 'Dear Grace, you hate being in this hospital, don't you!'

Grace looked like a child caught stealing from the cookie jar. 'How can you tell?'

'It's just . . . well, it's just so obvious. You're dying to straighten the sheets, or fill the water jug or take my temperature.'

Grace gave a wry smile. 'You're too smart by far, Robin. I thought I was doing rather well.'

'You're doing wonderfully but I can see it's a struggle for you. Your days of looking after other people are over, Grace. You're awfully good at it but there are other things you want to do now.'

Grace nodded. 'But I don't want to let you down.'

Robin laughed. 'You've never let anyone down in your life and you're not doing it now. Help me work out something else. Look, I'm not hard up, maybe I could find a retired woman, a nurse or a carer, who'd share the cottage with me.'

'Could you cope with that? A stranger living with you? You've lived alone for years.'

'It's a compromise I may have to make,' Robin said. 'There are other possibilities that are worse. I need to be able to talk about it without you feeling guilty or thinking you're letting me down. The best thing you can do for me now, Grace, is to let go of feeling responsible for me and just help me sort it out.'

Grace bit her lip and looked away, nodding. 'You're right, of course. We need to look at all the possibilities.' She laughed suddenly and looked back at Robin. 'We'll do it your way, Robin. I promise not to take you prisoner!'

Robin lay back and closed her eyes. She thought about Sally and Steve, who seemed as much at ease as people who'd been together for years but were just as much in love as when they first met. She thought about the way Steve put his arm around Sally's shoulders as they left, the way he looked into her face, smiled at her, and she wondered what it was like to have something so perfect, so comfortable. It had never been like that for her. Decades of avoiding relationships, and then Jim. Well, she thought, some people get it right and others just don't. Almost a week had passed since Dr Chin had laid out the situation to her and she still had no solution, but tonight she was too tired to think about it anymore. She was tired, always tired.

'We'll go to your place for the weekend,' Sally had said a couple of days earlier. 'Is there anything you'd like us to do while we're there?'

'I just want you to see it,' she'd replied. 'Be in it. It'll give me so much pleasure to think of you there. Come back and tell me about the light on the water in the early morning, the smell of the ocean and the gulls strutting about on the rail around the deck. And see if Maurice is okay. I think he's moved in with Dorothy and Ted at the shop.'

'I'll take some photographs,' Sally said, 'and we thought we'd go on to Albany for a couple of nights.'

'Yes, yes please. And go to the bookshop, talk to the Tranters. They've been so good to stay on. Tell them I'll have something worked out soon. I can give you the name of the guesthouse where I stayed.'

They would be in the cottage now, Robin thought, curled up together by the fire. It was June and she had never seen it in June. The tears squeezed out between her closed eyelids. It was so unfair. She had done everything right, left Jim, made her own life, and now it was all being taken away. The cancer was a thief in the night, a thief who crept in while she slept and took everything she cherished. She wanted to rage against it but she didn't have the strength. There had been so many visitors – Grace this morning, then Alec with the draft of her will.

Visitors were so tiring. She wanted to see them all and then wanted them to go away because she had no energy for them. She was trying so hard to be strong, to convince them that she was okay, to banish the anxiety from their eyes by trying to keep the conversation light. It was hard work but she kept doing it, because perhaps by convincing them she could convince herself. She wondered what time it was – ten o'clock perhaps, ten-thirty? Steve and Sally would be asleep in her bed. It was a place for lovers and for very special friends. She imagined them there, the Gang of Four, cooking breakfasts in the kitchen, talking by the fire, walking up the cliff path and scattering their sand-clogged bathers and thongs across the deck. She was too tired to open her eyes to look at the clock. From the corridor she heard the low rumble of a trolley, and the phone rang at the reception desk. The door of her room was opened, the rubber sound excluder swishing heavily on the floor. She feigned sleep, not wanting to talk to the nurse, but then sensed that it was not a nurse and that someone was standing very still close to the bed.

She opened her eyes suddenly and Jim jumped in surprise. 'I thought you were sleeping, Robin,' he whispered. He looked strangely uncomfortable in the hospital room, his usual confidence missing.

Robin dragged herself into a sitting position and he moved forward to help her with the pillows. 'How did you get in at this time of night?' she asked.

'I just walked in. No one attempted to stop me.' He smiled. 'I guess I'll be discovered and evicted shortly. I came straight from the airport.'

'Father Pat called you?'

He nodded. 'I was in London, at a conference. I was able to juggle the bookings and get back a few days early.' He sat down on the bed, his hand on her arm. 'I'm so sorry, Rob. I don't really know what to say to you.'

Robin shook her head and looked away, finally unable to control the great well of sadness that had been growing inside her, sadness about her illness but most of all about lost dreams, the dreams they had had together, the dreams she'd had for her life after him. She began to cry and couldn't stop. Jim leaned forward and took her in his arms and she sobbed harder at the feel of him holding her, the familiar scent of his skin, the way he stroked her head and rocked her gently.

'I don't know what to do,' she told him, barely comprehensible through her sobs. 'I just don't know what to do. I can't be brave about this anymore.'

And he said nothing, just kept holding her, letting her cry until her sobs waned and she was too exhausted to cry any longer. He laid her back against the pillows and wrung out a face cloth in cool water, and gently wiped her face, which was burning from the tears, and he sat holding her hand until she fell asleep.

TWENTY-FIVE

Isabel had wondered how she would fill the time until she could head back to Portugal. Doug's visit had left her restless and anxious. She worried about how much she had hurt him and how he would feel once back at home. She called him more often, and he sounded as he had before he left Nuremberg: vulnerable, cautious and uncharacteristically introspective. He was very different from the ebullient, energetic man who had arrived on her doorstep on Christmas morning. He listened more attentively, and he asked her to find an Internet café in Nuremberg. He needed to write some of his thoughts to her and wanted to do it by email. He was busy, the new minister was an alarmist without the knowledge and background of his predecessor, so it meant more work for Doug and a great deal more irritation and frustration. He asked her again to come home early and again she told him she would return by June.

She had spent most of her life doing the right thing, being a good girl, first for her grandparents and then for Eunice. Her only real misdemeanour had been her period of hostility to Eric. The good girl had invariably let Doug call the tune. But she couldn't do it anymore. She was through with passivity and being taken for granted. Doug loved her, of that she was sure, just as sure as she was of her own love for him, but the relationship had to change if that love was to survive. Returning early with her own journey unfinished would destroy the future.

She made the most of Klaus's willingness to act as a guide,

reading and learning about the history of Nuremberg and Hesse, and taking trips to Berlin and Munich. She enrolled for a six-week course in German and contacted some women from the 5W network. She had already acquired some of the language and began to feel at home in Germany, enjoying the people and the disciplined way that things got done. By the end of March, by which time she'd still had no word of Antonia's return, it was growing warmer, the snow was gone and there were signs of spring. The air was cold and some mornings there was still a fine film of frost covering the grass in the park, but the evenings were becoming lighter and the sun began to deliver some warmth.

In the first week of April a letter arrived from Antonia. Her sister had died, she said, and she would be flying back to Portugal in ten days time. Isabel began to pack. She called Sara, arranging to spend a few days in Cascais before going on to Monsaraz, and Klaus drove her to the station and carried her bag onto the platform.

'*Ach!* Isabel, I shall miss you very much. I wish I can make you stay here.'

'I'll miss you too, Klaus,' she said, hugging him. 'You've been wonderful. Promise me you'll come to Australia soon?'

'*Ja*, of course,' he grinned. 'I love to come if Doug lets me, if he no longer thinks I have dishonourable intentions towards his wife.'

'He no longer thinks that.' She laughed.

'Then he is not wise,' Klaus said. 'My intentions are always dishonourable, but I keep them to myself. But truly, Isabel, I love to come. Maybe I come to have a hot Christmas like you have a cold one.'

'I think,' said Sara, 'that I should start a consultancy service for women who want to travel. You looked good when you left here but now that you've grown into the look, it suits you even better.'

'You probably saved my life,' Isabel told her. 'I wonder how far I'd have got with all those shoes and a complete wardrobe for all seasons.'

She had taken the train from Lisbon and Sara had walked to Cascais station to meet her. 'I had a call from Antonia this morning,' she said, waving down a cab to take them home. 'She wants to know when to expect you. I told her she can't have you just yet. I've been so looking forward to your visit and her brother's there at the moment. I hear you met him in Nuremberg.'

Isabel swung her bag into the boot of the taxi and climbed into the back seat beside Sara. 'Her brother? Yes, I met him. I only really said hello and then he ignored me for the rest of the evening.'

'She told me about him when we met. Did I tell you I had lunch with her a couple of times? I don't think they get on all that well. Antonia says he's very cold and silent, but women find him incredibly attractive – they fall at his feet.'

'Can't imagine what sort of women. Masochists, probably,' Isabel said, gazing out of the taxi window across the sea wall to the sunlit ocean. 'It's so lovely and warm here. German winters are a bit challenging when you're not used to them.'

She was impatient now. She wanted a resolution and wanted it quickly. But she was disinclined to head for Monsaraz while José was still there. Easter came and went. The streets, calm and solemn on Good Friday, were filled with coloured lights and music on Sunday. Statues of Jesus and the Virgin Mary led lively processions, trailed by small children dressed for first communion, white prayer books clutched in their white-gloved hands.

'José has gone,' Sara announced in the week after Easter as Isabel walked back into the house with a bag of groceries. 'The coast is clear! Antonia would like you to call her and tell her when you will arrive.'

'I'm going on Friday,' Isabel told her after she had made the call. 'I'm going to walk down to the station to book my ticket. Want to come with me and have a coffee on the way back?'

They strolled together along the main street, watching tourists queue for a sightseeing tour in an open pony carriage. 'Strange, really,' Isabel said, staring at the carriage as it disappeared down a side street. 'José, I mean. He and Antonia are so different. She's so gentle and gracious, and he's so distant and stand-offish.'

'Apparently there's some big skeleton in the cupboard from years ago. Seems they were very close as kids but they had some big fight when they were adults and it never quite got put back together after that.'

Isabel stepped up to the booth and ordered her ticket. 'So what was the fight about?'

Sara shrugged, waiting for Isabel to put away her change. 'Dunno, she didn't say really – but a woman, I think. It was yonks ago. José was working in France, the Riviera somewhere – Nice, I think – and she went up there to see him and . . . Oh look, that's all I know. But apparently it was all pretty dramatic at the time.'

Isabel's skin prickled. 'How long ago?'

'Oh, ages. Sixties, p'raps; no – earlier. Fifties, I think she said. I don't know the details. You'll have to ask Antonia about it.'

'How did you find all this out? You only met her a couple of times.'

'I'm a journalist.' Sara grinned. 'We have ways of making you talk.'

Sweat trickled down Isabel's back. The temperature in the bus was mounting and the window beside her seat wouldn't open. Alongside her an elderly woman dressed entirely in black nursed a wicker basket in which a rooster grumbled and squawked. The woman's head nodded forward until the bus turned the sharp corner for the upward climb to Monsaraz. Her head jerked up and she resettled herself, occupying even more of the seat. Isabel sighed and craned her neck to look ahead. It was just as she remembered – a mythical place, white and hazy in the afternoon heat. The bus rattled under the archway and clattered to a halt. The woman shuffled to the exit and Isabel handed the rooster's basket down to her, then, picking up her own bag, she swung off the bus into the magic stillness of the square. Heat bounced off the cobbles as she crossed the street into the shade to make her way up the hill. They met halfway.

'I was coming to meet the bus,' Antonia said. 'But it was a little early today.'

Isabel put down her bag, running her hand across her forehead.

'I'm so pleased to see you, Isabel.' Antonia reached out to take both her hands, and kissed her on both cheeks.

'And I'm so pleased to be here. I can't tell you how many times I've imagined coming back.'

Antonia picked up her bag and led the way back to the house. 'You must be exhausted. First a cool drink and a shower. We have the house to ourselves for a few days at least.'

Isabel looked around her room, loving the deep cool shade of the shutters closed against the afternoon sun. The church clock chimed four and the only other sound was the bleat of the goats on the hillside. She sighed with pleasure. It was like coming home. She wanted to savour every delicious moment with Antonia in this exquisite place, but she also wanted to rush things, to have quick answers to her questions, to probe and parry, and satisfy her burning curiosity. She took a cool shower and washed her hair, towelling herself dry in the white-tiled bathroom, trying to talk herself into calmness.

'And so, Isabel, your husband enjoyed his visit to Germany?'

Isabel poured some homemade lemonade from the jug and sat down beside Antonia on the balcony. 'Not really,' she said. 'It was a difficult time for us. Being away created a lot of changes for me. We both have to come to terms with that, find a new way forward, I suppose. And you? How are you, Antonia?' Ice clinked in the tall glasses.

'Ah, well. How can I say it? How can I begin? The time has been difficult for me, Isabel, since you left . . . I . . .' She paused, seeking the words. 'I was not entirely honest with you in Évora and then here . . .' Silence again.

'In Évora something happened between us,' Isabel said. 'Something I couldn't understand or name.'

Antonia nodded, looking down into her glass, clearly unable to speak. Isabel waited a moment and then went on. 'At first it was like . . . well, like a sexual attraction. It was so powerful, I thought you felt it too. But after that you shut me out. That energy

346

is still there – it's something intimate, as though we're linked in some way.' She knew she was rushing things, that it would be better to wait and let things evolve more naturally. But she had waited so long that every minute now seemed burdensome. Their silence hung heavy in the late afternoon. The town heaved and shuffled with the small sounds of people emerging from siesta, but Isabel and Antonia sat side by side as if cast in stone.

'You knew my mother.'

It was a statement not a question, and Antonia nodded and looked up at Isabel with tears in her eyes. 'Yes, Isabel, I knew your mother, briefly, in 1953. We met in Nice. I will tell you all about it. It is not easy for me, and for you . . . well, I don't know, I think maybe it will be hard for you to hear it. But I must tell you just the same.' She took a deep breath. 'José, my brother, was working for the government at the time, and he was posted to Nice. He and your stepfather became friends. It was through José that Eunice and Eric met.'

'How strange,' Isabel cut in. 'Your brother never mentioned it to me.' She paused. 'In fact, he barely spoke to me.'

Antonia shook her head. 'No, he would not mention it. He never speaks now of Eunice and Eric, it is a taboo subject. But I did tell him that you are Eunice's daughter.' She sighed again as though the effort of talking wearied her.

'Eunice and José, they were going out together. It was nothing serious, you understand, just a flirtation. Then, one evening at a party, José introduced her to Eric and the next thing was that Eunice and Eric were lovers. They very quickly became engaged to be married.'

'And José was jealous?'

'Oh no!' Antonia laughed lightly, reaching for the jug of lemonade and refilling her glass. 'No, José was not jealous, he was very happy for them. Eric was his best friend and José was a flirt. He had no serious intentions towards Eunice. He liked to play the field, as you say. He was pleased for them both. They were very happy.'

'She was living in Monaco then,' Isabel cut in. 'I went to the theatre, through the archives, I found a photograph.' She got up and picked up the folder that she had left on the table. She drew out the photograph and handed it to Antonia. Antonia stared at it in disbelief and Isabel, standing just behind her, saw her shoulders shaking with silent sobs. She put her hands on Antonia's shoulders. 'Antonia, what is it? I'm so sorry. I didn't want to upset you. I thought you'd be pleased to see it.'

Antonia shook her head. 'No, no, of course I am happy to see it, but it also brings memories, great sadness. Sit down again, Isabel. I have to tell you this. Maybe when you know you will want to leave here straight away, and of course I understand.' Isabel slipped back into her chair, looking again at the photograph, filled with anxiety and anticipation.

'So,' Antonia began again, 'I was living in Lisbon but I went to Nice to have a short holiday with José, and he says that he will take me to see Compagnie Fluide at the Théâtre des Beaux-Arts. It is a very well-known company, as you said yourself, Isabel, somewhat avant-garde, and I am a dancer myself, so of course I am delighted. It is a very special night because it is the birthday of the director and there is also a party. We will go to the party, José says, because he has a friend who is a soloist and she is fiancée with his best friend.'

Antonia picked up the photograph again, tapping it with her finger. 'It is this night, the performance for which I send you the program. The first time I saw Eunice was that night. She was like a spirit, such a dancer – oh, Isabel, if only you could have seen her. How she moved, such a presence on the stage. She was, how do you say? Bewitching. The audience was ecstatic.' She stopped and sighed. Isabel handed her the photographs that had been taken of Eunice that night and Antonia studied them, sighing deeply, her eyes filling with tears again.

'Yes, yes, this is it, but the photographs cannot really capture . . . do her justice.' She put the photographs on her lap and folded her hands on top of them. 'So we go to the party. It is a very beautiful party in the theatre, many important people. I was almost twenty and I thought myself very sophisticated. I hope I will have the chance to meet this wonderful dancer and suddenly there she is, taking my hand, kissing me and telling me she is so happy to meet José's sister. I thought I was in heaven. Eunice had such wonderful eyes, you remember? Hypnotic almost . . . well . . . How will I say this? There is no easy way.' She turned to face Isabel.

'We fell in love, Isabel. Eunice . . . your mother . . . and I. That night – like the song says, an enchanted evening, across a crowded room. Before they left the party I wrote her telephone number on my program. We met the next day, and three weeks later she came with me to Lisbon. We were lovers.' Antonia paused, seeming uncertain whether she should go on.

The sun was lower in the sky now, sinking slowly towards the horizon. Beyond the town wall a man called to the goats and they responded with plaintive bleats. Isabel watched the fading rosy gold light above the charcoal shapes of the distant hills. She had known it before Antonia had said it. She wondered if she had known since that moment in the cloisters.

'We were together for several months in Lisbon and then in October, Eric finally persuaded Eunice to leave and go back to France with him. He came to fetch her and we . . . we said goodbye. You are shocked, Isabel. I am sorry, it is not a nice thing to learn . . . you are angry.'

Isabel felt her own tears starting and she reached for Antonia's hand. 'No, oh no, please don't think that. I'm not shocked at all, or angry. Just, well . . . I don't really know . . . Surprised, I suppose, but not shocked. Tell me more, Antonia. You were happy together? How did it end?'

'Yes, we were happy, very happy. It was not easy, you understand – the times, of course . . . These days people are more open, but in the fifties, here in Catholic Portugal, it was difficult. We behaved outside like friends sharing a home. In the theatre, of course, these things have always been more acceptable, but one has to live in the world, which is more narrow. We were not open as one could be today. But I'll go back a little. There was a terrible time while we were still in France. A week or so after we met, Eunice came to the house where I was staying with José. He and Eric had arranged to go sailing on the yacht of the British consul, and they will be away all day. So I telephone Eunice and she takes

Eric's car and drives to Nice. It was our first chance to be alone together in private, intimately, you understand. We had met for a drink, for lunch, gone shopping together, but always we were in public places. Now at last we are alone. And we are in heaven with hours to spare because they would be away until the late evening, staying for dinner on the yacht. The whole day is ours. Except that it was not.

'There is a problem with the yacht, they could not go out, so the men come back to the harbour in the dinghy, they go to have lunch in their favourite restaurant and then, together they come back to the house. And we, Eunice and I, well, we do not hear them, but they hear us, and then they are standing in the bedroom doorway and it is . . . oh, I can't tell you how terrible. José is like the mad bull and Eric, poor Eric, he is devastated, weeping, angry . . . everything . . .' She paused as a tremor shook her.

'Always,' she went on, 'always I remember it, that moment and the days that followed.' Antonia shook her head, wiping her eyes. 'They treat us like children, keeping us apart. Listening if we make a phone call. And the anger and hurt is unbelievable. And for Eunice and I – we long so much for each other, if only we can just talk to each other. Eventually we are able to talk on the telephone and we decide we must go away together. Eunice tells the director that she is not well. It is easy to convince him because the strain, you know, it showed. She asks for one month *congé*, and she does not tell Eric. She can't bear to hurt him by telling him but she knows all the time it will hurt more when he finds we have gone. But we take the train to Lisbon together.'

The sun had sunk behind the hills and the balcony was suddenly cool. Antonia began to shiver and seemed unable to stop. Isabel got up, fetched a shawl and draped it around her shoulders. 'Can you tell me some more?' she asked, her hand on Antonia's arm. 'Or is it too painful?'

'No, no, of course I tell you. I tell you all you want to know. You have a right, and I have not talked about this for so many years. Just give me time.'

'Shall I make us some tea?' Isabel asked, and Antonia nodded, so she went to the kitchen, returning a few minutes later with a pot of peppermint tea and two delicate china cups. She poured the tea and sat down again. 'Did they know where you'd gone?'

'Oh yes, they knew. José guessed. He knew I had nowhere else to go. I was living in an apartment in Lisbon in the house of my aunt, the one you have in the photograph. My aunt was away but José was terrified that she would find out and will tell our parents. We are not in Lisbon more than perhaps two days and José and Eric arrive. There is more terrible fighting and weeping. Eric is quieter, so sad – he is bereft, as you say. But José, he is wild and angry. He blames Eunice, he is furious with her because she is older. She is thirty-two and I am not yet twenty. He says I am an innocent girl and she has seduced me. He calls her corrupt and evil, he tells her he wants to thrash her, she has ruined my life and brought shame on our family. If our parents discover what has happened to their daughter, it will kill them. For him there is great disgust. He is always what we say now – macho. The thought of two women together, it is disgusting to him. Not so for Eric, he seemed to understand. Love between two women, that in itself does not threaten him – it is Eunice's desertion and infidelity that destroy him.'

'Were you innocent? Did she seduce you?'

Antonia smiled. 'Oh yes, both, really. Yes, I was innocent. I have been on dates with boys, I have had some physical love, but I was a virgin, yes.'

'And other girls?'

'No, not me. I never even knew such a thing was possible before I met Eunice. That night in Monaco I could not understand how I could have such intense feelings and attraction for another woman.'

'And Eunice? What about her?'

'Eunice, yes. She told me she had lovers, both men and women. But nothing like this, she promised me, nothing so intense, so passionate . . . she had not been in love. Did she seduce me? Maybe, maybe not – I was more than willing, I adored her. It was strange and new, my sexuality, you know. I did not really understand this.'

'So what happened next?' Isabel asked. 'Eric and José didn't manage to break you up at that time. I've seen the theatre records.

She applied to stay away longer. It was October before she went back to Monaco.'

'That's right. We were together all that time. They couldn't separate us that first visit. But they would not leave us alone. There were all the time letters and telephone calls, they came back three times and each time it was terrible. In the end it was Eric who persuaded her. He wore her down. He told her always, "Your daughter, Eunice, you owe it to her, you must make a life for her. All this time you have left her and now you mean to stay here like this, it's not fair to the little girl." He was right of course, and he was genuine. He wanted her himself and he thought he could use you to persuade her, but his intentions were good. At the time I hated him for it, but that changed a long time ago. She did what she had to do, she needed to be with you. It was you she chose, Isabel. She loved Eric too, but in another way. She did the right thing. That was her consolation – and mine too, I suppose – to think that her child at least would have her mother, and that's as it should be.'

Isabel leaned back in her chair and closed her eyes, tears running silently down her cheeks. 'Her diary,' she said. 'The pages are gone for that period. She tore them out.'

'Yes,' Antonia nodded. 'I know, she tore them out and gave them to me when she left. I have them still, Isabel. If you wish you can read them, but I will never part with them. She was gone only a few weeks and then the accident. So cruel! I think she must never have recovered from that in her heart. To dance was every-thing – without that she would be desolate. But she had you and that would be what she lived for. Poor Eric, after the accident he thought it his fault, because he persuaded her to leave.'

Antonia sighed. 'It is like some storybook, the passion and the pain. I am sorry to have to tell you all this, Isabel. When I realised who you were, it was like some magic had brought you here. But I couldn't tell you. It was so many years ago, and I have not been able to talk about it. I had to pretend I knew nothing. And then in Évora, that moment in the cloister, I thought perhaps you knew. It felt as though you could see into my soul, saw it was like looking into Eunice's eyes. I already loved you – not just as Eunice's daughter, but as yourself. I wanted us to be friends, I did not want to spoil it, but instead I spoilt it by telling you nothing, by pretending. So, now you know it all and perhaps you wish to leave . . .'

Isabel was standing by the balcony rail, looking out across the flat plains to the tiny pinpoints of light of another hilltop village. She turned around to face Antonia, almost too full of emotion to speak. She paused, swallowing hard several times before she could manage the words. 'I don't want to leave, Antonia,' she said. 'I want to stay here as long as I can. I want to know more, and to tell you about Eunice, about her life after she left you. What you've told me is such a gift, it's as though you have given me back my childhood. You see, she was away so long, and while she was away she seemed such a magical creature, but when she came back she was broken, she seemed to have lost everything she cared about. I thought she just missed the dancing. I was angry with her because she wanted that back and didn't want to be with me. But I couldn't show her my anger, so I took it out on Eric, who treated me better than any real father. I thought she didn't really love me, you see, not in the way she should.'

'She adored you, Isabel, and she was so proud, always talking about you, showing your pictures, always promising to bring you to Portugal one day. She worked hard for you, you know. Oh, she danced because she loved it, yes, but she also worked hard because she wanted good things for you. When she came to Europe after the war she had nothing. The dance companies worked people to exhaustion. She wrote to me once from Perth saying that she knew she had done the right thing. In the end it was you who mattered . . . you were all the things she could no longer be – young and free and beautiful. She had her daughter.'

'And you, Antonia? What happened to you after that?'

She shrugged, pulling the shawl closer around her shoulders. 'I was alone for a very long time. I kept dancing. José's job brought him back to Lisbon and we shared the apartment but he made me feel like a child. I went to Spain for a while and then moved back again when José was transferred to Germany. There were lovers and I was married briefly, but it didn't work out. I think I was supposed to be alone – it has become my life. I chose it and it suits me. I am responsible only for myself and I give of myself only what I can afford to give. Eunice was my one real love, my sadness has been always to have to hide it, never to be able to publicly acknowledge the loss. But you, Isabel, have given her back to me. I see you now, a beautiful woman, loving and wise and forgiving. In the end, you see, I know it was worth the parting.'

TWENTY-SIX

'Y'know,' said Steve, battling his way through the cottage door with a basket of logs, 'I could've sworn that back in California you told me that Western Australia had a beautiful Mediterranean-type climate.'

Sally laughed and went to help him. 'We do. But it can get a bit full-on in winter sometimes.'

'Full-on? Ha! Some understatement, lady! There's a hurricane out there and listen to that rain.'

The kitchen door swung open again in the high wind and Sally ran to close it. 'It won't last long,' she said. 'Never does. In fact, the sun'll be shining again by this afternoon. The lovely thing about this place is that you can see the weather changes coming in from the ocean.'

'Sure,' said Steve. 'I can hardly wait. I'm never gonna believe you again. Give me the mild Californian climate any day.'

Sally's face fell. She was pathetically vulnerable and she knew it showed. 'Don't you like it here, Steve?' she asked in a small voice. 'It's winter, after all, and it's been lovely and sunny until today.'

He straightened up, brushing dust off his hands from the fire-place where he had juggled the fire to life. 'Sure, I love being battered by the elements,' he said. Looking up suddenly, he saw her crestfallen expression. 'Hey, Sally, I'm only joking, honey. I love it here. You know I do.'

'Really?'

'Really!' He grinned.

'Cross your heart and hope to die?'

'Cross my heart. Rather not die, though. There are other more interesting things to do in a remote cottage on a wet morning in front of an open fire.' He drew her down beside him on the couch and they sank into the softness of Robin's purple cushions. 'Trust me, sweetheart, I told you – I love it.'

'Yes, but . . .' She began struggling into a more upright position. 'Would you want to live here?'

'In this cottage? Hell no, too far from good coffee shops, movies and retail therapy.'

'I meant Western Australia.'

'I know, I know, I'm just teasing. You should know me by now. Yep, I reckon I could live here very happily. Beautiful place, clean air, magnificent scenery, very friendly people.'

'But would you *want* to live here?' she persisted. 'Would you consider it as a permanent option?'

'No,' he said. 'Definitely not. Unless, of course, I was offered some inducement.'

'Like what?'

'Like you agreeing to marry me.'

'That's emotional blackmail,' she said, smiling.

'Sure is!'

Sally got up from the couch to close the bedroom door, which was tapping in the draught.

'Be serious, Steve. We have to talk about the future.'

'I know we do,' he said. 'I'm just fooling around, not trying to avoid the issue, if that's what you're thinking. Look, I'll be straight with you, Sally. I love you and I'd go almost anywhere to be with you. What's more, I actually like it here, love it, really. I'd be very happy to live here and I don't mind leaving California, although I guess I'll get a bit homesick from time to time. There's just two hurdles as far as I can see. One – from what the immigration people told us, the only way I can stay here is if we're married. Two – will I be able to get work here? I'm concerned that I might not be able to earn a living. Perth's a small place and I don't think there's all that much demand for fifty-something photojournalists.'

'I've got a job,' Sally said. 'Teaching's very secure, I can probably keep us. Whole families live on a teaching income.'

'Sure they do, but while I like the *idea* of being a kept man, I know I wouldn't like the reality and I'd be bored. Maybe I could find a business of my own. I don't know what the answer is to that.'

Sally nodded. 'I know, and it's the same for me in California. In fact, I might not be allowed to work there even if we did get married.' She sighed. 'Why do they have to make it so hard?'

Steve reached up to take her hand and pulled her down onto the couch again, swinging her around so that she lay with her head in his lap. 'Thing is,' he said, 'it seems that if we want to be together we've gotta take a risk on one place or another.' He laced his fingers through her hair. 'I'm prepared to give it a go here if you are. I can probably get some sort of work and do a bit of free-lancing as well.'

She caught his hand and held the palm to her lips. 'You're so sweet.' He laughed. 'But you are,' she persisted. 'You're so easy to get on with.' She drew herself upright and looked him in the eyes. 'I never thought it could be this easy. Relationships have always been such a struggle. I don't mean fights and arguments, just such hard work to sustain – emotional hard work.'

He stroked her cheek. 'I've had that too,' he said. 'Imagine what it was like being married to Stacey's mother – she was Stacey plus! I said I would never ever get involved with a woman again. Just too hard.'

'P'raps it's because we're older, and maybe a bit wiser,' Sally said. 'How d'you think Stacey will cope with you coming here?'

'You can probably answer that better than me. You're her confidante these days – thank God!'

Sally laughed and lay down again. 'It's weird, you know. I really couldn't handle her at all at first. I'd actually built her up in my head to be some sort of monster who was determined to keep us apart.'

'Well, she *was* pretty obnoxious when she got back from London.'

'But, Steve, think how lonely she must have felt. Do you remember that night, the first time we went to bed together and she burst into the bedroom? Well, later, when you were asleep, I was sure I could hear her crying.'

'Maybe this is why I love you, Sally. Because you're so fair and reasonable, and you even make Stacey seem fair and reasonable. She'll be fine, I think. She was in a bad space and she felt left out and lonely. I wasn't there for her when she needed me. She and I have sorted that part out, and she thinks the world of you.'

'I like her too,' Sally said. 'I liked it that she came to me when she was in trouble, even if it was only as a last resort. We'll be okay. I like getting to share your daughter.'

'And your own daughter?'

'Ah well, I'm coping with that. What do you guys call it? Closure? I'm getting there.'

'So, I'll go back and sort out the stuff for the book and come back again?' he asked.

'When?'

'I can probably get back here for Christmas.'

She sat up again, put her arms around him and kissed him.

'It's a deal,' she said. 'Christmas it is. Don't be late!'

'No, ma'am!'

Grace lay on the bedroom floor practising her yoga asanas in an effort to calm her mind and body. However hard she tried, she didn't seem able to shake off the sense of responsibility she felt for Robin, or the growing anxiety about her life after hospital. She was having great difficulty controlling the desire to take charge, and while Robin was certainly considering the situation, discussing it, entertaining various possibilities, it was all too vague and slow for Grace's liking.

She sat in the lotus position and tried to meditate but today it wasn't working. Her head was spinning with the possibilities she wanted Robin to consider, but she knew she had to hold back. She couldn't just barge in and set it all out – numbered options, facts and figures – as she wanted to. Robin wasn't ready for that.

She'd made it clear that she wanted to work backwards, or at least Grace thought it was backwards. Instead of having a list of possible solutions with costings and then thinking through which she preferred, Robin wanted to get a sense of how she would like things to be and then try to create the perfect solution. Grace found it disconcerting. She had expected that Robin, with her legal training, would have approached it in a more ordered fashion. She was battling her old-style irritation at things not being done her way. 'Ah well,' she said aloud, standing up and stretching her arms behind her head. 'I guess I'm learning. A year ago I would have been in there laying it out in front of her and bludgeoning her into accepting my system and my choice.'

She pulled her bathrobe around her and wandered to the window. The dense Kings Park treetops swayed in the wind like a great moving carpet. There was more rain on the way. She wondered how Sally and Steve were enjoying being lashed by wind and rain in Robin's cottage – was it bleak and dreary or cosy and romantic? They were so wrapped up in each other and Grace was happy for them, but she also felt a sense of displacement. Sally was her closest friend but now she had to accommodate Steve's prominence in Sally's life. Grace knew that her friendship with Sally could never be quite the same again. She accepted it, but she was having a little trouble trying not to resent it.

And Robin – what about her love life? A few days earlier Grace had dropped into the hospital early in the morning and found Jim McEwan, looking very crumpled and drinking a cup of tea. He'd spent the night there, having gone straight from the airport to see Robin. He'd fallen asleep in the chair until the night nurse discovered him when she brought Robin a cup of tea at six o'clock. Grace wondered if the nurse had given him a dressing-down as she would have done twenty years ago. What would she do now? She thought she might just turn a blind eye. Must be getting old. So where was Jim going to be in all of this? Was that a flying visit or was he permanently back on the scene again? Robin hadn't said – maybe even she didn't know.

Grace sighed and wandered through into the kitchen to make herself some toast. Orinda's postcard of New Orleans stood on the windowsill propped up against a pot of African violets. She took it down, studied the picture and turned it over to read again.

Grace! Don't you forget our singing date! I got some great plans for your visit, sewing and singing and soul food. Did you book your ticket yet? Let me know when you're getting here and I'll start cooking! Love, Orinda.

She sighed again and put the card back in its place. Should she take the chance and book, or just postpone it all indefinitely until Robin was settled? And was it wise to spend all that money on fares? She stared out of the window hating the dilemma and the fact that she was letting it occupy her head space and take over her life. Two different Graces were doing battle inside her: the control freak who wanted to be needed and to take charge of everything, and the new Grace, who wanted to learn to let go of it and press on with the journey that had just begun. The phone rang and she jumped. It was barely after six, unusually early for a call.

'Hope I didn't wake you. What time is it there?' Vivienne said.

'Just after six and, no, you didn't wake me. It's great to hear your voice. Isn't it past your bedtime?'

'Yep, but I got some news I wanted to tell you. How are you, anyway? How's your friend?'

'Not good at all.'

'Does that mean *she's* not good, or *you're* not good at coping with it?'

Grace laughed. 'You're far too astute for me at this time of the morning. It means both, really. She's not good at all, the cancer wasn't just in her breast. And there's a problem with her heart . . .'

Vivienne sucked in her breath. 'So what's the situation?'

'Grim, really. They told her she has a few months, maybe more, but she's very sick and she'll deteriorate. We have to find some care for her but that's complicated. She's single, her family are all in England . . . well, you know. It's difficult . . .' Grace's voice trailed away.

'That's very sad, Grace, I'm really sorry. So how are you coping?'

Grace wanted to burst into tears. There was something essentially solid about Vivienne and it was much more than just her physical size. She had an ability to see around emotional corners, her bullshit detector was finely tuned and she was always straight to the point. 'I think I'm schizophrenic,' Grace ventured. 'Wanting to be in charge one minute, wanting to be free and run away the next.'

'Run away?'

'Perhaps that's not the right expression, but wanting not to have the responsibility.'

There was a pause and Grace could almost hear Vivienne analysing what she had just said. 'But you're not responsible, Grace, deep down you know that. And from what you've told me about Robin, she wouldn't think that either. You waved goodbye to all that when you didn't race off to Tokyo to look after your daughter-in-law, when you stuck with your plan for yourself.'

The tears had taken over now – there was relief in being able to talk about it to someone else. 'I know, I know. But, Viv, she's my friend, and there isn't anyone else.'

'Grace, there's always someone else. You just have to make space for them to move in.'

'Really, I don't think there is anyone. Sally's very involved with Steve, and she'll be back at work in a couple of weeks anyway. Isabel's not back yet. Robin's quite a loner – she's always travelled her own road.'

'In that case the last thing she'd want would be for you to take a detour from *your* road.'

'Viv, I know what you're saying is right. It all makes sense, but what I can't sort out is where the line falls between being a helpful and supportive friend and giving away too much of my own life in the process.'

'Dear Grace,' Vivienne said. 'Sometimes, you know, I really believe there is a God and that he's a man and he takes a sadistic pleasure in planning out the most perfectly designed tests for us. This one's really an Oscar winner.'

Grace smiled through her tears. 'Absolutely.'

'Look, love, I'm afraid I'm not going to make this any easier for you. I suppose if I were a different sort of friend I'd keep my news to myself until you've sorted this out. But I actually don't think it would be very honest. See, your idea for Vietnam, the business plan you wrote, the only hitch was that we didn't have the money to do it – yes?'

'Yes,' Grace said. 'It's going to be very expensive to get off the ground. I've no idea how to raise that sort of money. And I need to find work and try to live within my means, which I haven't been very good at in the past.'

'Well, that's what I rang to tell you. You see, the money isn't a problem, and nor is work. We've got it, enough to get it going and enough to pay you to do it.'

'What? How?' Grace's heart thumped.

'Remember Gary was taking some of the quilts to New York? Well, he hung three at some swanky exhibition, put ridiculously high prices on them and sold all three to a woman who's a merchant banker. Rich as Croesus and – wait for it – really committed to supporting projects that provide self-sufficiency for women in developing countries. She bought the quilts, one for herself, one to hang in the foyer of some ethical investment company that she's on the board of, and the other to auction at a ball for some women's project in Harlem.'

'Brilliant. That's wonderful. But that money will go straight back to the women who made the quilts, won't it?'

'Yes of course, but hang on, I haven't finished yet. A couple of days later she calls Gary and invites him for dinner and asks him more about the Patchwork Project. I had to email him some stuff in a rush because she was asking questions he couldn't answer. Anyway, the long and the short of it is that she was over the moon. Said she'd come up with some money for a specific project, so I sent her your Vietnam plan and she jumped at it. She'll cover the setting-up costs, including enough to pay you to do it.'

Grace could barely breathe. 'You mean it's all there? All we need?'

'All we need and more, Grace. You just have to get on that plane as planned, because Helena – that's her name, Helena Wells

– wants to meet you. She's keen to be involved all through. Says she doesn't want to interfere but she's really taken with the whole thing and she wants to take a personal interest, so she wants to make a personal connection with you. And, talking about connections, there's more. She's got great connections, she's going to set up a fund to support this, and she's going to help us market the best of the quilts from all the projects. It means that there is going to be some big money going back to the women, and you've got a job if you want it. Grace . . . Grace, are you still there?'

'Yes, yes I'm still here. It's fantastic. It sounds like a dream come true.'

'Well, it is. A lot of women's dreams have gone into this and Helena is just the sort of breakthrough that will make a huge difference. So there you are, Grace. Patchwork Vietnam is full-steam ahead.'

Grace's body was rigid with excitement. She had twisted the phone cable around her wrist so tightly that her hand started to tingle. 'So what have you told her? What happens next?'

'I've told her that you'll be in New Orleans by September and then you're coming on here. Helena wants you to go on up to New York and meet with her before you come to England. She'll pay the airfare, accommodation, everything. And while you're there she's going to introduce you to some other women in this women's ethical investment thing she's involved in. If you can talk up the projects she may be able to get us money to expand in some of the other locations. I'm going to email you background on all the projects so you can do your homework on them, bone up before you go. All you have to do is turn up as planned and start talking – so you'd better book your seat, Grace, and start swotting.'

TWENTY-SEVEN

'I'm not going to die, you know,' Robin said, pushing food around her plate in a desultory fashion.

'No?' said Father Pat, raising his eyebrows.

'Thank you for not saying "of course not". That would have been unconvincing. But I'm not going to die, I'm not ready for it. I won't be for a long time.'

'You're reading the book, though,' he said nodding towards *The Tibetan Book of Living and Dying*, which sat on the bedside cabinet.

'Well, something like this does make you think about forces greater than ourselves – what comes next, all of that. Have you read it?'

'I have.'

'And?'

'Wise and comforting, I think. After all, when it comes down to it we really know nothing. It's only a matter of the details of belief and the search for meaning.'

'Maybe you could suggest something else I could read as well.'

'Of course. I'll bring something in.'

She selected a forkful of mashed potato and savoured it. 'The food's not bad here. Not that I seem to be able to eat much of it. No bacon, though.'

He grinned. 'I found some first-class bacon in a roadhouse on the way back from Geraldton. I may have to drive you up there to sample it.'

'It's a date!

'Last night I dreamed that I'd died and gone to heaven and I was starting to like it, and then St Peter – well, I guess it was him – came and grabbed me and said I couldn't stay there because I was reading a book on Buddhism.'

'I don't think they'd ban that book in heaven,' he said, with a grin. 'But it was a ridiculous dream anyway – they'd never have let you into heaven in the first place.'

'Why not?'

'You're a lawyer. *They're* banned.'

She laughed and pushed the plate away. 'Aren't you supposed to give me spiritual comfort? I'll have to complain to the archbishop.'

'Much good may it do you – he told me that joke himself.' He got up and moved the tray away. 'Jim called me. I hear he came to see you.'

Robin leaned back on the pillows and stretched her legs out, pushing her toes down towards the mattress. She was sick of sitting in the bed. 'Yes, he came. I cried for what seemed like hours and then fell asleep. Then he fell asleep in that chair and got told off by the nurse in the morning. It helped, seeing him. I don't know why, but somehow he gave me permission not to be strong. Not to pretend to be on top of it all.'

'That's good.'

'Yes. It got a bit out of hand in the morning, though. He started saying he would leave Monica and devote himself to looking after me down at the cottage.'

Father Pat's eyebrows nearly shot off the top of his head.

'I know; ridiculous, really, but I believe he meant it when he said it. He always did mean it at the time. Anyway, it's not what I want, it's not right and it wouldn't work for me. I want to see him sometimes but I can't begin the relationship all over again. I only have enough energy for myself, barely that. Could we go for a bit of a walk?'

Cautiously she turned and hung her legs over the edge of the bed. It always felt as though she would fall down when she put her feet on the floor. Father Pat helped her with her dressing gown and they set off at a slow walk down the corridor.

'That woman had her mastectomy after me and look at her,' Robin said. 'She's almost back to normal and I'm a wreck.' The woman was dressed, ready to go home. She was moving carefully but comfortably, her hair done, face lightly made up.

'Your body has a hell of a lot more to cope with, Robin,' he said, patting the hand that was hooked onto his arm.

'Oh, I know, I know. I'm jealous, that's all. I want to be normal again, I want this to be over and get back to my life. I was having such a good time. Now I know life will never really be normal again – and there may not be much of it left anyway.'

'I thought you weren't going to die!'

'I'm not. It makes a difference, I think, being positive. Don't you agree?'

He stopped and faced her. 'Yes,' he said. 'I think it makes a difference. In some people it's the crucial difference between life and death, the determination to live. I've seen it many times. It defies medicine and science and all expectations.' He paused. 'Besides, you're not allowed to die.'

'Why not?'

'Because I love you. I told you, I fall in love in most unsuitable ways for a priest.' He leaned forward and kissed her cheek, and they walked on slowly down the passage.

She could smell the southwest air on their clothes, and their energy breathed life into the bland, colourless room. Their faces were rosy with happiness, shiny from walking in the wind. Sally's hair was tied in a bulky ponytail, she was light-hearted and more confident. They're good for each other, Robin thought, really good. Better than Jim and I ever were – perhaps if we'd met earlier, before he was married, perhaps twenty years ago we might have been like that.

She had got up to sit in the chair and they sat on the end of the bed facing her. Life had become a series of shifting scenes with different characters, and she felt as though she was watching herself perform from a great distance. Were these scenes sent to illuminate things for her? Were they just little windows for her

366

to see life outside? She wondered where she had got to with planning for her future care. It all seemed to keep slipping away. Sometimes she couldn't remember what she had considered and dismissed, and what had seemed a real possibility.

Steve handed her a package of photographs. She opened them and she was back there, on the deck, watching the setting sun, dodging the rabbits as she ran along the clifftop path, strolling down to the shop. 'Tell me you loved it,' she said, moving the photographs so that her tears wouldn't mark them.

'We loved it,' Sally said. 'Even in the storm we loved it.' She put a little cloth bag on Robin's lap. 'From your beach.'

Robin put her hand in the bag and drew out a handful of shells, small stones, bits of driftwood and seaweed. A huge lump rose in her throat as she lifted them to her face and breathed in their aroma. 'Beautiful,' she sighed, flicking away the tears. 'Better than drugs. And Maurice?'

'In cat heaven,' Sally said. 'Dorothy is spoiling him silly.'

'So did you go to the bookshop as well?'

'We did,' Steve said. 'It's there in the pictures.'

She went through them slowly. There were shots from every angle, on the street, inside the shop itself, the Tranters sorting books, David on tiptoe at the top of his ladder, Sue talking to Sally, and pictures of the upstairs apartment. 'So it looks as though you like the shop too. How are David and Sue? They must be fed up with me for not making a decision yet.'

'They're fine, Robin,' Sally said. 'They understand perfectly, but of course they do want to get away. And we ... well, we wanted to talk to you about it. Have you decided what to do yet? Will you keep it or sell it?'

She leaned back in her chair looking down at the photographs. 'You know, I realise it's not sensible but I can't bring myself to sell it quite yet. It would be like giving up. I've decided to find someone to run it for me short term. He or she could live in and manage it. Alec Seaborn has said he'll take all that on – advertise, interview, then get it down to two or three possible people and I can meet them and decide. Eventually I suppose I'll have to sell it because I'm never going to be able to run it. Don't you love the way they put those tall, round things with seats and shelves through the shop? It makes it so cosy.'

'Robin,' Sally said. 'If you haven't found anyone yet, would you consider us?'

Robin looked up at her in amazement. 'You? In the shop?'

'Yes, the two of us,' Steve said. 'Me managing it, but us living there –'

'And I'd transfer to a school in Albany,' Sally cut in. 'I've checked and there are a couple of vacancies coming up at the end of the year.'

Robin looked at Steve. 'But I thought you had to go back to California.'

'I do,' he said. 'But I'll be back here to stay before the end of the year. I have to do some research for my book and organise selling my apartment.'

'And in the meantime,' Sally said, 'I could take another six months' unpaid leave and run the shop. Then I'd go back to teaching in the new year.'

'You don't have to answer now, Robin,' Steve said, an anxious frown crossing his face. 'We probably dumped too much on you all at once. But I fell in love with that place, the shop, Albany, the apartment. Sally did too. Eventually we could buy it but I have to sell my apartment in Berkeley first. With the exchange rate and the California property markets as they are, I'll be quite well placed to buy here, but it'll take a few months. No hard feelings if you say no. Take your time, think about it.'

Robin reached out for Sally's hand. 'I don't have to think about it,' she said. 'It's more than I could have dreamed of. With you two there, I'll still feel close to it.'

'I'd understand if you want someone with experience,' Steve went on. 'I mean, I know quite a bit about books, though not the book trade as such, but I can learn, we both can.'

Robin threw back her head and laughed. 'Steve, really, it's perfect. I'm sure you know as much about books as I do, so does Sally – probably more. If I thought I could run it, why wouldn't I be happy for you to do it? This is the best idea that anyone has had in a very long time.' She reached out for his hand, and he took it in both of his and bent down to kiss her cheek. 'Got some other news too.' He grinned, looking across at Sally.

Sally blushed. 'It feels so strange,' she said. 'I never, ever thought I'd do this. We're getting married when Steve comes back at Christmas, so you just have to be well by then.'

Robin cried a lot that night. She cried with happiness for Sally and Steve, and with satisfaction for herself. She cried for what they had and she had never known and would now never know. She cried for the loss of dreams, and for all the things she had stuffed up in her life, and the things that had gone wrong in spite of her doing her best. And she cried with fear and panic and the terrifying sense that she had lost control of everything in a particularly unfair way. At eleven the night nurse found her still crying and made her a mug of Horlicks, and they sat together in the dark talking about life and death and love. Robin felt as though they were floating in a dark bubble totally detached from the rest of the world. The nurse encouraged her to take a sleeping pill and she rearranged the pillows and said goodnight. Robin lay very still wondering where the bubble would land and wishing that she could see Isabel.

Hours later, as the early winter sun crept between the slats of the venetian blinds, she opened her eyes and thought she was still in a dream. Standing at the foot of her bed, the sunlight striping her like a tiger, stood Isabel. A thinner, older but more beautiful Isabel, with a haircut and clothes that Isabel would never have worn, but a smile that was unmistakably her own.

TWENTY-EIGHT

Isabel had been in Monsaraz for four weeks when Grace's letter arrived. Antonia had gone to meet a client in Évora to discuss the translation of a guidebook and Isabel walked to the mailbox and back up the hill, her conscience pricking her as she looked at Grace's envelope. She had not been a good correspondent. The others would have seen through her cheerful travelogues and known that there was some far more complex emotional journey in progress. In contrast their letters had been rich in personal stories, honest and soul-searching. She knew hers hadn't done them justice, but until these last weeks in Monsaraz, she hadn't felt able to translate her own intense and confusing journey into words on paper. She walked up the hill in the late morning sunshine, enjoying the anticipation of reading the letter and reminding herself that it was already the end of May and she must soon start her journey home.

During her first week in Monsaraz she felt that she might never be able to leave. Now that she knew the truth she was desperate for more, she wanted to draw out every anecdote, every detail, every nuance. The Eunice that had returned to Perth in 1954 had been an enigma and had largely remained so until her death. 'She was always hidden from me,' Isabel explained to Antonia in one of their many conversations during the days that followed Antonia's revelation. 'It was as though there was a part of her that was never accessible to me. She wouldn't let anyone else come close either. Eric and I, and Grandma, were closest to her, but there was always a part of her that was shut off. I suppose she'd made a choice and she was doing the best she could to live with it, and of course with the results of the accident. It's terrible, to have lost so much – first you and then her dancing.'

'But there was always you and her love for you, and she must have been so proud of you, Isabel,' Antonia said.

'I wish so much that she had told me her story. It could have been so different between us. Imagine all that love and loss buried for all those years – all my confusion – such a waste.'

'It's easy to look back, always it is easier to be wise for someone else and wise after the event. It is water under the bridge, Isabel. It is best to let go now, I think. Eunice could not tell you because she thinks maybe you cannot accept it and forgive her. And Eric, she would not tell you for Eric's sake.'

'I know.' Isabel sighed. 'I can see all that. But I wish . . . I wish so much that I had known while she was alive. Now it's too late.'

'But it is not too late for you, Isabel, not too late for what this means to you, for what you will make of it.'

But what would she make of it? She felt she had been searching for the Eunice of the letters and cards since her childhood and had decided on this trip very soon after her mother's death. Was it death that gave her the freedom to find the original Eunice? It was spine-chilling to contemplate the serendipity that had brought her first to Portugal and then to Monsaraz. She had been searching for something to fill the void left by Eunice's death, but also to resolve the contradictions of her life. Eunice and Eric, the devoted couple in conservative fifties Perth, and the quiet companionability of the decades that followed, were so far removed from the passion and intensity that Antonia had described.

'Eric must really have loved her,' Isabel commented to Antonia one evening. 'To put up with everything, to care for her all those years. In the end, you know, she did love him. She depended on him totally. There was a gentleness between them – not passion but peace, I think. She was devastated when he died.'

Isabel put Antonia's mail on the kitchen table and took Grace's letter onto the terrace. It was a dull day, heavy and overcast. The distant hilltop villages, usually so clear, were blurred and grey in the haze.

Dearest Isabel

This letter is going to arrive near the end of your trip and I hope it won't spoil your last days or weeks. I wasn't sure whether to write but I think you'd want to know what's happened here.

A few weeks ago Robin was diagnosed with breast cancer and the doctors recommended a mastectomy. At first, quite understandably, she freaked out and disappeared down south, but after a week or so she called me and I went to collect her and brought her back. She had the operation a week ago and is recovering from it. The worst part, though, is the news that the cancer is also in her lungs. All that, combined with a genetic heart condition, means it's very serious.

Right now she's refusing to give in. She says, quite rightly, that lots of people manage to get the cancer under control and live for years. She's very determined. I think her determination is wearing her out.

At the moment we're trying to sort out some living arrangements. She wants to be independent but she'll need care and the options are fairly limited.

I'm not saying come home immediately, Isabel, there is still plenty of time. Even at the worst the prognosis is months – maybe a year. But frankly I'm hoping you'll be back soon and not just for Robin's sake but for all of us. I miss you, we all miss you. This situation makes me realise how very much you have been the lynchpin of the Gang of Four. Robin is very sick, Sally is madly in love and I'm trying to get a grip on myself and let go of my desire to control everything that's happening. I didn't tell Robin I was going to write.

I'm so looking forward to seeing you. Sally sends her love. You'll like Steve – he and Sally are so right together, I'm very happy for them. I'm hoping to set off for the US and then England again, in August. I saw Doug a couple of days ago.

He's looking a bit subdued since his German trip – I hope
everything is all right for you both. Hoping to see you soon.

Very much love,
Grace

Isabel read the letter twice before folding it back into its envelope. She ran upstairs to find her tickets and dialled the number for Qantas in Lisbon. Drawing a huge breath she made a booking for the end of the following week. Then she called Doug and told him that she was coming home.

It is the fierce intensity of the night that turns dreams to nightmares and unease to misery and panic. Waking in the darkness and silence, vulnerable to the terrors of both reality and imagination, pastels become bold primaries, the creak of a floorboard becomes the splutter of gunshots, mild pain becomes unbearable. Isabel opened her eyes and felt herself falling apart, abandoned, rejected and rejecting. She had risked everything, lost everything, ruined everything. She was terrified of going home. For hours she struggled with the night terrors; getting up to pace the room, returning to lie absolutely still in the hope that sleep might return and in the light of day everything would look very different. Eventually she slept but the morning brought little relief. Her fear and depression were a confused morass of cause and effect – guilt about her journey, about Doug, guilt about her decades-old treatment of Eric, confusion about Eunice, and countless other mental snapshots from the past that formed an album of pictures of her failures as a wife, mother, daughter and friend. Had she destroyed everything she loved?

'It will pass, Isabel,' Antonia told her. 'It will pass but you cannot force it. You're returning home, there are big challenges there for you. You took a big risk. You stepped out of a mould which was safe and familiar, you tested yourself. Now a part of you wonders if it was all worth it. Is what was gained worth what may be lost?'

It made sense, but it was more than that too. Underneath the chaos lay a grinding sense of loss and grief, feelings she had shouldered aside when Eunice died. Now they came back to haunt her, demanding their inescapable place and resolution. 'The word that came to me in the night was "orphan",' she said. 'That I am an orphan and that somehow it was my fault, for not asking the right questions, for not recognising and cherishing what was there.'

'We feel like this when the last parent dies,' Antonia told her, holding Isabel's hands firmly in her own. 'When there is no one left who knew us as children, it is as though that part of us also died with the mother or the father. For you I think it is harder because you are an only child. Now without Eunice, your childhood exists only in memory and imagination. It is not unusual. It is what you might have felt when she died, but somehow you postponed it.'

For several days Isabel was crippled by her grief and a resulting lassitude. On the morning of the sixth day she woke very early to find the pall had lifted and a new and sudden energy drove her out of bed. Still in her white cotton nightdress she ran barefoot from her room and knocked on Antonia's door. 'There's something I don't understand,' she said, flopping down on the end of the bed. 'Klaus, when he left here – what he said to you that day when he got on the bus. Does Klaus know about this?'

Antonia, fully dressed, was sitting at her dressing table, brushing her hair and twisting it into a loose bun. She picked up some large tortoiseshell hairpins and fixed it in place, her eyes meeting Isabel's in the mirror and holding them with a strange intensity. 'Yes,' she said. 'Klaus knew.'

'About you and Eunice?'

'Yes.'

'And did he know about me? That Eunice was my mother?'

Antonia put down the brush and turned to face her. 'Yes, he knew.'

'But I asked him,' Isabel said angrily. 'When I was in Germany I asked him about it. I told him about you sending me the theatre program. He said he didn't know anything about it.'

Antonia looked away, sighing. 'It is my fault, Isabel. I asked him, begged him, not to tell you anything. I didn't know what to do. It was such a shock to discover you were Eunice's daughter. When you arrived here I felt very close to you, almost as though we had met before, but of course you do not look like your mother, and you have a different name. Then you told us about her at dinner and I was shocked and confused. I didn't know what to do so I pretended I knew nothing. But in Évora, after that moment in the cloisters, I could not contain it anymore. I was tortured by these feelings – I was drawn to you as though you were Eunice, but also as though you were my daughter. I was mad with the feelings. That night in Évora, after dinner, I didn't go for a walk – I went to talk to Klaus.'

Anger was more energising than the grief and loss that had trapped her for the last few days, and Isabel felt its stirrings. 'You told him what you wouldn't tell me. Antonia, this was something so vital to me, something concerning me so completely, but you didn't tell me, you told Klaus, a friend who is unaffected by it all. How could you have done that?'

'Isabel, Klaus is not unaffected by this,' Antonia said. 'You see, there is one part of the story I have not told you. Since you arrived you have been so obsessed, quite naturally, with the story of Eunice and me, and how this affects you and your relationship with your mother. So, somehow, I cannot quite bring myself to bother you with the rest of it.'

Isabel, who had got up to pace the bedroom floor, dropped onto the bed again, staring at her. 'What?' she said. 'What else? Tell me now, please. I need to know.'

Antonia nodded and got up to open the shutters. Morning sunlight flooded the room, and she pulled back one shutter to filter the light and stood gazing out down the hillside. 'It was 1954,' she began. 'The year that Eunice and Eric went home to Australia. I felt no bitterness, I understood that she had to go, but I thought my life was ruined. José barely spoke to me – he is still so angry. I was young, of course. I still had not learned that one survives, that the loss of one love does not mean that one can never love again.' She paused, still looking out of the window, her slim frame silhouetted against the light.

'That was when I met Klaus again. We had not seen each other since we were children. He was a few years older than me and he was doing his research in Lisbon. He called me one day and we went out. I liked him, he was gentle and thoughtful, not like some of the other young men I knew, and he was easy to talk to. He was a delightful companion, so we did everything together but at the same time we behaved like friends. I did not know that Klaus was in love with me. He treated me with great respect. He was very Germanic in this – rather formal, you understand?' Isabel nodded, her heart beating faster, wondering what was coming.

'And then, he asked me to marry him,' Antonia said, turning to face Isabel. 'Well, it is a long story but I refused several times. Klaus knew I had been in love but did not know about Eunice. He said to me always, "You will recover, I will give you time, I understand." But it went on a long time and I could see that if I did not marry him I would lose him. He was soon going back to Germany and I had begun to depend on him. I did love Klaus, though not in the way that would make me want to marry him, but I was frightened of losing him, and finally I thought, he is a good man and I care for him. It will not be grand passion but it can be a good marriage. And so I agreed. We were married in 1955.'

Isabel gasped in amazement. 'You and Klaus were married! He's your husband?'

'Ex-husband. We were separated two years later, and divorced about ten years after that. It was a disaster. He was in love with me, I was not in love with him, and I grew to resent him. I hurt him deeply and I hurt myself too. I was still in love with Eunice, at least with the dream of her. It was a shock to Klaus when he discovered that my great lost love was a woman. In those days he was more conservative, he was wounded by this. It was almost twenty years before he came to terms with it and before we could talk about it together. Then we were able to be friends, dear friends. He is my most treasured friend. That is why I told Klaus, Isabel, because his life has been affected by this just as deeply as yours or mine.'

Isabel got up from the bed and walked to the window, putting her hands on Antonia's shoulders. 'Antonia, I'm sorry. I've been so selfish. All I've done is talk about the effect this had on me and my mother. I never even thought of asking what it all means for you.'

Antonia shrugged and put her arms around Isabel. They stood by the window holding each other. To Isabel it felt as though they were a scene in a tragic ballet danced across the decades.

Antonia stepped back and reached for the tissues to dry her eyes. 'What Klaus said that day – *verweile doch du bist so schön* – "please stay, thou art so beautiful". He said it to me many times before I left him. Now, after all this time, he says it always to me, and I to him, when we meet and when we part. That day, Isabel, you thought Klaus was saying something about you, but it is a talisman for Klaus and me. It is part of our special language for each other, our way of saying you are my dearest friend, I miss you, I love you, I am so happy to see you, don't forget me. You understand – a few words can mean so many things.'

Doug was standing in the arrivals hall facing the door, his hands clasped behind his back, wearing jeans and a navy sweater. At first she thought that he had lost a lot of weight since Germany, but a second glance told her that these were not new clothes and they fitted the way they always had done. He saw Isabel and walked towards her as she tried to steer the recalcitrant trolley between the barricades. For an instant she felt as though she was in a scene from a movie, a couple meeting, excitement, apprehension, love, anxiety. In the movie you knew something important would happen from this meeting. It was a turning point – whatever happened on those few inches of celluloid would be crucial to the future. She could scarcely breathe because suddenly she wasn't sure what she was walking into. His anger? The pain of her physical rejection of him? Pure confusion? 'I'll be there,' he'd said when she told him she had booked her flight.

'Well, I'm sure Deb'll come if you're busy,' she'd said. 'It's a Wednesday morning, and that's your regular meeting time with the minister.'

'Isabel, I said I'll be there,' he'd said with a calm purposefulness.

She slowed the trolley to a stop and they faced each other across it. He brought one hand from behind his back and in it were half a dozen heart-shaped foil balloons on red ribbons, each one with a legend: 'I love you', 'Missed you!', 'Be mine'. She smiled and then started to laugh in amazement. 'Doug?'

'You once said it was your dream,' he said, handing her the red ribbons.

'I did?'

'Yes. To have a really silly romantic welcome with balloons and roses.' He produced his other hand, clutching a bouquet of apricot roses.

'Doug, darling, that's so beautiful of you. I never thought I'd see you within five metres of a foil balloon.'

'Well, I did feel like a bit of a pillock standing here,' he said, 'especially when your flight was late. But actually, I rather enjoyed buying them!'

They hugged each other, the balloons and roses caught awkwardly between them, the other arriving passengers and their families crowding around and past them. She saw that there were tears in his eyes, and new lines around them. She leaned forward again and kissed him on the lips. 'I'm really pleased to see you,' she said, and clutched his arm with her free hand as he took over driving the trolley.

Doug nodded. He didn't say anything, just nodded as though he couldn't speak. But as they pushed their way through the concourse and out onto the pavement, he drew in his breath and smiled, and when he had lifted her bags into the boot of the car he put his arms around her again and they stood there in the busy car park, just a couple of people holding each other as cars shunted in and out, and people loaded and unloaded baggage and talked about the late arrival of the flight and what the weather had been like while they were away.

TWENTY-NINE

'What kept you?' Robin asked with a smile.

'Just a few thousand kilometres, and a bag full of intense personal crises,' Isabel said, bending down to hug her. 'I thought I told you to take care of yourself. I go away for a while and look what happens.'

'So much for the healthy lifestyle.' Robin laughed. 'It's wonderful to see you. You'll hate this but when I opened my eyes and saw you there I felt like a child seeing its mother!'

'You're right,' said Isabel with a grimace. 'I hate it. I've had enough of mother issues for a very long time.'

'You look different!'

'Everybody looks different,' Isabel said. 'Grace looks different – all those sharp angles have gone and she's positively blurred around the edges. Sally looks like a teenager and you . . .'

'Yes?'

'Well, you look different too, and I don't just mean you look sick. You look – how can I put it? There's something in your eyes, it's . . . I think "unequivocal" is the word. When I last saw you, you look tortured, confused, uncertain. Now, amazingly in view of the circumstances, you actually look quite calm and peaceful and strong . . . really strong.'

'Facing one's mortality has a dramatic effect,' Robin said, leaning forward and swinging her legs out of bed. 'Pass me my dressing gown and I'll sit in that chair. They're letting me out next week – on a short leash, you understand, but at least I'll get a change of scene.'

'Grace told me. She says you're staying with her for a while.'

'Yes,' Robin grinned. 'But a very short while. I have to get my act together and organise something quickly. It's not fair on Grace. All this stuff is interfering with her plans and making her very twitchy. You'll see it.' She smiled affectionately at the thought of Grace. 'She'll be in here being the new Grace, calm, centred and, as you say, blurry round the edges, and then something will trigger it and she'll start wanting to take my temperature and reprimand me for not having drunk enough water. Looking after me is the last thing Grace needs at the moment.'

'You can come to us, you know,' Isabel said. 'I talked to Doug after I talked to Grace. We'd love to have you while you sort out something more permanent.'

'Poor Doug,' Robin said, settling back into the chair. 'I'm sure he'd like to have you to himself for a while after all this time. He must be starving for some special Isabel-type attention.'

Isabel laughed and sank down into the other chair. 'Doug's okay,' she said. 'Much more okay than I imagined he'd be after all that happened. Since I've been back we've covered a lot of ground. I thought I was in for a battle getting him to accept the change in me and what that means for him, but it seems he's already done a lot of the groundwork on his own, or at least with some help from Deb. We had a disastrous time together in Germany and so I'd expected disaster here too, but it seems we are past the worst. I'm very lucky.'

'You've been very secretive about what's been happening for you.' Robin smiled. 'I'm learning that one privilege of being sick is that one can ask intrusive questions, and people feel it's their duty to talk.'

'Actually, I'm dying to talk about it,' said Isabel. 'But I want to know more about you first, and sort out the practicalities. By the way, did you know it was Doug who told Jim where you were?'

Robin nodded. 'I know, and I know he did it with the best of intentions. Don't worry about it. In the end it's all worked out all right. I've got all that Jim stuff to tell you too. Will we ever have time?'

'Well,' said Isabel, 'we will if you come to us when they release you. I'm sure you're right – the last thing Grace needs right now is a patient, and frankly the last thing you need is to feel you're holding up her plans.'

Robin leaned back and stretched out her legs. 'I think I fancy a walk down the corridor. Let's go and take a look at the view.'

They made their way from the room along the brightly lit passage to the picture window at the end that looked out across the Swan River to the tall buildings of Perth city. 'Strange place, isn't it?' Robin said. 'Perth, I mean. Perched on the west coast of this huge island, so isolated from the rest of Australia. It's quite weird, really. You, Grace and Sally went off to other places and became somehow different in different ways. I stayed close by and became different in a way I'd never bargained for. Now here we are all back again. D'you think we're still the Gang of Four?'

Isabel put her arm around Robin's shoulders. 'Of course we are. We didn't stop being it just because we weren't together.'

'I said something like that to Grace,' Robin said. 'Last year when I was on the edge of breaking up with Jim, I asked her if she thought we four would ever be the same again. She said no, it couldn't be. It had to be different.'

Isabel paused, considering the words. 'Well, she's right of course. We're all changed by the things that have happened in the last year. It will be different, but that doesn't mean it will be less than it was. I mean, look at you and Grace, you're closer now than you've ever been. And Sally, well – she's having to find out how she manages her friendships with us while being in a very intense relationship. And by the way, I really like Steve. I only met him briefly but he seems lovely.'

Robin nodded. 'He is, and he and Sally are so happy. You know they're going to take on my shop?'

'Yes, I do. That's good, isn't it, for them and for you. But now you, Rob. What do you want to do when you get out of here? Say you'll come to us.'

Robin turned away from the view to look at her. 'Okay, Isabel;

yes, I will. Thanks a lot. It's a much better solution for Grace and for me. But only for a short time. I promise to sort something out soon.'

'Don't worry about it in here,' Isabel said. 'We'll work on it together once we get you home.'

Robin was bored beyond belief. She couldn't concentrate for long enough to do more than read through the morning paper or flick through a magazine. The things she had always enjoyed didn't seem to work for her anymore. She would put on the headphones to listen to classical music and want to punch Margaret Throsby for sounding so deep and meaningful. She would switch to Radio National and find herself bored to tears by Phillip Adams talking more than his interviewees. The constantly changing voices on news radio were more suited now to her short concentration span and increasingly critical frame of mind.

An hour or so earlier on a great surge of energy she had written several pages of her journal. Now she was exhausted and could barely hold the pen. Her arm ached, her back ached, she felt nauseated and she had a pain in her chest. She wondered about the sudden changes, so much energy one minute, barely enough to breathe the next. And she wondered, not for the first time, how long this alien had been living in her.

'Think about how you've been over the last few months,' Dr Chin had asked her. 'When did you start to feel something different? Feeling sick?'

She'd been annoyed at first but finally admitted that not long after selling the house and buying the cottage in January she had started to feel very tired. She had stopped running so far and so frequently, convincing herself that she didn't have to be so obsessive about her running now she was living such a healthy, relaxed life. The pain in her chest had been bugging her again, and she had often felt nauseated but found that it wore off if she ate something plain like a piece of dry toast. 'The more I think about it,' she said. 'I suppose I haven't been feeling all that good for several months.'

Dr Chin nodded. 'It is well advanced,' he said quietly.

Had the cancer been there inside her for months or years? The day she left Jim? The day she moved south? At the pub in Pemberton? She pondered once more on where and how she would live. The thought of living with a carer was depressing and, despite the fact that she felt so weak, the prospect of not having any work to occupy her mind horrified her. The long, lazy, relaxing months at the cottage had always been temporary. Now more than ever she needed a sense of purpose to keep her going. She'd asked for her laptop to be brought in, but Dr Chin made Sally take it away again. Not for another few weeks, he had said. The writing she had begun at the cottage was shapeless although at the time it had seemed important that she keep on with it, but it was hardly going to occupy her seven days a week. She could maintain her interest in the bookshop for a while at least, until Steve and Sally were in a position to buy it. What she needed was something more practical, something demanding that would keep her focused and stop her from burying herself in her illness. She needed something useful to do. While Grace was pulling away from the need to be needed, Robin felt that she, now so dependent on others, needed to find some way of contributing something herself.

'You could always do some opinions for us,' Alec Seaborn had suggested when he visited her. 'We could really use you. There's so much you could contribute. You've been such a big part of it all for so long, it would be good to have you still involved.' Perhaps that would be it, she thought, although it hardly fulfilled the need to give something back, but at least it would occupy her and give her a focus. She told him she'd think about it.

'I think something will emerge,' Sally said confidently, sitting on the end of her bed. 'My mother used to say, "One door closes and another opens." It's just that sometimes the opening door takes a little while.'

'You've become extremely philosophical.' Robin grinned. 'Bringing out the ancient wisdom in times of trouble.'

'Well, I have reason for it,' Sally said. 'Not so long ago I was in the depths of despair, anger and frustration. Now look at me.

Anyway, I brought you some Tim Tams. I'm sick of seeing you push your food around – get stuck into these.'

They sat munching their way through the biscuits in companionable silence for a while.

'How long is Steve here for?' Robin asked.

'He has to leave at the end of August,' Sally said. 'As soon as he goes I'll relet my place and go down to Albany. The Tranters are going to stay on for a while to give me some training in the shop before they go to Tasmania.'

'And you think you'll be okay down there all on your own?'

'Why not? If you'd've been okay there on your own, why wouldn't I be?'

'It was my choice,' Robin said. 'An overwhelming passion made me buy it. It's different for you.'

'It's my choice now,' Sally said firmly. 'A choice that will allow me to indulge my own overwhelming passion – as soon as he gets back. And the teaching job is fine for the new year. It's a lovely school, I'm looking forward to it.'

And then there was Grace. 'I know what you mean,' she'd said. 'I could probably find you some work to do on the patchwork project but I sense it's not really your thing.'

Robin shook her head. 'It's not really. That doesn't mean I don't think it's a wonderful project, just that it's not really me. What's more, this is your baby, Grace, you need to develop it in your own way. And you're not responsible for finding work for me any more than you are for sorting out my living arrangements.'

Grace paused.'You are sure about going to Isabel and Doug?'

'Yes,' Robin said decisively. 'And I don't want to see you in here again, Grace, until you can show me an airline ticket to New Orleans, New York and London, booked and paid for.'

Robin was sitting up in a chair, picking at a quite reasonable mild chicken curry with rice and watching the ABC television news, when there was a tap on the door and Alec's new partner Diana Hooper popped her cheerful face around it. 'Am I disturbing you?'

Robin, her mouth full of curry, shook her head and flicked off the television with the remote control. 'Of course not,' she said, swallowing hard. 'Come on in and sit down, if you don't mind me finishing my meal. It's nice to see you again.'

Diana cleared some magazines off the other chair so she could sit. 'It's a bit of cheek, I know,' she said, blushing slightly, 'but Alec mentioned that you were looking for something to do and you might do some opinions for us.' She pushed stray hair back behind her ears and took a deep breath.

'Yes, he did mention it,' Robin said, wary of what might be coming. 'But I'd understand if you prefer me not to. After all, you're there now. Sometimes an old business partner is not the most welcome person to have around.'

Diana blushed more deeply and looked flustered, the jacket of her dark suit straining across her large breasts. She shook her head. 'Oh no, it's not that at all. I'd be delighted and we can certainly do with your experience – you know how much work there is. It's just that Alec said you talked about wanting to make a contribution and I thought, well, if you were looking for something different . . .' Her voice wavered. 'I mean, not if you don't like the idea or anything . . .'

'What, Diana?' Robin asked, finishing her curry and pushing her plate aside. 'What have you got in mind?'

'Well, I'm involved with the Women's Law Centre. I actually helped to set it up. You know we run on a shoestring, and we're always desperate for experienced lawyers to prepare cases and provide opinions, but we can't afford to pay.'

Robin felt a surge of excitement. 'Go on.'

'Obviously the women who come to us are in trouble – victims of domestic violence, some of them, others are having difficulty getting advice for divorce and custody settlements, some are women who've been charged with welfare fraud. You know the sort of thing – woman supporting her kids on a pension, new boyfriend moves in and doesn't contribute anything, she keeps claiming the pension but the department thinks he's supporting her.'

'Yes,' said Robin, so loudly she surprised both herself and Diana.

'Sorry?'

'Yes,' said Robin. 'I want to do it. It's exactly what I want. Tell me what you need and I'll do it. When can I start?'

'I, er . . . I don't think you'd be allowed to start yet, would you? I mean, the doctors . . .'

'Okay, next week. When I get out. Will you come and see me and we'll talk about how it'll work?'

Diana grinned. 'Absolutely. That's fantastic. We can work it on email, of course, if that's how you want to do it. Then, wherever you are, we'll be in contact with you. You sure it's okay, Robin? It won't be too much for you?'

'Too much?' Robin smiled. 'Diana, you'll think I'm exaggerating, but I think you just saved my life.'

Isabel stood in the bedroom contemplating the rose-pink velvet chair. There was a time before she had left for Europe when she had felt it was a bad omen and she should replace it with something new. Now as she was preparing the second bedroom for Robin's arrival, she decided that it might look nice in that room. She stood looking at the chair standing by the window as it had done for years, and realised that she didn't want to move it. She had made such profound moves within herself that moving the chair was no longer necessary – in fact, she rather wanted it to stay where it was. She would find another chair for Robin's room.

Doug looked in and, seeing her there, came over to sit on the bed. 'How's it going?'

'Good,' she said. 'She'll be comfortable in that room and she'll have the second bathroom to herself.'

Doug nodded. 'Good. I'm glad she's coming. I'm looking forward to it. I've always liked Robin. And what are you up to in here?'

'I was just looking at the pink chair. I was going to get rid of it but I've changed my mind. I rather like it.'

'I sympathise with the chair,' he said. 'It and I have something in common.'

'I was never going to get rid of you, Doug,' she said, walking over to sit beside him. 'I just needed things to be different between us.'

'I know,' he said, covering her hand with his. 'I'm just playing for sympathy. You know me. You were right, Isabel. I couldn't see it in Germany. I came home a complete mess, but there was only one way and that had to be up. Rather like having a new minister to cope with, new policy decisions, new priorities, new ways of working. I suppose I felt I could rise to the challenge or risk losing everything. It was hard in Germany. I thought it was the end.'

'I love you to bits, you know. I was never leaving you. But I'd reached a point where things had to change. Things between us.'

He nodded. 'I know that now, but I didn't when I left, and when I got back here I went into this huge rage. In the end it was Deb who laid it out in black and white. She was pretty brutal with me. I went there looking for sympathy – hah! She told me I was very complacent, and demanding. She virtually told me to grow up and get my act together. Bit confronting from one's daughter.'

Isabel leaned forward and kissed him, holding his face between her hands, and he put his arms around her and pulled her down to lie beside him on the bed. 'It wasn't all your fault,' she said. 'I colluded in all that, I let it happen and then suddenly I started to see it and resent it.'

They lay side by side, holding hands. 'You know,' he said, 'I was thinking that life had suddenly become so turbulent and uncertain over the last year, and then I thought that beside Eunice and Eric, and Antonia and Klaus, we're positively dull and boring.'

She laughed. 'Exactly! Isn't it all amazing? Who'd ever have believed all that was hidden away behind Mum and Eric's life. It seems so bizarre and yet it explains so much. But I still wish I'd known while she was alive. I don't think I'll ever stop wishing that.'

Doug pulled himself up onto his elbow and looked down into her face. 'Well, in a way you've recaptured something of the real Eunice. You can hang on to that. And look what you achieved – Klaus and Antonia coming here together for Christmas!'

Isabel smiled, putting her hand up to stroke his cheek. 'I know. Isn't it wonderful? Maybe they'll get married again and live happily ever after!'

Doug laughed. 'I think you should just settle for the visit. From what you've told me, Klaus and Antonia seem very happy with the status quo. I don't think they're going to go over that old ground again.' He bent his head, kissing her lightly on the lips. 'I love being dull and boring with you, Iz. I'm so glad you're back.' And he kissed her again as she put her arms around his neck and pulled him down onto the bed.

Grace stared once again at her ticket. She'd been sure she wouldn't be able to go ahead and fix it before Robin's arrangements were all in place. It was good that Robin had moved to Isabel's place. It certainly made it easier but she still worried about what the next stage would be, and how it would feel to get on a plane without some sort of resolution about Robin's future. She was restless for the hospital corners to be neatly tucked in. But at least she'd made the decisive move of booking her flight.

'Good on you,' Sally said as Grace helped her get the town-house ready again for more tenants. 'It's only six weeks and you'll be off.'

Grace finished wiping out the cutlery drawer and put the knives and forks back in place. 'Sometimes I can't believe it'll really happen,' she said. 'Orinda says we're going to sing in this piano bar in New Orleans where she's been going for years. Can you imagine it, me singing in a bar?'

Sally laughed as she straightened saucepans in the cupboard over the stove. 'What I wouldn't give to be a fly on the wall, Grace. And then on to do big business in New York?'

Grace picked a laptop off the workbench. 'This is Robin's, isn't it?'

'Yes, the doctor came in while I was there and made me take it away while she was still in the hospital. He says she's not supposed to have it for at least a month, she's not allowed to work. I think it's stupid. She's been out of hospital for ten days and she's getting frustrated and irritable. She needs to do something.'

Grace considered for a moment. 'I think you're right – she's really keen to get onto the women's law stuff. Why don't we take it around there when we finish here?'

'Good idea.' Sally closed the cupboard and leaned back against the worktop. 'Grace? What's going to happen? To Robin, I mean.'

'I don't know – we haven't found a solution yet.'

'I don't mean about where she'll live. I mean what's it going to be like for her? Is she . . . is she going to die?'

'I don't know, Sally. The prognosis isn't optimistic. It's extremely rare for people to survive this for more than a few months, or a year at most. The future doesn't look good. She'll slowly get worse, weaker, nauseous, she won't be strong enough to do much at all.'

'It seems so unfair,' Sally said. 'A year ago we were all cruising along with our lives and then all this change, and so much happiness for me, a whole new direction for you, Isabel really seeming calm and peaceful – and Robin's lost everything. Doesn't it make you want to know why things happen like this?'

Grace raised her eyebrows. 'You've had your share, your challenge and personal crisis in this last year,' she said. 'We all did in our own different ways. When I look back at it I think we all had things we needed to learn and, strangely, we chose to do things that forced us to learn very quickly.'

'Yes, but you can't say that about Robin. What's a terminal illness supposed to teach her?'

'I know,' Grace agreed. 'Or rather, I mean I don't know. I don't understand it either, Sally. It does seem totally unfair, really cruel and meaningless.'

Robin, wrapped in a cotton blanket, lay on a lounger on the deck looking through half-closed eyes across the rooftops to where the sun hovered crimson and gold above the horizon. Twenty minutes earlier she had been looking for something to occupy her, and Doug had suggested she take a look at the legal implications of a new policy document and give him her opinion on it. She had swept enthusiastically through the first eight or ten pages, jotting notes in the margin, fired up by having something useful to do, but now she was tired. She put down the papers and leaned back. Would her energy and concentration always burn out so quickly? If it did, she wasn't sure how much use she'd be to the Women's Law Centre. What had seemed such a wonderful idea while she was in the hospital now seemed to swamp her with its enormity.

She had been out of hospital for three weeks and was questioning if she really would be able to work again. She wondered if she would always feel like an invalid, or if there would be days when she felt normal and healthy again. She sighed deeply. Perhaps she should just rest a while and try to work out some solution for her living arrangements. She really couldn't impose on Isabel and Doug for too much longer. Back at the other end of the house she heard the front doorbell ring and the steady plod of Doug's sock-clad feet on the polished boards of the passage. Robin hoped it wasn't anyone to see her. She just wanted to close her eyes and sleep.

'Come in, come in,' Doug said. 'Isabel just popped out to get some milk. She'll be back any minute.' He drew Father Pat inside. 'Robin's asleep on the deck. Come into the kitchen and have a drink.'

'I'd love to,' Father Pat said, 'but I've got a friend with me. Could I bring her in too?'

'Sure, of course,' Doug said, opening the door wider and looking out into the street. An unlikely looking young woman dressed in black leather with spiky blonde hair was leaning against Father Pat's car. 'That's your friend?' Doug asked, raising his eyebrows.

'It is indeed.' Father Pat grinned and beckoned Josie into the house. 'A friend of mine and an old friend of Robin's. I think she'll be pleased to see Josie.'

Doug took them through to the kitchen and opened a bottle of wine while Josie looked around in approval. 'So, how do you know Robin?' he asked her, carefully drawing the cork.

'I was a client – a legal aid client.' Josie grinned. 'A fallen woman – Robin picked me up!'

'Then you must be Josie,' said a voice from the doorway, and Isabel walked in with a litre of milk. 'Robin's told me all about you.' She walked over to shake hands and then impulsively they hugged each other.

'How is she?' Josie asked.

'Up and down,' Isabel said, putting the milk in the fridge. 'More often down than up. She has real highs and lows, and the extremes are hard on her.' Isabel turned to Doug. 'Is Robin still out on the deck?'

'Yes, she's asleep. I thought we might leave her for another ten minutes or so. She ran out of steam rather suddenly.'

Isabel nodded then looked at Josie and Father Pat. 'Why don't you stay for dinner? There's heaps, and Grace and Sally are coming over soon.'

Josie looked towards Father Pat and raised her eyebrows. 'He's the boss man!'

'Ha! That'll be the day. But thanks, Isabel, that'd be delightful if it's not too much trouble.'

'Let me help,' Josie said, slipping off her jacket. 'Kitchens are my thing.'

'Oh, of course,' said Isabel. 'Well, make yourself at home. Could you start on the salad?'

The two men sat on stools at the bench drinking their wine while Isabel got out plates and cutlery, and Josie rummaged through the fridge. 'I may have a solution for Robin,' Josie said, scoring through the skin of an avocado and easing the flesh away from the stone. 'Can I try it out on you first?'

'Of course,' Isabel nodded.

'My partner Dawn and I have this place in Pemberton.'

'Yes, Robin told me about it. It sounds beautiful.'

'Well, we have a small cottage in the grounds, separate but quite close to the main building. It's fully furnished and equipped. We've let it occasionally to guests who want a self-catering arrangement for a few weeks, but most of the time it stands empty and we keep telling each other we ought to make better use of it. When Father Pat told us about Robin we – Dawn and I – thought maybe she'd like to live there. She could be independent but – well, you see, we're always there, we could put in an intercom in case she needed us in a hurry, stuff like that. She'd have her own place but there'd be someone close by. There's always somebody there – even if we're out, one or two of the staff are always around. She could cook for herself when she wanted to or just call on the intercom for a meal. It would be easy for us, because there's two of us and we have help, so it means it wouldn't all fall on one person.'

Isabel put the plates on the bench and looked straight at her. 'It sounds brilliant. She's talked about you and Dawn, and how lovely the place is. And you obviously realise we haven't managed to come up with a solution. Is that what you've come to ask her?'

Josie nodded. 'Yeah! D'you think it's reasonable? Okay to put it to her?'

'More than okay, Josie, I think it's a wonderful and generous offer. My bet is she'll jump at the idea.'

Doug put another bottle of wine into the fridge. 'Great idea,' he said, refilling Josie's glass. 'But would you be able to handle it and the business as well?'

'Oh yes, until – well, until it becomes more complicated. I mean, unless she actually needed nursing,' she said. 'We can easily manage it – in fact, we'd love it.'

Isabel spread the cloth on the table and then changed her mind. It might be winter but it was still warm enough to sit on the deck. 'Shall we eat outside?' she asked, and handed the tablecloth to Father Pat. 'Why don't you go out and put the cloth on and wake Robin up gently?'

She pulled out a tray and began to stack the crockery on it while Josie tossed some sliced cucumber into a yoghurt dressing.

'Would you cut some bread, please, Doug,' Isabel said, and picking up the tray she went out through the lounge to the deck. The sun had disappeared, leaving only traces of rosy wash above the horizon.

'You could have put the lights on, Father Pat,' she said, setting the tray down on the table and turning back towards the switch.

And it was then, as she turned, that she saw the silhouette of

Father Pat crouched beside Robin's chair, his head in his hands, the tablecloth a crumpled heap on the floor beside him, and she knew with a sickening dread that the solution to Robin's future had always been beyond their control.

THIRTY

'Where do you think, then?' said Sally, shoving her hands into the pockets of her coat and looking around. The wind whipped her hair across her face and made her eyes sting. They stood together on the headland, shoulders hunched, their collars turned up against the wind. Overhead the gulls shrieked and swooped, their cries harsh one minute, swept out to sea the next.

Isabel lifted both hands in a gesture of indecision. 'I don't know. Grace, you came here with her when you collected her. What do you think?'

Grace looked behind her and then ahead up the cliff path. 'Further up there,' she said, 'where the path curves. That's where she used to run. She told me that on the way back, when she got to that bend and could see the cottage, her heart would lift.'

They struggled on up the hill against the wind, the first drops of rain stinging their faces, until they reached the bend.

'Here?' Isabel asked.

Grace turned and looked down to the point where the cottage just came into sight. 'Yes,' she said, clutching the urn against her chest. 'Here, I think.'

'How do you think we should do it?' Sally said. 'It feels as though there should be some sort of ritual.'

'Suppose we sit down on that rock and each tell our favourite memory of her,' Isabel suggested, 'or say what we loved most about her. Then we can open the urn and take it in turns to scatter the ashes.'

They headed for the rock and sat looking out across the waves that crashed high and wild. 'Robin loved this sort of winter weather,' Grace said, shaking her head in incomprehension. 'She said it was energising and invigorating. I never could understand that – perhaps you never get over coming from the northern hemisphere.'

The silence was broken only by the roar of the wind and water.

'Okay,' Isabel said slowly, 'shall I go first?' The others nodded.

'I loved her for her mind. She was so quick at understanding things and analysing them. You could give her a really difficult document to read and she'd speed-read it and have the measure of it in minutes – something that would take me hours. That and her independence, the way she just got on with things on her own. She never expected anyone to help her or to take some of the responsibility. She was very singular and strong.' Isabel put her hand up to brush away the tears. 'But the night she told me about Jim, she was so vulnerable, so concerned about what we'd all think of her. It made me realise how important our friendship was to her. I loved her for her vulnerability as much as for her strength.'

Sally sighed. 'Yes, I loved that too, her strength and her straightforwardness. She always said she was a dark horse, but I never felt that, I felt that she was very open and honest. It was only the Jim thing that she hid, and that was understandable. There were so many best moments, but I suppose that weekend I took you guys out to do some painting. Remember? We went down to Fremantle, the Round House, and you two did really well, and Robin just couldn't get it. She kept scrapping it and starting again, knocked over the water jar and got paint everywhere, and she was so frustrated she was nearly in tears. Then when she stood up she knocked over the easel and had a bit of a hissy fit, and we all sort of stared at her in amazement because it was so unlike her. Then she came and hugged me and apologised, and told me how hard it was to admit that she couldn't do something, or at least couldn't get the hang of it instantly. I loved her for that. Her ability to apologise and admit that about herself. I'll miss her so much.'

Grace clasped her hands between her knees and unclasped them again. 'I was always a bit nervous of Robin,' she said.

'I never knew why at the time but now, in the last few months, I worked it out. I think at some level I felt she could see through me, although at the time I didn't realise there was something to see through to. She used to make me feel like an impostor and I didn't know why. Now I think she could just see through my obsessive behaviour.' She paused and sighed.

'There are two favourite memories, the first while you two were away and she was frantic about Jim and she came to my place early one morning looking like death. We were both very vulnerable that morning. Neither of us would have chosen the other as a confidante if either of you had been around, but we talked carefully, we were feeling our way. It was a turning point. The other was in the hospital when she told me she knew how her illness and the hospital itself was bugging me. I realised she was as concerned about me as she was about herself, which was an incredible thing considering how sick she was. I feel as though, just as we moved into a deeper level of friendship, she was snatched away.'

The rain was falling faster now, soaking the shoulders of their jackets. 'Shall we do it then?' Isabel asked after a few minutes, and she stood up and unscrewed the urn. Slipping her fingers into the ashes she took a handful and, turning her back to the wind, she opened her hand.

''Bye, Rob,' she called as the ashes were swept seaward. 'Peace and love wherever you are.'

Down in the village, Dorothy, removing a poster from the shop window, looked up at the cliff and saw them standing there, buffeted by the wind. She saw Sally take the urn and then Grace, and watched as they put it down on the rock and stood hugging each other, three figures merging into one against the grey sky.

'God bless you, Robin,' she whispered, crossing herself. 'I'm going to miss you.' And she picked up Maurice and turned back into the shop.

'It's very lonely here,' Sally said, adding a couple of logs to the fire and stirring it with the poker. It leapt into life and the flames licked around the new wood. 'Wonderful for a holiday but I wouldn't want to be here for months on my own, like Robin was.'

'Me neither,' said Grace, sorting through the collection of mail Dorothy had given them from Robin's mailbox. 'I'd go raving mad very quickly. But she loved it.' She picked up a bundle of junk mail. 'These can all go,' she said, tossing them into the fire and watching as the flames devoured the brightly coloured pages.

Isabel came through from the kitchen with three mugs of tea and a packet of Tim Tams. 'Look what I found in the pantry. She was such a healthy eater, but she loved Tim Tams, didn't she? I think she'd want us to finish these.'

Sally sank down onto the couch where she had so recently lain with Steve. 'What would she think if she could see us?' she asked.

Isabel gazed into the fire, sipping her tea, and shrugged slightly. Grace stood up and helped herself to a biscuit. 'She'd think we did the right thing, bringing her back here,' she said. 'This was where she wanted to be. When I came to collect her for the mastectomy she told me she felt more at home here than she had anywhere else in her life. You're going to faint when I say this, because it's not a me sort of thing, but it's as though I can feel her, as though she's here with us.'

Sally smiled. 'I know what you mean and it *is* a you thing, Grace. You, now! A year ago you would have laughed if one of us had said that, but you're a very different person these days.'

Isabel nodded. 'Yes, you are. And I feel her presence too. Perhaps that's why she left the cottage to us. Remember what she said in the will? That it was to be shared between us, to use as we wished, for holidays or retreats, together or alone or with others we love. I wept when Alec read that – where she said she would always be with us, that wherever we went and whatever we did, in the cottage we would always be the Gang of Four.'

Grace gasped, swallowing a sob. Clasping her hand across her mouth she stood frozen for a moment and then dropped onto the couch, putting her head in her hands. 'I wasted so much of my time with her, with all of you. Being so obsessive and prickly, especially with Robin, and now she's gone just as I was beginning to get it right.'

Sally moved closer and put her arm around Grace's shoulders. 'Oh, Grace, it wasn't wasted time. She loved being in the Gang of Four, she mentioned it to all of us during those last days at the hospital. It meant the world to her. You're part of that, and you grew so much closer in the last year.'

Isabel fetched a box of tissues from the kitchen and put them down beside Grace. 'Sally's right, Grace. Robin knew how it was, she loved you and she respected you enormously for so many things, and most of all for how you've dealt with what happened to you this year.'

Grace sat up and blew her nose. She straightened her shoulders and stiffened her body. 'Sorry,' she said in a harsh, decisive tone. 'Very self-indulgent, crying. I never cry.'

Isabel and Sally looked at each other and then at Grace, a smile tweaking the corner of Isabel's mouth. Sally stifled a laugh and cleared her throat. Grace stared from one to the other. Her face, which had changed moments before from the crumpled looseness of grief to a tightly controlled mask, began to soften again. 'Well,' she began, 'I mean, I never used to ... but ...' She stopped again, watching as the other two collapsed in laughter.

'Did you hear that, Robin?' Isabel said, walking over to the framed photograph of Robin on the mantelpiece. 'Did you actually hear what she said?'

Sally fell back laughing, and Grace shook her head and her mouth broke into a wide smile.

'I suspect Robin is deeply shocked, Grace,' Isabel said from the fireplace, trying to keep a straight face. 'Her dearest wish was that this should be a place for the passion of tears as well as for laughter. And I think she'd also say that it's about time we stopped sitting around eating Tim Tams and got on with sorting out what needs to be done here.'

Sally got up and dragged Grace to her feet. 'Right!' she said. 'To work – let's organise the new headquarters of the Gang of Four. And to start with, I want to see one of your own patchwork quilts on the bed in the main bedroom, Grace.'

'And I want to hang one of your photographs here, Sally,' said Isabel, pointing to the wall above the fireplace.

Grace dried her eyes again and picked up a large cardboard box she had brought with her. Taking off the lid she took out one of several dozen thick white candles and, reaching down further, extracted a curved black wrought-iron candleholder and a box of matches. She pressed the candle onto the holder's central spike and struck a match. 'And I want to make a rule,' she said, holding the burning match to the candle, 'that every time any one or all three of us are here, we light a candle each day for Robin and for friendship.'

They watched as the wick caught.

'For Robin, and for friendship,' said Isabel, raising her mug.

'For Robin and for friendship,' echoed the other two.

'Now,' said Grace, 'let's get the beds made up – and please remember, I want those hospital corners nice and neat!'

'Yes, Sister!' Isabel and Sally laughed in unison, and together they pulled the linen from the press and began to make up the beds.

MORE BESTSELLING FICTION FROM
LIZ BYRSKI

Food, Sex & Money

It's almost forty years since the three ex-convent girls left school and went their separate ways, but finally they meet again.

Bonnie, rocked by the death of her husband, is back in Australia after decades in Europe, and is discovering that financial security doesn't guarantee a fulfilling life. Fran, long divorced, is a freelance food writer, battling with her diet, her bank balance and her relationship with her adult children. And Sylvia, marooned in a passionless marriage, is facing a crisis that will crack her world wide open.

Together again, Bonnie, Fran and Sylvia embark on a venture that will challenge everything they thought they knew about themselves – and give them more second chances than they could ever have imagined.

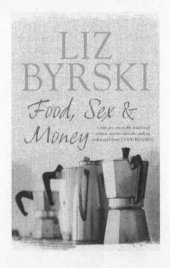

Belly Dancing for Beginners

Gayle and Sonya are complete opposites: one
reserved and cautious, the other confident and
outspoken. But their lives will converge when they
impulsively join a belly dancing class.

Marissa, their teacher, is sixty, sexy, and very much
her own person, and as Gayle and Sonya learn about
the origins and meaning of the dance, much more than
their muscle tone begins to change.

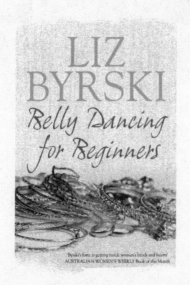

LIZ
BYRSKI
Belly Dancing
for Beginners

'Byrski's forte is getting inside women's heads and hearts'
AUSTRALIAN WOMEN'S WEEKLY Book of the Month